GUTTER CHILD

GUTTER CHILD

a novel

JAEL RICHARDSON

HARPERAVENUE

Gutter Child
Copyright © 2021 by Jael Richardson.
All rights reserved.

Published by Harper Avenue, an imprint of HarperCollins Publishers Ltd

First edition

HarperCollins books may be purchased for educational, business or
sales promotional use through our Special Markets Department.

HarperCollins Publishers Ltd
Bay Adelaide Centre, East Tower
22 Adelaide Street West, 41st Floor
Toronto, Ontario, Canada
M5H 4E3

www.harpercollins.ca

The author gratefully acknowledges the support of the Ontario Arts Council.

ONTARIO ARTS COUNCIL
CONSEIL DES ARTS DE L'ONTARIO
an Ontario government agency
un organisme du gouvernement de l'Ontario

Library and Archives Canada Cataloguing in Publication

Title: Gutter child : a novel / Jael Richardson.
Names: Richardson, Jael Ealey, 1980- author.
Identifiers: Canadiana (print) 20200358855 | Canadiana (ebook) 20200359045
ISBN 9781443457828 (softcover) | ISBN 9781443457835 (ebook)
Classification: LCC PS8635.I33345 G88 2021 | DDC C813/.6—dc23

Printed and bound in the United States of America
LSC/H 9 8 7 6 5 4 3 2 1

A Note from the Author

This book is a work of fiction that explores a perilous world rooted in injustice. As in life, the effects of injustice impact many of the characters. Take care with your heart and your mind as you read. Pause and rest as required. These are difficult times.

For Earline, Dorothy, Sherri, and Derryl,
and all the women who struggled so I could soar

To be a poor man is hard, but to be a poor race in a land of dollars
is the very bottom of hardships.
—W.E.B. Du Bois

WHEN I DREW PICTURES OF MOTHER AND ME, I USED PEACH for her and Chestnut for myself. "Why is your skin named after something soft and sweet and mine is something hard and bitter?" "Because you are so much tougher," she said. I thought that was a very good answer. And maybe it's true. But I am forced to be tough. It takes a particular kind of strength to exist in a world where you are not wanted that doesn't feel like strength at all. Like giving up or giving in would be easier, smarter even. Maybe that is my chestnut, my toughness. The fact that I am still here.

LIVINGSTONE

1

THE DRIVER LOOKS IN MY DIRECTION, FULL OF WORRY. Her lips are red, glossy and pouted, and there's a crease in her forehead, like she's the one with problems, not me. I stare out the window wishing I could go back and put my old life back together, which is impossible, I know. So here I am instead. Hours away from the only home I've ever known and driving up a long gravel road through a tunnel of trees with branches that reach down like fingers, hungry for touch.

"This is Livingstone Academy," Miss Femia says, as we pull up to a grand white house with black shutters and a door that's green like a swamp.

The car slows to a stop under a droopy willow, and I step out in what feels like a whole different world. I take one deep breath and close my eyes, and when I open them again, Miss Femia is standing in front of me with her tight bun and waxy mouth.

She takes my hands in hers, rubbing my scar with her thumb— the hideous X on the back of my right hand that's ugly and raw. She sighs, and I wonder if it's sadness in her eyes, because it's hard to tell with Mainlanders. Pity looks very much the same.

"I know this wasn't the plan," she says. "But let's make the most of it, hey?"

Her voice is high and hopeful, and I hate the way it sounds, like forgetting the life I had is my best option. Like that's even possible.

"I really think you might like it here. I think your mother would have really liked this place," she says.

I want to tell her that what Mother would probably like is to be living instead of dead, to be back home with me instead of wherever it is she is now. But Miss Femia doesn't have children, and people without children always share silly bits of wisdom, like it will all go to waste if they don't.

"Yes, let's make the most of it," I say, turning up the corners of my mouth as high as I can manage. Which isn't much.

"You can do this, Elimina," she says, wrapping her fingers around the doorknob, holding the swamp-colored door with her back. "You can find happiness here."

But happiness isn't something a kid like me can afford to hold out for.

THE MAIN ENTRANCE of Livingstone Academy is large and impressive with tall columns and a wide, carpeted stairwell that curves like a bow. Framed pictures of open landscapes and wide fields hang on brightly lit walls.

At least it's not the Gutter, I try to tell myself as I turn and take it all in.

"Miss Femia," a man says, emerging from a hallway in a sharp tan suit, followed by a girl in a gray dress with a crisp white shirt underneath.

The tall man with slick brown hair takes large steps across the room to greet us, kissing Miss Femia on the cheek and smiling down at me after. I stare back with wide eyes because, other than Mother, no Mainlander has ever looked at me this way. Like they're actually pleased that I've arrived.

"Elimina, it's a tremendous honor to have you here at Livingstone Academy. I'm Headmaster Samuel J. Gregors. But Mr. Gregors will do just fine."

He smiles and pauses for a moment, raising his chin in a way that makes me wonder if I'm expected to curtsy or applaud.

"While the circumstances that brought you here are less than ideal, I believe that Livingstone is exactly where you need to be," he says. "Elimina, I sincerely believe that here in our tidy little academy, you'll find a home that propels you into an excellent future."

He looks down at the girl in the gray dress whose hair is pulled into two round ponytails. Her skin is like mine, the color of oak trees and coconuts, as Mother would say whenever she rubbed lotion onto my skin that smelled like a spring rain.

"This is Josephine. She's one of our best students," he says, nodding in Josephine's direction as she takes a step forward, so we're close enough to touch.

Josephine tilts her head, taking in my shaved head and raising one eyebrow.

Mother started shaving my head when I was five years old because I had curls that refused to submit to her—hair that grew out instead of down. "It's impossible to deal with. There's just nothing else I can do," she said, lifting me onto a tall stool, where a pair of scissors lay resting on the countertop. She cut one messy ponytail, and when I gasped, she cut the other quickly before grabbing a razor to take the rest. When she was done, when tiny black curls were scattered around her like feathers, she held my face between her hands, tilting me this way and that, marveling at the richness of my skin, held in her moon-colored palms. She smiled, like she was proud of the result—the smoothness, the even shape, how clean I looked. "Perfect," she said. "You look perfect, Elimina. A beautiful, ebony goddess."

Her eyes were wet, but no tears fell. And I believed every word she said. *You are perfect. Beautiful. A goddess.* But when I looked in the mirror, I saw someone I didn't recognize. I saw a head that was naked and shorn like a bird born too soon, one that would never grow up and fly. And I knew that she had lied.

"You made me ugly," I yelled, and when I said those words again, shrill and loud, she called me vain and selfish.

"Elimina?" Miss Femia says, placing one hand on my shoulder. "Mr. Gregors just asked you a question, dear."

I look up, my heart racing wildly, like I've just been caught doing wrong. "I'm sorry, sir. I—"

"Never you mind. It was a very long drive," he says, waving one hand in my direction like it doesn't matter at all. "Josephine will take care of you today, and I'll meet with you tomorrow after breakfast. After you've had some rest."

"Yes, sir. I'm sorry, sir."

"Don't be sorry. And don't be late," he says, pointing in my direction. "It's a basic tenet of the work we do here to always be on time. I consider tardiness a sign of disrespect. Let's not get off to a bad start."

"Yes, sir."

"Josephine, show her around, and do it proper," he says. "No shortcuts. Leave nothing out. Get her a uniform and be sure to take her to Nurse Gretchen. I want her ready to go when I meet her tomorrow. I'll have Violet inform Miss Darling that you'll be away for the duration of the day."

"Yes, sir. Thank you, sir," Josephine says, nodding her head.

Miss Femia moves closer, placing her hands on my shoulders

and opening her red mouth, like she's going to say something, but when she looks back at Mr. Gregors and Josephine, she presses her lips back together like now is not the right time.

"Miss Femia?" I say, hoping she'll reconsider and say what's on her mind.

"It's not important," she says. "You've got enough to worry about right now, Elimina. Go on with Josephine. Get settled in. I'll swing by another time."

She wraps her arms around me, and I don't squeeze back or cry, but when Miss Femia whispers in my ear, "You'll be fine," I feel a stick in my throat that hurts so bad it makes it hard to swallow, like a knife cutting from the inside. "I'll see you soon," she says.

But somehow, I know this is a lie.

JOSEPHINE LEADS ME down a long hall with high, curved ceilings, our footsteps clicking against the floors. When she reaches the tall set of doors at the end of the hallway, she places her palms on the brass panels and turns toward me, the Xs on both of her hands standing tall. For a moment, I'm not sure I'm breathing at all.

"You ready?" she says.

But I don't answer. I just stare and follow her slowly through the doors, feeling somewhere deep in my gut that this is all wrong. I should turn and run.

The dining hall is filled with long tables and wood chairs. It reeks of fried meat and steamed vegetables, and when we enter the room, students in matching gray uniforms turn and stare. But I just look down at all of the hands that look just like Josephine's—two scars instead of one, like mine.

I stop, and when Josephine turns to me, I whisper the only

words I can manage, my throat still thick and tight: "I don't belong here. You're all . . . I'm not . . . I'm not a Gutter child," I say.

But Josephine just hands me a tray and shakes her head, like I've got a lot to learn.

2

TREES WITH WIDE GREEN TOPS AND THICK, RUGGED trunks line the campus as dirt paths curve and swirl between buildings surrounded by colorful flowers.

"You alright?" Josephine says.

Two girls in white aprons stroll by, staring and pushing a cart packed with cleaning supplies.

"You hardly said anything over lunch. You've hardly said anything at all," she says.

"I'm alright," I say, trying to smile. But I keep thinking about Capedown and Mother and what lies ahead for me now.

"You should consider yourself lucky. Other academies are not as nice as this," she says. "Trust me, it could be much worse. You're lucky they sent you here, Elimina."

I want to tell her that I've never felt lucky, especially now. But maybe I've got it all wrong. I thought it was unlucky to grow up in Capedown, where no one looked like me, where my face and my X disgusted everyone. Now I'm not so sure. Maybe I was lucky then and now I'm not. Or maybe what I've always known somewhere deep inside is really true after all. Maybe I was born unlucky. Marked for a horrible life.

Along the path, two boys inspecting a tree stop to watch us.

"Why is everyone staring?" I say after we pass them.

"People always stare at new kids," Josephine says. "I can't imagine anybody's ever met a project kid before. Someone who's lived out there with Mainlanders, like a Mainlander. Word travels fast around here."

Josephine stops in front of a large statue of a man hunched over a cane, his glasses angled down on the tip of his nose. A plaque under his feet reads: "Mr. Henry Livingstone—Founder of Livingstone Academy. A man dedicated to the growth and development of Gutter children pursuing greatness."

"Have you ever seen such an ugly mug?" Josephine says, and for the first time we both smile at the same time.

The only statues in Capedown were of General Colin Covey— the Founder and Father of the Mainland, whose name appeared all over town. There was Covey Court and Covey Lane and the C1 Covey Overpass, which connected Capedown to towns all along the Sunset Coast and throughout the Mainland. Unlike Henry Livingstone, General Covey was incredibly handsome, as though his sharp jaw, broad shoulders and black wavy hair destined him to be powerful, as though he was meant to be carved in stone.

Inside schools and hospitals and every Mainland government building, there were paintings and statues of Covey, featuring his most famous words: "For the greatness of the country."

Whenever Mother and I went on walks, Mainlanders would say these words with tense expressions, their eyes fixed on me. "For the greatness of the country," they would say to Mother in a way that sounded more like a warning.

"For the greatness of the country," she'd mutter under her breath—the last line from that long quotation in my history book: "Every Gutter man, woman and child will toil and struggle, and when they succeed, when they rise above their circumstances and redeem their place on this land, we will celebrate their toil and their labor. 'For the greatness of the country,' we will shout."

"Am I from the Gutter?" I remember asking Mother.

"You were born in the Gutter. But you *live* here, Elimina. You are as much a Mainlander as I am."

"Then why do I have this scar?"

"Because you are my special gift. Because you are a gift to all of us."

"Then why does everyone hate me?" I would say, and she would shrug her shoulders and hold her palms up like this was a mystery that we might never solve.

THE SINGLE PATH that stretches from the back of the Main House splits toward three buildings beyond the Henry Livingstone statue: the West Hall, where the girls sleep, the East Hall, where the boys sleep, and a large red barn known as the Fieldhouse.

Josephine takes the center path toward the red barn, where boys in black rubber boots plant flowers and turn soil with sharp spades.

"Most of the boys work in landscape and maintenance or agriculture. They spend their days down here in the fields or the Fieldhouse, sunup to sundown," Josephine says, as we move down the path. "There are a few girls who work down here, but I wouldn't recommend it. Frankly, you don't look like the type."

I stare at her, unsure of what she means or how to respond, like she's speaking in a whole other language I don't know.

"Mr. Gregors will ask you tomorrow, about housekeeping or kitchen work," she says. "I'd figure out what you want to say sooner than later, or who knows where you'll get assigned."

In Capedown, and in all Mainland cities, kids weren't allowed to work until they were eighteen. When they weren't in school, they could play sports, read, join the band, dance, perform, draw. Anything but work. "Play Now," the billboards read. Although, for as long as I could remember, Mainlanders who saw me in the grocery store or walking along the street would say something quite the opposite.

"You should put that girl to work or she'll get ideas," they would say to Mother.

I was never sure what kind of ideas they meant.

"Guess this is a bit of a demotion for you," Josephine says. "Way we heard it when we were growing up is that project cases had it all. Lived like kings and queens out there."

"Hardly," I say as I kick a rock down the path.

"Look, I had a hard time when I came here too," Josephine says. "But you won't always feel bad."

"I miss my mom," I say with a small, shaky voice, and Josephine nods like she understands.

A tall boy with long arms steps out of the Fieldhouse, and when he sees Josephine, he smiles and heads toward us. They spread their arms wide and squeeze each other so tightly, Josephine's feet lift high off the ground.

"This is David," she says when he finally puts her down. "And this . . . is Elimina."

"Nice to meet you, Elimina," David says with a smile that's full of crowded, crooked teeth.

Even though he can't be more than sixteen, his face seems grown-up somehow, like he's too old to be here, like the rest of us are just kids.

In the distance, a Mainlander in a security guard uniform makes his way toward the East Hall with a dog that's pulling hard on its leash, barking and sniffing the ground.

"That's Mack. I should go," David says with a long sigh.

"Us too," Josephine says, stepping away with a nod.

She pushes me toward the Fieldhouse, waving me ahead, and when I start down the path, I see David pull on Josephine's arm and whisper in her ear. She smiles and he holds her face in his hands for a moment, kissing her on the cheek before he goes.

When Josephine sees me watching them, she heads toward me quickly and grabs me by the arm.

"Let's go," she says, squeezing so tight it hurts.

"Ow. Josephine—"

"Best to keep your eyes, ears and nose on what you need to know and not what you don't. That's a good rule to follow around here, Elimina," she says. "Or this won't be the only pain you know."

THE FIELDHOUSE IS a labyrinth of hallways filled with gated stalls for animals and large cupboards for storing supplies. Josephine leads us through the main entryway, where some boys push wheelbarrows full of manure and others spread fresh straw.

"Jimmy, take that pile out to Will on field two," one boy says.

"Coming through," another shouts, carrying a long plank of wood.

The sour stench of manure is so thick that I can feel it in my throat and taste it on my tongue. But Josephine just keeps going, talking to me like it doesn't bother her at all.

She points at tools and explains the role of the field hands, stopping at a stall where a girl with crooked braids sits on a low stool and scrapes mud from the hooves of a horse. A second girl stands next to her, brushing the horse and humming a song.

They're both dressed in white T-shirts and worn gray pants,

just like the boys, and when I look at their faces, I notice fresh bruises running all the way around their necks in a dark band. I stare at the marks closely as the girl on the stool picks up a piece of manure and flings it, barely missing my nose.

"Don't you know it's rude to stare, project kid," she says, and I feel my face go red.

"I'm sorry. I'm so sorry," I say.

I look at Josephine, worried that I've done something wrong, and the two girls hold on to their bellies, laughing hard at my expression and the manure that's splattered on the wall.

"Ally and Sam are about as crazy as they come," Josephine says, heading farther down the hallway. "Rumor has it Mr. Gregors tried to get them to wear dresses and do housekeeping when they first got here. But when he saw that they could work like the boys, only cleaner, well, he can get more for them doing that, so why not," she says.

We hear shouts from somewhere near the front entrance and we rush toward the doors, where a boy with thick muscles is dragging a skinny boy in a red vest into the Fieldhouse while the other boys gather around.

"What's going on?" Josephine says to one of the boys.

"Rowan is about to fight Louis."

"Well, I can't say I'm surprised," she says, shaking her head as Ally and Sam join us at the back of the crowd.

"Let me go, Rowan!" the red-vested boy says, pulling at his collar, which Rowan has gripped in his fist. "I'm warning you. Let me go!"

Rowan looks at the boy and grits his teeth, slamming him against the side wall.

"You better let me go, Rowan. I swear to god. Do you know what I can do to you?" Louis shouts.

But I can tell by his thin arms and the sharp, pretty bones of his face that if this turns into a fistfight, Louis doesn't stand a chance.

"Louis, you can't do a damn thing. You talk, but no one listens, man," Rowan says.

"Rowan! Rowan! Rowan!" the boys who've gathered around shout, their voices growing louder and louder as Louis looks at all of them, trying hard not to show that he's scared.

"Mr. Gregors won't believe you," he yells. "I'm the one he listens to!"

The walls of the Fieldhouse start to shudder and shake as the boys bang their shovels, some grabbing slabs of wood or metal and clapping them together. "Rowan! Rowan! Rowan!"

I think of the times in Capedown when people surrounded Mother and me and shouted "Gutter" over and over, and I press my hands against my ears and close my eyes, but I can still hear everything.

"I'm about to end you and that stupid red vest," Rowan says.

"Then do it," Louis says, nodding his head toward Rowan and the others, pretending he's tough just for show.

Rowan reaches back and punches the wall next to Louis's head so the wood bends and splinters, and suddenly Louis looks genuinely afraid, like he knows his face is next.

"I will get you leashed, Rowan. Two days. A week even, you hear me? Like I did with those two," Louis squeaks, nodding toward Ally and Sam, their hands instinctively reaching for their necks, their faces filled with worry. "And not one of these Gutter-fools who are calling your name will be able to stop me."

Louis smiles, slow and wide, as though an idea has suddenly come to him. "In fact . . . maybe instead of leashing you, I'll put one of them on the leashes instead."

The cheering quietens, as though this threat is actually working, as though they're all really worried.

But Rowan just turns to the crowd and raises his fist. "Woof, woof, woof," he says, and the boys bark in response. "Woof! Woof! Woof!"

Rowan smiles and bounces on his toes closer to Louis, then farther away, fists raised, like he's waiting for Louis to step up. But Louis just stands there, wide-eyed and terrified, as the barking and banging get louder.

"Woof, woof, woof!"

"Stop. That's enough. Stop it, Rowan!" a voice from behind the crowd says.

The cheering gets quieter as David makes his way through the group, shovel in hand, blade up like a scepter—the tallest of all the boys, looking somehow like royalty.

"Let him go, Rowan," David says.

Rowan grabs Louis by the collar of his shirt again, his other hand ready to strike. "But, David, he—"

"Save your fists. Do you want to get leashed?"

Rowan rolls his eyes like this threat is unconvincing, keeping his hand in a tight ball.

"The Decos will be back for afternoon check-ins soon," David says, loud enough so everyone can hear him. "You want them to find you all here, doing nothing good? You all want the leashes?"

Ally and Sam scatter off quickly, like that's all the warning they need, followed by a few of the younger boys. But the older boys nervously eye each other, unsure of whether to back Rowan up or listen to David and go.

"Get back to work. Go on. There's no fight today," David says, and when Rowan finally releases his grip on Louis, the boys groan and head back to work.

"Always nice talking to you, Rowan," Louis sneers, slithering out of reach.

"Today was your lucky day, Louis."

"Whatever, Rowan. I'm not afraid of you," Louis says. But when Rowan makes a move toward him, Louis ducks behind David, who stands between the two of them.

"Enough, Rowan. It's not worth the trouble it'll cause," David says.

Rowan reluctantly steps back, shaking his head as Louis heads toward the doors to the Fieldhouse. "I've got my eye on you, Rowan! You step out of line and I got you next time."

"Alright, Louis, that's enough," David says as he follows Louis out of the Fieldhouse, nudging him with his shovel to speed him along.

When everyone is gone, Rowan grabs a dry rag from the wall and cleans the blood off his fist, spitting on the back of his hand and wiping it with the cloth. "If I had known we had real ladies in the room, I might have given Louis a swing just for show," he says, smiling at us and moving closer.

Josephine rolls her eyes, pulling me toward the door like it's time for us to go.

"So, you're the project kid," he says, stepping in front and blocking our way.

"Her name is Elimina and you're really lucky David stopped you today, Rowan."

"Louis needs a good punch in the face," Rowan says, smirking and shrugging his shoulders.

"Maybe. But you could have gotten yourself into a whole lot of trouble."

"Ah, Jose, you and David worry too much. Don't they worry too much, Elimina?" He smiles at me, waiting for me to respond, and I nod.

"We gotta go, Rowan," Josephine says, shaking her head like she's disappointed in me for taking his side. "Try and stay out of trouble."

"Does that mean you care about me, Jose?"

Josephine doesn't answer, but when I look back at Rowan, he winks and smiles. "See you around, Elimina."

"See ya around," I say as Josephine pulls me toward the door.

"Look, don't talk to him, okay?" she says, stopping outside of the Fieldhouse and crossing her arms.

"Who?"

"Rowan! Just . . . keep your distance," she says.

"Why?"

Josephine shakes her head. "Just take my word for it."

WE TOUR THE fruit trees and the greenhouse, where academy students grow spices and herbs for the kitchen and for sale at the local market, before making our way to a cobblestone courtyard behind the Main House.

A pair of long, thick chains are attached to the wall with cuffs that lay open on the ground.

"Are these for the dogs?" I say, looking around.

Josephine bites down hard on her lip and shakes her head. "Those aren't for dogs, Elimina."

"Then what are they for?" I say, my skin suddenly cold, tiny bumps rising along my arms.

"Those are the leashes. That's what Louis was talking about back at the Fieldhouse . . . It's what they do when you don't follow the rules. It's where you sleep. It's where you eat. It's where you take a piss. And they make the rest of us come out and bark at you."

I think of the boys barking in the Fieldhouse like dogs.

"Who? Who makes you do that?"

"Louis. Mr. Gregors."

"For how long?" I whisper. "How long do they leave you here?"

"One day. Sometimes two. Ally and Sam—the girls from the Fieldhouse—they just finished three days."

I think of their bruises, the dark marks around their necks. "Why?" I say, my voice high and broken, my hands pressed against my face.

"They got caught sneaking around the East Hall after hours."

I walk over to the chains, and Josephine follows, her eyes peering up at the window, like she's checking to see if we're being watched. I lean over and feel the metal chain and the collar, both hot from the sun.

"They can't do this," I say, and Josephine scoffs and shakes her head.

"Of course they can. This is an academy. This isn't Mainland City or whatever fancy place you've been living. We're here to work. This is how it is for people like us."

I swallow hard, my throat dry and tight like it may close up entirely if I don't keep swallowing. *People like us.*

"Just so we're clear, you're not to tell anyone about what you saw today," she says. "You understand?"

I nod, unsure of what exactly she means—the kiss from David or the fight between Rowan and Louis.

"Tell Mr. Gregors you had a perfect tour of this fine, prestigious academy," she says, in a voice that's high and fancy. "Tell him you're excited to be here and that you want to do whatever job he's got for you. But do not mention anything else. Do you understand?"

She watches me closely, waiting for me to respond.

"I don't belong here," I say. Tears start rolling down my

cheeks, like they've been waiting days to fall, and when I feel a ringing in my ear and a sting in my cheek, I look up at Josephine, shocked by the force of her hand.

But she's calm and relaxed, like she'll slap me again if I don't stop.

"Listen, Elimina. We've lived in two different worlds, and we are not blood, but in this place, we are going to treat each other that way anyway. I will look out for you and you will do the same for me and for every other Gutter kid who's just trying to make it out of here and get on with their lives. You may just have the one scar and you may have lived differently before now, but you are here, just like the rest of us."

I look down at the scar on my right hand, and when I look back up, I nod. But deep inside, I want to believe that Josephine is wrong.

X 3

MR. GREGORS IS STANDING IN FRONT OF A LARGE WINdow that runs along one side of his office when I arrive the following morning, tired from a restless night. It's the kind of office I imagine important Mainland officials having, the kind full of sunshine and light, and I pull my shoulders back in my new Livingstone uniform, just like Mother would want. *Stand tall and confident, Elimina.*

The floors, the shelves and all of the furniture in Mr. Gregors's office are a deep reddish-brown and the air smells like stale cigars. A white General Covey statue sits on a pillar in the corner while an antelope with sprawling antlers stares from the wall—glossy black eyes, mouth slightly open, like it was killed mid-cry as a prize.

"You're right on time. I like that," Mr. Gregors says, turning slightly as the sun streaks through the glass. "How was your tour?"

"It was good, sir."

"I trust that Josephine was helpful, that she showed you just what a magnificent place we have here."

"She was very helpful, sir."

He sits down at a desk covered in files, gesturing toward one of the chairs and inviting me to sit down.

"I have to say, there was a part of me that was rather worried about your arrival," he says, picking up one folder from the small stack in front of him and reading the label before setting it aside.

"Worried, sir?"

"I understand that this is your first time being with children who are . . . like you, shall I say. But from what I can tell, you are handling it with an excellent measure of grace."

I sit there, unsure how to respond, unsure how to feel about his words "quite like you." *I'm not a Gutter child. They're not like me at all.*

"Where is it you lived again?" he says, still searching the files, lifting and checking them one at a time before placing them off to the side.

"Capedown," I say. "On the coast."

"Ah, yes. Of course. Capedown. I traveled there once, on a fishing excursion," he says. "Not a bite to be had, in the water that is, but the food was absolutely divine. The town has a quaint feel despite its size, if I recall. All those little shops. There was this delicious seafood restaurant. Marty's, was it?"

"Molly's Seafood Shack," I say.

It's the most popular place in the whole city, but I've never been allowed to eat there.

"Yes. Yes. Just the most delicious salmon steak. I daresay it's the best I've ever had."

He picks up a file and gives it a flick of approval, raising it up, like he's found the one he wants. I see my name typed on the label on the left-hand side as he lays it down: Elimina Madeleine Dubois.

"Elimina, my students usually come to see me on their first day for a little chat," he says, and I notice how he pronounces his words so precisely, so the richness of his speech matches everything he wears and the decor of his office. "We talk about the kind of work they've been doing and the kind of work they would like to do here at the academy. But I know things have been *different* for you. So I have something else in mind. If you're open to it."

I nod and he smiles, like this pleases him.

"Your debt is almost negligible, which is a fantastic way to start. It's one of the reasons—"

"My debt?"

"Your Gutter debt," he says, as though this should be obvious.

I look at him, and he stares back, tilting his head.

"Miss Dubois must have told you about your debt?" he says and I sit taller, wiggling awkwardly in the chair.

Mr. Gregors leans forward, placing his elbows on the desk, like he's confused or maybe even angry. "You do know why you're here, don't you? I mean certainly you know that."

I bite down hard on my lip, wiggling my mouth side to side.

"Oh for heaven's sake," he says. He lets out a long, slow exhale, pressing his fingers together and bringing them close to his mouth like he's not sure where to start. "Let me ask you, Elimina: Do you consider yourself a Gutter child?"

I look down at my hands before I respond, trying to relieve all the tightness in my chest, trying to keep my voice steady and calm. "Mother said I was only *born* a Gutter child. That that's not who I am or how I should be treated or what I should be called, sir."

Mr. Gregors raises his eyebrows and pauses for a moment, squishing his mouth to one side. "Well, first of all, let me just say that I'm truly sorry for your loss. I lost my mother when I was a teenager, and it nearly ruined me. It certainly ruined my father. It's a terrible thing to go through. For any child. But . . . regardless of what Miss Dubois told you, or what she *wanted* before she died, it's important for you to know that *legally* you are a Gutter child.

You are a ward of the nation. And there are rules and laws that dictate what that means for you, *especially* now that Miss Dubois has passed on. That scar still means something, Elimina. Even if you have just the one."

When I was growing up, Mother told me that my scar was just like a birthmark. Special. Unique. She said it didn't matter what others said to me about it, and it didn't matter how I got it. "Now, my dear, is all that matters," she said.

When I asked her more questions, she refused to answer. "Not now, Elimina," she would say, like I was somehow being difficult.

Eventually, she told me that my mother had given me up on the day I was born because she knew she couldn't take care of me. She wanted me to be a part of a special project that meant I could have everything I wanted in life, just like a Mainlander. When I asked her why she couldn't tell me more, she told me it was because she wanted me to live *unfettered*, a word that sounded so beautiful and boundless, like a bird on the wind—a word that made me trust that she knew best until it was too late to know better.

In the hospital, I thought of all the questions she had never answered, and I prayed for her to wake up, whispering all my questions in her ear as though it might bring her back: "Where am I really from? What happened to my other family, the ones who look like me? Are they in the Gutter? Is it true what they say, that that's where I belong?"

But she never woke up. And when her brain shut off completely, when the beeps on the machine by her bed turned to one solid scream, I knew I had waited too long to ask.

There's a light knock on the door and, on Mr. Gregors's command, a slender girl with a tight, dark ponytail that swirls like soft ice cream enters the room.

"Do you need these right away, Mr. Gregors?" she says, holding up a handful of files just like the pile on his desk.

"No, Violet. Leave them with Miss Templeton," he says.

She turns to leave but Mr. Gregors calls her name before the door closes all the way.

"Violet, before you go," he says, moving toward her and leaning in, lowering his voice. "Have Miss Darling prepare the red jacket."

"The red jacket?" she says, emphasizing *red*.

"Yes. Have her check the buttons to see if they need tightening, and then bring it here as quickly as you can."

She looks at Mr. Gregors and then at me, tightening her jaw so all of the bones stick out pointy and sharp. "Of course, Mr. Gregors," she mutters.

"Another bright academy student. Just an impressive lot of them, if I do say so myself," he says, once the door closes and Violet is gone. "Now where were we, Elimina?"

"You were explaining my debt," I say.

"Ah yes. Of course. How could I forget? The Gutter System. A fascinating topic. I could quite literally talk about it for hours. I studied it in university and it never gets old. But don't you worry, Elimina. I'll spare you the torture of all those lectures," he says, smiling at me with all of his straight teeth.

"Please, sir, I'd like to know," I say. "Mother . . . didn't tell me much."

Mr. Gregors nods like he understands, but I wonder if he can.

"Your debt, your scar and your status as a ward of the nation are all tied together. Part of a very intricate economic system. It's important for you to understand that, Elimina."

I nod, swallowing hard.

"The Mainland is built on one of the most advanced economic

systems in the world. It's a model of revolutionary forward-thinking. Thousands of books have been written about it, and nations from all over the world have tried to copy what we've done," he says, using his hands in grand gestures as he moves along the walls of books. "But I truly believe that what we've done here can never be duplicated in quite the same way. That's how impressive it is."

He pauses at a painting of a Mainland ship pressing through waves in a storm.

"Tell me, Elimina, what do you know about the way the Mainland was founded?" he says.

I think back to the history lessons Mother provided, and the books we took out of the library. "I know that Mainlanders landed on the Sunset Coast a few hundred years ago. I know that's how the Mainland became the Mainland."

He smiles and nods proudly. "It was a remarkable time of travel. Mainlanders were just explorers at the time, and we were welcomed with open arms. Given places to live and observe and study the land and the people who lived on it. We brought gifts, of course, to make it worthwhile," he says with a small laugh before moving toward the Covey statue, adjusting the head by turning it to the left.

"We saw the Sunset Coast as a prime location for future trade. Plenty of people had stopped here before, but all the things that had been written about it implied that beyond the coast, this place was just a wasteland of heat and dust, a wild jungle. Can you believe that? I mean, we're inland now, and it's simply beautiful," he says, moving toward the window and staring out at the grounds.

"Did you know that this is the largest floating landmass in the world? No one had ever said that back then, but it's true. It's one of the reasons we decided to stay. To build something great on this massive land and to raise its people up at the same time. But nation-building is complicated work," he says, moving to his bookshelves, his finger and thumb pinched around his chin. "I mean there were over fifty-four tribes living here, speaking different dialects of a very complicated language that was virtually impossible to understand or translate in any meaningful way. So when we decided to stay and do the hard work of building a nation, we had to take on the responsibility of drafting the first agreement—guidelines about how this future nation would be governed and developed, how it would grow with all of us in mind."

He selects a book and flips through it, turning the pages and sliding his finger up and down each page.

"Now, I'm a little embarrassed to say this, but I've been trying to think of what you folks called yourselves initially. It's on the very tip of my tongue. Either way, we called this place the Mainland for obvious reasons. I mean, if you've only ever lived here, you might not know that there are small islands and medium-sized places all around the world. But this one is the biggest. The Main Land," he says, lifting his hands. "The land of all lands, as we like to say."

He continues to turn pages, searching for a particular part of the book, then smacking the page suddenly.

"Sossi!" he shouts, and I jump, placing one hand on my chest. "That's what they called this place! Sossi territory. Sossi people. How could I forget that?"

"Soh-see," I say, letting the word roll around on my tongue.

"Yes. Exactly. Sossi people lived very simply at the time. Simple homes and villages. Which is a perfectly lovely way to live, don't get me wrong. I mean, we could all stand to live with a little less, to trust the weather or the universe to guide us. But that way of life is less than ideal for building a nation. That story-and-drum-and-sit-around-the-fire country life is quaint. But it's just not ideal for really prospering. Do you want to have a look at this?"

He holds the book out to me, and I take it: *Building a Nation: The History of the Mainland* by Norman Holloway. The pages are filled with small print, scattered with drawings of Mainland soldiers and Sossi people in thin strips of cloth or animal fur.

"Go on. Have a read," he says, waving me on, like he wants me to read it out loud.

"'Sossi people lived like great creatures of the land, marvelous beasts roaming the earth, guided by the animals they killed to eat of their flesh and adorn on their bodies—tawny skin they strip from the bones of God's creation and stitch into cloth from miraculous feats of brute strength.'"

I close the page and Mr. Gregors smiles, pleased not only by the words of the book but my ability to read them so well.

"Feel free to take it out and read it whenever you like," he says. "It's fascinating. Impeccably written."

"Thank you, sir," I say, holding it in my lap.

"Now, the tribes who lived here didn't write anything down, if you can believe it. They had never formally documented anything. They had never seen an agreement like the one we created when we arrived—a written document that took years to create and craft, that defined and established a nation. But when the Mainland Agreement was done, we all sat down together and signed it into law. It was an exciting time, of course, but one of the most important aspects of the agreement, and one of the things I studied closely as an undergraduate, because to me it is the heart of the matter, was the care that was taken to spell out the values of this nation and how the land would be developed. There's no sense having a bunch of huts and firepits on land that's got valuable resources. That's just bad economics. We wanted this land to prosper, so hard choices had to be made for the greater good. And I truly believe that everyone understood that—at least initially. You see, the Sunset Coast was a major draw. But it was the place where many Sossi tribes were already well-established. The development of the Mainland as a nation required us to develop the Sunset Coast into a place with more modern accoutrements."

"So the people who lived there had to move?" I say, turning to drawings of Sossi people carrying their belongings with wide, toothy smiles on their faces.

"They weren't forced. No one pushed them out, despite what some say. Sossi people were given useful incentives to go farther inland and to develop new areas, in accordance with the Mainland Agreement—to create more growth by developing the resources we all needed to survive. For the greatness of the nation, as we say. The mistake, if you can call it that, was the way land developers handled relocations. There were taxes and fees that weren't care-fully explained. Gutter folks had never had to pay for their homes, and they didn't like the change. They didn't understand how it benefited all of us," he says. "Eventually, most of the fifty-four tribes decided they didn't like what they'd agreed to and that it was time for us to go. Well, you can imagine how that went."

"That's what led to the Great War," I say, and Mr. Gregors nods, looking out the window with one hand against his waist.

By the time Mainland kids start school, they all know about the Great War, which went on for three years and took more than ten thousand lives in a hard-fought war of ideals.

"It's important to know, Elimina, that there was a process for grievances that was built into the governance model embedded in the Mainland Agreement. It's not talked about as much as it should be, but it's important to note. This wasn't a unilateral experience. But instead of following procedures, Sossi people resorted to what they knew. They attacked places all along the Sunset Coast, setting fire to important buildings and critical military hubs. And they did so quite recklessly," he says. "But Mainlanders are resourceful, and after all we did here, we weren't going to leave the nation we had started without fighting back."

I look down at the book, turning to pictures of Mainlanders standing in fields, guns raised and pointed.

"The real tragedy of this rebellion is not just that it happened, but that so many people died along the way. Sossi plans were poorly conceived and particularly violent. In my opinion, they demonstrated a lack of military knowledge that cost far more lives than necessary. They had signed an agreement, and then they went back on their word, fighting us with the very weapons that were bestowed upon them when we arrived. They killed generals and soldiers, one of whom happened to be one of my great-great-great-grandfathers. They left women without husbands and children without fathers, and is there anything worse than that?" he says, shaking his head.

I think of the Victory Day celebrations, the biggest national holiday on the Mainland, when everyone celebrates the day the war ended and the point where the economy began to soar. A day when everyone remembers the Mainlanders who sacrificed their lives.

"Which brings us to the Gutter System," Mr. Gregors says, clapping and extending his hands, like he's finally arrived at the point. "Despite the victory—or perhaps because of it—Mainlanders felt very strongly that after the war there should be clear consequences to prevent something like this from happening again. If nothing was done, what would stop another group from turning to violence to solve their problems when they got upset about something, rather than trusting the processes that were built into the Mainland Agreement?" He gestures toward the Covey statue with a nod. "Which is why General Covey established the Gutter System."

"The Gutter *System*," I say, like I'm making notes in my head, like I'm finally going to understand exactly why I'm here and everything that's ahead now that Mother is gone.

"The Great War was the destiny of this nation. Despite its losses, the war was an important part of establishing the Mainland's presence in the world. We wouldn't be who we are without fighting for what we believed in, without defending what we built and what we wanted. It's why we remember it so fiercely. The war taught us that struggle and sacrifice, and the success that follows, would define us as a country. Struggle and sacrifice make us great. And the genius of the Gutter System is that it's built on this same premise, that people need to struggle *and succeed* for their own good and for the good of the country."

I think of what Mother used to say about hard work and sacrifice, of her response to the tears that came when I wished for friends or when I prayed for people to stop staring at me. *Struggle makes you stronger, Elimina.*

"To pay back the Mainland for the lives that were lost and the damages that were incurred, and to prove they wanted to be here and build with us, Sossi people were fined for their role in the rebellion. They were required to work off their individual debt and earn back their freedom. The Gutter System is built on the premise of Redemption Freedom," he says. "It is rooted in the long-held belief that freedom is something you fight for and earn."

"So I'm not free?" I say, pausing and staring at him, unsure what this all means. "Sir, I don't understand."

"You might *believe* you are free," he says, tilting his head side to side. "You probably *feel* free in some ways based on your upbringing in particular. But like most Gutter folks, as they're now called, you *are* a ward of this nation, with a debt that's assigned and passed down until it's paid off."

"But Mother . . . But I don't . . ."

Mr. Gregors shakes his head, raising his hand so I'll stop. "The Gutter Enhancement Project—the initiative that brought you to Miss Dubois—does not protect you from your past. So long as you have that mark, Elimina, you are a Gutter child and you are in debt."

I sit back with my arms crossed over my chest, my throat thick and tight as I think quietly about this for a moment while Mr. Gregors waits. "Why wouldn't Mother tell me any of this?"

"Perhaps Miss Dubois had her reasons, perhaps she thought you would be debt-free before you discovered you weren't. I don't know," he says, shrugging his shoulders. "At least you got a proper education out of it. It's more than what most get."

"I never went to school, Mr. Gregors."

Despite the approvals Mother received to enroll me in Capedown Elementary, I never attended a Mainland school. On my first day, crowds gathered and yelled for me to stay out, to go back home. They carried posters on wooden sticks with pictures of my face covered in a big red X. "Go home, Gutter," they said. And I wanted to. I wanted to go back to our house on Harriet Street as soon as I saw them. But I knew what they really wanted to do was send me to the Gutter.

Mother insisted that once I was inside the school, I'd be fine. "The teachers and the police, they're here to protect you," she said. But when she left for her shift at the restaurant, a group of students pulled me into the washroom and stuck my face in a toilet that hadn't been flushed, and when I stepped out into the hallway, students scrunched up their faces and pinched their noses, calling me shitface.

I locked the door to the bathroom and sat on the floor until I heard Mother's voice calling sometime later. "Elimina? Elimina, are you in there? It's okay, honey. I'm here."

When I finally came out, Mother stormed down the hall, pulling me hard by the arm. "I have worked too hard for too long with Elimina for you to go and ruin her now," she shouted at the teachers and the principal who stood cross-armed in the halls to watch us go.

Mother taught me from home after that, receiving small monthly checks from the Seaside School Board on contract as a substitute teacher. But I never forgot that first day. That was the day I decided that being a Gutter child was some kind of curse, and that I wanted no part of it. Mother was right. I was just like any other Mainlander. I could do or be anything. I belonged to the place I had lived all my life, not to a place I had never even visited—a place I never intended to go.

"I'm shocked to hear that you were treated that way. Disappointed, in fact," Mr. Gregors says when I tell him the story. "But it will not be like that here at Livingstone. I assure you of that."

I nod, fingering the book in my lap. "How much is my debt, sir?"

Mr. Gregors opens my file again and uses his index finger to search for the amount.

"You will graduate from Livingstone Academy with a debt of $25,000. That covers your room and board here, and it's well below the national average, which seems to increase at an appalling rate every day."

"Twenty-five thousand dollars?" I whisper, trying to breathe evenly, which suddenly feels hard. "How am I supposed to pay that off?"

"Through hard work and discipline. Which is exactly what we teach here, Elimina. We'll help you secure a job and work it all off."

"But, sir, how long will that take?"

"It depends on your employer—on your salary and their investment—which will all be determined by your hiring package. But we will help you with all of that," he says. "The national average for Gutter children graduating from a school like ours is $75,000. Some more. Some less. Every situation is unique. But it's rare, Elimina, to have a student with less than $50,000 of debt. Families just aren't doing their part, and it all falls on these young kids, who have to leave home and figure things out on their own. But, if you're looking for an age, I would say that most people on the academy track are looking at Redemption Freedom by the time they're about sixty years old."

"Sixty?" I say, my throat catching, like there's something stuck inside.

"Sometimes sixty-five," he says. "But students here fare a bit better than the average, and your freedom will come much faster based on your debt and your training here and your Mainland experience. I expect you'll be forty years old at most. And if you get a good employer, it could be even earlier," he says. "And we've got an outstanding reputation at this school. I really don't want you to worry."

But all I feel is worry. Mother was forty years old when she died.

"As I said, students from Livingstone Academy fare far better on the Mainland than those from other institutions. They do far better than the kids who come from other academies and certainly far better than those who are working for this from inside the Gutter. You have the best chance of doing this, Elimina. Best chance I've seen in a long time."

"Chance," I say, rubbing the lines of my scar.

"The scars are barbaric, I admit that," he says. "No one has been able to agree on a better way. There's been talk of turning to papers, but there's concern over how to keep track of folks and how to know who is in debt and who's Redemptioned out. Can't get everyone to agree, and so nothing is done, I'm afraid. Fortunately, you just have the one."

There's a knock at the door, and I place the book down on the desk as Mr. Gregors rises quickly, like he's anxious to change the subject. When he opens the door, Violet is standing in the doorway with a red garment draped over her arm, looking in my direction with a scowl.

She opens her mouth to say something, but Mr. Gregors just takes the coat and closes the door.

"Sir?" she says, extending one hand and sliding it forward to keep the door from closing.

"Now, now, Violet. Go on and get back to work," he says. When the door is closed, he holds the coat proudly toward me. "Well, come along now, Elimina. This certainly isn't going to fit me."

I stand up and touch the fabric, running my hands over a material that's red like the feathers of a beautiful bird. The gold buttons send flickers of yellow light around the room, dancing around the ceiling and across my face as Mr. Gregors shakes it again.

"Well, don't just stand there looking foolish. Try it on," he says with a grin.

I slide my arms through each sleeve as Mr. Gregors helps lift it onto my shoulders. It's a mixture of a light blazer and a shawl, and it's the most incredible thing I've ever worn.

"Now I know you've had a hard week, and I know this was a lot to take in," he says. "I wish I wasn't the one to tell you all of this. But this coat is very special, Elimina—a symbol of my absolute confidence in you. You are going to do great things here at Livingstone Academy and beyond this campus as well. Do you understand that? Do you understand how much I believe in you?"

I nod with my lips pressed tightly together.

"You said that a Gutter child is not who you are but simply the place you were born, and I think that's a tremendous way for you to look at things, especially now. You are not like anyone else here. You *are* special, and I will do everything I can to help you see that, to help you get Redemption Freedom as quickly as possible. I believe this coat will help."

"This coat? But how, sir?" I say, staring down at the fabric and the buttons, fingering the outline of the hood.

"The red coat is reserved for Livingstone's most trustworthy and important students," he says, guiding me toward the window. "You will be my eyes and ears out there, Elimina. When employers see this red coat, they'll know that you are the best of the best."

I watch the students working, sweat dripping through their shirts, my red coat glowing in the reflection of the window, vibrant like the tip of a match.

"Students at Livingstone Academy are happy to be here," Mr. Gregors says. "And it's good for everyone if it stays that way. You will keep me and all of the students on campus safe and satisfied. As a Red Coat, you and Louis will maintain happiness, as I like to say."

"Louis—the one with the red vest?" I say, thinking about the boy from the Fieldhouse.

"Yes. Louis is one of my senior students. He turned his coat into a vest because he's . . . well, he's very particular about how things look," Mr. Gregors says with a laugh. "But I tell you, he's the best Red Coat I've ever had. You will learn a lot from him."

I think about the fight in the Fieldhouse, and all of the things that he said.

"Will I have to send people to the leashes?"

Mr. Gregors smiles and puts his hand around my shoulder. "The goal—the hope—is always that it never comes to that, Elimina. I, for one, would prefer it if we never needed the leashes at all. But sometimes it's necessary, and I always leave that up to my Red Coats to decide."

I stuff my hands in the pockets of the coat. "So, this is my job?" I say. "To be a Red Coat?"

Mr. Gregors smiles. "It's part of it. But that's hardly enough work to keep you busy day in and day out. And a busy life is a happy life. Or is it the other way around?" he says, pausing for a moment to think before dismissing the thought with a wave of his hand. "Louis works in housekeeping—he's very good with a needle and thread. But my plan for you, Elimina, is that you will work here, in the office, with Miss Templeton."

"The office, sir?"

"Well I don't suppose you can cook or clean?" he says, and when I shake my head, he laughs again. "Don't worry. Violet is not the domestic type either, and she works here as well, as you saw. I'm certain you two will get along."

But when I think about the way Violet looked at me when Mr. Gregors wasn't watching, and the way she handed him the coat, I know that Mr. Gregors is wrong. Violet is not going to be happy about this at all.

4

M R. GREGORS'S ASSISTANT IS A THICK-BELLIED WOMAN with white hair and pointy glasses. She moves around the office in a colorful knee-length dress explaining the filing system and the different kinds of work I'll be doing while Violet does inventory in the West Hall.

"Let's just hope Mr. Gregors knows what he's doing," Miss Templeton says as she busies about the main office, making room for a second station next to Violet's, where I can work.

She selects two small packages and instructs me to follow her out of the office and down the main hall, her chunky heels pounding against the floor and echoing off the walls.

"The departments for employment are very important at Livingstone Academy, Elimina," she says. Her voice is high and wavy, her words rising and falling like a song. "They define all the types of work students can do to prepare for their future. You'll want to memorize all six of them quickly. I want you to know who runs them and how they like things, and I want you to get real familiar with the students assigned to each department as well. Every student. First and last. You understand?"

"Yes, ma'am," I say, swallowing hard at the thought of knowing all seventy-three students at Livingstone Academy by name.

"Each department is headed by a Department Coordinator—we call them Decos for short. The Decos monitor the work and progress of their students. Most of them are in charge of about ten to twenty, some have more, depending on the department and the work that's required. There are a few exceptions, of course. But let's start with all the Decos' names, shall we?" she says, pointing at the notebook and the pen in my hand, as we reach the top of the stairs.

"Yes, ma'am," I say, ready to write.

"Miss Dora Darling (Housekeeping), Chef Boris McCain (Kitchen), Mr. Timothy Smith (Landscape and General Maintenance) and Mr. Marcus Warren (Agriculture)," she says, speaking a little more slowly than before but not slow enough, as I scribble down the names.

She points out all of their offices as we make our way around the second floor, and I write down the room numbers and any notes about special delivery instructions.

"Never enter Miss Darling's office. And when I say never, I mean never. Even if there's a fire and you think you can save her, never go in there, you hear?"

I nod, thinking about my neighbor on Harriet Street who told Mother to keep me away from her house and everything she owned, including her garbage.

"Speaking of never," Miss Templeton says, moving quickly down the hall, "Chef Boris is never in his office and prefers that all of his things get delivered to the kitchen. He's made himself a little office there in an old storage space. It's not much, but you'll hardly ever find him sitting anyway, so I don't think he cares much at all," she says, pausing for a moment before heading back down the stairs. "Do you have any questions, Elimina? I don't like to say things twice, but I understand you are just starting out, so you go ahead and ask whatever you need to know."

I pause, looking over the names on the page, pressing my front teeth into my bottom lip.

"Elimina, if you've got something to say, best to say it," she says.

"Umm . . . you said there are six Decos, but . . . I think you only named four," I say, looking down at the list again and praying I didn't make a mistake.

Miss Templeton's scowl loosens and she pats me on the shoulder, smiling like she's proud. "Well done," she says. "I do this all the time when I train new students. I get a fair number who can barely get one name down, let alone all four. And I can count on one hand how many have asked for the missing two on their own. I've been known to tell Mr. Gregors that it's just not going to work with some. But I think I'll keep you, Elimina."

I smile back at her as she stops just outside the office.

"There are two Decos who do not have any students to train in any official way. Nurse Gretchen is in charge of the nurse's quarters, monitoring students' health and managing any bumps or breaks that don't require a trip to the hospital, which is miles out of town. Did you see her yesterday with Josephine?"

I nod.

Nurse Gretchen is a sour-faced woman with thick glasses that hang on a string, and when Josephine took me to her office, she barely spoke to me, handing me a cup and nodding toward the washroom, like she couldn't be bothered with words.

"The other Deco is Miss Ida Mason. She's a Gutter Deco," Miss Templeton says. "She handles Aesthetics and Personal Care, and she's very well-liked by the students."

While Mainland Decos drive in from the city to work every day, Gutter Decos live on campus, working six or seven days a week, depending on their hiring package, which in Ida's case includes a living space in the basement of the Main House, next to a studio-office she uses for appointments. According to Miss Templeton, Ida Mason came up through a redemption academy—a place just like Livingstone—and is nearly halfway to Redemption Freedom.

"Which is very impressive for someone of her ilk," Miss Templeton whispers, and I nod as though I know what *ilk* means, even though I don't.

"It's one of the best kinds of jobs you can get, with room and board all built in. Securing housing can be tricky for Gutter folks. Gutter Decos are a perfect example of the kind of good-paying opportunities that are available to you if you work hard," Miss Templeton says as she steps back into the office. "You remember that, Elimina."

VIOLET IS BACK by the time we return, but even when I'm standing right next to her, she barely acknowledges I'm there. We organize files without speaking while Miss Templeton opens mail, so that all that can be heard in the main office is the shuffling of paper.

"Well, well, I can see you two are already getting acquainted," Mr. Gregors says, stepping out of his office and standing in front of Miss Templeton's desk while he watches the two of us work.

Violet and I look at one another, then over at Mr. Gregors, smiling with only our cheeks, as though the one thing we've agreed on without ever speaking is that we will not be friends.

"I told you this would be a good fit, Miss Templeton," he says.

"Yes, you did, sir," she says without looking up from her papers.

"I feel like we should celebrate," he says, clapping his hands and rubbing them quickly together.

"You know, sir, that's a really good idea," Violet says, moving closer to Mr. Gregors. "I was just thinking that since it's Elimina's first real day at Livingstone and since she is the new Red Coat, that it might be a good idea for you to introduce her to everyone, sir. Personally. Perhaps you could give a little speech. Maybe at dinner? The students love your speeches, and what a great way to celebrate our new student. Our *new Red Coat.*"

Miss Templeton clears her throat, arching up her eyebrows and shifting in her seat. But Mr. Gregors claps his hands again and smiles.

"Violet, I think that's a wonderful idea. Why don't I take both of you down and we can do it right away over lunch?"

"You're right. There's no use waiting, sir," Violet says, smiling at me with a fake grin. "And while I would like to go, of course, sir, there are some packages that arrived for Nurse Gretchen that I really need to take down to her. I already grabbed a bite from the kitchen before coming. I'm so sorry, sir," she says, hand to her chest like she's pretending to be full of regret.

"No matter. Best not to keep Nurse Gretchen waiting. Come along now, Elimina," Mr. Gregors says, clapping twice more and heading out of the office as I follow quickly behind him.

Mr. Gregors marches straight to the podium at the front of the dining hall, and adjusts the microphone as I stand next to him, shifting from side to side.

"Students of Livingstone Academy," he begins, but everyone is already staring at my red coat.

I watch Josephine straighten up in her seat, shaking her head and whispering to a group of girls with her hand covering her mouth.

"The best of the best come to Livingstone," Mr. Gregors says, pausing for effect before sharing a few words about the role of the Red Coat and gesturing to Louis, smiling in a front row.

"Please join me in welcoming a new Red Coat: Elimina Madeleine Dubois," he says.

No one claps when Mr. Gregors steps back from the microphone, not even Louis. Everyone just stares, and I wish more than anything that a strong wind or an angry tornado would pick me up and take me away.

"Come on now," Mr. Gregors says, clapping into the mic so the sound booms like a drum. "Let's give Elimina a big round of applause, Livingstone. Let's give her a proper welcome."

Josephine stands, clapping slowly, her mouth tightly clenched. And when the rest of the students join her, standing and clapping slowly, Mr. Gregors smiles and grabs me tightly around the shoulders like his speech was a great success.

I STAY IN the Main House for as long as possible, helping Miss Templeton tidy up the office, and cleaning up the cafeteria when all of the other students are gone. When I arrive in the West Hall just before evening curfew, the Lower Room is quiet and empty, and when I reach the top of the stairs, all of the girls are gathered around my bed.

Josephine and Violet are standing in front, and I squint my nose up at the smell that's thick in the air, tickling the back of my throat.

"What is that?" I say, placing one hand over the bottom half of my face.

"Well, Elimina, I'm glad you mention it," Violet says, tossing her hair over her shoulder and placing one hand on her chest.

"We all came up to the Upper Room because something at Livingstone stinks."

The girls part, so I can see my bed. A dead rat carcass is lying in a pool of red, the word "RAT" written on the wall in blood.

I stare at the mess as Violet leads the snickering girls from the Lower Room downstairs, and the girls from the Upper Room climb into their beds. I try not to gag at all the blood and guts. I just wrap the small rodent up in the sheets and run off to find something to clean up the mess with before lights-out.

"Take your time, Elimina. Don't worry," Josephine says as I open the closet in the bathroom, searching for a cloth. "You can stay up as long as you want, can't you? I mean, no one can rat on a rat, can they?"

I look at her for a moment, her own face tight with anger and hurt, as though I betrayed her somehow. As though she didn't hurt me by putting a dead rat in my bed. I push past her with a bucket of soap, remove my coat and scrub hard at the wall until the blood is nearly gone and most of the girls are fast asleep.

When the room is quiet and dark, I gather the bundle of sheets with the carcass inside and sneak out the back door of the West Hall. I toss the carcass into the forest and cover the sheets with dirt and ashes at a small firepit, where I sit on an old tree stump and look up at the sky.

"I don't want to be here," I say, crying into my arms to muffle the sound.

A SECURITY GUARD and a dog move in the distance, and I lift my head. I feel a pinch in my chest because I left the red coat in the Upper Room and now I'm here at the firepit after lights-out, which is against the rules.

I lie flat on the ground where small pieces of chopped wood cling to my clothes as the guard circles all of the buildings before heading back toward the front gates.

I sit up, ready to sneak back the same way I came. But before I can move, I see Josephine slip out the back door of the West Hall and sprint toward the Fieldhouse, and before she steps in, she looks around like she's hoping no one is watching her.

5

LOUIS IS WAITING IN THE SUNLIT COURTYARD WITH HIS back against the brick wall, his red vest fitted neatly around his thin frame. It's been two weeks since Mr. Gregors named me a Red Coat, but Louis and I have barely spoken. "We should talk," he says, stepping onto the path and blocking my way.

"I have to get to work," I say, pointing up at the window of Mr. Gregors's office, where he stands most mornings, watching everything.

"He's off-site today," Louis says. "Besides, you don't have to worry about that. You're a Red Coat, Elimina. You don't need to be walking around scared."

Two girls from housekeeping pass us, shaking their heads, and I lift my chin, like I've been doing for weeks, pretending it doesn't bother me.

"Don't worry about them either. Believe me, I got far worse than your rat. They'll get used to it. And so will you," he says.

"I don't know if I can ever get used to this," I say as I move into the shade.

Violet and Josephine barely look at me, and every day, someone in the West Hall leaves a note for me on my bed: "Dear Rat, your hair is ugly." "Dear Rat, go home."

"Well, this is all you've got," Louis says. "Mr. Gregors gave you that red coat because he thinks you're special."

"I am special," I say.

"Well, to me you look about as un-special as they come, Elimina Madeleine Dubois," he says, emphasizing my name with a scowl.

"I don't care what you think of me, Louis."

"You know what, Elimina? I think you do. I think the reason you're moping around this place is because you care too much about what everyone else thinks. And I'm going to do you a favor by helping you out."

I take a deep breath and lean my head back against the wall, unsure whether I should be annoyed or grateful. I've been watching Josephine for two weeks and I still haven't caught her sneaking out again. Even though I'm still mad about the rat and the letters, part of me just wishes that she would acknowledge I'm here. Because the loneliness is unbearable.

"The fact is, Elimina, I'm in charge when it comes to Red Coat business," Louis says. "And I don't want you to screw this up for me. I've spent a lot of time being a Red Coat and making things good. So I've talked about it with Mr. Gregors and we decided that you're going to be my Junior Red Coat. I'm going to train you proper."

He looks up at the sky and nods, bobbing his head and smiling like he likes the sound of his own thoughts, and I wonder if he's actually talked about this with Mr. Gregors at all.

"You know what? *Junior* has a nice ring to it. How about I just call you that instead of Elimina?"

"Fine, Louis. You're in charge. Call me whatever you want. But I'd like to get to work now," I say, even though it's not true. I'm never in a rush to spend a day with Violet, especially when Mr. Gregors is gone.

"Woah, woah, woah. Slow down, Junior. As of right now, you've got nowhere to go till I say so."

I sigh, trying to decide which option is worse, a morning with Violet or Louis.

"Consider this your official Red Coat training," he says.

I shake my head and slide down to the ground, legs crossed at the ankles.

"Now, Mr. Gregors gave you that red coat. But the way I see it, you still have to earn it. You have to make it count, and to do that you have to know the rules," Louis says, waving his hands as he paces back and forth.

"I know the rules, Louis," I say.

"But do you know what happens when folks break them?" he whispers, leaning in close, and when I shrug and shake my head, he points his finger too close to my face.

"Exactly," he says. "When folks obey the rules, life is good. But when folks break the rules at Livingstone, their debt becomes the least of their problems."

I take a deep breath and exhale because whenever I hear the word *debt*, I feel like all that money I owe is piled high on my shoulders.

"Our job as Red Coats is to enforce the law," Louis says.

"Mr. Gregors said our job was to 'maintain happiness.'"

"They're the exact same thing. Enforcing the law for those who need reminders means happiness for everyone."

I think about these words together—*enforcing* and *happiness*.

"You see, Junior, you've been around Mainlanders your whole life. You're used to folks acting right, obeying the rules—am I right?" Louis says, placing his hands behind his back and intertwining his fingers.

I nod.

"But Gutter folks don't like rules—especially Mainland rules," Louis says. "It's that rebellious spirit. Truth is, if Gutter folks really want to get Redemption Freedom, knowing Mainland rules and following them is key."

I think about the rules that kept me from going into Capedown restaurants and stores, and the rules Mother had about staying inside—how we spent most of our time in our small house because of what others might do or say.

"I didn't grow up in the Gutter either, Elimina. Never even been there. And I never intend to go if I can help it," he says.

I look over at him, surprised, like I'm not sure I heard him right.

"My mama got herself knocked up while she was in an academy just like this," he says.

"Where is she now?"

He shrugs like it doesn't matter. "She went back to work, and I got sent to a junior academy. Nobody wants kid debt on top of their own debt. You'll never get out if you do that."

"So they have junior academies too?" I say. "For babies?"

Louis nods. "Junior academies take in MMEs, like me. Mandatory Mainland Entries. Babies born out here to mothers working their way out. I practically potty-trained myself. I could cook and do general maintenance before they even sent me to a senior academy, which is one of the reasons I became a Red Coat. I know how to do all of this work, and Mr. Gregors knows he can trust me to keep an eye on things."

"So you've never been to the Gutter?" I say.

He shakes his head. "My first academy was a few hours away, other side of Haven. But I learned how to do things and how to survive, just like you. See, you and I, we have to teach them what we know." He points across the campus, toward the start of the road that leads to the Main House. "You see those security guards, those old guys near the gate? The security guards keep folks out, but we are the real law and order, Elimina. We teach them to work hard. You hear me?"

I nod.

"Our most important job is to keep an eye out for students who need a *reminder* about why they're here, who can't seem to follow the rules," he says, pacing slowly. "See, I could get Rowan leashed for what he did, pulling me around like he did that first day I saw you. And I could punish any one of them fools for taking time away from their work. But what good would that do me? That's what I have to ask myself. Rowan's going to do what Rowan's going to do. That boy doesn't listen to nobody. He is who he is and I don't have time for that. But the rest, they need to be taught. They can still be taught."

He heads over to the leashes, and I follow him to the chains that are staining the concrete with rust.

"Don't you think there's something wrong with chaining people up like dogs?"

Louis laughs like I just don't get it. "Do you know what will happen to them if they steal food or try to escape from an employer after they're hired?"

I shake my head.

"The Gutter. And do you think they know that, Junior? Do you think they really understand that and how that impacts their families? No. They don't. Because if they did, they wouldn't disobey. Nobody wants to go back to the Gutter. There's nothing but shame and pain if you get sent back with nothing to offer your family but a bigger dose of debt. No matter how bad it seems here, what everyone really wants is to survive on the Mainland," he says.

"So, what do you want from me?"

"Well, that's easy," he says, smiling and sliding his hands in the pockets of his pants. "Information. You know those girls who were so awful to you when you got here?"

I nod, thinking of Josephine and Violet standing with all of the girls, and the stink of dead rat in my mouth.

"You're going to keep an eye on them. They're always scheming in there, just like they did with that rat prank. I was the one who caught Ally and Sam sneaking into the East Hall, and I'm willing to bet someone in one of the dorms knew about their plan and didn't say anything. So you're going to tell me everything you learn in the West Hall as soon as you learn it so *we* can keep this place running good. In exchange, why don't I see if I can stop those nasty notes from showing up."

"You can do that?"

"Do we have a deal?"

I think about Josephine and the night I saw her run into the Fieldhouse. But I don't tell Louis. I just extend my hand the way Mainlanders do when they're hoping to seal a promise. "Deal," I say.

6

THE BASEMENT OF THE MAIN HOUSE IS GRITTY AND cold, with concrete floors, stone walls, and pipes that hover low. At the end of a long hallway, past the rumble and heat of the laundry facilities and the clanging of the maintenance department, I find Ida Mason's living quarters and a studio that looks like a small version of the salons Mother went to in Capedown.

A black leather chair with a metal base is bolted to the floor in front of a mirror surrounded in lights, and there's a small sink in the corner with a long counter covered in bottles.

When I enter the room, a full-bodied woman in a gray dress appears from around the back corner, sweeping bits of hair into a pile. She has a white apron tied around her waist and a colorful scarf wrapped around her head, like a crown.

"Miss Mason?"

The woman stands tall and graceful and part of me wants to bow, but I just hang my head low and pass her the note, scratching at my scalp.

My hair has grown quickly since arriving at Livingstone, but I have no idea what to do with it. Yesterday, I started pulling at the knots with a comb, hoping it would help, but I only made things worse. When I showed up at the office, Violet laughed into her hand and Miss Templeton sent me down to the basement right away with a note: "Ida, fix this."

Ida reads the note and shakes her head, tossing it in a garbage bin and opening her arms wide. "Baby girl, I'm glad you finally made your way down to see me. I was wondering when you'd come."

I step into her slowly, and she hugs me so tight I feel swallowed in warmth. I wrap my arms around her and squeeze back, hoping she doesn't let go.

"You're okay. You're safe here," she says, and I sob into her shoulder, leaving dark stains on her chest.

"I'm sorry. I'm so sorry, Miss Mason," I say when I lift up my head, wiping my tears away with the back of my wrist.

"Don't be sorry, baby girl," she says, pulling me in again to show that it's really okay. "And it's Ida in here. Just Ida when you talk to me."

I step back, and she hands me a handkerchief.

"Well, this coat is fancy," she says, sliding her hands down the sleeves with a strange look on her face, and I don't know whether to feel proud or ashamed.

"I . . . I . . ." But I don't know what to say.

"It'll help. That's for sure," she says, shrugging her shoulders. "You take your help where you can get it, baby girl. I know how that goes. But you don't need all that in here, so you can hang that coat right outside the door when you come in from now on."

I nod, hanging up the coat just like she asked, and settling into the chair.

"Never combed your own hair, have you?" Ida says, touching my hair as her mouth bunches like a prune.

"No, ma'am," I say, trying to look anywhere but the mirror.

When I was younger, I used to stare at myself for hours. I'd study my face and the strangeness of it in comparison with the faces I saw at the park and on the covers of Mother's magazines. I would gaze at every feature, and I would ask myself the same questions, tilting my head this way and that to see it at different angles. *Am I pretty? Am I kind of pretty or really pretty or almost pretty? How about now?*

When Mother asked what I was doing in the bathroom and why I was taking so long, I would tell her I was studying. And it was true. I was studying how I looked, creating a list of the things I liked, things that made me happy or proud—like the round of my head and the shape of my eyes. I liked the way I smiled and the way my top lip slipped up over my gum, like it was too big to hold inside.

But eventually, I saw uneven teeth, an oversized grin and a head that was bald like a boy's. I longed for hair like Mother's, with skin just as fair and scar-free. And I started to wash my face and brush my teeth with the lights off or with my eyes closed, like my own face was something no one else should have to see, including me.

"You never had a Gutter woman do your hair?" Ida says, and I shake my head. "Weren't there any Gutter women in that town where you were raised?"

I watch Ida standing behind me, hands on my shoulders, waiting for me to respond.

"Miss Ida, you're the first Gutter woman I've ever met. First one I've ever spoken to as far as I can remember."

Ida closes her eyes and shakes her head before clearing her throat. "Now then, you're going to have to tell me what it was like being out there with all of them Mainlanders instead," she says.

I shrug. "It was different."

"Well, I figured that much, baby girl. But when you've lived something no one else has, you have to tell folks what it's like as though they can't see and they're asking you what red looks like. When someone asks you for a picture, you got to spell it out in color for them," she says.

I try to think of how to explain Capedown, but I can't find the words. "How long have you been here?" I say.

"Left the Gutter when I was five years old for the academy track. Spent ten years at North End Academy, which is a place I don't care to remember, that's for sure. I worked down the way for a bit until Mr. Gregors hired me. Been working for twenty years maybe, so . . . thirty years on the Mainland is my guess. Though I'm sure my debt manager could count it better."

"Thirty years?"

"Sounds like a whole lot, I know. But the truth is, it doesn't feel that long at all. Besides, I got it real good here," she says with a toothy smile that's full of gaps and one tooth that's mostly brown.

"How much longer till you're done? Till you get Redemption Freedom?" I say.

She takes a comb and pulls it through my hair, and when a piece of the comb breaks off, she grabs another from the pile and tries again.

"I'll be done in twenty or so, I think. But truth is, I'll probably work as long as I can. Maybe I'll buy a house in the city and come in with the Mainland Decos," she says. "But I gotta keep going."

"Why?"

"I got family who are counting on me. I was the one that got out to make the way. When I get Redemption Freedom for myself, I get to give it to one other person. I figure I can get one of my grand-nieces out, hopefully one with a baby. That way I can get two more generations out at the same time—set our family up right for the future. But there's still others. There's always others. Don't think I could enjoy my own life knowing they're still in the Gutter—that I didn't do everything in my power to help," she says.

"In Capedown, you aren't allowed to work until you're eighteen. And even then, it's optional," I say. "Mainlanders can't start until eighteen. It's the law."

"It's the law that you can't work?" she says, and when I nod, she shakes her head, like the unfairness of it is almost too much.

I tell her about the Kids-Being-Kids Legislation and the Youth Enjoyment Opportunities, how Mainland kids are encouraged to explore and how Mother used to take me to Capedown museums during the day—when other kids were at school—where they'd let us in at twice the price.

Ida shakes her head again, her jaw stiff with anger. I feel a sharp pain in my scalp as she pulls the plastic comb through my hair a little harder.

"Do you miss your family?" I say through gritted teeth, and Ida nods.

"Most days I miss them fine, just in passing. But some days, I'll admit, it's hard. Knowing they're there. And I'm here. That the little ones don't know anything about me, except what I write down in letters. But I try not to worry because nothing good comes from it. All worrying can do is bring a sickness that starts deep inside. And I got no time to be sick, baby girl. I got to stay well up here most of all," she says, tapping her finger against the side of her head. "Besides, I'd rather be here making a way than waiting in the Gutter. Can't complain about that."

But there's a lot she could complain about, and I think about telling her that it's another way Mainland life is different.

Mainlanders get up-in-arms angry when things don't go their way. And when they complain loud enough, the Mainland government usually does something about it.

The year before I was supposed to attend Capedown Elementary, the school board established tests to ensure that all students were on track and making good progress. The Mother's Alliance made signs and yelled outside the board offices and in the lobby at city hall. They said standardized tests were the equivalent of work and should be against the law, and the tests were banned, just like they wanted. One year later, those same people grabbed new signs and stood in front of Capedown Elementary to protest my enrollment in a school that had always been exclusively for Mainlanders—in a town that prided itself on the same. "Keep the Mainland for Mainlanders," they said, and when Mother dragged me out, never to return, they got their way again.

I ask Ida if there's a way to change things for her or her family, but she shakes her head.

"It doesn't work that way for us," she says.

She sprays my hair with water, picking at the tips with a few sharp tugs, and I try not to let her see how much this hurts.

"I wondered about you project cases—how you would do out there with no one," Ida says, scowling at my hair before starting again. "I only got five years in the Gutter with my family, but those five years mean everything to me, especially now that I've been gone for so long. I can't imagine what it was like to have no one—to know nothing."

I tell her about a photograph of a Gutter family I saw in a library book before I could read, how I ripped the picture out and studied those faces carefully for signs that we were related. I had never seen faces like mine before, and I decided they were my long-lost family. I gave them all names, and I held that photo inside one of my books until it was so thin and worn it fell apart in my fingers.

"Is that all you know about your own—that picture?" Ida says, with her eyebrows pushed down toward her nose.

"Mr. Gregors told me things, and Mother taught me history for school," I say.

"Don't believe everything them Mainlanders tell you," she says, shaking her head like I'm making her tired and sad. "And don't believe what you read in those books either."

She stops working and takes a long, deep breath, looking down at the hair that's still tightly packed and knotted, like she's ready to give up.

"Please don't. You just can't," I say, my voice wobbling as my eyes fill with tears.

"Baby girl, what's wrong?"

"Please don't cut it."

"Baby girl, this side here is just knots on knots."

I look in the mirror, horrified, and when she turns the chair, I drop my head and press my palms against my face.

"What's wrong, baby girl?"

"When my hair got too long or too hard to comb, Mother just cut it off. She always cut it off. And I didn't know how to stop her. But I want it back," I say, tears thick in my throat.

Sharing this feels like a betrayal, like I'm turning on Mother. She lived alone because of me. *It's only hair*, I told myself. But it always felt like something more.

"You ever met your real mother?" Ida says, hands on my shoulders. "Ever even seen a picture of her?"

I shake my head, unsure whether "real mother" is a fair term. I've never known how to feel about the woman who gave me up to be raised by a Mainlander. I've tried to just feel grateful to Mother for giving up everything to love me.

"A girl learns who she is from the woman she sees loving her," Ida says. "She learns what's good and what's lovely about herself, and the further apart she is from that woman, and the more different they are, the harder it is for her to know what to love about herself. Especially when everything around her tells her she's not right. You know what I'm saying, baby girl?"

I nod and Ida smiles.

"I remember watching my mother twist her hair. I remember her weaving her fingers through my roots. I remember what she told me when I left. 'You are beautiful and strong, Idalaye Mason. The loveliest of lovelies. You have been chosen,' she said."

Ida turns my chair back to face the mirror, leaning over so our faces are close together, so we're staring at our reflection.

"You are lovely, Elimina. Really lovely," she says.

She repeats these words over and over, and I cry so hard my whole body shakes, because I desperately want to believe her. When I stop crying, she places both hands on my shoulders and squeezes gently.

"What do you want your hair to be like, Elimina?"

I look at her in the mirror, then close my eyes. "I want hair that sits around my shoulders, that I can pull up or let down. I want hair that I can twirl around my finger when I'm thinking— the way Alice Day did on the front stoop of the house next door. I want hair like Violet. Hair that will make me feel like a woman. A real woman," I say.

When I open my eyes, Ida is smiling, like saying all this makes me brave.

"Can I have it? Hair like Violet. Can I do that?" I say.

Ida laughs, a big, hearty laugh that rattles her whole body. "Violet's got something that don't everybody got, so her hair does things that not everyone's can do. You, baby girl, are no Violet," she says.

I stare down at the tips of my shoes peeking out from underneath the white cloth.

"Now, I'm no Violet neither," Ida says. "Nobody but Violet is Violet, so don't go mourning that, baby girl. Don't you go feeling bad because you got your hair and not hers. That kind of thinking will take what little you've got and make it so you've got nothing. I tell all you young ones that when it comes to beauty, don't go looking for your reflection in someone else's mirror. You hear me? You are lovely as you are. And you're a woman either way, no matter if your hair is short or long."

I stare into the mirror trying to find the girl I saw before, the face I loved when I was little, as Ida tugs at the scarf around her head, unwinding all of the fabric until her hair falls down in thick strands, tight black ropes of hair.

"This something you might like?" she says, leaning over and adjusting a few strands so they fall around my face.

I nod, smiling wide.

"It will take time," she says. "And if you want to make it happen starting today, you're going to have to suffer a little. But I never knew anything good that didn't come without a bit of hurt."

"I'm ready," I say, and Ida grabs the comb and starts to work, pulling through the tight knots.

I bite back tears to show Ida that I am brave, that my life in Capedown did not make me weak. But it hurts so bad that I close my eyes and curse under my breath, trying to hold back the tears.

When Ida finishes combing, she twists and knots my hair in

small sections, something she first saw her mother do and practiced on the other kids at her academy.

"Gutter folk are poor in position, but don't nobody do family like us," she says. "And we don't have to be family to be family, if you know what I'm saying. Wherever we are, we find family."

I nod, thinking about Josephine, wishing that were true. I didn't have a family member alive in the world, and the only person at Livingstone Academy who would speak to me was Louis.

"Do you ever get angry that your family sent you away?"

Ida shakes her head. "The only reason my parents sent me here was because we all want what those Mainlanders got from birth, that Redemption Freedom, that sense of being fully free, not an animal that can be marked or leashed or put to work for someone else. When a creature is trapped, they'll cut off their own arm to save their body. That's what Gutter folks do. We cut off our own body for the chance to save the family."

I think of how Ida has a whole family depending on her, and I wonder if that makes it harder, if I should be grateful to be doing this alone.

"Should I be happy to be here, Ida?"

She stops and sighs, resting her hand on my shoulder, like this is a question she's not sure she can answer. "You have lived a different life, baby girl, seen different things. So I can't answer that for you. I don't know if I have happiness . . . But I found purpose, I suppose. That's what drives me. Perhaps you can find that too. If you ask me, purpose is far more useful than happiness. Happiness is like sugar—sweet, but quick to go. But purpose is really something, baby girl. Purpose gets you through whatever comes."

When she's finished with my hair, I touch the ends, tilting my head to get a better look, smiling into the mirror.

7

I PAUSE AT THE DOORS OF THE FIELDHOUSE AND STARE INTO the dark, waiting for things to take shape—the wood posts, the stalls, the tools that hang on the walls. But all I see is black, and when someone grabs my arm, I jump and clasp my hand around my mouth to keep myself from making a sound.

"Did you follow me?" Josephine whispers, holding on tight.

For weeks, I had been watching Josephine at night, waiting for her to sneak out, so I could find out where she went that night they put the dead rat in my bed. When she stayed awake tonight, watching the other girls fall asleep before stuffing her sheets with pillows and heading for the back stairwell, I did the same and followed her to the Fieldhouse in my red coat.

"Ow, Josephine, you're hurting me," I say.

"You are such a rat, Elimina," she whispers, shaking my arm. "Did you even check to see if you were followed?"

"Did you?" I say, and she grips my arm tighter, pinching the skin.

"Did Mr. Gregors ask you to do this? Did Louis? Have you told them?" she says, and I can hear in her voice a desperate kind of anger. "What have you told them, Elimina?"

"I haven't told them anything."

"You're lying!" she hisses.

"I'm not lying. I came on my own. No one knows I'm here," I whisper, pleading for her to believe me, frustrated that I can't be mean and ruthless like Louis after all that Josephine has done.

"But you're going to tell? That's your plan, right?" she says.

"Josephine, relax. It's okay," someone says from the dark.

I squint into the shadows as a figure with wide shoulders and a thick, stocky frame moves closer. I hear a snap and then a hiss that glows into a flame as Rowan lifts a match to the base of an oil lamp, raising it up so his face is covered in an eerie yellow glow.

"Go on, Josephine," he says.

Josephine looks at me, then back at Rowan. "But, Rowan, she could—"

"I'll take care of it, Jose," he says.

Josephine clenches her jaw and loosens her grip on my arm. But when Rowan nods for her to go on, she sighs and heads deeper into the Fieldhouse, leaving the two of us alone.

"What are you guys doing here?" I say.

"I'm about to show you, Elimina. But first, I need to know if you can keep a secret. Or if that red coat means you're with Louis."

"I can keep a secret," I say.

He holds the lamp out with one hand so the light spreads wide around us, pointing his elbow in my direction the way Mainland men do when they're asking a woman to dance at a fancy party. I slide my hand into the bend of his arm, pressing my lips tightly together to keep my smile small.

"Being a Red Coat has advantages, Elimina," he says as we make our way down one hallway and turn down another. "But the real advantage is knowing when and how to use it."

At the far corner of the Fieldhouse, past horses and cows that shuffle as we pass by, a second lamp flickers in the corner stall. I can hear voices whispering low. Josephine and one other, maybe more.

"So, you won't tell?" he says, stopping and leaning in close.

"I won't tell. I promise," I say, closing my eyes at the gentle feel of his breath against my skin.

David, Josephine and Violet are sitting on blankets that are spread over the concrete floor, and when Rowan leads me forward with his hand pressed gently against my back, they immediately stop whispering.

Josephine doesn't look at me, and when David makes room for me to sit down, Violet glares at him like she doesn't want me here at all.

"Welcome to our little gathering," Rowan says, sitting down next to Violet.

"No way in hell is that Red Coat welcome," Violet says, crossing her arms over her chest.

"Violet—"

"Don't even start with me, David. She's not one of us," she says, and I cover my bare hand with my scarred one so I look like I belong.

"Am I the only one who's bothered by this?" she says. "She's a rat. She's *friends* with *Louis*."

"We're not *friends*. Louis is just the only person who'll talk to me," I say. "We're supposed to work together."

"You're a rat, Elimina," Violet says, and when I look over at David and Josephine, I can't tell if they agree or if they're nervous about something else.

"Violet, calm down," Rowan says. "Maybe it's good to have someone keeping an eye on things. I mean, if she's got that red coat, it's better she's with us than against us."

"If she's willing to work with Louis, she can't be trusted," Violet says. "That's just facts, Rowan."

"I don't know, Violet. I think Rowan's right," David says.

"She's ruining everything," Violet says. "There's barely enough work in the office as it is. God help me if I get sent to housekeeping on account of her! If she replaces me, I don't know what I'll do."

"There's nothing wrong with housekeeping," Josephine says.

"Not for you," Violet says, waving her arms and pouting her lips.

"Well, maybe when Elimina does take your job, she can arrange to put you in the Fieldhouse instead."

Violet gasps and the two boys cover their mouths to stop themselves from laughing out loud.

"You'd certainly have plenty of work. There's plenty of manure for you to shovel here," Josephine says.

"Don't even think about it," Violet says to me.

Josephine looks over at me and we both fight back a smile, covering our mouths and laughing along with the boys when we can't hold it in any longer.

Violet huffs, and when the laughter doesn't stop, she reaches under a blanket and pulls out an old blue book, tossing it in front of her so it falls against the ground. "Let's get on with things," she says, crossing her arms again.

David reaches over and picks up the book, turning the pages gently until he reaches a spot near the center. When everyone is quiet and comfortably settled, he reads a poem about a dream that seems forgotten, a dream that's bright like the sun.

I can feel Rowan watching me, studying my reaction as David sounds out words that flow together like music. When he pauses to clear his throat, Violet continues the poem from memory. She doesn't stop or pause or falter as she recites the words, but her voice gets quieter near the end, and I lean in so I can hear all about the whirling dreams that shatter darkness.

When she finishes, I close my eyes, letting the words hover around me like a beam of light, flooding me with fire.

"What do you think, Elimina?" Rowan whispers.

I open my eyes and find all of them looking at me, waiting for me to speak, but I just shake my head because I don't know what to say. Because I don't know how to put what I think and feel into words.

"Did you write that?" I finally say to Violet.

She shakes her head. "I found it in my mother's side table. It's how I learned to read, and it's the only thing I brought from the Gutter. It's the only thing I want to remember from that place."

I think of all the books Mother made me study for school— poems and stories about men searching for big adventures that never made sense. "I can't believe it. It's incredible," I say.

"What, did you think we were idiots because we weren't raised in a fancy Mainland city?" Violet says.

"No. I . . . I didn't think that at all. I don't think that," I say, looking at Violet and then around at the others. "That's not what I meant."

"Did you read a lot where you lived?" David says with an expression that's both kind and curious.

"Mother liked to read. She read to me a lot. And I read on my own. But nothing like this," I say.

"I didn't read much before I came—even less when I got here," Rowan says. "I came when I was seven years old, but when I heard those poems, I felt like you, Elimina. Like it was a good song or a favorite meal from back home. It feels different, right?"

"You've been here at Livingstone for that long?" I say, and he

66

shrugs with a smile that's more cheeks than mouth, like he's not sure if he's embarrassed or proud.

"I'm a special project too, I guess, Elimina," he says with a dimpled grin.

"Rowan's a fighter," Violet says, patting him on the arm like he's a child she's taking care of. "He was brought here to train to become a boxer. He'll be the talk of the Mainland and the Gutter, and he'll be out sooner than all of us. Redemption Freedom and all."

She smiles at him and when he winks back at her, I see the way she straightens up her shoulders, like she wants more.

"I'm the youngest student they've ever brought into Livingstone," he says, raising his arms and flexing his muscles while Josephine rolls her eyes. "They built a whole space for me to train in the basement of the East Hall, and they brought the older boys in to help me. Everyone else was at least twelve or fourteen. But I held my own."

I look around at all their faces, how comfortable they seem together. "Have you all been on the Mainland that long?"

"Violet's the only normal one. She came out right at five. Started at a junior academy, just like you're supposed to," Rowan says.

"Bayshore Academy," she says proudly, like this should mean something.

"What about you?" I say to Josephine and David. I think of that day on the path and the closeness I see between them now.

"I came about five years ago. Straight from the Gutter," David says, looking down and then at Josephine before continuing. "There was a fire and I ended up here. My parents didn't plan it this way, but . . . I'm making the best of it."

"Me too," Josephine says. "I came out the same time as David. Same kind of thing."

"And this?" I say, gesturing at the stall and the lamps and the book in David's hand. "How did this happen?"

The four of them all look at each other, like they can't decide who should speak first.

"David and me . . . just wanted to . . . meet up sometimes," Josephine says slowly.

"She was having trouble sleeping," David says, and she looks at him and nods. "Somehow Violet and Rowan joined too. I don't even remember how. But one time, Violet pulled out the book and read to us."

"It helped so much," Josephine says.

Violet smiles, squeezing Rowan's arm, while David and Josephine sit close, and I feel a pain that pulls at my stomach, an ache for what they have.

"Being so far away from family for so long . . . I don't know . . . it felt like we made a family of our own," David says.

I feel a catch in my throat at that word, and it reminds me of my conversations with Ida. "I don't have a single bit of family anywhere," I say, mostly to myself, but when I look up, I see how this saddens Rowan, Josephine and David, how they really seem to care.

"She just wants you to feel sorry for her," Violet says.

"Violet, what the hell is your problem?" Rowan says.

"She's a Red Coat, Rowan!"

Josephine frowns. "Being a Red Coat means it's difficult to trust you, Elimina," she says. "You being here—do you understand what that means, what we could all lose if you turn on us?"

"I wouldn't do that. You can trust me," I say, trying hard not to sound desperate, even though that's exactly how I feel.

"And we're just supposed to believe that? You could get us leashed. Or worse," Violet says.

"You could have us moved," Josephine says, and I hear the fear in her voice. I see the way she looks at David and he squeezes her back, their need to be close.

"You could report me as well," I say. "You could tell Louis I was here and you could have me sent away too."

"Not without telling him about the group and wrecking it anyway," Violet says, rolling her eyes like this is not a strong argument.

"I won't tell anyone," I say. "I promise."

WE LEAVE UNDER the night sky in shifts. Violet first, then me and Josephine, leaving the boys to put out the lamps and close the doors. We run down the path quickly, my heart full and light, like the joy from tonight is greater than all my fears of being caught.

When we reach the back stairwell, we stop at the bottom of the stairs with our hands against our knees to gather our breath.

"So, you and David?" I say, and she looks over at me like she's not sure what to say. "Is he your . . . Do you like him, Josephine? Is that what you don't want to tell me?"

She shakes her head.

"Josephine, I know you don't know me," I say, taking one of her hands in mine. "But I've always wanted a friend. And I'll be a good one."

She looks down at our hands, then up at me, our faces close in the dark. "David is my brother," she says.

I clutch my chest, like the pain and longing I've felt for as long as I can remember is suddenly stronger, more sharp. "Your brother?"

"No one else knows but Violet and Rowan," she says, her voice tiny and low. "It's against the rules, family being together.

I don't know why I'm telling you now. Especially since you're a Red Coat."

She takes her hand and puts it to her mouth, like she suddenly regrets sharing this.

"You can trust me. I will never tell Louis or Mr. Gregors about any of this," I say.

"David's the most important thing I've got here. He looks out for me and he reminds me of home, and I miss my family, Elimina. I miss my parents so much. I need him like you just don't know. So you can't tell anybody . . . And you can't let him leave here without me. You have to tell me if you hear anything about him or about me in the office. Don't let him leave me here alone," she says, gripping my arm tightly, the red fabric wrinkling under her hold.

"I'll tell you everything I know," I whisper, and when I lean in, she squeezes me so tight it fills me with hope that I can help, that somehow I can keep their family from splitting up again.

8

JOSEPHINE AND I OPEN THE DOOR THAT LEADS OUT OF THE
back stairwell and wait, just like we do each time we head
out to the Fieldhouse. We watch for Mack's flashlight before
racing down the path, our nightgowns bunched high in our
arms to protect them from mud as a messy rain drizzles across
campus.

When we reach the Fieldhouse, David is waiting just inside
the doors. We dry ourselves off, and the three of us make our way
down the halls, whispering in the dark.

To keep up appearances, the group agreed that it would be
best if I continued to be a friend of Louis's. Which means that
other than sharing a few subtle smiles when Josephine visits the
office or when the boys are in the dining hall, I still feel very much
alone.

"In here, you are our friend, Elimina," Josephine had said at
our last meeting, taking my hand in hers. "But out there, you're
a Red Coat. And you need to appear like a good one, even when
it's hard."

I remind myself of her words whenever I hear the laughter of
the other girls in the Upper Room or when Violet is particularly
unkind, because I don't want to lose these nights at all.

"I don't know what side of the Gutter you lived on, Violet, but your home's no better than mine," Rowan says in a low growl, when we reach the stall.

He's standing in the middle of the space, facing Violet, with the lamp flickering on the ground near his foot.

"What are you going to do, Rowan?" Violet says. "You going to hit me? Practice your fight skills on me?"

Rowan shakes his head and she shoves him hard as David moves the lamp and steps between them.

"What's wrong with you two? Do you want us all to get caught? Violet, sit down," David says, pointing to the corner of the stall.

"Why don't you tell him to sit down?" she says.

"You first," David says.

When she finally takes a seat, everyone sits down slowly, while Violet pouts.

"What the hell is going on?" Josephine says, looking at both of them.

"Can we just read?" Violet says, crossing her arms, the way she does when she's annoyed.

"You want to read, Violet? That's what you want?" Rowan says. "Fine. It's whatever *you* want."

She bites her lip and reaches between the folds of a blanket, retrieving the book and flipping through the pages until Rowan snatches it out of her hands.

"You know what, I'm tired of you having your way all of the time," he says. "This time, Elimina picks."

He hands me the book and I hold it gently, running my fingers along the edges. The pages are worn and gray, full of long, elegant strokes where each letter floats into the next like wings. I see a poem that begins like a letter, and I read it. It's a short piece, written to a woman, that's consuming——the touch of her skin, her heart and her soul so deeply wanted by the person writing to her.

When I finish the last word, no one speaks, and the rain drums harder against the roof, surrounding us with noise.

"I don't like that one much," Rowan says.

"It's not a very good one. Definitely not one of our favorites," Violet says, and I hear the satisfaction in her voice.

"I wonder who the woman is—the woman the letter is written to. I've always wondered that," Josephine says.

"Probably some crazy woman," Rowan says with a nod toward David, but David just stares at the lamp in the middle of the stall, like he's barely here.

"Nothing's as painful as love," David finally says.

I wonder if he's loved someone the way this writer has and what that really feels like. But when he looks up at Josephine, his face soft and fallen, I see that David is talking about a different kind of love—the kind of love we're all missing, and a deep sadness fills my belly and squeezes at my throat.

"Love that's taken is the worst," David says.

"When you know it, when you have it, and then it's taken . . . Nothing else has ever hurt so much," I say, and I wonder if maybe Louis is so mean because he's never known that kind of love from anyone.

"The Mainland woman who raised you, she was good? She was kind to you?" Josephine says.

I shrug and nod at the same time, thinking of all the good things she did and trying to ignore all the ways I feel hurt now that she's gone.

"She kept so much from me. Things that would have helped. And some days I hate her for that," I say. "But I miss her too. I miss her a lot. I feel guilty and sad and angry. I feel all of those things, sometimes all at once."

They nod, like they know what I mean, and I close my eyes and take a few deep breaths, listening to the rain.

"No one told you about anything?" Josephine says.

I shake my head. "I didn't know anything about my debt."

"How is that even possible?" Violet says. "Didn't you see Gutter folks?"

I wiggle my mouth, trying hard to remember all the things I saw when I was little. "I remember when I was seven, Mother took me to a beach just outside of Capedown. It was a school day, so it was quiet and pretty empty. She put her towel down on the sand so carefully. It was a big towel with pink flowers, and when she lay down, it was like she was lying down in a garden. She told me she just needed a quick rest after the drive. She closed her eyes, and I tried to make a castle out of sand, but the sand was too fine. I needed water to make it hold, so I went to the ocean with my pail. And I saw this man. A Gutter man," I say, slowly, like I'm just remembering it all again. "He was older but not old, you know. He was carrying this thick yellow garbage bag, and he was walking along the beach picking up cups and food wrappers. His skin was like mine, and I remember watching him so closely. I remember wondering if he was my father. Maybe he was looking for me, you know. But the weird thing is, I didn't know whether I should run *to* him or whether I should run away. I didn't know whether to be happy or scared. So I just stood there. When he got closer, I noticed the two Xs. And I felt afraid. I thought maybe he was going to take me to the Gutter, away from Mother. And I didn't want to go. But I couldn't move."

"What happened?" Josephine says when I stop and look away.

"He smiled, and I smiled back," I say, grinning at the thought of him. "He said hello, and I remember his voice was really deep. Really low. Mother must have opened her eyes just then, because all I remember after that is her scream. 'Elimina, no! Elimina, get away from that man!'"

"Why did she want you to get away from him?" David says.

I shake my head, looking down. "I don't know," I say. But maybe I do. Maybe Mother didn't want me around Gutter folks. Maybe Miss Femia was wrong. Maybe Mother wouldn't want me here at all.

"Elimina?" David says, and I look up quickly, lost in my thoughts. "What happened to the man?"

I squint, like I'm not sure I remember. "He . . . he just apologized to Mother, and when she pulled me away . . . he just kept going, walking along the beach with his yellow bag. Mother packed up all of our stuff and we left, and I cried because she promised we would swim in the ocean, and we never did. It was the last time we ever left Capedown. We barely left home after that."

Thunder snaps and rumbles, and we all jump, hands to our chests. We sit there, waiting for the next bolt to strike, but nothing comes.

"Do you think Ida is lonely here?" I say as I touch the tips of my hair, which she tightened earlier today.

Everyone just frowns and shrugs their shoulders like they're not sure.

"I wonder if she could leave campus if she really wanted to, or if part of her package is that she has to stay here?" Josephine says.

"Would they do that?" I say.

"Employers can do almost anything with those contracts," Rowan says.

"Do you think if she fell in love, she could get married, though?" Violet says.

Josephine picks up a piece of straw and splits it in two. "I thought she did have someone."

"Yeah, but he's long gone now," Rowan says.

"Oh yeah, the maintenance Deco. You remember, Jose, the one before Big Tim," David says. "That was right when we got here."

"There was another Gutter Deco before?" I say, and Rowan nods, eyebrows raised, like this story is a good one.

"He used to come to the ring and spar with me, help me train for my matches. He was pretty good, too. He'd talk about how he wanted kids someday. How being in the system wouldn't stop him from having that," Rowan says. "But Ida wanted to save for her family back home, not start a new one. He said she needed to start living forward, not backward. But she didn't change her mind. Eventually, he got transferred out. Mr. Gregors brought in Big Tim and he went somewhere else."

"Why?" Violet says.

"I don't know. Maybe to start a family," Rowan says. "Or maybe Mr. Gregors wanted to get back at Ida. I remember he was pretty mad about it."

"Why would he be mad at Ida?" Josephine says. "Do you think that Deco was here for her?"

"Maybe. Which is why I was so impressed," Rowan says.

"Impressed?" Violet says, like that doesn't make sense.

"Ida didn't want to have kids and stuck to it even though it cost her love. That's brave. Debt for one is plenty enough," Rowan says. "I think she did the right thing."

"Do you think they could have had a family? Do you think Mr. Gregors would have let her?" Violet says.

Rowan scowls at her. "You think Mr. Gregors is just going to let Ida raise a family here while she pays off her debt?"

Violet shrugs.

"Violet, you're crazier than I thought," Rowan says.

"Don't call me that, Rowan. I'm not crazy."

"I'd like to think that there are employers who let you have kids and get married. I mean, it must happen. You'd be more likely to do your best work, wouldn't you?" David says.

"I can't see Mr. Gregors going for it," Josephine says.

Rowan shrugs. "I think Ida has her own way of living that's none of our business."

"She never leaves campus," Violet says. "She hardly leaves the basement."

"Is that Mr. Gregors's doing or is that how she wants it?" Josephine says.

"Who would want to live like that?" Violet says. "I've been to those employer fairs, helping Mr. Gregors. Rowan has too. There's not much choice involved. I bet anything she's not allowed to leave. It's probably in her hiring package."

"I heard she's terrified of the dogs and the guards," Josephine says. "Because of her last school. Maybe she just prefers to be alone."

"She's got a whole business of her own making bags down there that Mr. Gregors sells. For a good bit of extra money," David says. "Whatever her reasons, she's doing good for herself and her family."

I imagine Ida sitting in the basement, weaving banana leaves together, and I wonder if she's happy or if she's lonely like I was in Capedown, trapped in our house, afraid to go anywhere.

"I don't think I want to be a mother," Josephine says, and David turns to her abruptly.

"You don't want to have what Mom and Pop have, Jose?"

She shrugs, swallowing hard, like the very mention of her parents is too much. "It's not as easy as that out here, David. Maybe that's why Ida doesn't want to have kids. I mean, Louis doesn't even know who his parents are. He's been in an academy his whole life. He has no one."

"But Louis doesn't have the burden of freeing up a family either," Rowan says. "He's lucky that way."

"Family's not a burden, Rowan," David says.

"It is if you have to pay their debt."

"Or if you have to spend your life away from them," Josephine says, but David shakes his head like they've got it all wrong.

"I don't know that life's really worth living without family, without someone," he says. "I can handle all of this, if it's for someone or something. But what's the point if it's just me? I don't know if I could do it that way."

I look at David and try to smile like I agree. I think about what Ida said about happiness and purpose, how David seems so clear about his, while I still feel so lost.

"Sometimes I think being in the Gutter with family wasn't so bad as being here, fighting for everyone," Rowan says. "My dad— my pops—geez, I don't even know what to call him. He taught me how to fight when I was barely able to walk. You can make good money at rings in the Gutter. He was raising me to make it from the start."

"Is he who you're going to buy out?" I say, and everyone looks down, like this is something I shouldn't have said.

"He disappeared a few weeks before my seventh birthday," Rowan says, clearing his throat.

"Do you remember the day you left?" Violet says.

Rowan nods, tilting his head back against the wall.

"I remember it like it's right here in front of me now," she says. "Tasting the river water in my mouth, hearing those Healers sing those songs, holding on to me on that bus in shirts that smelled like the petals on the flowers in our yard. I was so glad to get out.

Other kids were crying. But not me. I didn't cry at all. I smiled when I went through that gate and crossed over that bridge for the last time."

"I didn't smile," Rowan says, as he looks up at the ceiling. "Momma was standing at the fence with my sister. I thought they could come all the way to the main gate. But the guards said no. When we passed through the chain-link fence, I turned to her, but the guards held me back. They kept pulling me away, and Momma started to cry. I didn't want to leave. I wanted to run back, but I kept thinking about my pops and the way he got so angry whenever I cried or made a fuss. I had to be tough. I was the man of the house. And I was going to take care of us. So I just walked away. I got into a van and we drove through those Gutter gates slowly. I remember sitting in the backseat as the gates swung closed. They clicked, like locks on a cell. They made that noise. I was seven years old, and the thing that sticks out most to me now is the sound of that gate clicking shut. I never saw the Gutter that way until that moment. I never realized we were trapped in there until I was on the other side."

For a second, the rain seems to slow down, like it might be ready to stop, but when I close my eyes, it picks up again, faster and harder this time, like the clouds are not done feeling sad.

"Funny thing is, I've always thought of my pops as the perfect parent because he wasn't the one who made me walk out those gates. He didn't give me away. Maybe, if he'd been there, he would have stopped it all, you know. Maybe I'd still be home," he says, clearing his throat again. "Truth is, my pops gave me the only worthwhile skill I got—the one thing that might get me out of this mess."

I smile, small and sad, and he looks at me and does the same, lifting the corners of his mouth before letting them fall.

"Do you want family, Violet?" David says. "Is that why you want to know about Ida?"

She shakes her head. "I didn't have a good family," Violet says. "Maybe that's why I've always wanted a family of my own. To do it well . . . But maybe Rowan's right. Ida too. Maybe it's better to do this alone."

But as I watch Josephine and David together, and as I look around the stall, rain pounding against the Fieldhouse walls, I think maybe Violet, Rowan and Ida have it all wrong. Maybe alone is the hardest way of all.

9

ON THE LAST FRIDAY OF EACH MONTH, LOUIS HOLDS
Red Coat meetings in the Main House courtyard, where
we discuss difficult students and suggested punishments.
At the meetings, Louis almost always pushes for the
leashes and I always plead for alternatives.

"Can't he just miss a meal or do some extra work in the
Fieldhouse?" I said at the last meeting when we discussed a maintenance student who had been late five days in a row.

Louis shook his head, hands pressed firmly against his waist.
"Punishment and discipline are gifts, Junior. Why would you
withhold the opportunity to give your peers a gift when you know
it will further their learning?"

When I arrive at the meeting, Louis is standing near the
leashes with Murray Smith, a new student with a crooked smile
that bends under a scar that runs from the corner of his eye to the
point of his mouth.

I try not to show how bothered I am that Murray is here at the
meeting, given that he's not a Red Coat, but I can tell by the way
Murray and Louis are both smirking that my discomfort doesn't
bother them at all.

Murray Smith transferred to Livingstone Academy two months

ago, taking one of five beds that became available on campus after a handful of older students were hired at a recent employer fair.

Murray is only fourteen, but his body is thick and wide like an oak tree. His skin is covered in scars that run along his arms, legs and neck, each one neat and round like a coin or the end of a cigar. According to Murray, the scars were caused by his father, who hated the look of his own son so much, he took it out on him every day. But whenever Murray says this, he smiles as though it's the very thing that makes him strong.

Murray insists that his five years in the Gutter with the meanest father on the planet made him brave and untouchable, and that it's his purpose in life to create that same kind of inner strength in others, which is exactly why Louis likes him. He's stocky and strong like Rowan but tall, with a permanent just-give-me-a-reason-to-punch-you look on his face, and Louis treats him like he's his own personal bodyguard.

"Alright, Elimina, why don't you start?" Louis says, raising one hand over his brow to shelter his eyes from the sun.

"No, you start, Louis—seeing as it's Murray's first time. Why don't you show him how this works," I say, and Murray grins with his crooked mouth.

"Fine. Let's talk about May Bennet," Louis says.

May Bennet arrived on the same day as Murray Smith. She was the last one to exit the small van of transfers who came from an academy that was shut down abruptly by the Mainland government for reasons no one really knew. May had a soft belly and a round face, with freckles so perfectly placed on the bridge of her nose they looked like they'd been drawn on with pencil. Her curls were messy and wild, and her skin was always red and splotchy from crying.

May slept in the bed next to me in the West Hall, and every

night, she tossed and turned, flailing her arms and groaning like she was running from something that would catch her eventually if she ever slowed down. By morning, I would find her in such a deep sleep that I'd have to shake her and call her name loudly over and over in order to get her up.

"Please. I just want to go home," she would say as I helped her into her clothes. "Please, Elimina. I just want to go home."

Most students at Livingstone Academy were terrified at the thought of going back, afraid to be seen as failures. Once or twice a year, students wrote home to say thank you for this amazing opportunity, promising Redemption Freedom with letters that were full of love. No one wanted to go back and admit they had lied—that they'd had a difficult time and were now adding to their family debts and difficulties by returning empty-handed. But May Bennet didn't care. She just wanted to go back to the Gutter.

"She's not pulling her weight in the housekeeping department," Louis says, and Murray nods as I adjust one lock of my hair.

"She's not even making her *own* bed," Murray says, and I wonder how he got that information. Who told him what goes on in the West Hall?

"It's clear something needs to be done," Louis says.

"Louis—" I start to say, but Murray interrupts me.

"It's like she's forgotten why we're here," Murray says to Louis, with his eyes fixed on me, and for a moment I'm not quite sure if he's talking about me or May Bennet.

"Well, then she needs a reminder. Don't you agree, Junior?" Louis says, and I shrug because I don't like the way it feels to be up against Louis and Murray.

"We should definitely do something," Murray says.

"We?" I say, rolling my eyes because I don't want to admit that they're right.

May Bennet sits by herself at every meal, moving her food around her plate but barely eating anything, which causes trouble for the kitchen staff, who are punished by Chef Boris for wastefulness, as though not eating a meal is a sign of poor work. According to Josephine, May sits in the corner and cries all day instead of folding sheets or sweeping hallways, and Miss Darling and all of the housekeeping students are losing their patience. They're tired of taking on the tasks she never completes and sending her off to Nurse Gretchen.

"We can't let her keep going on like this," Louis says. "She needs to learn. She can't graduate if she doesn't know better. There are standards for Livingstone graduates that we have to maintain."

"She doesn't want to be here," I say.

"It doesn't matter what she *wants*, Junior. Mr. Gregors *needs* her to work," he says. "She's letting us all down by not doing her share. Other people have to pick up her slack, and I don't think that's fair—do you?"

Murray nods, scratching at a scab near his elbow.

I let out a long, deep exhale. "What do you think we should do, Louis?"

"What do *I* think we should do? Why am I always the one who has to do this kind of work for you? I don't know why Mr. Gregors gave you that coat if you're not willing to do the work that goes with it," Louis says, and Murray nods again, their heads bobbing in unison.

"Look, Louis, May's not pulling her weight, but she's not a mean person. Let's give her a warning. We'll let her know that if she doesn't start pulling her weight by the end of the week, she'll get the leashes," I say.

"A warning? You want to give her a warning?" Murray shouts, arms wide and raised, like the very idea offends him.

"The leashes work best when students are given a chance to change first," I say to Murray. "That's the ultimate goal, right, Louis? To change her behavior, to get her to do her job so she can graduate? Isn't that what you said?"

Louis puckers his lips and pulls on his chin like he's not sure how to follow through on his own words without appearing weak in front of Murray.

The leashes at Livingstone Academy were meant to be used on students who stole something or hurt someone, or who ignored the rules like Ally and Sam did. They had never been used on someone like May Bennet, who seemed to suffer from what I could only describe as an overwhelming sadness.

"I'll warn her, and if she doesn't change, it's the leashes. Willful disobedience," I say, one of Louis's favorite reasons for using the leashes.

"Fine, Junior. But when she doesn't do what she's asked—and Junior, I can bet you right now that she won't—you'll be the one to deal with it. You'll be the one to snap the leashes around her neck," he says, and Murray picks up a rock and throws it, like this whole meeting was a waste of his time.

AFTER TWO CLEAR warnings and three more days of tears, I sentence May Bennet to one full day on the leashes for failing to complete mandatory work requirements and for willful disobedience. On the day of the leashing, the sun is bright and warm and the birds soar overhead, chirping and happy, as Louis and Murray cool the concrete with a bucket of water.

May leans into me, squeezing my arm and pressing her face into my shoulder, as we make our way to the courtyard, like she's too tired to stand on her own. I resist the urge to hug or console her, because I warned her and she didn't change. I just try to think about what Mr. Gregors said when he gave me the red coat as I swallow the angry lump in my throat. *Sometimes it's necessary.*

When May sees the chains lying across the concrete, she starts to shake, and I wonder how she'll survive twenty-four hours. If she cries too much, Murray said she could choke on her own spit or vomit and die—that it had happened to someone he knew.

"I mean, they didn't die, but it was close," he said, like part of him was disappointed.

I lead May up to the concrete block and grab the metal collar, holding it open and standing in front of her as Louis and Murray watch. She looks at me, gray eyes pleading.

"I'm sorry. I'm so sorry," she says through tears, the same way she did with each warning. "I don't know what's wrong with me."

"You need to stop crying so I can put this on properly," I say with a sharp edge in my voice that frightens her and makes me want to look away.

She looks sad and wounded, and when she sees the anger and disappointment on my face, she cries even harder.

"Stop it, May," I say in a whisper that's mean and snakelike. "Do you want to die with this around your neck?"

She takes one deep breath and then another until the tears slow. But when I snap the collar closed with a click, she opens her eyes wide, lips quivering, tears starting again.

"Listen to me," I say, grabbing her face with both hands. "It's one night. You have one night to keep it together."

"I'm sorry, Elimina," she says, and I turn away.

Louis leads the Livingstone students to the courtyard after dinner, when May has been on the leashes for a few hours. She's red and sweaty from the hot sun, and when she sees the crowd of students, she starts crying again until Murray threatens a second day.

When all the students have gathered around, Louis instructs us to bark. I bark soft and quiet, barely opening my mouth while everyone barks around me. But when Louis shrieks at us to do better, to bark louder, I close my eyes and open my mouth, barking so loud I hardly recognize myself.

When I open my eyes, I find Louis watching me, smiling and nodding his approval, as though I've finally earned his respect.

DAVID FINDS ME at the back of the Fieldhouse when the sun is sinking behind the trees.

"Elly?" he says.

I turn and try to smile, wiping away tears with my wrist. "How did you know I was here?"

"I watched you," he says, sliding down beside me. "I waited a little while. Thought you might need some time alone. You okay?"

I breathe in, trying to stop my own tears from falling, wondering if whatever May has is contagious, if her incurable sadness is in me as well. "I didn't want to do it," I say.

"I know," he says.

He puts his arm around my shoulder, the way he does with Josephine, and I lean in close and cry into his chest. There's mud on his jeans and his shirt, and I feel it rubbing on my skin and clothes, but I don't care. Being this close feels good right now, and part of me hopes he never leaves.

"I barked, David. I barked loud. And I don't know why I did that. For Louis? For Murray? For this stupid red coat? What is wrong with me?"

"You've got to do what you've got to do," he says.

"What does that mean, David?"

"It means that we do what we need to do in order to survive," he says, shrugging his shoulders and shaking his head, like he's saddened by his own words as well. "You've got that red coat and you've got to keep it, Elimina. And if that means dealing with cases like May Bennet and barking when you're told, then you do what you need to do."

"People probably hate me now," I say.

"I know you didn't want to do that."

"But you're different, David. What about everyone else?"

"Well, maybe I'm the only one whose opinion should matter," he says, smiling at me, and I almost manage to smile back.

I stare out into the forest, at the layers of trees and leaves woven together like fabric. I try not to think about May sitting in the court-yard with nothing but a trough of water and scraps of leftovers and a collar around her neck, but I can't get her face out of my head—those freckles, those teary eyes. A kid who misses her family.

"May will be fine, Elimina," he says, like he can tell what's on my mind.

"Will she though? Will she be fine?" I say, turning to him.

"You can't make life easier for her, Elimina. There are rules."

"I'm so sick of the rules. There are so many rules, David. And I hate them all."

"I know. But we have to survive. Surviving is the only thing I think about. Surviving means paying off my debt so I can get away from these rules once and for all. And sometimes that means fol-lowing rules I don't like. You think I like that I have to sneak out to see my sister, that I'm not supposed to see her at all? You think I don't want to hug her every time I see her? But I don't. Because graduating from Livingstone means doing things we don't want to do, so we can get out."

"But what happens then? I mean, where do we even go when we get out, when we pay our debts?"

He shrugs. "There are places we can go. Places just for us. That's what our parents told us."

"Have you ever met someone who's done it, who got out and went there?"

"I try to just focus on what's next," he says, and I nod, leaning my head against his shoulder, letting him pull me close.

"Do you really think she'll be okay?"

"If she can't make it here, then she really won't make it with a Mainland employer," David says. "You're helping her survive, Elimina. May is going to have to find a way to get working. It's not easy going back. People aren't the same."

He takes my unmarked hand in his and smiles down at it, and I wonder if seeing it gives him hope, if it reminds him of what Redemption Freedom might look like, or if it makes him feel sorry for me because I'm alone.

"What if we let her come read with us?" I say. "That's what helped me, and I know it helped Josephine. And you. What if it helped her too?"

"You're not like May, Elimina."

"How do you know that?"

"Do you know how Violet and Rowan started meeting with us, how the four of us got together?"

I shake my head because they have never shared the whole story.

"Violet saw Josephine sneaking out, just like you did. And she followed her, just like you—probably hoping it would get her that very red coat you're wearing. And Rowan. He's always been a wanderer. Up late training. Preparing for matches. Sitting in the stalls, sulking after a loss. I think he used to come and sit with the animals for comfort. Fact is, we all went looking for something. We all broke the rules for something, not knowing what we'd find."

"But—"

"Elimina," he says, squeezing my hand. "You are not like Louis or Murray. This is not your fault. And you can't save May by giving her what you got because she's not you."

He lifts his hand and moves a strand of hair off my face, smiling at me in a way that seems both sad and happy, a look I don't understand.

"You're special in ways you don't know, Elimina," he says.

I lean into him as the sky turns pink, thinking about those words and the look on his face and the feel of his arm around me.

10

JOSEPHINE AND I ARRIVE AT THE FIELDHOUSE ON A NIGHT when the blackness of the sky swallows the moon so that all that's left is a thin sliver of light. We make our way down the halls and find David staring into the lamps and Rowan lying on his back, looking up at the ceiling, while Violet talks loudly.

"All I do is laundry. It's never-ending," Violet says.

The boys smile when we arrive, but I don't smile back. I just slide down next to David quietly.

"It's exhausting and sweaty and steamy. And boring. It's so unbelievably boring."

Violet has been working in housekeeping for three weeks, after Miss Templeton informed her that it was time to "diversify her skill set." Miss Templeton had tried to move her two months after I arrived, but I begged her to let Violet stay longer, claiming I needed the help. I thought that maybe if she got to know me better, if we worked together long enough, things would change. But the longer I was there and the more Miss Templeton or one of the Decos praised me, the meaner Violet got.

"For god's sake, Elimina, who the hell taught you to write? Is this supposed to be a *J*?" she yelled in earshot of Miss Templeton after one of the Decos complimented my work. And in that moment, somehow I knew that Violet would hate me no matter what I did or didn't do for her.

So when Miss Templeton asked me again, a few months later, if I would be okay on my own, I told her I could easily manage, and the next day Violet was gone. Now Josephine lived with her daily complaining, while I lived only with the regret that I didn't send her away when I first had the chance.

"Elimina, are you okay?" David says. "You look—"

"You look awful," Rowan says.

"I . . ."

"Elimina?" Josephine says.

"I—"

"For goodness' sake, say something!" Violet says, annoyed at having lost their attention.

"You're . . . graduating," I say, head down. "Violet, David and Louis are going to the employer fair next week. Mr. Gregors asked me to come and help."

Violet stares at Rowan while Josephine turns to David. He tries to pull her close, but she holds her hand up to stop him.

"Just David?" Josephine says. "Not me?"

I bite my lip, remembering the promise I made to her in the stairwell the night I followed her to the Fieldhouse because I desperately wanted a friend.

"We came at the same time," Josephine says, her eyes glassy and wet. "We have the same age on paper. Why don't they take me too?"

"I thought you had to be sixteen," Violet says. "I'm not sixteen. I won't be sixteen for a few months."

"You know how it is—how it goes with money and Mainlanders. They send kids whenever they want, whenever there's a need, or whenever an employer with deep pockets asks," Rowan says, but I can hear in his voice that this is hard for him as well.

"Is that why they sent me to housekeeping?" Violet says. "Because they're looking for housekeepers? Is that what Mr. Gregors expects me to do?"

"It's good to have more experience, Violet," Rowan says, trying to reassure her. "It's good to be able to do more things. Mr. Gregors was probably just—"

"Do you know how to fold sheets and clean toilets, Rowan?"

"You're going to have to work like the rest of us at some point," Josephine says, her tone sharp and angry. "No one's going to hire you to do the kind of work you're doing in Mr. Gregors's office."

"Oh really, Josephine! What do you know about that?" Violet says. "You've never even been to an employer fair."

"Violet, please," David says.

"Don't, David," Violet says, pointing at him. "Don't use your please-calm-down voice on me. I've been at an academy longer than all of you. And while Rowan gets to travel around, throwing punches and meeting important people, I've had to work. My parents didn't sign me up for an academy. They aren't waiting for me and hoping for me. My dad was a drunk and my mom was just a shell of a person. My sister left me with them, and it was horrible. I had to find my own way. I've had to fight for everything, and I will not do crappy work for crappy pay. I will not spend my life being miserable and unhappy."

"Violet, I'm sorry. I didn't mean . . ." David begins, but Violet just shakes her head and turns away so it's clear she hates the pity on his face just as much as his calm-down voice.

"I want to be done with this debt. I want to pay it off as fast as possible. And that's not going to happen cleaning houses. I shouldn't have to do housekeeping if I can do things that make more money, and I don't care if that bothers you, Josephine. I really don't care what any of you think of me."

"You talk like you're better than everyone else. Like you work harder," Rowan says. "I'm sorry you had a crappy family, but I've been working in this Fieldhouse since I was seven years old, doing my training on top of it. I work hard. We all work hard, Violet."

"I'm sure you do. But it's not the same for you, Rowan, and you know it. You know you'll get paid well. You'll be out quick. Whether Josephine wants to admit it or not, it's different for us," she says.

I look down at the ground, wondering if what Violet says is true, if it will be hard for us to find good work after the academy.

"Elimina, why is it just them?" Josephine says, her voice small and shaky.

"Mr. Gregors just said he's taking a small group and that I'm coming along to get some experience."

"Am I going?" Rowan says.

"He said to make sure your schedule is clear so you can help with the luggage and stuff."

"He always needs my muscles," Rowan says with his dimpled smile, but no one laughs.

"So everyone's going but me?"

"We're coming back, Jose," I say. "Rowan and I are just going for the day."

Josephine looks up at David. "We're supposed to go at the same time, to the same place."

"I know, Jose. I know that's what we wanted. But it doesn't always work out," David says, and I see a sadness in his face as he looks around the whole stall, like he doesn't want to leave any of us.

"Elimina, can't you do something?" Josephine says.

"She doesn't have any control over that, Josephine," Violet says.

"Can't you suggest me to Mr. Gregors? Maybe they can make a deal with someone."

"I . . ."

"Please, Elimina, you promised!" she says, and Violet rolls her eyes and sighs.

"We'll be okay, Jose," David says, but she shakes her head, burying her face in the curve of his shoulder and sobbing so hard we all sink back and close our eyes.

"Well, the good news for all of us is that Louis is going too," Rowan says, raising his hands and smiling like this is a fact that's worth celebrating.

"Can't you be serious for once?" Violet says.

"I think everyone is being far too serious," Rowan says. "You all need to lighten up."

"We're leaving, Rowan! This—all of this—it's over. We may never see each other again," Violet says, and Josephine sobs even harder.

"I don't understand what all your fuss is about! I mean, I get why Josephine is sad. But you? I thought you'd be dying to get out of here," Rowan says.

"It's not that simple."

"But it is. The sooner you get hired, the sooner you can get Redemption Freedom. Isn't that what you want?" he says.

"Not if I get hired for housekeeping. I'd have to do that for the next forty-five years. I'd hate every minute," she says. "And what if my employer is terrible, or what if the people I work with are like Louis? Or worse, what if it's bad, really bad? We've all heard the rumors. What do I do if that happens?"

Josephine looks up at David and he squeezes her tightly, like he's telling her everything will be okay.

"What rumors?" I say.

"That the debt managers keep money for themselves," Violet says. "That the living conditions are terrible."

"Those are just rumors, Violet," David says. "There are good jobs and good employers and good debt managers out there. Just like there are good academies like Livingstone. Ida is happy enough . . . and Albert seems happy too. It doesn't have to be terrible."

Albert Cootes delivers mail to Livingstone Academy and is set for Redemption Freedom in just under a year, on his sixtieth birthday. Once his debt is paid, he'll be the ninth Livingstone Academy graduate to achieve the honor.

Albert delivers mail to the academy every day, and when the weather is nice, he parks at the gate and walks to the front door, just for the exercise. If things are slow in the office, Miss Templeton lets me meet him partway, where he almost always gives me candy and tells me stories. He talks about the food they make back home and the places he drives to on the Mainland that remind him of his time in the Gutter.

"Albert loves what he does. I'm sure you will too, Violet," I say.

"Well, I'm glad you're so smart and confident," she says.

"This is a new start, Violet," Rowan says. "Out there, our debt will go down instead of up for the first time ever."

"Rowan's right," David says, and Josephine pulls away, like he's jabbed a knife in her stomach. "The sooner we get out of here, Jose, the sooner we can have what we really want. It's why Mom and Dad sent us here. We always knew it could happen at some point."

Violet closes her eyes, holding the palms of her hands against her face, like it's all too much.

"We're Livingstone Academy kids, Violet. The best of the best. You'll be okay," Rowan says.

We all sit quietly for a moment as Violet fidgets with her fingernails and Josephine sniffles and clings on to David.

"Do you think that place exists? The one where all the Gutter folks went after the war, the ones who didn't go to the Gutter?" Violet says to Rowan.

I remember the book Mr. Gregors gave me and the small paragraph about the Sossi folks who paid their way out.

"The Hill definitely exists," Rowan says. "Ma talked about it all the time. It's where she wants to live when we get out. Fancy houses, clear water. Sossi people with real money and no debt just walking around everywhere."

I try to imagine a place like that, filled with faces like mine, but even when I close my eyes, I can't quite see it, like it's too impossible to be real.

"I want it to be true more than anything," Violet says as we all stare at the two lamps sitting on the concrete, fire bending and waving inside.

"Can we read one more poem?" Josephine says.

David nods and when Violet hands him the book from its spot underneath the blankets, he reads a poem about all of the things that can happen when you wait too long for a dream—a stench, a heaviness, an explosion.

"I knew you would read that one," Josephine says when he's finished, and David closes the book and smiles, holding it out to Violet.

She takes it and clutches it to her chest, instead of returning it to its hiding place, and I realize that in addition to losing Violet and David, we're also losing the blue book of poems.

"That poem is my favorite too," Rowan says, and we all just sit there quietly.

"We should go," David finally says.

Everyone nods except Josephine, who sobs into David's arm as he squeezes her close, carrying her out of the stall like a child.

Violet follows them, but I stay seated on the floor, thinking about the raisin that dried up, about the sweetness and the festering and the possible explosion. I wonder what will happen while I wait for my dreams—if I'll dry up or explode without these friends and these nights reading poetry.

Rowan offers his hand to me and I look up, unable to move, like I'm stuck. "I need you to let me know if there are any changes. Tell me anything Louis or Mr. Gregors says about the fair. Okay?" he says, and he waits until I nod back before pulling me up.

When we reach the doors, Violet is standing in the shadows while Josephine continues to cry with David's arms wrapped tightly around her. It's the sound of heartache, and it reminds me of the way I felt when Mother suddenly got sick, like the whole world, the ground itself, was splitting apart and leaving me alone.

11

ON THE DAY OF THE EMPLOYER FAIR, JOSEPHINE WAKES up sweaty and pale, shivering and curled up in a ball of damp sheets, like her body's too cold but also too warm. When she tries to get out of bed, I tell her to rest.

"It's the stress that's making you sick," I say.

She shakes her head from side to side, like I've got it all wrong. "I have to say goodbye."

"Mr. Gregors will get suspicious if he sees you making a fuss over David. I'll keep track of where he goes, and David will work with whoever hires him to get you there too. You won't be apart for long. It's going to be okay."

Josephine looks up at the ceiling, sighing and nodding her head, like she doesn't want to listen but knows she should.

"Stay in bed, Josephine. Rest. It'll be okay," I say again.

But I wonder if this is really true—if everything will be okay with David gone, or if she'll end up broken like May Bennet, who still moves around campus like a ghost.

"Elly," she says, grabbing the sleeve of my blouse as I head to the door. She pauses for a moment, biting her lip until it looks like it might burst. "You'll tell Mr. Gregors and Miss Templeton I'm sick? I don't think I can make it to Nurse Gretchen."

"Of course. I'll tell Miss Templeton on my way out."

"You're a good friend," she says, voice wobbling.

"You're my first friend, Josephine. My best friend. You're my David," I say, and she buries her face into her pillow and sobs as I head down the stairs.

WHEN I ARRIVE in front of the Main House with all of the paperwork for the fair, Violet is sitting on a bench wearing a yellow dress with a shiny white belt and a pair of white gloves. Her hair is pulled into a neat bun, and when I tell her she looks like the girls from the Mainland magazines, she smiles at me for the first time I can remember.

"I'm so nervous," she says.

I think maybe she's going to say sorry for being so awful to me from the moment I arrived, but when Rowan and David appear carrying the trunk with David's belongings, she lets go and heads toward them instead.

Rowan whistles and Violet twirls at his command, her dress floating up in perfect waves as she holds her gloved hands against her chest.

When Mr. Gregors pulls the van up to the front of the academy, the boys load all of the crates and trunks in carefully. Rowan climbs into the middle row next to Violet, and David sits in the back row with me while Louis holds the map up in the front seat.

At our last meeting, Louis made a ceremony of his departure, entrusting Murray and me with information about where to store the keys for the leashes and how to submit Records of Mischief, which he always insisted on doing himself.

"We're gonna keep things running, Louis. No worries here,"

Murray said, placing his arm around my shoulder and squeezing me close. "We got this. Right, Junior?"

"Don't call me Junior," I said, stepping away from him with a shove. "You're not a Red Coat. And if you do happen to become one, you'll be *my* junior. Got it?"

"Okay, boss," he said, raising his hands and smiling sarcastically, like it was only a matter of time before Mr. Gregors offered him the job.

David stares out the window as the van pulls away from Livingstone Academy, his mind somewhere else altogether as we maneuver down long country roads. On more than one occasion, he asks Mr. Gregors to slow the van down and take it easy on the curves, fearing he might be sick, and I wonder if he's really unwell or if it's his worry for Josephine that's making him ill.

I place my hand on his, and he locks his fingers between mine, and this is how we stay for the rest of the drive, holding on for the last time.

MR. GREGORS PARKS the van on a gravel road beside an open field in the town of Haven, where a large white tent is pinned to the ground with tight ropes and wood pegs. Above the tent, a billboard displays shackled Gutter hands and a Mainland flag with large black letters: "Welcome to the Site of the Battle of Haven where Mainland Believers defeated Gutter Betrayers."

I stare out at the field, then up again at the sign as Louis and Mr. Gregors continue toward the tent, leaving the rest of us behind.

"Remember what Ida always tells us," Rowan says, leaning close. "This land was ours before it was theirs."

I close my eyes and nod, but I can't help thinking about the way Mainlanders in Capedown looked at Mother whenever I was around—like she had somehow betrayed them by taking me into her home.

At the fair, Mainland men in fancy suits mingle and laugh while students in academy uniforms set up markers and displays, pointing at Rowan as we pass.

"That's the fighter, the one who's going to fight on the Mainland," one boy says.

"Saw him fight at an academy match. Busted a kid up so bad he could hardly see after," another boy whispers.

"What I wouldn't give to see him knock out one of them Mainland boys," says another.

But when the students see me walk by in my red coat, all I hear is "rat."

I PLACE THE graduate markers out on the Livingstone Academy tables, just like Miss Templeton instructed, while Louis, Violet and David unpack the items they brought for their displays.

LOUIS JOHN
LIVINGSTONE ACADEMY RED COAT, SEWING & TEXTILES
CREATIVE | ORGANIZED | DETAIL-ORIENTED

DAVID HAMBLE
LIVINGSTONE ACADEMY, GENERAL LABOR & CARPENTRY
STRONG | CAPABLE | DILIGENT

VIOLET MASTERS
LIVINGSTONE ACADEMY, HOUSE MANAGEMENT
INTELLIGENT | ARTICULATE | LOYAL

Violet arranges a color-coded filing system on the table along-side samples of her penmanship and calligraphy, while Louis displays a few vests and an assortment of ties in a variety of colors. David sets a log, some tools and four wood carvings on the table between them—a soldier, a moving car, a train that whistles and a statue of a woman with a child held close to her chest.

"It's the first thing I made when we got to Livingstone," David says when I pick up the statue of the woman and child, sliding my finger along the edges.

I examine the way the mother and child are joined, wondering if this is what it feels like to have a mother who carried you in her body and loved you from the start—forever connected and bonded, even when you're apart.

"It's beautiful," I say, placing it back down and stepping away as an employer approaches David to talk about his work.

I stroll up and down the rows of tables and displays, studying each of the sixty graduates from the ten Mainland academies that have come to the fair. Half of the graduates are boys who are slated for maintenance, agriculture or general labor. Every girl other than Violet is slated for kitchen work or housekeeping—including all eight girls from North End Academy, the school Ida Mason graduated from and refuses to talk about.

The girls from North End Academy have torn shoes and patched uniforms. Their legs and arms are bony and thin, and all of them have short hair. A girl named Shanta Cinder shivers like she's cold, her whole body quivering despite the warmth. I move closer to see if she's okay, but when she sees me coming, she turns to the girls beside her, covering her face like she's scared.

"Leave her alone," one girl whispers as Shanta stands behind her. "We don't like rats around here."

"I just . . . I didn't mean," I say, stepping back and heading quickly for Mr. Gregors, who is looking out over the fair in a sharp gray suit, hands against his waist.

"It's quite the turnout," he says.

I nod, but I don't look up because I can feel the North End Academy girls watching me as I stand with my headmaster.

"Sir, what's wrong with the girls from North End Academy?" I whisper, turning my back to them. "Why do they look like that?"

Mr. Gregors looks over at the North End Academy tables, before returning his attention to the crowd. He shrugs like there's nothing unusual about them at all. "Everyone will walk away happy today, Elimina. Don't worry about appearances," he says. "They remind me a bit of you when you first arrived, and look how well you've turned out."

I frown at the comparison, tugging at the ends of my hair. "They don't seem very happy, sir," I say.

"Some schools don't put much weight or care into the happiness of their students, Elimina," Mr. Gregors says. "Happiness is not a very lucrative business model, at least when it comes to your employees. I can assure you that those girls will be very happy to be leaving North End Academy for good today. That is what I love about days like this," he says, with his hands held out in front of him. "It's the one place on earth where everyone wins. Students get work. Employers get workers. And everyone else gets paid. Win win win."

"But, sir, I thought it wasn't good for kids to start working so young. I thought that's what all the Mainland studies said. That kids should enjoy being kids," I say, looking around at the fair. "Some of these graduates look younger than me."

"They probably are, and you're absolutely right, Elimina. But it's hard to enjoy life when you're saddled with debt. So for Gutter children, perhaps it's best to get right to it."

We watch as a woman with curly black hair stops in front of Louis. He shows her his work, holding each piece up and turning it over, explaining all of his stitchwork.

"See how poised our students look? There's no comparison," Mr. Gregors says.

I look over at the North End Academy tables, where Shanta Cinder is responding to an employer by nodding and shaking her head.

"Imagine if I had sent you here right when you arrived? Imagine how much more confident you'll be in a year or so. Especially as my top Red Coat."

I stick my hands deep into my pockets as Mr. Gregors embraces an old friend. The two of them move farther away just as Rowan reappears for the first time since our arrival.

"Where have you been?"

"Around," he says, shrugging his shoulders.

We stand there for a while watching David, Violet and Louis talk with employers, smiling at the ones who look nice, as though it might help.

"Do you like coming to these things?" I say.

Rowan curls his mouth to the side, like he's not sure how to answer. "I like seeing graduates get hired. I like the change of pace," he says. "But it's tough to be here and just watch it all happen, you know."

"What do you mean?"

Rowan looks around and points at a man with thick eyebrows talking to a small academy boy with a display of potted plants. "See that kid over there?"

I nod, standing on the tips of my toes so I can get a better view.

"See that guy in the white suit that's walking up to them—the headmaster?"

I nod again as Rowan retrieves two small wooden crates for us to stand on to get a better view. We watch the man with the eyebrows pull out stacks of bills.

"The money he's showing the headmaster? That's the hiring deposit," he says. "Which the debt manager will take—"

"Those fancy guys at the door?"

"Yup. They get assigned when you're hired, and they're in charge of tracking your debt until it's paid," he says. "And if they die before you do, they just hand their cut to whoever's next in their family line, usually their kids."

"So we have to pass down our debt, and they get to pass down the money *we* earned?" I say.

Rowan frowns and nods.

I feel a sharp turn in my stomach, and I place my hands around my belly as the two men and the young boy move to the debt manager—a man with slick black hair and a shiny watch. The three men talk for a moment while the young boy looks on, and when the headmaster signs the paperwork, the man with the shiny black hair takes the bills, licking the tip of his finger before he begins to count.

"That conversation that just happened was the most important discussion of that kid's life," Rowan says. "He's what, twelve, thirteen? He didn't say a word. But they just decided what he'll earn for the rest of his life and how long it will take him to get Redemption Freedom. And sometimes when I think about that, I don't know, it messes with me. Like I just want to hit somebody. Anybody."

When the employer leaves with the boy, I watch the debt manager and the headmaster shaking hands, pulling each other close and smiling as they pat each other on the back.

"The debt manager keeps all of that money?"

"They take it and redistribute it. A portion goes toward the kid's debt. Some goes back to the school. But the largest portion of that deposit goes directly to the headmaster as a commission," he says, lowering his voice and leaning in close. "A personal payment for raising a solid graduate."

"The headmaster?" I whisper, thinking about the young boy.

Rowan nods. "Mr. Gregors gets a good chunk for every one of us who gets hired."

I look through the crowd and spot Mr. Gregors laughing with a group of debt managers. "Do you think Mr. Gregors is a bad person, Rowan?"

"It depends on what you're looking at, Elimina. He's helped me, that's for sure. But he'd have to do a lot of things differently if I was going to call him a good person, starting with telling that headmaster from North End Academy not to beat and starve his students."

I look over at Shanta Cinder and the rest of the girls from North End Academy, then back at Rowan.

"Only ones who eat proper at North End Academy are Red Coats," he says, and I bite down hard on my lip, staring at Shanta and thinking about Ida. "Kid I boxed against said Red Coats get fed for ratting, even if they lie about it."

I stuff my hands in my pockets and rub my stomach, which continues to rumble like I've eaten something awful.

"Mr. Gregors may be nicer than some, Elimina. He may do things differently. But he's one of them. You can't ever forget that," Rowan says, resting one hand on my shoulder. "But he also holds our whole future in his hands. So no matter what you think about him, it's best to stay on his good side."

x

THE GIRLS FROM North End Academy are hired quickly, and while the boys are hired more slowly, they go for nearly double the rate.

"I can tell you how many crops a Gutter kid can cut and how much that'll bring me. But how in the hell am I supposed to make any money off the old lady's clean floors?" I hear one employer say as a group of men laugh.

Despite all of the introductions and interest, two hours into the fair, no one has hired Louis, David or Violet, and I wonder if Mr. Gregors has made a horrible mistake—if the more mature Livingstone Academy students with higher rates are less desirable. But Mr. Gregors doesn't seem worried, and by late afternoon, a large crowd begins to gather around them, studying their markers and shouting out questions.

Louis brags about his ties and Violet shows off her penmanship. But it's David's quiet carving that creates the biggest draw, as he forms a three-legged stool from the log.

"What else can you do?" a man in a black cowboy hat yells.

"I can make anything out of wood—fences, cabinets, sheds. But that takes me a bit longer," he says, and the crowd laughs.

Despite all of the interest in David, Louis is the first Livingstone student to get hired when the owner of a clothing store in Garrett City makes an offer. The woman proposes a solid deposit, few conditions and an admirable rate to take him on as one of her tailors. When the contract is signed, Mr. Gregors places his arm around Louis, who smiles up at him like a child who's made his father proud.

"You'll never find an employee who's more loyal and trustworthy. He's never spent a day in the Gutter, and it shows," Mr. Gregors says, and the woman smiles.

"It's always nice to have a young man who knows how to behave, if you know what I mean," she says.

Louis steps closer and pats me on the shoulder as he leaves. "Take care, Junior. You keep an eye on things over there," he says without looking at Rowan, who's standing beside me, clenching his fist.

By the time Louis leaves the tent with his contract and hiring package in order, there are only ten other graduates left, including David and Violet, with most of the remaining employers gathered nearby.

"Why are they just standing around watching?" I say.

"People want the best deal," Rowan says. "David's the last boy because of his hiring rate. But he's also the best candidate. Those employers think that if they can outwait everyone, they can get him for less. And it's true, in a way. I mean, if no one takes him by the end of the fair, that will happen. But folks want David. Trust me, they're going to pay."

The crowd buzzes and employers check their notepads as they watch David work.

"What if more than one person's interested in David?" I say. "What happens then?"

"That's the best part," Rowan says with a sly grin. "If there's more than one offer, they'll bid for him. Like an auction. Or a boxing match. Employers love to fight over graduates. And people love to watch. Especially for a kid like David."

"Because he does woodwork?"

"Yeah. But also because he's calm and easygoing. Mainlanders like to see guys like me get angry and fight in a ring. But they love to *hire* guys like David," he says with a strange curl of his mouth.

When the man in the black cowboy hat approaches Mr. Gregors, followed by a short old man, Rowan rubs his hands together and smiles all teeth and dimples, like we're about to see something good.

"Ladies and gentlemen!" Mr. Gregors says, voice raised so everyone in the tent can hear. "I'm pleased to announce that David Hamble is going to auction."

The crowd cheers, whistling and gathering closer as Mr. Gregors places the cowboy and the old man a few feet in front of him. Just as David moves toward Mr. Gregors and faces his potential employers, a commotion causes everyone to turn toward the entrance.

"What's going on?" I say.

Rowan and I step back onto the crates to get a better view of a well-dressed couple moving calmly toward the Livingstone Academy tables. The woman is wearing a plum skirt and a green blouse with a tan hat pulled down to one side, while the man walks alongside her in a collared shirt and a black bow tie, carrying a briefcase in his hand.

Only they're not Mainlanders. Their skin is rich and warm like mine, but their hands are unmarked.

"Do you think . . . ?" I say, turning to Rowan.

"They must be from the Hill," Rowan says. "They're real, Elimina."

The couple moves through the crowd, stopping between the cowboy and the old man, like they're interested in David as well.

"Can we get this thing going?" the cowboy says, lifting his hat and combing wet hair off his forehead.

"Yes, yes. Yes, of course," Mr. Gregors says, watching the couple closely before placing his hand on David's shoulder. "Let the bidding begin. Can I get one thousand dollars?"

The cowboy raises his hand, and when Mr. Gregors increases the price, the old man raises his also. They go back and forth, and I turn to Rowan, lips pouted in confusion because the Hill couple have not said anything. It's like they just came here to watch.

"We've got ten *thousand* dollars," Mr. Gregors says. "Can I get $10,500?"

The old man squints, shaking his head, as the cowboy grins.

"Going once. Going twice," Mr. Gregors says.

But before Mr. Gregors can finish, the woman in the plum skirt steps forward. "We would like to take that last offer, from the gentleman in the cowboy hat . . . and double it," she says.

Rowan and I look at one another, our mouths wide open like caves. *Twenty thousand dollars.* The cowboy removes his hat and shakes his head, and when Mr. Gregors is certain no one else can beat the offer, he invites the couple to step forward to make it official.

"Mabel and Harold Freeman," the woman says.

"Samuel J. Gregors," he says. "Congratulations. This young man is an incredible talent. You chose well."

"We're very excited to bring him to the Hill," the woman says.

Rowan and I smile and Violet stands a little taller, like she's hoping to be seen and hired by them as well.

Mabel Freeman tells Mr. Gregors that they've traveled a long way to get to the fair, which is why they were so late. "We came by ferry and then by car, and we'd like to make it back as soon as possible, if you don't mind."

Mr. Gregors nods and instructs Rowan and David to go with Mr. Freeman and transfer David's belongings while he and Mrs. Freeman finish the paperwork.

"That was quite the show you put on," Mr. Gregors says as I hand Mabel Freeman the hiring contract.

"That was no *show*, Mr. Gregors. That was a young man's future we just decided on," she says, studying the pages closely as Mr. Gregors gives a polite smile.

"Of course," he says.

"And while we're on this topic, I would like to discuss how we might go about negotiating the percentage of your commission. My interest is in helping that young man. The Mainland rules around hiring here are very particular, as you know, but David will be doing all of the *real* work going forward, so I'd like to see him get most of the reward, starting now."

I watch Mabel Freeman, studying her voice and the poise of her body, like it's something I can copy.

"Well, of course, I want to be open, Mrs. Freeman—"

"I believe that with an offer such as ours, there is room for you to get the sizable commission you expected—plus a little more—without taking too much from the young man. It's his debt that is of utmost importance to us."

"Yes, of course," Mr. Gregors says, straightening his shoulders and lifting his chin. "I think it's important to note, however, that the rigorous training of these young people does come at a tremendous cost to the school and to myself. But, as you said, with the generosity of your offer, I believe your requested adjustment is still more than fair."

He looks down at the clipboard and scratches a few notes onto the page, and I watch the way Mabel Freeman signs the documents, handing the debt manager the money from the briefcase like it's the most normal part of her day. When she turns to me, I almost feel afraid.

"What's your name, child?" she says. She takes one step toward me, leaning close, and I feel faint, like the ground is moving away.

"Elimina," I say softly.

"That's a very pretty name," she says. She takes both of my hands in hers, and when she turns them over and sees the single X, she looks up, clearly unnerved.

"Just the one?" she says. I nod, and she turns to Mr. Gregors. "She's a project case? The—"

"Yes," he says. "She joined the academy last year, after the woman who adopted her passed away suddenly."

Mabel Freeman looks at him oddly, like she's angry or annoyed. "And you have her on the academy track?"

"Project cases are wards of the nation, Mrs. Freeman. It's out of my hands."

"Of course. This place and its rules," she mutters, shaking her head. "How soon will she be graduating, then?"

Mr. Gregors looks down at me, hesitating for a moment. "Well . . . as you know, the government requires us to keep her until she's sixteen, and . . . they're being very strict about that with Elimina, for reasons I'm sure you can understand," he says.

Mabel Freeman leans closer to me, turning up the corners of her mouth. "How old are you, Elimina?"

"I just turned fifteen," I say.

She smiles at me and squeezes my shoulders the way Mother used to do when she wanted me to be brave, like she's trying to fill me with courage and hope with only her touch and her gaze.

"Well, then it will only be a year," she says.

"You're going to hire me?" I say, and when she nods, I feel like I might burst, like there's too much happiness in me to hold inside.

"Well, Mrs. Freeman, I think that sounds like a lovely idea," Mr. Gregors says, guiding her to the table where Violet stands. "But may I also introduce you to Violet Masters. She is another one of our graduates, and she's ready today. She has a very similar skill set as Elimina."

"Mrs. Freeman, I just want to tell you that I would love to work for you," Violet says with a quick bob of her head.

"Perhaps we could make an arrangement to tie her hire in with David's, a packaged deal?" Mr. Gregors says, leaning close to avoid being heard by anyone else.

Mabel Freeman backs away from the table with a polite nod, commenting on Violet's lovely penmanship before turning around as Mr. Gregors follows. "We are not interested in *deals*, Mr. Gregors. Especially the kind that make it harder on these kids," she whispers. "It's clear Violet is an excellent student, and I'm sure with all of your skill and persuasion, you will find an excellent opportunity to help her on her way. You know as well as I do that there are very strict regulations surrounding how much we can spend while we're here, and I will not make this young girl's life harder just to make yours easier."

Mr. Gregors smiles politely, but I can see his irritation with Mabel Freeman and his frustration over Violet's state as he surveys the tent. Only five older girls remain, including Violet, and nearly all the employers have left.

"As soon as Elimina is free to graduate, I would like to make arrangements to hire her. Perhaps we can avoid the whole mess of the fair altogether. I believe she's earned that," Mabel Freeman says to Mr. Gregors, just as Rowan and David return.

To be with the Freemans on the Hill with David is almost too much to believe, and when David looks at me and smiles, I wonder if my life is not unlucky after all—if luck just has bumps and curves.

"Hold on to this for me," David says, handing me the carving of the woman and child. When I start to protest, he interrupts. "Elimina, I want you to have it, to take care of it, until we're back together. So you don't forget me."

I smile, squeezing his arm. "I'll see you soon," I say so only he can hear as he leans over and holds me tight.

"Maybe we can find a way to bring Jose too," I whisper.

He steps back and bites his lip. "Take care of yourself, Elly. It'll be okay," he says.

ROWAN HELPS THE fair organizers move the four other girls to the tables next to Violet, so that all the remaining hires are standing in a row—older girls in their academy uniforms, Violet in her yellow dress.

"I shouldn't have let her wear that," Mr. Gregors says under his breath, rubbing his hands through his hair as two tall men with messy beards enter the tent.

"We are late it seems. I just hope we are not too late," the taller man says when he reaches Mr. Gregors and the other headmasters.

"Not too late at all," Mr. Gregors says, extending his hand and stepping in front of the others. "Samuel J. Gregors of Mainland Academy."

"Eli Jung. My brother, Sebastian, and I are new to the Mainland. Newlanders, we call ourselves," the taller man says with a grin that makes me shiver.

"We own a travel company," Sebastian says, walking past the girls and studying them closely.

"You own a travel company?" Mr. Gregors says.

Violet straightens and smiles.

"Yes, we make arrangements for business people—flights, hotels, hospitality. We are looking to expand here on the Mainland. Get bigger. Much bigger. We were wondering if these young ladies might do well, working for us. Help us expand."

Violet clasps her hands in front of her as Sebastian tilts his head and looks at her, tapping one finger against his lips.

"Our biggest question for the ladies is travel stamina, you know? There will be a lot of it. A lot of here, there, going, going," Eli says with a wave of his hands.

"Violet is an excellent traveler. She is skilled and disciplined. She will train well," Mr. Gregors says, standing next to Violet as the remaining headmasters echo the same pitch.

"Lovely," the Jung brothers say with a nod. "We will take all of them."

Mr. Gregors and all of the other headmasters clap and nod to show their enthusiasm, clearly relieved. But when the arrangements are made, the Jung brothers propose rates that go far below their proposed contract, and while none of the headmasters seem happy, all of them accept. Violet gets the best offer, but all five girls are hired for the lowest rates of the day.

"I'm going to be traveling the world," Violet says as she packs up her belongings.

Her voice is high and tight, and it's impossible to ignore what we all know as she follows the Jung brothers and the other four graduates out of the tent: this is exactly what she feared, a hiring package that will require her to work well beyond sixty in order to earn Redemption Freedom.

THE SKY IS navy and smooth on the way back to the academy. Mr. Gregors whistles from the front seat, fiddling with the radio, while Rowan and I sit in the back and look out our windows, our heads leaning against the glass.

"You worried about Violet?" I say.

"Nah. She'll be alright, I think."

But I can tell by the way he looks out the window, with his leg bumping up and down, that he's just as worried as I am.

"I don't have a good feeling about those Jung brothers," he says.

"Me neither."

We sit quietly for a while, listening to the tires rumble and grind against the road.

"We're going to be okay, Elimina," he says.

He tries to smile, and I do too, but there's a heaviness in my chest that only grows as the van gets closer to campus and the iron gates come into view.

Should I tell Josephine that I'll be going to the Hill with David? Or should I wait until we can work something out for her too?

"Rowan," I say, turning to him and placing my hand on his arm, "I don't think we should tell Josephine about the Hill until . . ."

Before I can finish the sentence, the van stops in front of the Main House, where a dozen vans with "MG" stamped on the side are parked—the vehicles of the national defense service, the Mainland Guard.

"What the hell?" Mr. Gregors says, turning off the engine and climbing out. "What the hell is going on?"

He steps toward a crowd of Mainland Guards who are holding guns and long black flashlights that remind me of clubs, their dogs pulling on their leashes, barking loud.

"What is going on?" I say, but Rowan just shakes his head, helping me out of the van as Miss Templeton runs toward Mr. Gregors, her hair tumbling down, her makeup smeared like she's been crying.

She pulls Mr. Gregors aside, and despite her best efforts to keep her voice down, Rowan and I hear every word: "Josephine is missing."

12

DOGS BARK AND GROWL, BARING SHARP WHITE FANGS, AS the Livingstone Academy security guards and the crowd of Mainland Guards wait for direction in front of the Main House.

"How does this even happen?" Mr. Gregors says, his voice high and loud.

"We'll find her, sir," Mack says. "She can't hide for long. That forest is deep. Real deep. No way she survives out there and no way she got me at the gate."

"Well, let's find her already, then, Mack. For heaven's sake, it's pitch-black out. I don't know why everyone's just standing around doing nothing. What are you all waiting for?" he yells. "You've searched all of the buildings?"

"Our guys have been all over campus. Searched every building," Mack says.

"But the dogs. Have you sent the Mainland Guard dogs?"

"Well, no, sir—"

"Then do that. Have those dogs tear through every building until she's found."

"But sir," Mack says, "if we want to make some ground, I think—"

"Listen to me," Mr. Gregors shouts. "We're going to find her. But before we do, I want all of these kids to see those dogs, so they know what's coming if they decide to follow Josephine's lead."

Mack nods and heads over to the Mainland Guards, who turn on their flashlights and shout out orders before spreading out in organized lines.

"Sir, should I tell the Decos to go home, or do you want to talk to them? Do you want them to help with the search?" Miss Templeton says, her voice quiet and gentle, like she's almost afraid to be heard.

"I have no interest in talking to them right now, Miss Templeton. But what I do want from them is a written account of every action they performed today. I want to know everything Josephine did and every person who saw her, and I want every car searched inside and out before they go anywhere."

I GRAB A flashlight from the supply closet in the office, but instead of entering the front doors of the West Hall and climbing into bed, I head down the path toward the back stairwell. If Josephine ran away to be with David, she would need to hide in a place where she couldn't be found until she got word of his whereabouts.

"Josephine? It's me, Elly. Are you here? Josephine?" I say in the loudest whisper I can manage, holding the door open with one hand and pointing the flashlight at all the dark corners.

When I hear footsteps coming down the path behind me, I stick the hem of my coat in the door so it doesn't make a noise when it shuts.

"Tell me again what happened," I hear Mr. Gregors say, his words choppy and staggered, as though he's out of breath.

"She was sick. According to everyone I spoke to, she stayed in bed. She was there all day . . . I think," Miss Templeton says with a shaky voice that's so quiet, I have to put my ear against the small crack in the door to hear.

"You *think*? Did anyone check on her?"

"No. I mean, I don't know," Miss Templeton says as the two of them get closer. "No one I spoke to had checked on her."

Mr. Gregors exhales loudly, stopping in front of the door. "This is why they go to the infirmary if they're not well, where Nurse Gretchen can supervise them. This is why we have rules, Miss Templeton!" he says, like he's talking to a child.

"I'm sorry, Mr. Gregors."

"Who saw her last?" he says slowly, trying to remain calm.

"Elimina was the one who told me she wasn't feeling well."

"Elimina? You mean to tell me this happened before we left? And no one saw her after that? We've been gone for twelve hours, Miss Templeton! You're telling me she's been missing for twelve hours?"

"I don't know . . . I'm sorry, sir."

"Do you even know if Elimina was telling the truth? Is it possible it could have been longer?"

I hold my breath, resisting the urge to defend myself.

"I-I-I don't know. I can check," Miss Templeton stammers. "Let me go check. I can go ask Elimina right now."

I prepare to run up the stairs to get to my bed.

"No. Leave her for now," he says, and I exhale quietly. "I'll talk to her in the morning."

"Do you think she's involved?"

"I don't know what to think right now!" Mr. Gregors says. "But if Elimina was the last one to see her, we've got a very large search area to cover in a short period of time. And if she lied, or if she was involved, it's even worse. Damn it, Miss Templeton!"

"What can I do to help?" she says.

"Nothing. You can do nothing. But I would like these dogs to rip through this forest until they find her. Alive preferably. Although I just might kill her myself when she finally turns up."

I PULL THE hood of my red coat over my head and make my way to the only other hiding spot I can think of. I move my flashlight around the Fieldhouse, whispering Josephine's name. When I hear a shuffle in the corner of the back stall, I point the flashlight toward the noise, where a figure is huddled in a ball on the floor with one hand raised toward the light.

"Turn that off, Elimina!"

"Rowan? What are you doing here?" I say, crouching down and creeping forward in the dark until we're shoulder to shoulder against the wall.

"What are *you* doing here? Why aren't you back in the dorm? You want them to send the dogs for you too?"

"She's gone," I say, even though he knows this, and I bite my lip to stop the tears from coming down hard. "Why would she do this? What will they do if they find her? What if they make me leash her? We need to find her, Rowan."

But Rowan just waves his hands across the ground, moving the straw.

"You need to go to bed, Elimina."

I tell him about the conversation I overheard between Mr. Gregors and Miss Templeton and he shrugs.

"You were the last one to see her, that's all. Just tell them what you know."

"But I don't know anything! I just told Miss Templeton she

was sick and that she'd be staying in bed, and now they think I was involved."

"Then tell them what you just told me."

"Something bad must have happened. I've got to find her."

I put my hands on the ground to stand up, but Rowan grabs me.

"Don't, Elimina," he says.

"But, Rowan, those dogs. Did you see those dogs?"

"If they find you out there, don't you think they'll be suspicious? You'll get in even more trouble."

"I'm a Red Coat, Rowan—"

"That red coat doesn't make you invincible, Elimina! That's the Mainland Guard out there. Not Mack and his gang. Real Mainland Guards with their marked vans that will take you away to god-knows-where. You think they care if you're the campus snitch?"

I turn to him, sitting up tall, my finger pointed toward his mouth. "I'm not a snitch."

"Josephine broke the law. That's all the Mainland Guard know or care about. And so long as they're here, that's all Mr. Gregors is thinking about as well. He's going to try to save face, Elimina. If they *think* you're involved or if they *want* to think you're involved, that red coat isn't going to protect you, and running around out there when you're supposed to be in bed isn't going to help. God, that coat is not a magical shield. It's just a stupid coat."

"She's my best friend, Rowan," I say, swallowing the hurt. "You might be fine doing nothing, but I can't just let those dogs find her and tear her apart."

"So you'll let them tear you apart? That's just silly, Elimina."

I grab the flashlight and stand.

"Don't go looking, Elimina. It won't help," he says, rising to follow me as I head down the hallway. But I don't stop moving. I slide my hands against the walls and make my way to the entrance based on touch until Rowan grabs me and pulls me back.

"Stop, Elimina. Don't do this."

"I'm going, Rowan, whether you like it or not," I say, trying to pull away.

"Don't, Elimina," he says, and something in his voice makes me pause and study him closely, like there's something he's not telling me.

"Rowan, what is it?"

He grasps his hands behind his head, his elbows pointed out wide. "She's not here," he says.

"What do you mean she's not here?" I say, moving closer as he steps away. "How can you be so sure?"

"Don't worry about it. Just know that she's not here," he says. "When they talk to you tomorrow, just tell the truth. Just repeat what you know and you'll be fine. She was sick, and you told her to lie down, and then you left for the fair."

"What's going on, Rowan?"

Flashlight beams slice through the walls, growing brighter and brighter as the voices get louder, as the dogs and the guards move closer. Rowan pulls me into a stall with one of the horses, and crouches down, wrapping his body around me with his hand pressed tight across my mouth.

"Listen to me carefully," he whispers. "Don't fight me or scream or this could go very badly. Just trust me and stay really quiet and really still. Do you understand, Elimina? You gotta trust me."

I nod as the dogs sniff their way through the Fieldhouse, closer and closer, until one of the guards shouts, "We've got something!"

"Boss, we found something too!" another guard says, his voice much farther away, like he's coming from the south yard.

"What is it?"

"Shoes. Found them near the forest."

"Uniform was found in one of the stalls."

"Found a shirt on the other side of campus," another guard says.

"Her scent is all over. Someone tell the headmaster that the girl planned this, and that she probably had help. For now, we'll have to get the dogs to scan the perimeter on all sides, then tackle it section by section. It's going to be a long night for everyone. Where is campus security?"

"Right here," we hear Mack say.

"Any truck or van comes in or even pauses in front, you check. Especially if it's driven by a Gutter. You know how they help their own."

"Yessir," Mack says.

When the guards are all gone and it's quiet in and around the Fieldhouse, I stand and turn to Rowan as the dogs bark in the distance. "What is going on? Did you put Josephine's things all over?" I say, but he doesn't respond. "Tell me, Rowan!"

"He's her brother," Rowan says, like this explains everything. "What else was he supposed to do? If you had seen her when she arrived here, you'd get it. She was May Bennet, Elimina. She couldn't make it without him. But she'll be fine at the Hill. We don't have to worry. They're going to be fine, Elimina. They won't turn her away or report her."

"The Hill?" I say, stepping away from him.

I think about the way David was so sick in the car whenever Mr. Gregors went too quickly or stopped too abruptly, the way Rowan kept disappearing from the tent, the way they both ran off so quickly to move his belongings when David got hired. I think of the look on David's face when I mentioned Josephine and said goodbye, and I feel my legs wobble, my skin turning cold.

"She was in David's trunk."

I can hear the muscles on Rowan's face shift into a crooked kind of grin, as though he's proud of what they did. But I don't grin back at him.

"She's gone? To the Hill?" I say, like repeating myself will help it sink in.

Rowan nods, and I shove him as hard as I can. "What the hell, Rowan? How could you do that?"

"Do what? Help a friend?"

"What if it had been someone else, some other employer?"

"But it wasn't," he says.

"But what if it was? What if they didn't want Josephine? What then?"

"What employer wouldn't want two kids for one price? I mean, that's why it's so great that they went with the Freemans. That's what they do. They rescue kids like us. And now they've helped two. It's going to be fine. It worked out better than we could have imagined."

"For who? For Josephine?"

"Yes."

"But what about her debt? How is she going to pay off her debt if she's not even supposed to be there?"

"She's at the Hill. I'm sure they can figure something out."

I shake my head, my face warm and squeezed in a scowl.

"David loves Josephine and she was a mess. He had to do something," Rowan says, stepping closer. "They'll figure it out."

"He shouldn't have done it," I say, placing my hands on my waist. "They shouldn't have done that."

Rowan tilts his head, as though he's confused. "Ooooh, I see. You're worried the Freemans won't hire you now. You think that if they have another girl, maybe they won't need you. This isn't about Josephine at all."

"That's not true," I say. But maybe it is. What if having Josephine means the Freemans won't come back, that I'll have to go to an employer fair? "You should have told me. You all should have told me."

"Were you planning to tell Josephine about the Freemans' offer?" Rowan says. "That they asked to hire you next year?"

"It's not the same thing," I say.

"It's exactly the same thing."

"I would have told Josephine eventually. Once I knew that she was going too. I would have been doing it to protect her, until I knew for sure."

"And if you were going to the Hill without her? Would you have told her? Would you have stayed behind and given it all up for her?"

I look around the Fieldhouse and clutch the flashlight against my chest. I think of how Rowan let me into the group, how just last week he coached me to keep an eye on things in the office, to report back to him if there were any changes with the fair. I feel a pain in my chest that makes my whole body ache, like there's a wound on the inside of my bones.

"You . . . You all used me. You used me from the start," I say.

Rowan shakes his head. "That's not true."

I move backwards toward the door, tears filling my eyes.

"Elimina—"

"You told me to watch out for Mr. Gregors, Rowan. Don't trust him, you said. But it's you who can't be trusted. I can't trust anyone here."

"That's not true. Josephine, David, they're your friends. I'm your friend, Elimina."

"No. I don't have any friends! I've never had any friends," I hiss.

Rowan steps toward me, careful and slow. "Elimina, you think Mr. Gregors cares about you, but it's Mr. Gregors who's been using you. It's why he made you a Red Coat. To keep you from us."

"Well, maybe I should have listened to him," I say as Rowan moves closer.

"Elimina, why do you think he didn't let the Freemans take you now? You think he cares about some Mainland government rule? If someone comes for you who's willing to pay more than the Freemans, he will hire you out. He's making sure he's got the highest bidder, Elimina."

I stare at Rowan, horrified.

"You saw how Mr. Gregors pushed you aside to try to get the Freemans to take Violet. You saw the way he hired her out for almost nothing when he saw that that was all he could get. Mr. Gregors does not care about us."

"Shut up, Rowan. Shut up. Shut up!" I say, turning away and placing my hands on the door, leaning my head against the wood.

"Listen, Elimina, those were the only friends I've got, other than you, and now they're gone," he says, placing his hands on my shoulder and turning me around. "They're the only people I really know in this world and I helped them leave. And I would do it again. I would do it for you too. Please. Don't tell Mr. Gregors. Please, you're all I've got," he whispers, and all I can think about as I stare at his face in the dim light is whether the tears that are filling up his eyes are real or part of the act.

"If Josephine gets caught, she won't be coming back here," he says softly as I open the door to leave the Fieldhouse. "Mr. Gregors will find a way to make some money, to punish her, but she will never see any of us again. Whatever you're feeling right now, think about that, Elimina. Please, I was going to tell you, I swear. But I didn't want you to have to lie. I was just—"

"Goodnight, Rowan," I say, before heading toward the West Hall.

I can feel Rowan standing at the door to the Fieldhouse as I make my way down the path. I can feel him watching me, waiting for some sign that I've forgiven him, that I'll protect Josephine and David. But I don't pause or hesitate, and I don't look back. I just walk toward the dorm as the Mainland Guard dogs on the other side of campus growl and bark in the darkness.

13

MR. GREGORS IS STANDING BY THE WINDOW WEARING the same gray slacks from the employer fair when I arrive in his office the next morning. His pants are stained, his shirt is untucked, and his hair is loose and messy so that he looks wild and unkempt in a way that's unsettling. I can tell from the way the pillows are bunched at the end of the couch and the way his jacket is draped on the chair that he slept in his office last night—and that, like me, he slept very little.

"You wanted to speak to me, sir?"

He continues to stare out the window, pausing for a long moment as though he hardly knows that I'm here.

"I'm very concerned about Josephine, Elimina," he says. "The Mainland Guards searched all night. They found pieces of her uniform all over campus but no significant scents to follow into the forest. I find that very strange, don't you?"

"Yes, sir," I say with a small nod of my head. "That's very strange."

"Do you know how this makes me look, to have all these people here thinking I don't know how to run an academy, that I can't keep track of my students?"

I'm not sure if this is a question I'm meant to answer, so I don't say anything, and Mr. Gregors moves closer, like a dog approaching its prey.

"What do you know, Elimina?"

I shake my head side to side. "I don't know anything, sir."

"I made you a Red Coat for a reason, Elimina. So you would keep an eye on things. So you would know what's going on on my campus. And you're telling me you don't know anything?"

"I don't know anything, Mr. Gregors."

"I have heard from other students that you and Josephine were friends. Is that true?"

I can smell stale liquor on his breath and I try not to breathe in through my nose.

"Elimina, were you two friends?"

"I don't know where Josephine is, sir." And as soon as I say this, I regret pulling the real story out of Rowan last night, because lying makes me nervous.

Mr. Gregors stares, watching me carefully, puzzled by the tightness in my jaw, the way I drop my head and trace my scar. When I look up, he's pressing his thumb and his index finger against his forehead and moving them in circles, like he's trying to think more and think less at the same time.

"What happened when you saw her, Elimina?" he says quietly, careful with each word. "I understand you were the last one to see her. I'd like to know what she said, every detail, no matter how small."

I nod. "She didn't want breakfast," I say. "That's how it started. When I went to get her out of bed."

"And this is unusual for her?"

"Yes, sir. Very unusual. She loves food."

"You told Miss Templeton she was sick," Mr. Gregors says, like he's waiting for more.

"Yes. Her skin was really hot."

"Her skin was hot?"

"It was damp, sir. Like she'd been . . . Like she'd been . . . tossing and turning all night with a fever or something," I say, and I wonder if she was sweaty from dropping her uniform all over campus or if that was something Rowan or David did for her.

"So you're a nurse?" he says, pouring himself a drink.

I can hear the meanness in his tone, the anger from last night rolling into today, but he raises his glass for me to go on.

"I put my hand on her head. Like Mother used to do. And she was really hot, sir."

"But you are not a nurse?" he says, his face reddening as he swallows his drink down quickly, wiping his mouth with the back of his hand.

"No, sir."

"Did you send her to see the nurse?"

"No, sir."

He walks past the window again, past the shelves, holding his empty glass and studying it carefully with a scowl that creases his brows and the skin around his mouth. "If she was too sick to work and if you are not a nurse, why wouldn't you send her to see Nurse Gretchen, Elimina?"

Because Nurse Gretchen would have just told her to eat something like she did with May Bennet. "I don't know, sir. I'm so sorry, Mr. Gregors."

"You're sorry?"

"I made a mistake, sir."

"You're goddamn right, you made a mistake!" he says, slamming the glass down and leaning over the desk like he needs it to hold him up. "Do you know how much money I lost with this little escapade? Do you know how much money I lose when one of you Gutter kids decides to go and lose your goddamn minds?

Who do you think has to pay for all these Mainland Guards? Who is going to pay for what I lost yesterday chasing that little . . . ?" He wanders over to the window and looks out on the field, running his hands through his hair, so that it sticks up on one side. "And you. What a disappointment you are. I thought you were different, that you were raised better. But all you've got for me is 'sorry'? 'I made a mistake'?"

He laughs an ugly laugh, shaking his head and pointing in my direction.

"I hate losing money, Elimina," he says, grabbing a file and whacking it against the desk. "I hate losing money!"

He pulls a chair from the other side of the room, so that when I turn to him we're face to face at eye level.

"In all my years, I've never lost or misplaced a child. Do you understand me, Elimina? Never. This happens in other places, but it has never happened here. And now you're here. And it does. Is that a coincidence?" he says.

"No, sir. I mean, yes, sir," I say, biting down on my lip.

He leans forward, his face red and stony, nostrils flaring like wings.

"Did you do this, Elimina?" he says, watching me carefully.

"No, sir. I didn't do this," I say, looking him straight in the eye.

He stares at me for a long while before shaking his head and turning away.

"I thought I could trust you, Elimina. I really thought you were a different kind of student. That you were special."

I feel a sharp pain in my belly when he says this, like the tip of a knife is pressed into my skin. I want to yell, *I'm not like them*, the way I did when I first arrived, but I don't know if that's true. I don't know what that means anymore.

"I can't believe you would do this to me," he says.

"I didn't help Josephine, Mr. Gregors. I wasn't involved in any way. I swear. Please believe me."

He looks at me, tired and annoyed, but I can tell that he almost believes me.

"Yesterday was a good day," I say. "You made good money. And I'm going to bring you another good day just like that. The Freemans . . ." I pause, thinking about Josephine arriving and settling in, before clearing my throat. "The Freemans want me. They will pay well. Please believe me: I didn't know anything. And all I want—all we both want—is to get to that day."

Mr. Gregors rubs the bridge of his nose.

"Elimina, there are problems in these kids, ways of thinking that you've avoided by growing up on the Mainland. But I worry that they've already got to you somehow, damaged you. That you don't know right from wrong."

"I'm not damaged, sir," I say, but he keeps on talking as though I haven't spoken at all.

"It's the hardest part of my job here, you know—convincing students that life here is far better than whatever it is they think they remember about living in the Gutter. That's why parents send their kids to us. For a better future and reliable work and food and shelter. Don't I care for you all better than those other headmasters, Elimina?"

"Yes, sir," I say. "But—"

"I would like you to turn over that red coat," Mr. Gregors says, extending his hand, ready to receive it immediately.

"The coat?" I say, one hand against my chest. "Why?"

"You are, at the very least, an unknowing conspirator in Josephine's disappearance," he says. "You didn't follow health protocol and as a result a student has gone missing. Your actions threaten my entire reputation and the reputation of this school, and on that basis alone I *should* get rid of you. But you're right. You are valuable to me, and so I will squeeze every penny I can out of you to make up for what I've lost. When it's time for you to graduate, those Freemans are going to pay. They're going to pay a lot or I'll find someone else who will. I'll make that money back somehow, Elimina. But for now, I want that red coat. I will not have you walking around campus like you've done nothing wrong. Perhaps Louis was right. Perhaps you are too soft for the job."

"But who's going to be the Red Coat?" I say.

"Murray Smith will serve as the campus Red Coat, and I believe he's best suited to doing it alone. And I'm going to tell him to keep a special eye on you," he says.

Mr. Gregors holds his hand out and stares at me with a kind of loathing I haven't seen in him before. I look down at the wood floor, my face red and warm, angry and afraid at the same time.

"The coat, Elimina," he says, moving to the door, like the meeting is done.

I give Mr. Gregors the coat, and when I step out of the office, Murray Smith is standing next to Miss Templeton's desk. When he sees my plain gray uniform, and the red coat in Mr. Gregors's hand, he winks at me with a wicked, crooked smile.

14

THE STUDENTS AT LIVINGSTONE ACADEMY TREAT ME differently without my red coat. Some return to taunts and cruel notes—payback for all the time I spent being the campus Red Coat. Others smile and nod their support, convinced that I somehow helped Josephine, and that I'm a hero of sorts.

Ida doesn't ask me about the red coat when I visit her. She just holds her arms out wide, like she knows that's what I need right now. When she finally lets me go and guides me to the chair, one arm around my shoulder, I wonder if looking at me in that red coat was always difficult for her, if she's grateful that it's gone.

When Ida asks me about the fair, I act like I hardly remember it, even though I've hardly thought of anything else for the past few days. "It was . . . unexpected," I say as I climb into the chair.

"It always is, baby girl."

I tell her about Shanta Cinder and about the bad deal Mr. Gregors made with the men who hired Violet, and Ida shakes her head.

"At least you got a teaser before you go for real," she says as she twists the roots of my hair. "When I went, it was a mess, people touching and pulling at me, like I was fruit at the market.

I wondered if what was coming up ahead was worse than where I'd been. Lucky for me, I was wrong. I left hell that day and I ain't never going back to something like that. No way."

I tell Ida about the Freemans and the way they stepped in and hired David, but Ida just nods. When I tell her that the Freemans want to hire me too, that Mr. Gregors said I could go in a year without having to go back to the fair, she nods again, smiling with only the corners of her mouth.

"Going to the Hill? My goodness, ain't that something, baby girl," she says with a voice that's strangely high.

"Did you know that the Hill is a real place, that there are folks like us with no scars, Ida? You should've seen their clothes. They were so beautiful and colorful. Mabel Freeman looked like a queen, and Mr. . . . ."

Ida's jaw tightens in the mirror, her fingers moving quick, tightening each lock, like she's only pretending to listen when what she really wants me to do is stop.

"Ida?" I say, waiting for an explanation or a response.

She sighs, closing her eyes. "When I was growing up at the junior academy and even at North End Academy, there was talk of them guardian angel Hill types, baby girl. People who'd come save us," she says. "There's a Hill Coalition that helps Gutter folks. But they never come for North End kids. I figured if they didn't come and save us from a place like that, they couldn't be real. Because no guardian angel would ever leave a kid in that kind of place."

Her fingers weave at the roots of my hair, and when she's done, she gives me a handful of pins and shows me how to use them to style my hair by lacing the strands together or pinning them up at the sides. I watch our faces in the mirror, wondering what it might have been like to grow up with Ida for a mother.

"Is it true that you don't ever want to have children?" I say.

She squints her face the way people do when they've eaten something sour. "Who told you that?"

"I heard that you were in love. That there was another Gutter Deco who worked here, who left because you didn't want kids."

She nods slowly, like the question brings back memories that are hard. "He was a dreamer, baby girl. Thought we could have it all—children and happiness and freedom, all in one lifetime. But that's not how it works for us. Truth is, I don't ache for a child the way some do. And I don't ache for a man. I suppose I've got enough to worry about that those things don't seem so interesting to me."

I think about the things that worry me: Murray Smith, whether or not I'll get to the Hill and whether it'll be good.

"Do you think I'll like it? At the Hill?"

"Do you even know who they are?" Ida says.

"They're the ones who paid for their Redemption before the Gutter began."

Ida looks at me and sighs, like she's suddenly remembered who I am and how I got here—how little I know and why. She lowers my chair and pulls another seat close, so we're facing each other, my legs tucked between hers.

"Baby girl, I'm going to tell you the truth every Gutter child is told before they walk out of those Gutter gates—a story we hear so much from the time we're born, we can tell it ourselves from memory with our first words. Because if you go to the Hill, you should know where you're heading and who you're heading to," she says. "Now, I know you're grown, but I'm going to tell you this story the way my mama told me, because that's how I remember it. And who knows, one day you may need to tell it to a child of your own."

I watch as Ida takes my hands, clasping them between hers, pressing my fingers down so my fingers link together.

"Thousands and thousands of years ago, the world was good and healthy, connected just like your fingers—land, ocean and sky, all happy, good friends. But one day, the sky got jealous that the land and the ocean were together, and the sky was very alone, and the sky cried angry tears that made the oceans overflow."

She leaves my hands clasped and raises her hands high, wiggling her fingers down like raindrops.

"It was a rain that seemed to last forever. And when it finally stopped, the sky—still bitter with jealousy—turned cold, and everything froze."

She wraps her hands around my clasped fingers and squeezes tight, pressing my fingers until they cramp.

"Eventually, the sky got tired of the cold and the loneliness, so she sent the sun high like a bird with flames for feathers. But it was too late, and when the ocean melted, the earth cracked into pieces and spread apart."

She pulls my hands apart slowly, my fingers tingling as she rests them against my legs.

"The earth floated in different directions, and the ocean filled up the cracks. Rivers and streams and small lakes came up everywhere, and the people moved with it, floating and moving up and down and around, mapping new land and territory. Those who survived the Freeze and the Thaw built homes and villages wherever they landed. There were people who lived inland and people who lived by the sea, people who lived in houses built on the mountains and others who lived amongst the trees," she says, shaping each place with the motion of her hands. "There were small islands that you could cross by foot before dinner, and larger ones that took days. But our people lived on the Great Land, the largest body, the one shaped like wings. We were *Sossi* people—people with skin the color of earth, some as fair as the sand along the ocean, some as dark as fertile soil. We grew fast in numbers after the Thaw because of the abundance of our love and the sturdy bellies of our women," she says, placing her hands on her stomach and tapping her belly like a drum. "We were Sossi and we were strong."

She frowns, lowering her hands. "But when they came on ships, everything changed," she says.

"Mainlanders?"

She gives a small, tense smile and turns my hands over, pointing at where the skin is pale and light.

"We called them *Olo*. People of the Sky. People the color of the moon and the clouds," she says. "At first, the Olo said they were not staying for long. They were not farmers, like us. They settled along the shade of the mountains, and plunged into the earth with sharp machines, breaking rock and root to bring things out that could make light. They wanted to take it back to the place where they came from. But they did not return. They had run out of land and they wanted ours. We should have seen the dark sky that lived in their hearts, that jealousy that led to the rain and the cold. Mama told me, 'You should never follow people who don't know the way to their own joy, who seek it out in other places.'" Ida taps me on the chest. "She said joy starts right here, in your own heart. But our people did not remember that, and they agreed to let them stay—these people who are only happy when they get more from someone else."

I think of Mr. Gregors at the fair and the morning after Josephine disappeared—the way money filled his face and his eyes with something so ugly.

"Olo wanted this land so that they could be seen and known by others. But that is not our way. Our people don't long for that same thing. We are guardians and farmers and shepherds," she says, bringing my hands together in prayer.

"Is that why they fought in the Great War?" I say, and she nods sadly.

"Sossi people did not always agree, baby girl. There were many tribes and ways of living back then. There were loud fights about what should be done. Our people fought like thunder. You see, Olo are tricky. They knew how to divide so that the fight is smaller," she says. "They met secretly with each of the tribes and bargained, giving different leaders whatever they needed— weapons and supplies—in exchange for more land. Sossi people believed the Olo would show honor the same way we show honor, that they would not take too much, that they would leave when asked. But Olo people are not Sossi people. They don't think like us, baby girl. And we did not realize, until it was too late, that Olo people are *joda*," she says, smacking her hands together with a loud clap.

"*Joda?*"

"It means 'one who devours.' But not like food. Olo are *joda* because they devour like fire. They had begun to consume our Great Land with a fire no one could tame."

I think of Capedown, where buildings were always growing, where there was always a push for bigger and more, and I see how Olo ways are Mainland ways, how we are what we know.

"Olo say that promises made on paper are the only promises that stand. And when Sossi tribes signed papers to give away land, to move away from the coast so that this *nation* could grow, they gave up their rights to everything else."

"But that's not fair."

"The rules are only fair for those who make them, Elimina."

"But couldn't they—"

"We did not have proof that the land was ours, only stories told in a language they couldn't understand. And what are stories but lies that are told too often, Olo said. But stories, baby girl, stories *are* life. They are on our tongues. They are with us now," she says, holding my hands to her mouth.

I think of how those poems from Violet's book fed me in a way no other story has.

"Olo took the land along the coast to build their nation. They gave Sossi some land that was farther away, hard and dry, and they made us pay for this and for that, again and again," she says. "Our families got smaller and hungrier and thinner. Our babies did not survive. And Sossi fought each other in ugly ways over what we had left. While the Olo built and laughed."

I shake my head, full of something hot that burns as Ida talks, a rage that's too hard to hold down.

"There was talk of sending Olo away, of putting out the *joda* fire with fire of our own. Some believed we should fight, risk our lives for what we loved, for what was ours. Others believed that things would change with time, that we should work with them, learn from them. 'Be patient,' they said. But you see, baby girl, Olo know how to devour not just the land, but who we are. In my mama's last letter before she died, she said that that's the slow death you don't see coming, the hardest one to fight. The one that comes for your mind."

Ida smiles with her mouth but her eyes seem to frown.

"Sossi fought the Great War because we wanted our lives and our land. But not everyone fought. Those who had gotten rich working alongside them hid, waiting for things to settle down. But when more Olo dropped from the sky on ships, bringing their weapons, the ones in hiding came out and surrendered, fearing for their lives."

"The ones who fought must have been angry," I say.

Ida nods. "Those Sossi who hid had a different way of surviving. They spoke the Olo language well, so they negotiated with Covey and paid their way to the Hill, while we were taken to the Gutter—a tiny bit of land that dangles off the edge of the Mainland, connected by a bridge you cross only once in your lifetime."

I think about Ida's mother telling her this story before she left—by her crib at night, over dinner. I study my hands, the scar that matches Ida's, the unmarked one that looks like Mabel Freeman's.

"Are you mad . . . at the people on the Hill? Are Gutter people angry?"

Ida takes a breath. "I don't know, baby girl. Hill folks have the life I'll never have, and for that, I feel something," she says, turning her hand into a fist and holding it near her belly. "They come back when they can, or when they want, to help a few. So there are many in the Gutter who believe in them, who trust in the Hill Coalition. But there are many who think little of them because they put themselves first long ago. Because they left so many behind."

Ida grabs a broom and starts sweeping so the bristles scratch against the floor like claws as I think of David and Josephine on the Hill with the Freemans.

"But they're helping, aren't they? The people on the Hill. They're good, right?"

She stops sweeping and turns to me. "Mainlanders said they were helping you when they took you from your birth mother. But it's not right for a child so young to be separated from a mother. And that project proved that."

"My birth mother wasn't forced to give me up," I say. "She volunteered."

"There's no such thing as volunteering when it comes to something like that, baby girl," she says, her voice tight and angry. "Mainlanders build things in such a way that giving a baby up is the best option you've got. Don't you see how your mother *couldn't* keep you? My mother too? They had nothing to offer us, and they believed what we're all told from birth: From the Gutter to greatness. For the greatness of the country."

"For the greatness of the country," I repeat as Ida shakes her head.

"We are told that over and over, and now that I'm here, I see how they lied, how nothing here is great, how there's so much greatness back in the Gutter with my family."

"Do you want to go back?"

"You cross that bridge only once. And then you bring others along after. That's what my mama told me. So that's why I'm here and why I stay. To be great for her and for the rest of my family. No matter what. No matter what I now know or think."

"I want to be great, Ida," I say, tears filling my eyes, like it's a truth I've always known but never been able to admit because I don't know how.

Ida leans the broom against the wall and places her hands on my face, bending over so we are close, so I can feel her breath on my face. "Then be great."

"How can I be great when I've got nothing but debt?"

Ida takes my hands in hers again. "You fight for whatever you can take, bit by bit, baby girl."

Before I leave, Ida reminds me to repeat the story every night, and when she pulls me in close, I hold her tight and promise to never forget.

15

THE WIND WHIRLS LOUD AND HARD, SO I CLOSE THE
Fieldhouse doors slowly, using all of my strength. When
they're shut, I lean up against the wall and my whole body
shakes—like my bones and nerves know it's not safe to be
here, especially without the red coat.

Rumors are spreading about what's become of Josephine, and
Murray is determined to find answers, but all I can think about is
when I can finally leave Livingstone Academy for good, and this
worry keeps me up most nights.

I creep through the halls of the Fieldhouse until I reach the
back corner where a single oil lamp flickers near Rowan's leg. I
stand there watching him for a moment, wondering if I should sit
down or head back to the West Hall.

"I wasn't sure you'd come," he says, sitting in the corner, his
legs spread wide like a V. There's a red gash on his temple, and a
bump on the bridge of his nose.

"What happened to you?"

"Don't worry, I won," he says, smirking at me as I stand over
him. "It's still so weird seeing you without that red coat."

"Why did you invite me here?"

"I needed someone to talk to."

"No. The first time. You weren't surprised when you caught me. You weren't bothered like the others," I say. "You just let me right in like it was nothing. Did you do it because you needed a Red Coat to keep an eye on things? Were you always planning on making me take the blame?"

"There was no master plan, Elimina," he says, leaning his head against the wall. "I didn't ask you to come here or let you join just so you could help Josephine. I didn't know all this would happen."

"So it was luck?" I say, sitting down a few feet away. "It was just dumb luck that you welcomed me in and then used me to take the fall?"

"I knew Mr. Gregors would try to . . . that you didn't know the way things are here. I knew that the first day I saw you," he says, shaking his head. "But I didn't know that you would follow Josephine. How could I? And I fought for you to be here because I wanted you to be here . . . and because I thought you needed it."

"Needed it?" I say with a laugh, and Rowan frowns.

"We shared the book with you. We told you things about our lives that no one else knows."

"And then you lied. You all lied," I say.

I've tried to write the poems I can remember from Violet's book in an empty notebook I took from the office. But every poem is broken and unfinished, fragments of what we read. Lately, I've started writing things of my own—unfinished thoughts about all of the things I don't understand and the things I don't want to forget, including the story Ida told me about the way things began.

"How do I know any of that was real?" I say. "What am I supposed to think?"

"Everything we told you about our lives was true, Elimina. And we didn't lie to you about Josephine. We just didn't tell you. We couldn't risk it," he says. "David wanted to tell you but—"

"And Josephine?"

"She . . . said you weren't a very good liar."

"And you?"

"I agreed with Jose," he says, lowering his head.

I think of my talk with Mr. Gregors and how hard it was to lie, how difficult it's always been for me to hide the truth, and the fact that they knew me so well makes me even angrier.

"We thought it would be better if you could say you really didn't know, if you didn't have to pretend," he says softly.

"Why are we here tonight, Rowan?"

He looks over at me, reaching his hand along the ground, like he's not sure what to say or do next when we're so far apart. "I know what it's like to feel alone here, Elimina. I know how hard it is to have no one."

My lip quivers and I close my eyes, taking deep breaths in and out to keep everything—all the anger and the sadness and the loneliness—somewhere deep inside.

"You used me from the start."

"I'm not *that* smart," he says with a smile.

I try not to smile back, but when the corners of my mouth wiggle upwards, he smiles even bigger, like he's proud to have broken me down.

"None of us planned to be at Livingstone Academy," he says. "My mother sent me because she thought boxing was the best way to get out. Your mother died. We didn't plan this or ask for this. But we ended up here anyway. And all we can do is try to survive."

There's a long quiet where I just sit and think, listening to the wind. Part of me wants to be angry, but part of me wants to forgive. And I lift my knees and put my head in my hands because I don't know which feeling to let in.

"I'm going out there to fight next week," he says, moving closer and wrapping his arm around my shoulder.

I lift my head and nod at the bruise on his eye. "Looks like you already started."

"This was just a practice," he says with a sly grin. "And you should see the other guy."

"Oh, really?" I say.

"I've got a big match in five days, and then I'm off."

"You're leaving?"

I try not to sound as horrified and desperate as I feel, but Rowan squeezes my shoulder like he doesn't want me to worry.

"Not permanently. At least for now. They've entered me in a tournament. A real Mainland one. Outside the academy league. This match is just a warm-up, to see how I'll rank," he says. "I'll go into the circuit after that. And then, if I do well, I'll be making real money."

I run my fingers along the hem of my gray dress, thinking about Rowan's new life.

"Soon enough, I'll be making enough to get Redemption Freedom for myself and my mom, and she'll bring one of my sister's kids, I'm sure. Cuz you can bring someone under five with you, cuz they're not a whole person with debt yet. Maybe I can make enough to bring my sister eventually too, who knows?"

"You have a sister?" I say, reaching for a blanket and stretching it over our legs.

"She was twelve when I left. She got married, has a few kids."

"You're an uncle!"

"Uncle Rowan," he says, smiling and nodding at the title.

He fiddles with a piece of straw, peeling it back in thin strands, and I wonder if he's thinking about all the time that's passed since he left, all of the family that's happened without him.

I reach out and touch his face—the stitched-up gash on his head and the bump on his nose—and even though I do it gently, he flinches from the pain.

"Does it hurt—when you get hit? Does it hurt right away?"

"Yeah, it hurts," Rowan says. "Although it's not until I sit down that I really feel it, you know."

I nod, even though I don't know at all.

He picks up another piece of straw and begins pulling it apart, one strand at a time. "Do you think I'll do okay on the Mainland?" he says.

I think of how it felt to walk around Capedown—the staring, the curiosity, like I wasn't supposed to be there, like I was some-how dangerous. But I don't share any of this with Rowan. Maybe they'll treat him differently on the boxing circuit, a place where he's invited and wanted. Maybe it will be different for him.

"Do you think they'll be better fighters? Because they're Mainlanders?" he says.

"I don't know."

I can tell he's disappointed by my answer, like he was hoping I would share more, and I wonder if that's why he wanted to meet, so he could talk to someone who lived where he is going. I slide my hand over his and squeeze it the way David did when I was sad about May.

"Those boys you'll be fighting will be more afraid of you than you can ever be of them," I say.

"I'm not afraid," he says, pulling his hand back.

"It's normal to fear what you don't know, Rowan. There's nothing wrong with that."

Rowan's lips tighten and he starts fiddling with the straw again, his knee bobbing up and down.

I think about what Ida says about telling things clearly so that people can really understand, and I wonder how I can explain things to Rowan in a way that will help as I stare at the other side of the stall where David and Josephine sat.

"They would never even look at me," I say.

"Who?" he says.

"Mainlanders. People in Capedown. They would never look me in the eye. Especially the boys," I say softly. "I told myself that they didn't look at me because they were afraid they would fall desperately in love with me, that I had special powers. I made up stories like that so it wouldn't hurt so much."

I pick up a piece of straw, pulling it back bit by bit, just like Rowan.

"I used to love reading and spelling. One year, Mother fought to get me into the local spelling bee. I must have been in fifth grade."

"Spelling bee?" Rowan says.

"It's like a boxing match. Well, kind of. Except instead of punching each other, you take turns spelling words."

"Yuck," Rowan says, and I laugh.

"Well, the spelling bee is a pretty big deal in Capedown, and I ended up making it to the final round with Edgar Turpentine. I was wearing my favorite dress—red and pink with swirling flowers. It was a dress Mother got at a secondhand shop for a really good deal. Looked brand-new. We were both standing there, facing a crowd of Mainlanders, waiting for our last word. He was given *miscellaneous*."

"Miss-a-what?"

"Miscellaneous."

Rowan scowls. "I don't think I would like spelling bees," he says, and I smile.

"Well, Edgar spelled it wrong, and then I spelled *metamorphosis* for the win. Metamorphosis. M-E-T-A-M-O-R-P-H-O-S-I-S.

Metamorphosis," I say, as though I'm back in that auditorium in front of those judges, waiting for folks to cheer. "But they didn't cheer when I won. They just watched me. Like what they really wanted to do was boo. I looked at Mother and she looked back at me with so much pride and joy that I realized right there on the stage that everyone else was hoping I would lose."

Rowan shakes his head, wrapping his arm around me and pulling me closer.

"It was all over the local news. 'Local Boy Chokes in Face-Off with Gutter Child.' No one came to my house for an interview like they did with the other winners—the ones from the years before. All everyone talked about was how Edgar Turpentine choked. And Edgar's family was furious."

I rub my finger against the blanket, remembering those stories, the conversations that whispered around me every time I left the house.

"They said it was unfair, that it was rigged, that the organizers *wanted* me to win for ratings, which was silly and untrue. They had tried to keep me from participating. But no one cared about the truth."

"And Edgar?" Rowan says.

I pull at the straw, strip by strip. "Kids in the neighborhood tormented him. To have lost to a Gutter child was beyond humiliation. I thought it would eventually die down and that Edgar and everyone else would forget about it. But Edgar never forgot."

I shake my head, remembering not just the spelling bee but what came after, the thing I never told anyone.

"A year later, maybe a month before the next bee, I saw Edgar on the street while I was waiting outside a coffee shop for Mother. He pulled me into the alley and pushed me against a brick wall, squeezing my neck until I couldn't breathe, until I was gasping for air. He used his other hand to grab me, to touch me underneath my dress. He said, 'You're so dark I can hardly tell if this is working. I can't tell if you're dying or if you're enjoying it.'"

Rowan bites down hard on the back of his teeth, so the bone of his jaw juts out.

"I never went to another spelling bee," I say, as the tears fall down hard and I wipe my face with my hand. "I told Mother I was done with them. And that's what makes me mad. That I gave up. That he won."

I turn to look at Rowan, my face puffy and wet, his tight and full of anger. I think about that first day, when he was ready to fight Louis, when he punched a hole in the wall.

"That's what you need to take with you, Rowan. That anger you feel right now. They may be clever and big, and the crowds may never cheer for you, but maybe that can be your advantage."

He looks at me, his brow scrunched and wrinkled, like he doesn't understand.

"They want to win. But what do they lose if they don't—their pride, their confidence? That's nothing. You're strong because you have to be. You've got no choice. Everything rides on you winning each match. Use that."

I lean my head into his shoulder, listening to his breath.

"You do have special powers," he says.

Rowan removes his arm from my shoulder, and when I lift my head to look at him, he places his hands on my neck, kissing me on the forehead, then gently on the lips. He sits back for a moment, then leans in again, pressing his lips against mine, harder this time, opening my mouth with his tongue. I close my eyes and let my skin turn warm with his touch. But when I feel his hand slide under my nightgown, between my legs, I jump.

"It's okay, Elimina. Trust me," he says.

There's a confidence in his voice and in his touch that's hard not to trust—as though it's wise to let go and give in to everything he says and does. I feel nervous and needed and afraid all at once, and I don't know which feeling to let all the way in or all the way out, so I close my eyes and hold my breath.

"You're beautiful," he whispers.

I smile with my lips pressed tightly together, pain pressing between my legs. I open my mouth, ready to scream or cry, or shout for him to stop, but I clasp my hand over my lips and hold it all in instead.

"Relax, Elimina," he whispers, his face resting in the groove of my neck. "You're beautiful. You're amazing," he says again and again.

I breathe in and out slowly until my whole body starts to believe him, until my mind and my body give in completely.

16

WHEN I MAKE DELIVERIES TO THE DECO OFFICES IN the Main House, I take the long route through the Hall of Heroes, where the eight portraits of the Livingstone Academy graduates who have achieved Redemption Freedom are hung. I gaze up at the portraits, and I whisper each name, adding my own to the list, hoping Redemption Freedom will happen for me too: "Colson Harper, John MacDonald, Samuel Prince, Freddie McDouglas, Thomas Baker, Timothy Jones, Morris Taylor, Harry Dennis, *Elimina Madeleine Dubois.*"

Two months ago, when Albert Cootes was delivering mail to the campus, he told me his debt was almost entirely paid off. "There are still processing fees and formal applications to be made, but sometime in the next year, I should officially be a free man," he said, which would make him the ninth Livingstone Academy graduate to join the Hall of Heroes.

When I see Albert smiling and moving briskly up the road, I wonder how he does it—how he gets more happy and hopeful with each passing day instead of the other way around.

Albert is holding a bundle of flat envelopes with a thin red box pinched under his arm, and when I meet him partway up the driveway, I ask him if we'll see him at all once he's done with his debt.

"I got no plans to stop working just yet. Got a fine-looking lady and a bunch of grown kids out there who got a ways to go," he says with a shrug. "Might as well help them out."

"How many kids do you have?"

He looks up at the sky, counting in his head. "Six in total. Well, five now. Youngest died a little while back."

I tell him how sorry I am, but he just waves his hand in the air, like he doesn't want me to fuss.

"I got two that are still on the Mainland, working their way, just like their old man. Three landed themselves in trouble and got sent back, best I know. Hard to keep track of them now. But this job helps. I find out what I can from folks here and there along my route. I told you about my old lady, right?"

I nod.

"So long as I can see her, I feel good and fine. I've always loved having a lady in my arms. Probably why I got so many kids," he says, laughing and grinning pink gums and teeth separated by large gaps.

When we reach the steps to the Main House, Murray Smith is standing under a tree, watching us in his new red coat, a jacket with shiny gold buttons. Albert lays down a few packages, turning his body so Murray can't see. He hands me a few envelopes, and when he opens the box I see an assortment of tiny chocolates.

"Try them out, Elimina," Albert says, winking as he wiggles the lid. "I brought them just for you."

I look closer at the box and spot an envelope pinned under the lid, my name printed neatly in the middle. It's the first letter I've ever received, and I can tell from the handwriting who wrote it.

"Had to make sure this one got to you proper," he says. "Couldn't let this fall in the wrong hands. You know how it is."

The mail that comes in and out of Livingstone Academy

arrives by way of the Mainland Postal Service, where Albert once worked on the mail room floor and is now a deliveryman based in Mainland City. According to Albert, the MPS can legally check any mail addressed to Gutter folks as part of the Treason Prevention Act, so Gutter folks use the Gutter Underground Network instead.

Josephine got a letter from her parents through the Network during her second year at Livingstone, but once they had both read it, David forced her to burn it, so they wouldn't get caught.

"I wish I could still look at their handwriting every day," she said, while I just wished that I had someone who would send me anything.

I take the bundle of envelopes from Albert and slide the letter discreetly into my pocket, selecting a chocolate and shoving it into my mouth before Albert heads back toward the gate.

I OPEN THE letter in the back stairwell of the West Hall, bursting into tears at the sight of her handwriting because I've missed her and resented her since she left: "My dear friend, I'm sorry. Life is fine."

I show Rowan the letter when we meet in the Fieldhouse, and I can tell that he's relieved to know she's okay, that her words have brought him peace too. I hold the note in my hands, and I feel my heart squeeze as I try to forgive all the way.

"This guy was huge, Elimina. Huge," Rowan says, standing and moving around the stall like he's still in the ring, while I sit quietly, closing the letter inside my book. "I had him the whole time. I was here and moving fast and he was just standing there, swinging heavy, like I wouldn't see his fists coming."

We don't talk about what happened the last time we were

together, but when he finally sits down again, he wraps his legs around me, holding me inside his arms in a way that makes me remember. I smile and close my eyes, relaxing into him, because it feels good to be held and wanted.

Next week, Rowan will leave Livingstone Academy to compete in the Mainland Boxing Circuit. He'll travel all over the Mainland under the direction of a boxing promoter and a specialized debt manager who, according to Rowan and Mr. Gregors, have both worked with the best of the best in the MBC. They've promised to get Rowan Redemption Freedom faster than a Gutter boxer who did it in just five years a few years ago.

"And he wasn't as good as me," Rowan says.

"Is he still boxing?"

"Nah. He died. Went to sleep and didn't wake up. He was only twenty-three," Rowan says, and I shake my head at the cruelty of working so hard to get free only to die before you can really enjoy it.

I decide to be happy that Rowan is moving forward, even though I have five more months to go before I turn sixteen. I try not to worry that I will never see him again. But the thought of Rowan leaving causes a squeeze in my chest that makes it hard to breathe. *Please don't leave me here alone.*

"You're going to be okay, Elimina," he says. "It won't be that much longer for you too."

He tells me that when he's done on the circuit, he and his mother will come to the Hill so we can all be together. "You'll be fine," he says with his lips close to my ear.

We sit in the stall and imagine what the Hill might look like and what it might feel like to be there. We imagine busy streets full of fancy shops and restaurants where we can sit at a table with a view of the mountains or under a large umbrella.

I think of the colorful dresses I might wear, and Rowan imagines all the money he'll be able to spend. "Maybe a coat or a car or a house," he says, and he smiles so big I can feel his cheek press against my face.

We imagine David owning a wood shop, and Josephine taking care of it and managing all the customers. We talk about the parties the four of us will go to, like the kind they have on the Mainland, and we stand in the stall to dance even though there's no music and neither of us has danced with anyone before.

I place my head against Rowan's shoulder, and we move around the stall, standing so close I can feel his heart race against me. He spins me around and when he tries to dip me low to the ground, we both fall and laugh so hard we have to press our hands over our mouths to stay quiet.

Rowan crawls toward me and asks if I'd like another dance, his dimples deep, his smile wide and bright. But I frown and turn away, shaking my head.

"What's wrong, Elimina?" he says.

"You're leaving," I say. "And I'm staying . . . And I don't know . . . All this *dreaming* . . . it's just . . . making it harder."

He sits next to me and pulls me under his arm. "Elimina, it's okay," he says, but I shake my head harder.

"I can't stop thinking about the Hill, and Josephine and David, about you and the boxing circuit, about being here alone. For months. Sometimes the Hill . . . sometimes I feel like I imagined it," I say, looking up at him. "Like I made the Freemans up."

"But you got that letter from Jose. You know it's real."

"But what if Mr. Gregors finds someone else? What if I end up like Violet?"

Rowan holds me tight, rubbing my back and rocking me in

his arms. "It happened, Elimina. It's real. And the Freemans are coming. You're going to the Hill," he says.

When my breathing finally slows, Rowan lets go and leans back against the wall, staring into nowhere, like he's thinking about the possibilities as well. And I hate how I've done this, how I've ruined all of our fun.

"I'm sorry. I didn't mean to spoil things or make you sad too," I say, reaching out and placing one hand over his.

But Rowan doesn't respond. He just keeps staring into the darkness.

"Rowan, what's wrong?"

Eventually, he looks down, wiggling his mouth side to side before speaking. "Sometimes I don't feel like myself, Elimina."

"What do you mean?"

He shakes his head, like he's trying to get his thoughts or his words in the right order. "When I'm moving around that ring, I . . . I can feel the good side of me that's focused on winning and technique, that's all controlled. It says, *Go and stop, and punch, punch, punch, okay, stop*," he says, palms raised in front of him. "But the bad side, this . . . other side of me, it says, *Keep going, keep hitting*. And not just in the ring. The bad side of me is walking down the street saying, *Don't let them look at you like that. Make them stop*. And, Elly, the bad side feels like it's getting stronger. Especially out there. On the Mainland. I don't feel like I do in here."

I turn to him and hold his face in my hands, just like Ida does with me when she tells me something important. "You're a good person, Rowan. You're a good man. Your mother would be so proud of you," I say, and when he bursts into tears that come down hard and fast, I'm not sure how to respond.

I hold my arms out and he leans in, gripping me tight, like he's been waiting years to let it all out. As he cries, I sing a song Mother sang whenever I felt scared, a song that only comes to me now: *"Come cool waters of paradise. Come find me in the waters of paradise."*

Rowan looks up at me with wide, wet eyes as I sing, and when he sits up, I hold his face again and wipe his tears with my thumbs.

"Come cool waters of paradise. Come find me in the waters of paradise."

When I'm done, he pulls me closer, staring at me so deeply I can almost feel his hunger.

"Again," he says.

I sing the song again, and this time, he places me on my back and climbs on top, a wide, heavy shadow hovering above me.

"Again," he says.

And I close my eyes and sing the song over and over, whispering it like a prayer.

17

FOR WEEKS I'VE BEEN FEELING UNWELL, AND WHEN MISS Templeton finds me in the workroom lying on the floor, unable to respond, she screams and splashes me with water. My eyes flutter and I wipe the water from my face as Miss Templeton asks so many questions so quickly that I struggle to keep up with her words.

"What happened, Elimina? Elimina, what happened? Are you hurt? Can you hear me?"

"I . . . don't know," I say, squeezing my eyes shut and opening them again until everything stops moving and the room becomes clear.

"What were you doing when you collapsed? Do you remember? Elimina, look at me. Do you remember what you were doing when you collapsed?" she says, leaning in closer.

"Collapsed . . . I . . . ?"

"What's the last thing you remember?"

I look around and spot an envelope on the floor, next to the table where I was just working. "I was opening the mail . . . I . . . I had just come back from walking . . . with Albert."

"Was it the heat? Were you out there very long? It's very hot out."

I shake my head, slowly, so it doesn't hurt too much. "I don't know."

"Elimina, look at me. What do you remember?"

I squint up at Miss Templeton's red face, so close I feel her breath.

"I . . . I just wanted to lie down."

"Did you hit your head on anything?" she says, and I shake my head, even though I'm not sure.

Miss Templeton reaches out and touches the back of my head, looking down at her fingers and pressing in different places, checking for blood.

"I just need to sit," I say.

She holds out her hand and helps me up, and when I'm seated, she sits down next to me and continues. "Is this the first time something like this has happened to you?" she says.

I nod because even though I've been feeling dizzy for weeks, I've never fainted before. I try to convince Miss Templeton that I'm alright, that I just need to eat, but she insists on escorting me to the nurse's office.

"Can't we just stay here?" I say. "I'm starting to feel much better."

"You need to go to the nurse," she says, and I can see in her scowl that there's no room for negotiating.

"I haven't been sleeping well. That's all," I say when I'm seated across from Nurse Gretchen, watching the string dangle down from the sides of her glasses.

"How long has this been going on?" she says, holding a pen and a clipboard while Miss Templeton watches.

"A week, maybe," I say, even though it's been more like four.

I keep telling myself I've got what May Bennet had, that Rowan's departure and the loneliness of Livingstone are making me feel tired and heavy. But when Nurse Gretchen asks me to pee in a cup, and she shows the results to Miss Templeton, they both look at each other and shake their heads.

MR. GREGORS STARES down at a file with my name on it, like he did on my first day. But this time he looks up at me with an expression that's difficult to read, his mouth wrinkled tight, and I'm not sure if he's pleased or bothered.

"I'm feeling much better, sir. It won't happen again," I say, hoping that he'll tell me everything is okay and that it's time to go to the Hill.

"Unfortunately, I don't think that's true."

"Sir?"

"You're pregnant, Elimina," he says, studying my reaction.

"Pregnant?" I say.

I think about the nights in the Fieldhouse with Rowan, about the closeness he seemed so hungry for, that maybe I wanted as well.

"Elimina?" Mr. Gregors says. "Do you understand what I just told you?"

I nod but part of me wonders if Nurse Gretchen got it wrong. "I think there's been a mistake," I whisper, as though there's not enough air in my lungs.

"There is no mistake, Elimina. You're going to have to go away for a while," he says.

"Away . . . for a while? What do you mean?"

"Until the baby is born," he says, looking back down at the file. "Which, based on Nurse Gretchen's calculations, will be in about eight months."

"Eight *months*? Sir, I'm supposed to go to the Hill in four!"

"Yes, well, your new situation changes things, Elimina," he says, waving his hand toward my belly.

"But, sir!"

"It's only four more months, Elimina. Surely you can manage that," he says.

"I can't," I say, shaking my head.

"You can and you will."

I feel something thick and sour in my throat, and I bite down on my lip, pressing against my stomach and rubbing in circles, so that whatever is stirring stays still.

"Sir, you told the Freemans a year. They're expecting me soon."

"Until that child is born, your hiring will need to be delayed," he says. "This is not a discussion or a debate. You are pregnant. You cannot get hired in your condition, and you cannot stay here."

"But what if they take someone else? What if, in eight months, they don't want me anymore?"

Mr. Gregors waves a hand at me as though this is hardly a concern. "They will pay for you or they will lose you to someone else who will," he says, and I see a coldness in his expression that makes me feel angry and ashamed.

"Sir, please," I say, but he raises his hand to stop me from arguing further.

"I will tell the Freemans that there's legal paperwork that requires a little more time. I will delay as much as I can. But I will not make any promises, Elimina. This is your doing and these are your consequences to bear."

I see in his face the same expression I saw when he took the red coat back, that tight-jawed disappointment, and I remember what Rowan said about Mr. Gregors holding our future in his hands.

"I don't want to go, Mr. Gregors. Please don't make me go," I say.

"Elimina, there are rules and laws for these situations, and I have a duty to enforce them. That's my job."

I think of my conversation with Ida about children and the Deco she sent away because he wanted to have a family, how she didn't want to bring a child into this world.

"Where am I going?"

"Somewhere where they can take care of you. Your things are packed. There's a car waiting for you."

I lean forward, rubbing my forehead. "What will happen to the baby?"

"The baby will go to a junior academy. Perhaps the same one where Louis grew up," he says.

He smiles, but I don't smile back at him. I just hold on to my belly as my stomach bends and swerves.

"Focus on taking care of yourself, Elimina—delivering the baby and staying well, and getting back here as soon as you can. I can reduce your debt if the child is healthy, and the child can have a strong future too—minimal debt, good work ethic. These are the kinds of students all academies want."

I look up at him, letting his words settle slowly.

"I will encourage the Freemans to wait. I'll take care of things as best I can. No one else needs to know," he says. "You'll be back in no time, Elimina."

I nod with both hands on my belly, thinking about the child that's growing inside me, and all the changes that lie ahead.

RIVERSIDE

18

Miss Charlotte's Home for Troubled Girls is a lonely gray house at the southern tip of Riverside—a town that takes so long to get to, it's a whole other day by the time I arrive. I pause for a moment as I read the sign on the lawn because "troubled" is exactly how I feel right now, and I wonder who else lives inside.

"Is this it?" I say, staring up at a house with a long covered porch surrounded by bright-colored flowers.

The driver nods as he takes my bag and places it on the front steps. He's an old Gutter man with a curve in his shoulders and a crackling rasp in his voice. "If you need to reach your people, your family or whatever, find Duncan. He's the Network man down here," he says before hopping back into the car.

I don't tell him that there's no family for me to write to. I just stand on the grass and watch him pull away as a pear-shaped Mainland woman walks out of the house, followed by two Gutter girls in matching gray dresses.

"Isobel, did you move your belongings into the other room like I asked?" the woman says, wiping her hands with a tea towel.

The younger girl nods as she pulls her black hair over her shoulder and weaves it into a braid that almost touches the curve of her belly.

"I don't see why the new girl gets her own room," the other girl says. "Is it because she's a project case? Cuz I don't think it matters who raised her, Miss Charlotte. Besides—"

"Matilda, that's enough," Miss Charlotte says, raising her hand. "Why don't you go over and show some good manners by properly introducing yourselves?"

Matilda makes her way over to me with movements that are labored and slow. While the younger girl is tiny everywhere but her belly, Matilda is thick all over, with a wide stomach that moves and sways as she walks. I smile at both girls even though standing in front of them makes me feel awkward and small. Other than the sick, dizzy mornings and the red lines that have begun to form around the lines of my underwear, my body hardly feels different at all.

"I'm Tilly, as in Matilda. But I prefer Tilly. *Always* Tilly," the older girl says, looking back at Miss Charlotte as though this clarification is just for her. "And this here is Isobel. Never Izzy."

"Tilly and Isobel," I say, and Isobel smiles.

"Why don't you join us for a walk, Elimina?" Miss Charlotte says. "I daresay you've been cooped up in that car for far too long. You could use a little exercise, and I'd like to get you registered in town."

"Yes, ma'am," I say, wanting to be obedient, even though I'd much rather lie down.

"Delightful. Isobel, take Elimina's luggage upstairs, and Tilly, show her the bathroom on the main floor so she can freshen up before we go," Miss Charlotte says, tossing her towel over her shoulder and returning to the house.

Tilly leads me down a narrow hallway covered in black-and-white pictures of Mainlanders with round chins and thin lips.

"Those are Miss Charlotte's people, if you couldn't tell," Tilly whispers over her shoulder, and I cup my hand over my mouth to stifle a laugh because they all look the same, each one more miserable than the next.

In Miss Charlotte's living room, there's a piano and a coffee table, and two heavy quilts that are draped over the back of a couch and a chair. The rugs on the wood floors and the metal ornaments on the walls make everything look neat and tidy like a display—a room you're only meant to admire.

"How long have you been here?" I say, and Tilly stops, one hand on the back of the chair, the other resting on the side of her belly, her Xs pink and rough.

"I'm almost six months along," Tilly says. "Hid it longer than most cuz the nurses at my academy weren't quite on top of things and, well, I've always been a big girl. Got here after Isobel, but I'll be heading out first. Been here about two months."

"So it's just the two of you," I say, nodding at the thought of living with two girls who seem nice enough so far as I can tell.

"It's just the two of us now," Tilly says. "Three with you. My roommate, Sarah, left last week. Other girl left a month or two before that. Supposed to have a full house again by next month, so I guess we got one more coming. Is it true you came all the way from Mainland City?"

"Yup. Capedown before that, on the Sunset Coast," I say, looking down at my scar and thinking about my arrival at the academy two years ago and how much has changed since then.

"From the Sunset Coast to Mainland City to the gates of the Gutter. You sure been around," Tilly says, smiling and shaking her head, like she's almost envious.

"The Gates of the Gutter? Is that what they call this place?" I say, because it sounds like a terrible name.

"Well, that's what it is," Tilly says. "I can practically see the red gates from my window when the sky is clear. Riverside's the last stop on the Mainland, and Miss Charlotte's house is about as close as you can get."

Tilly opens a narrow wood door and steps back, pointing into a small room with a large, deep sink and a small toilet. But I just stare at her, shuddering at the thought of being so close to the Gutter.

WHEN I RETURN to the front of the house, Tilly shows me the river that wraps around the back of Miss Charlotte's. I watch the water move fast and noisy like it's headed somewhere in a rush.

"Gutter looks different from this side," Tilly says. "Although you probably don't remember it at all. Did they really take you straight away? Were you always raised with Mainlanders?"

"The only person I had in my life before I got to the academy was Mother, and she was a Mainlander," I say, and Tilly shakes her head like this is impossible to imagine.

She points at a bridge that crosses over the river and at the wall on the other side where tall pipes spit yellow smoke somewhere far away.

"Well, that's Dead Man's Bridge. And that wall, well, that wraps around the entire Gutter. So I guess this is kind of your welcome home," Tilly says, smiling and wiping the sweat off her brow as the sun beats down hard.

I stare at the bridge and the wall, imagining those red gates as Tilly's words echo in my head. *Home.*

In Capedown, Mother read the *Mainland News* every day. By the time I was eight, she encouraged me to follow along to help develop my reading skills. The paper was filled with all kinds of articles about the Gutter: "Guards Attacked in the Gutter,"

"Ten Gutter Employees Fired for Fraud," "Gutter Births on the Rise—Will They Take Over?" The articles included pictures of angry Gutter folks, their teeth bared and sharp, or pictures of sad children in oversized clothing. Whenever I looked at the paper, I always felt grateful to Mother. Grateful I wasn't there. Grateful I wasn't them.

Now, here I am, closer than ever, separated by only a bridge. And despite what I'd heard from Josephine, Ida and Albert, something about being this close makes me afraid. As though the Gutter is a magnet, a powerful force, that can pull people away from their dreams.

Main Street runs through the center of Riverside, splitting the town neatly in two. The street is crowded with marked vans and curious Mainlanders who watch us arrive in a line that's led by Miss Charlotte, with Isobel and Tilly following behind me.

"As you can see, Elimina, Riverside is quite the busy little town. Everyone knows most everyone here, so it's very friendly," Miss Charlotte says, raising her voice and turning her head so I can hear her over the crowds. "Despite our location and our proximity to the Gutter, you'll find that Riverside is one of the safest cities on the Mainland. I say that as a woman who finds herself alone in a big house on occasion. I've always taken great comfort in the fact that the Mainland Guards outnumber the civilians."

Miss Charlotte waves at acquaintances and pauses to chat with a friend while the three of us wait in the shade. Isobel keeps her head down, gripping Tilly's hand tightly, and whenever folks snicker or stare in Tilly's direction, she raises her chin like she's proud to have won their attention.

"Wait right here, I just need to pick up some chicken for dinner,"

Miss Charlotte says when we reach the Riverside Country Store, where the sign is shaped like an apple.

She enters the store, just as five Mainland Guards exit, pouring onto the street in their muddy-green uniforms, heads shaved low. They laugh and wrestle as they move across the street, punching and grabbing one another as drivers in the marked vans honk on their way by.

"Seeing them makes me so mad," Isobel says somberly.

"You been around a lot of guards, Elimina?" Tilly says, rubbing Isobel's shoulder and holding her close.

I think about the guards on my first day at Capedown Elementary and the day Josephine disappeared. "Just a few times," I say.

"You'll figure out pretty quick how this guard town works. Most everyone here works for them in one way or another," she says.

We watch the guards lean up against a building across the street, laughing and yelling loudly as Isobel scowls and shakes like she's cold.

MISS CHARLOTTE TAKES me to Riverside's Mainland Guard Detainment Facility while Tilly and Isobel head back to the house with dinner. Gutter men are crowded in a small cell in the corner while a drunk Mainlander sits in a stall of his own, yelling and cursing at the guards.

A guard standing behind a tall counter asks for my information—the name of my academy, my total debt, my expected field of employment. When I answer his questions, he takes a picture of me with a camera that flashes loudly while Miss Charlotte removes a photo of a young girl with thick braids from a wall of photographs and tosses it in the garbage. The wall includes photos of Tilly and Isobel, posted under a sign that says "Registered," but I stare at the photos marked "Wanted." I look at each Gutter face, studying their features, looking for some kind of resemblance.

"You grew up on the Sunset Coast, did you, Elimina?" Miss Charlotte says as we step out of the detainment facility. "I've never been there before. But I've heard it's beautiful."

"Have you always lived here?" I say.

The sun is hot and strong, and I raise my hand over my eyes as Mainland Guards pass us on the street, greeting Miss Charlotte without acknowledging me at all.

"I slept in the very same room where you'll be sleeping for my entire childhood," she says. "My parents bought the house when there was practically nothing here other than the Mainland Guard Detainment Facility and a few dorms for the guards. My father built an addition a while back, and I can't imagine living anywhere else or calling any other place home."

I feel a sense of envy at the way Miss Charlotte talks about Riverside and the way Tilly spoke about the Gutter. And I wonder if I'll ever feel that way about a place—like it's somewhere I belong and somewhere I want to stay. I wonder if I'll find that at the Hill.

We head back to Miss Charlotte's on the other side of the road, passing stores with neatly drawn signs—a deli, a bank, a tailor and a shop for paper and cards. Miss Charlotte points out landmarks, and I gently rub my belly, which is moving and stirring like something might come up if I don't.

"When I was growing up, my very closest friends were Gutter girls," Miss Charlotte says. "Dad practically ran the whole town, so Mother opened up our home to young Gutter women who needed a place to go. It was quite the controversy at the time. But they were always such sweet girls, and the people in town came around. They always do. I grew up with those girls, and I adored them. I often wonder how they're doing. I never really knew what became of them after they left. You remind me of one of them, in fact. Leeza. She had hair just like yours."

Miss Charlotte tugs gently at a lock of my hair, and I tilt my head slightly out of reach.

"I tried to do the same thing to my hair once and Mother lost it. I made quite a mess of it. She nearly had to cut it all off," Miss Charlotte says with a smile.

I try to smile back, but I can feel my whole body slowing down, like the walk is getting longer, like we're getting farther and farther away from the house.

"It was different back then. Things have changed. The girls are just not as friendly, I find. Which is a real shame."

I pause on the sidewalk, waiting for things to stop spinning, hoping I don't fall like I did in the academy workroom.

"Elimina, are you alright?"

I shake my head, unable to talk.

"It's the heat. You're not used to it yet," she says.

Miss Charlotte places her hand on my back and guides me toward a tall tree in front of a large pink house. I lean over the fence, covered in shade, and I wait as my skin starts to feel cooler, my head more settled while Miss Charlotte rubs my back.

On the front porch of the pink house, a Gutter man with a thick black beard tinged with gray and an old Gutter woman watch us.

"Good afternoon, Miss Charlotte," the man says.

"Oh, hello, Duncan. And hello and good afternoon to you too, Miss Lulabelle."

The old woman has thick white hair, and she squints in our direction as the man leans closer to her. "Momma, Miss Charlotte said hello."

"Who?"

"Miss Charlotte, the woman who takes care of all of them girls."

The old woman continues squinting at us.

"See you got yourself a new girl, Miss Charlotte," Duncan says, nodding in my direction while I read the message under the sign for Cranberry Manor Assisted Care: "Hope for a Better Tomorrow."

"Yes. This is Elimina," Miss Charlotte says, watching me closely to see if I'm okay.

"She alright?" Duncan says.

I lift up my head and try to smile, raising one hand to show that I'm alright.

"Could I bother you to grab a glass of water and maybe a cracker or two from the nurses?" Miss Charlotte says, and Duncan nods.

"Momma, don't you go anywhere," he says, disappearing into Cranberry Manor while the old woman watches me closely.

Miss Charlotte rubs my back in slow circles, searching her purse for something to eat but finding nothing. "You're eating for two now. You've got to pay attention to when you eat and how much. You can't overdo it," she says.

Lulabelle stands and heads toward us, moving slowly, her expression eerie and still like a ghost.

"Lulabelle," Miss Charlotte says, as the old woman gets closer. "I think Duncan wants you to stay up on the porch."

Lulabelle ignores her, and when the old woman is standing in front of me, she takes both of my hands in hers and stares at them before letting out a long, loud wail.

"Momma," Duncan says as he rushes out of the Manor.

When he reaches her, Lulabelle looks up at him and starts crying, like her whole body hurts.

"Momma, Momma, it's alright," he says, holding her close. "It's alright. It's going to be alright."

"Lulabelle? Lulabelle? It's me. It's Miss Charlotte. Lulabelle, let her go. Elimina, don't worry. It's okay," she says. But when people stop and stare, Miss Charlotte whispers through clenched teeth, "Duncan, do something."

"Shhh. Shhh. Shhh, Momma. It's okay, Momma," he says as she cries into him. "She's okay. It's okay, Momma."

Lulabelle doesn't let go, but I feel her grip relax as she places my unmarked hand against her face. She turns to her son, and when he nods, I'm reminded of Josephine and David—the way they shared secrets and memories without words.

"Lulabelle, please let the girl go," Miss Charlotte says, pulling at Lulabelle's fingers while I stand there, watching everything.

"*Come cool waters of paradise. Come find me in the waters of paradise,*" Lulabelle moans through tears.

I think of the times Mother sang this song, how it comforted me when I was filled with thoughts of monsters hiding somewhere in the dark. I think of the night I sang the song to Rowan, how it helped him too, and as the tears start to trickle down my cheeks, I sing along with her: "*Come find me in the cool waters of paradise.*"

"Lulabelle? Let go, please," Miss Charlotte says, her eyes begging me not to encourage her.

Lulabelle doesn't let go and I don't stop singing, and when I look down at her hands gripped around mine, and at Duncan's resting on her shoulders, I notice that their scars are not Xs but splotches that look like dark puddles.

"Miss Lulabelle," I say when she finally stops singing. "My name is Elimina."

The old woman shakes her head hard, like I've got it all wrong. "You are Lima. You are Lima Jenkins Sinclair. And you are home. You finally came home," she says as she holds my face in the palms of her hands.

19

I HEAR A LOUD POP FROM SOMEWHERE OUTSIDE THE HOUSE, and I sit up in a dark bedroom, alone. It's my first time sleeping in a room by myself in more than two years, and I feel restless and jumpy at the shadows that bend and curve on the walls. I move to the window and press my forehead against the glass, but all I can see are glowing streetlamps and the quiet storefronts along Main Street.

I listen for movement from Miss Charlotte, or from Tilly and Isobel, and when I hear the sound again—a loud pop, followed by another—I climb out of bed and step quietly across the hall. I knock softly, placing my ear against the door, and when I hear "Shhh-shhh-shhh" on the other side, then silence, I knock again.

"It's me, Elimina," I whisper, and the door creaks open.

Isobel and Tilly's room is similar to mine, two beds separated by a narrow stretch of floor that leads to a small window. Only their window looks out on the river.

The two girls are sitting on their beds, facing each other with their backs against the wall. Tilly's legs are stretched out in front of her, while Isobel's are tucked underneath her like a bow. As soon as I see them, all I can think about is Josephine and those nights we spent talking in the Fieldhouse.

"Were those gunshots?" I say, walking toward the window and peering out into the backyard, where flecks of moonlight sparkle on top of the water.

"I'd step away from the window if I were you," Tilly says, and I step back quickly, sitting down on the edge of Isobel's bed.

"Why? What's going on down there?"

"Headhunters lie out in that grass every night, waiting for Gutter folks trying to make it out. I don't trust Mainlanders with loaded guns. Especially when it's dark."

"Make it out where?" I say.

"Out here. To the Mainland," Tilly says.

"Nobody's going to hire them without a hiring package. Where are they going to go?"

"Well, you know that and I know that, but they don't know that," Tilly says. "They think they can get somewhere better if they can just get past the wall. Truth is, they're dead as soon as they try."

"Is that why they call it Dead Man's Bridge?" I say, and Tilly nods.

"They should call it Dead Man's River. That's where they die. In the water," Isobel says softly.

"Mainland folks know it as South River, but in the Gutter, they call it Fadahe River, Freedom River," Tilly says, shaking her head and removing the lid from a tin beside her pillow. "But that river don't bring freedom to nobody. At least not in the way folks think."

"When you're desperate, you try anything," Isobel says with a tired sigh.

"Well, the only place that river's going to take you is straight to the devil himself," Tilly says. She takes a cookie out of the tin and savors the taste slowly as she swallows each bite.

"Do you know Miss Lulabelle?" I say.

"Everybody knows Miss Lulabelle," Tilly says.

"She is crazy," Isobel says, leaning into her pillow.

"I swear it gets worse every day. That old lady shouts things from her porch, and poor Duncan just sits there with her, listening to all of it," Tilly says. "I mean, it's his momma, I get it. But still. Keep your distance, Elimina. Crazy is contagious."

I nod like I agree with them, but I think they're wrong about Lulabelle.

In the office at Livingstone Academy, there were files for every student on campus, and when Miss Templeton was away from her desk and Mr. Gregors was out of the office, I looked at mine, recording the things that I saw in my notebook. There were pictures of Mother when she was young along with pictures of the two of us together, and at the back, there were two documents of record. The adoption papers loosely addressed the arrangement of the project with a signature from Mother. But the official record of birth provided details I never knew about my birth. According to the record, my birth mother, Rosalind Sinclair, died on the same day I was born. Milton Jenkins, who was listed as my father, died eight months earlier. At the top of the document, a name was handwritten in careful letters: *Lima Jenkins Sinclair.*

And all I can think about since I ran into Lulabelle is how she could possibly know that name when she saw me in front of Cranberry Manor.

"I still can't believe you grew up with a Mainlander, living like them, with them," Tilly says, shaking her head.

"It was just Mother . . . She never married . . . And she died a few years ago. Which is how I ended up at Livingstone . . . Which is how I ended up here," I say.

I look down at my belly, touching it gently, wondering if I'll look more like Tilly or Isobel when it grows.

"Lover or leader?" Tilly says.

"Pardon?"

"Was he someone you loved or was he one of the leaders? A Deco. A boss, a headmaster, you know?" she says.

Isobel looks down, biting her fingernails.

"Uhh. He was a friend. I guess. I think," I say, unsure how to feel about Rowan and how to explain him to Tilly.

"Do you miss it? Your home?" Isobel says quickly, like she wants to change the subject.

"I don't have a home," I say with a shrug, and Isobel nods.

"I miss home. So much," she says.

"How old are you, Isobel?"

"Fourteen."

"And you?" I say to Tilly, who lifts her chin high, like she's proud.

"Seventeen. Been on the Mainland for twelve years now. Just an hour or so away," Tilly says, looking out the window and tightening the short twists in her hair with one hand. "When I first got here, to Riverside, I'll tell you the truth, it felt good to see home. But it's hard now. I look out at that bridge every night, and it breaks me up knowing that the people I love are so close but so far away."

I look out at the bridge and then at Isobel. "Do you feel that way too?"

She shakes her head quickly, scowling at the window. "That is not my home. My family, my people, we are not Sossi. We are not Gutter."

"What do you mean?" I say.

She looks around the room, thinking carefully about what she might say, like the words she wants to use are new and hard to find. "In my home, the sky is bigger. The leaves on the trees, they are long and wide. And the water is clear. You can see fish at the bottom, swimming and crawling," she says, smiling and using her hands like this is the best way she can describe it.

"You weren't born here?"

She shakes her head. "The island where I lived cracked open and leaked fire. I was ten," she says. "Our elders said it was the dead rising. We all had to leave. So we took our boats and we sailed away. My home got smaller, and everything turned red."

"So you came here?" I say.

"We landed on the Mainland. On a small beach that curved out. Like this." She makes room on her bedsheet and traces the line of the beach with her finger.

"Mama said it was *mataiolo*—a welcome mat. This was where we were meant to rest. The land was welcoming us. But she was wrong. We were not welcome here at all," Isobel says, shaking her head.

"If you're not from here, then how did you get your scars?"

Isobel looks down at her hands and frowns, grabbing a pillow and squeezing it tight. "The Mainland Guard found us. At the camp we built near the ocean. They called us thieves. But Papa said, 'We are not thieves. We are *kiipa*. Visitors. Friends.' But they say we are Gutter. Gutter," she says, snarling and spitting it out with contempt, like she's imitating the guards. "No. We are Ruwai. Water People. *Kiipa-Ruwai*,' Papa said. 'Friends from across the water.' Over and over, he says this. But they called us Gutter and thieves."

Isobel points at everything in the room, scowling like the guards. "They point at our huts, our fire, our food. 'Thieves,' they say. This word means taking things that are not yours. But they tried to take us. They are the thieves. So we fight back. *Hakala anowei*," she says, waving two fists in the air. "This means . . . when you are pushed, you fight."

"Damn straight, Isobel," Tilly says, fists raised high like she's ready to throw a punch. "*Hakala anowei*."

I smile at the two of them, raising my fists as well. "*Hakala anowei*," I say, and for a moment, Isobel smiles.

"We fight. But most of my family did not survive. Me, my brothers and my sisters. Six of us hid. But they found us. They marked us," she says, showing her scars. "I cry and I cry, not from pain, but from the hurt in my heart."

I reach out for her and she leans her head into me as Tilly grabs another cookie and shoves it into her mouth.

"I was taken to Healers. They taught me to speak like them, like now. But I am not very good. They taught me from their book. And I read and I read and I learned as much as I could."

"Where's the rest of your family?" I say.

"I do not know. But the Healers, they are kind. They are very kind to me."

"I don't know about that, Isobel," Tilly says with a scowl. "I don't think they're kind at all. No Mainlander who keeps you from your family is kind, if you ask me."

"They feed me. They give me a house. They teach me to read and write. I work for them. They are nice."

"You think they're nice, Isobel? Tell her how you got knocked up, then. Tell Elimina. Lover or leader, Isobel?"

Isobel looks up at Tilly, her face red and angry. "You don't know, Tilly!" she says, growling into her pillow, like she doesn't quite know what to say.

"Isobel, it's okay. You don't have to tell me," I say.

"It's not right, Isobel," Tilly says gently.

"They don't have babies. Lady Ann. She can't make babies."

I turn to Isobel, staring down at the neat curve of her belly as she starts to cry. "Isobel, are you having a baby for them?"

"They were so kind," she says, nodding and squinting like she's not sure what to say. "They needed my help. They pay me for the baby. And when I go back to them, I work like before. No one will know."

"You know the reason they picked her is because of the way she looks. They're hoping the baby looks exactly like Father Healer, that the baby will be light enough to pass for his and Lady Ann's. They're probably on their knees right now praying that baby's got none of your brownness."

Isobel shakes her head, biting on nails that are so short there's hardly anything left.

"Tilly, come on, leave her alone."

"Look, Elimina, I love Isobel like she's my little sister. But it's not good for her to talk about those Healers like what they've done is helping her."

I wrap my arm around Isobel, and we both look out the window, watching and listening to the quiet that's come since the headhunters moved out of earshot.

"I love the sound of water," Isobel whispers.

"Me too," I say, smiling down at her.

"Did you know," Tilly says with a grin, "that Freedom River is the longest river on the Mainland, that there's a waterfall at the end that's so steep folks say it's the straightest route to heaven or hell, depending on who's doing the falling?"

I look up at Tilly, my face curled tight, wondering how she knows this and why she's sharing this now. When Isobel sees my expression, she bursts into laughter, stuffing her face back into her pillow, while Tilly pretends to bow.

"Seriously, Tilly, how do you know this?" I say, as Isobel continues laughing.

"We had a Deco who knew just about everything there is to know about the geography of the Mainland," she says with a shrug. "I asked lots of questions. Too many probably. Got me in trouble more times than not. Did you know there's a Gutter bird—an actual bird that won't ever leave the Gutter? Even though the sky is open and even though the walls are not that high, the birds just stay there. They sit on the wall, going nowhere, with feathers that are red like blood."

"Is that true?" Isobel says.

"It's called the gavanje bird," Tilly says.

We sit there for a moment quietly thinking about those red birds.

"Do you think I am stuck here, like the birds? Do you think I will ever go home and see my family?" Isobel says.

Tilly takes a long, deep breath, letting her shoulders drop as she breathes out slowly. "You know, I don't know, Isobel. I wonder about that myself sometimes, but I really don't know."

The two girls slowly lie down in their beds, and before I go, I pull their sheets up over them like Mother used to do when I was little.

"Do you think the babies can hear us?" I whisper to Tilly. "Do you think they know what's going to happen to them, that we're going to give them away?"

"I try not to think about that," Tilly says. "The advice I got from Sarah and the girls who came before her was that it's best not to get too attached. So that's what I'm trying to do. Don't think about it. Don't get too attached, Elimina."

I cross the dark hallway and climb back into bed, where I lie down with my hands on my belly, thinking about Tilly's advice. *Don't get too attached.*

20

ON THE WALLS OF THE RIVERSIDE MEDICAL CLINIC, there's a large map of the Mainland with "Our Home, Our Land" written in thin, curling letters. Next to the map, there's a row of framed degrees and certificates with shiny gold seals. When a man in a long white coat emerges from a door at the back of the clinic, I know that he's the person who earned them and the one we've come to see: Dr. Thomas D. Luca.

"Charlotte," he says, bending down and kissing her on each cheek while I stare at a head so pink and bald it seems to reflect light. "It's always a good day when you come by."

"Well, that means a lot coming from you, Thomas. I know how busy you are. I came because I wanted you to meet our new girl. This is Elimina."

"Oh yes, Elimina, the project case. All the way from Mainland City. It's quite an honor," he says, removing a pen from behind his ear and placing it in his chest pocket, his fingers long and bent like a spider. "How are you liking Riverside?"

"It's fine, sir."

"Oh, you don't have to call me sir, Elimina. Doc or Doc Luca will do just fine."

"Do you have a minute?" Miss Charlotte says, looking around at the quiet clinic, where a receptionist is clicking away on a type-writer.

"Is everything okay?" he says.

"Well, no, actually. We had a bit of a scare yesterday," Miss Charlotte says.

"What kind of a scare?" he says, looking at me with concern.

Miss Charlotte looks over and nudges me.

"I almost fainted," I say, biting down on my lip because all this fuss over what happened in front of Cranberry Manor is embarrassing.

"I think it was the heat. Although she hadn't eaten much either. You know how those academies can be," Miss Charlotte says. "She's well fed now. But I wanted to make sure everything's in tip-top shape—that there are no problems or concerns. She said this happened at the academy as well."

"Of course. Always good to check everything. Let's have a look," Doc Luca says.

He leads us through a door that opens into a room where a large silver lamp hangs over a medical bed with wheels and metal levers. The bed and the lamp are positioned in the center of the room, with machines and trays full of surgical tools lined up along the far wall. I stare at the jars of cotton and the containers of gauze on the counter, thinking about Mother's last days in a place that also felt stiff and cold.

"So how are you settling in?" Doc Luca says as Miss Charlotte sits down in a chair in the corner of the room. He pulls out two long metal arms with plastic grooves, which extend from one end of the bed.

"Good, sir," I say, anxiously watching as Doc Luca prepares a tray of tools.

"Lulabelle Turner had one of her episodes in front of the Manor. She mistook Elimina for someone else and just cried all over her," Miss Charlotte says, pulling a magazine out of her purse. "I don't know if you heard about that."

"No, I hadn't heard," he says.

"Scared Elimina half to death," Miss Charlotte says, shaking her head and wagging the magazine in front of her.

I want to say that's not true, that I wasn't scared at all, but I just stand there, listening quietly.

"Nurses had to come and take her away. She made quite the scene."

"It was that serious?" he says, and Miss Charlotte nods.

Doc Luca takes a gown from a hook on the wall and hands it to me, pointing to a curtained-off area in the far corner of the room.

"Remove everything and put this on," he says.

I pull the gown on and step out from the curtain, holding my arms tight against my body and biting down hard on my lip. The fabric is thin and worn, and suddenly I feel cold.

Doc Luca asks me to climb up on the table, and when I'm lying flat on my back, he points at the grooves at the end of the metal arms, instructing me to rest my heels on each one. "Bend your knees and slide down. Yup, just like that. A little bit lower. Almost there," he says, until my hips are at the end of the table, my legs spread open, the gown draped over my knees like a tent.

Doc Luca sits on a stool with wheels, rolling around to collect everything he needs, before moving between my ankles. I turn my head to the side and feel every muscle tense, horrified at the sight of this strange man looking inside me.

"Relax, Elimina," Doc Luca says, pulling on a pair of rubber gloves.

I try to distract myself by studying the letters on Miss Charlotte's magazine and trying to make out the words. But all I can see is a giant turkey on the cover, roasted and placed on a platter surrounded by fancy decor.

"You're sixteen?" Doc Luca says as he taps and scrapes and presses.

I nod, trying to ignore the feel of his breath on my legs.

"And this is your first time in Riverside?"

I nod again. But what I really want to say is *Stop. Please, stop touching me.*

I close my eyes and think about Mother, wondering if this is the curse of poor choices, the shame troubled girls deserve.

"How far along are you again?" Doc Luca says.

"Around twelve weeks," Miss Charlotte says without looking up from her magazine.

I think of the last time I saw Rowan, the night he cried and I sang to him, about what Josephine told me when I met him on my first day at Livingstone: *Don't talk to him. Keep your distance.* And I wonder how different things would be if I had listened.

"Well, good news. Everything looks fine," Doc Luca says, snapping off his gloves and tossing them in the garbage. "You've kept yourself quite nicely. No problems at all, from what I can tell. Should we take a look at that baby, just to be sure?"

"We can see the baby already?" I say.

"I guess *hear* would be more accurate," he says with a smile, his teeth so straight and white they almost look plastic. "Should we have a listen?"

I nod, stretching out on the center of the mattress while Doc Luca wheels over a machine with buttons and knobs. He rubs a thick liquid onto my stomach and presses a handle to my skin, moving it through the liquid and adjusting the dial until there's a clear whirring sound. He pushes deeper and lower, side to side, until I hear a fast drum.

Thump-thump-thump-thump-thump.

"There we go," Doc Luca says with a satisfied smile.

Thump-thump-thump-thump-thump.

"That's the baby," he says, nodding toward the machine.

I look at my belly and then at Doc Luca, amazed at the sound.

"It's a good little heartbeat," he says.

I listen closely, and I think about Rosalind carrying me in her belly. Had she heard my heart beating? Did she know what I sounded like before she gave me away?

"I think that's enough for now," Miss Charlotte says, turning off the machine so the room is suddenly quiet, the heartbeat gone.

But when I close my eyes, I can still hear it. *Thump-thump-thump-thump-thump.*

"Well, everything looks really good, Charlotte. I see no problems at all," Doc Luca says, removing his gloves and washing his hands at the sink. "Nothing to be worried about. She probably just needed some food and a little less of this Riverside sun."

"That's good to know, Thomas. I'm pleased to hear that. Elimina, you can get dressed now."

I head to the curtain slowly as Doc Luca and Miss Charlotte continue talking. I remove the gown and rub my hand over the small curve of my belly. I think about the sound, and I remember Tilly's advice. *Don't get too attached.*

MISS CHARLOTTE INSTRUCTS me to head straight home to help with chores while she visits with friends on the other side of town. But when I see Duncan standing by himself in a small shop with a spool of thread stenciled on the window, I open the door and step inside.

Duncan is leaning over a radio, listening to music, and when he turns around to face me, he smiles like he was expecting me.

"Why do you and your mother have those scars?" I say.

"Well, I usually like to start my day with good morning, Elimina. Especially on a fine one like this."

"Good morning," I say, smiling only a little. "Why do your scars look like that?"

He holds out his hands and studies them for a moment. "This is what Redemption Freedom looks like," he says.

"You're free? Like free-free. Redemption Free?"

He nods but he doesn't smile.

"I thought they removed them."

"Can't remove these kinds of scars, Elimina. They can only change how they look," he says.

I look down at my own X, trying to hide the disappointment of knowing it will always be there.

"How long have you been in Riverside?" I say.

"Been here long as I've been out. About sixteen years."

I look out the window, biting on my lip.

"What is it, Elimina? Say what's on your mind."

"If you're free, why would you choose to live here? Why not go somewhere far away?"

He gives a hearty laugh. "You're not wrong to ask it. That's for sure. I guess the truth is that we did do a bit of wandering at first. Momma and I. Never made it far. Not with much success, that is. It's not easy, you know, being free on the Mainland. And Momma likes being close to home."

"But you can do whatever you want, go anywhere."

"It doesn't work so much like that," Duncan says, scratching at his beard. "Truth is, paying off debt isn't enough for some. It doesn't change much. In their eyes, we are rebels and troublemakers. That's all they see when they look at us. No matter the scars."

I move toward a mannequin dressed in a Mainland Guard uniform and touch the buttons, the Mainland flag, the stitched-on awards. "So, you're a tailor."

He nods, adjusting the mannequin's collar, pulling at a loose thread. "When we got here, the old tailor had just passed and the guards were in need. Momma knew how to sew, and turns out you can make a decent living fixing guards' uniforms, which rip about a hundred times a day."

"And you like it?"

"I'm not sure that much matters," he says. "But I do alright for myself, and that's something."

A new song plays on the radio, and Duncan smiles, showing all of his teeth, including the spaces where some are gone. "This song will just heal your soul if you let it. You ever learned to dance, Elimina?"

I think of the night in the Fieldhouse when Rowan and I played pretend, when we danced even though there was no music. But I don't think that counts, so I shake my head. Duncan holds his hand out and waves me forward, placing my hand inside his. He puts my other hand on his shoulder and places his on my waist, telling me when to step and where to move until we're hopping and swinging around the room. We move slowly at first, then quicker as the music speeds up. Even though he's much older, his body moves smoothly, and I think about the baby feeling all of this as I try to keep up. I imagine the baby twirling and dancing along with us.

When the song is done, Duncan tells me about the instruments and the musicians who are playing, about the way the melodies carry joy even when the songs come from sadness. But when he asks if I'd like to stay longer and join him for a cup of tea, I remember Miss Charlotte's instructions and the girls back at the house, and I know that I have to get going.

"Can I come back tomorrow?"

"You can come back anytime, Elimina."

I move toward the door, then turn back before leaving. "Next time, can we go see your mother? I'd like to ask her something."

He hesitates for a moment and I step closer.

"Please, Duncan?"

He takes a deep breath, like he wants to say no. But when he looks at me, he sighs the same way Mother used to whenever I begged for something I really wanted that she wasn't sure I should have.

21

THREE DAYS AFTER I ARRIVE IN RIVERSIDE, DUNCAN takes me to see his mother after I finish all of my chores. When we arrive, Lulabelle is knitting in a rocking chair in the corner of a small room with yellow wallpaper that's covered in tiny pink flowers.

"She loves her knitting," Duncan says as Lulabelle zips her knitting needles in and out of a red scarf that swirls in a pile on the floor. "Only problem is, she can't seem to want to end, and we're all too afraid to take it away and tell her it's done. Lulabelle?" he says.

She looks up at him and frowns. "Is it dinnertime already? I am not hungry, Jack. Why do they always want me to eat? Eat, eat, eat. All I do here is eat."

"It's not time to eat just yet," Duncan says before turning to me. "Jack is my father. Been dead since I was ten. But some days, she thinks I'm him. Or one of the nurses. She almost never recognizes me as me."

I watch the two of them chat, and for a moment I wonder if I've made a horrible mistake—if Lulabelle is too sick to help after all.

"I brought a friend," Duncan says, sitting down on the end of the bed and placing one hand on her shoulder.

"My best friend on Sixteenth Street was Martha Lewis. Do you remember Martha? She came to our wedding," Lulabelle says, smiling up with gaps in her teeth that look just like her son's.

"This is Elimina," he says.

"Martha had fat thighs. Really fat thighs. So fat she could never find a pair of pants to fit. Always wore skirts and dresses. Boys used to try and sneak a peek because they knew she got nothing under them. See, she couldn't find no panties to fit neither," Lulabelle whispers, laughing to herself. "Poor girl. Poor, poor Martha."

"Elimina's going to have a baby soon," Duncan says.

"You don't think I know that?" she says. "Come over here, girl. Let old Lulabelle have a look at you."

She puts her knitting down and reaches out, touching the places where my waist is tight and stretched, before placing her ear against my belly.

"That's a good and healthy boy you got there," she says.

"Doc Luca said there's no way to know if—"

She waves her hand in the air dismissively. "Child, doctors are men who know books. They don't know bodies that carry babies," she says in a way that reminds me of Ida. "Those men know things they can study, things they can see and prove with their eyes. But we *feel*. Even you, young as you are, know more about your baby than that doctor. You know that? You can feel him, can't you?"

I nod as I think about the baby's heartbeat, which feels like a voice I can't seem to turn down. *Thump-thump-thump-thump.*

"What's your name again?" Lulabelle says.

"Elimina," I say, looking up at Duncan, who smiles and gives a small nod.

Lulabelle pauses, and for a moment I wonder if she remembers what she said the other day: *You are Lima Jenkins Sinclair.*

"I knew an Ellaree. She was a bit loose, but she never went hungry," Lulabelle says.

"It's Elimina," I say again, and this time Lulabelle takes a long, deep breath, her lip quivering as she holds out her wrinkled hands.

"Little Lima," she whispers, tears pooling under her eyes. "I'm glad you made it back. I'm real glad. But I think we done messed you up good, child. And I'm sorry for what I've done. I'm sorry every day." She looks down at the X on my right hand and shakes her head. "Took my own kind and gave them away. Said at least they saw a face like their own when they came into this world. That's what I told myself. But that's not enough. That's not near enough."

I'm not sure what to do or what I should say, and I look over at Duncan, who's staring down at the ground, closing his eyes, like he can't bear to look up.

"Rosalind. Sweet Rosalind," Lulabelle says.

"You knew Rosalind? You knew her?" I say, but Lulabelle doesn't answer. She just lets go of my hands and picks up her needles, knitting and singing again: "*Come find me in the waters of paradise.*"

"Lulabelle. Please," I say, and when she doesn't respond, Duncan takes the needles and the yarn from his mother, setting them down on the bed.

"Let's go outside, Momma," he says, helping her stand, then nodding for me to follow. "It's a beautiful day. Let's go sit on your chair."

DUNCAN AND I sit on a wicker couch on the front porch of Cranberry Manor, which is wide and spacious with plants and flowers sprawling from every corner. Lulabelle sits on a rocker next to us, tipping back and forth with her eyes closed. I see right away why Duncan brought her outside. Being here calms her.

I listen to the creak of the chair, the buzzing insects and the birds' fluttering wings. But when I close my eyes and smell the flowers, sweet and rich, all I hear are Lulabelle's words.

"Duncan, your mother . . ." I start to say.

He nods his head, like he already knows what's on my mind. "I worked in the Medical Center back in the Gutter, down in the clinics they opened up in the Lower End. But Momma was a midwife. She was known for delivering babies, and she was good at it, which is why she was asked to deliver 'special babies' for a government project," he says.

I look at Lulabelle and then at Duncan. "The Gutter Enhancement Project?" I say, and Duncan nods slowly.

"She . . . delivered me?"

"I helped her with the project. We both brought you into this world," he says with a smile that disappears quickly. "We delivered one hundred babies, and the folks in government gave them to Mainlanders . . . That's how me and Momma ended up on this side of the bridge with these scars."

He looks down at his hands, then toward the river and the bridge, shoulders drooped like there's a heavy weight bending them down. "See, I had a wife and two kids back in the Gutter. Two girls," he says, scratching the back of his head with his knuckles. "A few years before the project, a real bad sickness came through. Took the girls, then my wife. I didn't handle it well. Momma took care of me, trying to make ends meet and save up as much as she could. But it was hard. When they asked Momma if she would help with the project, and they told her she could get freedom for both of us in return, she said yes right away. But I mostly think she did it to save me. I was taking a lot of things to feel better. But the project gave me hope that I could start over."

"So you knew my mother, Rosalind Sinclair?"

Lulabelle opens her eyes, like the very mention of Rosalind rouses her. "One hundred," she says, shaking her head.

"You were the last child to be born in the project," he says. "The last one we gave away. Number one hundred. We always remember you and Rosalind. She was all alone. No family. Just you."

"Just me," I say, quiet and slow, thinking about my own baby, how it's just the two of us too. "My file said she died on the same day I was born. Were you there? Did you see her?"

Duncan nods as Lulabelle rocks her chair back and forth, gripping the handles tight.

"Momma knew right away that something was wrong. When we got to the block where she lived, she was lying in the alley. She was far along, so we just set up right away and got you out. But once you were born, Rosalind started bleeding everywhere. Momma told the guards to put her in the van and take her to the clinic, but they wouldn't do it."

"Why was she in the alley?"

"She was trying to get away from us," he says, as the skin around his mouth and his eyes sags low. "People didn't like what we were doing. Those mothers—they agreed to give up their babies for the project, but they didn't really know what it meant. Once folks saw babies leaving, and once those mothers who gave them up were left with nothing but a small paycheck . . . well, there was a lot of regret. And the ones like Rosalind who were due later started having second thoughts about the whole thing. Rosalind was the last one."

"She was trying to get away . . . with me," I say, like it still hasn't quite settled in.

"When Gutter kids go on academy track, folks have time with them. They're told Sossi stories. They know the names of their family. While they're making their way, parents get letters. But project kids were taken right from the start. And once they were gone, mothers had no way of knowing where they were or how to find them. Rosalind really didn't want to go through with it anymore. She didn't want to give you up, Elimina."

I close my eyes and place both hands on my belly, breathing in and out slowly. Rosalind wanted to keep me. Rosalind got too attached.

"Dancing walls," Lulabelle says.

"That's right, Momma," Duncan says, sadly. "You were born in an alley in Block 15. Right under this painting that looked like dancing bodies."

He leans over and rubs the back of his neck like he's tired.

"I took you to the van and got you cleaned off, and we brought you across the bridge with us. But there was nothing we could do for Rosalind."

"Lima Jenkins Sinclair," Lulabelle says, slow and deliberate, smiling.

"That's what Rosalind named you," Duncan says. "That's what she wanted to call you, so that's what we put on your record of birth."

"Lima Jenkins Sinclair," Lulabelle says again.

"But how did your mother know it was me?" I say, thinking back to my first day in Riverside. "Miss Charlotte called me Elimina. How could she know it was me if Mother changed my name? Did you know it was me, Duncan?"

He hesitates for a moment, then nods.

"How?"

"I saw your scar."

"But it could have been anyone," I say, and he shakes his head.

"The other project cases—they're all gone."

For a moment the street and the birds go quiet, like everything is paused, and I press my hands into my chest because it feels like I can't find any air.

"They died, Elimina," he says, and Lulabelle starts to sing.

"*Come find me in the waters of paradise.*"

"What do you mean, they died? All of them? How can that happen?"

"Most died at their homes on the Mainland, with the people who took them in. Slips and falls. Hunting mishaps, boat trips where they never returned," he says. "Some just . . . disappeared. Vanished. Like they were never there."

"Ninety-nine kids died. And no one did anything?" I say.

Duncan scratches his beard, running his teeth along his lip. "Around the eighth or ninth year of the project, when you-all were approaching your tenth birthday, there was about thirty kids left, best Momma and I could tell. We were keeping track as best we could. That's when folks from the Hill Coalition got involved. They argued that the project wasn't right. Unjust and inhumane, is what they said. But it took right up until the tenth anniversary of the project for folks inside the Mainland government to listen or do anything. By then, only twenty-one were still alive. Your momma was the only one who fought to keep you when the rest were pulled from those homes."

For my tenth birthday, Mother threw me a party. She did my nails and we sat around in swimsuits and robes, surrounded by candles. A call came through that made her so upset she left her cake and peeled off her nail polish. For weeks, little bits of red were stuck in her white rug.

"I will not give her back. Not now. Not ever. Do not call me again," she said, slamming down the phone.

That night, we slept in the same bed, and Mother wrapped her arms so tightly around me I found it hard to breathe. "I love you so much, Elimina. I will never let anyone hurt you," she said, and I waited until I heard her breathing slow to a snore before I got up and climbed into my own bed.

"If they were pulled, then where are they now, the other twenty?" I say as Lulabelle wanders into the garden, checking the flowers and placing her nose in the petals.

Duncan leans back, locking his fingers behind his head. I can't tell if he wishes I would stop asking questions, or if he's relieved to be able to talk about this with someone other than Lulabelle.

"They were going to send them all back to the Gutter. They didn't understand that those kids were not babies anymore. Those kids didn't know the Gutter, and they didn't want it. They had lived with Mainlanders their whole lives. All they knew about the Gutter was whatever their Mainland families told them. And most of it wasn't good. And who were they going to go back to, anyway? Most of them were like you. No family to even go to. A lot of those mothers were in trouble before they signed up for the project. Don't think many were still alive by the time those kids were pulled out of those homes."

"Do you think that's why they picked us?"

"I'm sure of it," Duncan says, nodding his head. "Rumor was they were going to send them to academies like the one you attended, but the Hill Coalition was fighting that too. They wanted them to be released right to the Hill. Network folks had thoughts on that, though. But when the fire happened, none of that mattered anymore."

"What fire?"

He looks down at the ground. "They were staying at an old academy while things were being discussed, supervised by Mainland Guards and a few Mainland government folks. The building burnt down with all twenty trapped inside and not a single Mainlander. They said it was an accident. Bad wiring. But Gutter folks know better."

I'm not sure whether to be sad or angry or what to do with my thoughts, but I feel something heavy in my heart and in my belly as I sit there with Duncan—a deep kind of hurt.

"You're still here," Duncan says, like he can see the pain rising. "You got to hold to that, Elimina. There's got to be a reason."

I stand and look at Duncan, suddenly furious. "Is there a *reason* they all died? Is that what you're saying? I'm here for a reason, so they died for a good reason too?"

"Elimina, that's not what I meant," Duncan says, reaching out for me, but I pull back hard.

"How can you live with yourselves?" I whisper, and before he can respond, I step off the porch and run down the street toward Miss Charlotte's, my eyes blurry with tears.

22

MISS CHARLOTTE DOLES OUT CHORES WITH JOY, LIKE she's proud of all the different ways she's able to make us work. We dust furniture and mop floors and scrub tiles because, according to her, staying busy is the sign of a well-made woman. Sometimes I wonder if she considers herself well-made given that all she does is watch.

"It's good for the babies to have an active mother rather than one who just sits around growing bigger," she says with her eyes fixed on Tilly.

We work from breakfast until lunch, and then all afternoon, and I wonder if this is good for us, all this bending and cleaning and doing. But part of me is grateful for the distraction. I am trying hard not to think about Duncan and Lulabelle and the project.

"Spot free, dust free. Healthy, healthy," Miss Charlotte sings as I wipe down the furniture in the sitting room. When she finds Tilly in the kitchen, resting in a chair during chores, her singing turns to yelling. "Matilda, how many times do I have to tell you to get to work?"

"How many times I got to tell you, Miss Charlotte, that my name is not Matilda, it's Tilly?"

"Your mother named you Matilda for a reason," Miss Charlotte says, "and I intend to honor that."

"I'm seventeen years old," Tilly says, with her finger pointed at Miss Charlotte. "I haven't seen my mother in twelve years. If she's still alive and I happen to ever see her again, I imagine a whole lot of things will have changed, Miss Charlotte. My name being just a start."

Miss Charlotte storms out the front door, mumbling about girls with no manners, and when she disappears down Main Street, Tilly takes a tart from the fridge and shoves the whole thing in her mouth.

Isobel and Tilly are wiping down the windows while I sweep the porch when a black car pulls into the driveway.

"New girl's here," Tilly says, leaning over the railing.

A young Gutter man with thick, curly hair steps out of the car and places a blue bag on the steps. "Is . . . Miss Charlotte here?" he says, and the three of us shake our heads.

I can see a girl hunched over in the backseat, and the driver looks nervous, like he's not sure what to do next.

"This girl's going to need some help. Is there a doc around?"

He opens the car door and wraps the girl's arm around his shoulder before lifting her carefully out of the car. When she stands and squints up at the sun, I gasp loudly.

"Violet?"

Violet pauses for a moment, lifting her head like she's confused. Her hair is cut short and her body is covered in purple bruises, but underneath her white dress are the budding signs of a small, round belly.

"I was told to bring her straight to Miss Charlotte's in

Riverside," the man says. "She was like this when I picked her up, I swear."

"I'll call Doc Luca," Tilly says, heading into the house.

"Violet? Violet, it's me, Elimina," I say, pulling her thin body close and helping her up the stairs.

When the driver sees that I've got her and that I know her by name, he gets back into the car and drives away so quickly his tires squeal up the main road.

When Violet sleeps for two days, barely eating or leaving our room, Miss Charlotte instructs me to take her outside for fresh air and exercise. Violet's hardly said a word to me since she arrived, and I worry that our time at Miss Charlotte's will go the same way things went at the academy, full of awkward silences and unkind words.

Her bruises are healing, and when she walks around the yard, picking up rocks, I can tell that the soreness that made it so difficult for her to sleep on her first night is improving as well.

"Do you want to talk about what happened?" I say.

She nods at my belly. "Do you?"

I sit on the bench and stare at the river, where a small red bag hanging from a branch is pulled by the water.

"Was it Rowan?" she says, and when I look back at her, I pause and then nod.

She grabs a rock and drops it in a jar she took from the kitchen, shaking it so the stones spread and settle.

"I'm sorry," I say, even though I don't know what I'm saying sorry for.

"Don't say sorry," she says.

"But Violet—"

She raises her hand to get me to stop. "Until I got here and saw you and figured out about you . . . and Rowan . . . I thought he might be hoping for me. Missing *me*," she says, clearing her throat with a cough. "At one point, when things were really bad, I thought maybe he might come and rescue me. I heard about his boxing matches nearby, and I know it sounds crazy, but I thought . . . I thought he might come for me. But that only happens in books, right? In stories. Like the ones Mr. Gregors let us read in his office. And this is Gutter life. Don't feel sorry for me, Elimina."

"Violet, what happened?" I say.

She turns to me, combing her fingers through her short hair. "What happened when I was young or what happened after Livingstone? Which story do you want?"

"I don't know," I say. "I guess whichever story you want to tell."

She shrugs, sitting down on the bench, her jar of rocks beside her. "My stories are not worth telling, Elimina."

She looks over at me with her chin raised high, the way she did at Livingstone, except this time her eyes are shimmery wet, like she's only pretending to be okay.

"I want a story where a Gutter girl wins, where things turn out well, like they do for Mainlanders. But the truth is, I don't know how that story goes. I don't want to tell the stories I know, okay?"

I place my hand on hers, hoping she doesn't pull away, and when she grips my hand tightly, we sit there like that, listening to the river, watching the red bag as it breaks away and floats down the river.

THAT NIGHT, VIOLET pulls the blue book of poetry out of her bag and hands it to me. I hold it against my chest, clutching it tight, and she smiles a little, like she's glad to see how much it still means to me. I flip through the pages, moving my fingers across the words, reading one poem, then another.

I tell Violet we should read a poem every night for the babies, but she says there's a power to those words that she can't take in every day, so I tuck the book under my pillow and vow to do it quietly on my own.

"How was everything after I left?" she says, picking up the carving of the mother and child and sliding her finger along the curves.

I climb onto her bed, so we're shoulder to shoulder, and I tell her everything—about Josephine's disappearance and Rowan's boxing, about the day I met Duncan and Lulabelle and the day I was born, and the truth about the Gutter Enhancement Project. I tell her about the fire that killed the last twenty project kids, and she listens thoughtfully, waiting until I'm done before saying anything.

"So Duncan and Lulabelle gave all those babies to Mainlanders, and for that they got Redemption Freedom?"

I nod.

"And now all those kids, except for you, are dead?" she says. I nod again as she exhales loudly, like it's too much to take in. "Are you angry?"

"At Duncan and Lulabelle?"

"At everything," she says. "At Josephine? At the project? At all of it."

"Most days, I'm just sad. That I don't have family. That I'm alone. And when someone makes that happen for you, the way that Josephine did, and Duncan and Lulabelle, it's hard not to be angry. But I'm also just hurt because I feel, in a weird way, like Josephine and even Duncan and Lulabelle are the closest thing that I've ever had to family since Mother died. And the truth is, I don't want to be angry with them. I don't want to lose everyone I care about."

Violet pauses for a moment before responding in a low, quiet voice. "I know I wasn't good to you at the academy, Elimina. But maybe now we can be each other's family, you know? Maybe family are just the people you meet who are worth forgiving, so you can keep them close."

I smile. "I would really like that," I say.

When I crawl onto my own bed, Violet lies down and falls asleep while I stare at the streetlights and the stars. I pull out the blue book, and before I go to sleep, I whisper a poem to the baby about a strange garden.

23

ON SATURDAYS, MAINLAND GUARDS HEAD TO MAIN Street and Covey Road, where bars built from old, splintered wood sit on all four corners of the crossroads. They stroll into the bars, sober and tired, and stumble out hours later, crashing on a bench or on the steps of their dorm-style apartment building.

"Stay inside. No exceptions," Miss Charlotte says as she heads out the door to play her weekly game of poker with Doc Luca and a few of the Main Street shop owners.

The first few Saturday nights after Violet's arrival, the four of us played cards and baked bread, staying up as late as we could manage. But on my eighth Saturday in Riverside, I convince Tilly and Isobel to help me plan a surprise party for Violet. We bake a cake and make fancy hats out of paper bags when Violet is napping, and after Miss Charlotte leaves for poker, I set up everything while the other girls keep Violet outside.

"Surprise!" we shout when she comes into the house. "Happy birthday!"

Violet stares at the decorations and the cake with an expression that looks more confused than excited. "It's not my birthday," she says.

"I know. But I also know that you've never had a party. And we all deserve a party sometimes," I say.

She smiles slowly, her eyes turning red and watery. But before she can cry or say anything else, Tilly punches her on the shoulder.

"Oh, stop it," Tilly says. "It's not that big of a deal."

We show her all of the things we made, and when Violet hugs me tightly and whispers a little thank you, I almost cry too.

Tilly uses a thin pair of scissors to style Violet's hair, and I fiddle with the radio while Isobel places flowers she found by the river behind our ears. We sit at the table, where I spread out a cloth and place two lit candles in the center like they do at Mainland restaurants. I grab the blue book and read a few poems, just like we used to do in the Fieldhouse. When I finish, Tilly and Isobel applaud, demanding we celebrate by eating the cake.

I hand Tilly the knife, and when we sing "Happy Birthday," she cuts the cake, lifting each slice with a knife and two of her fingers to keep it from falling. Crumbs fall everywhere and larger pieces follow with clumps of gooey icing. When Tilly is done, she spreads a streak of icing on Isobel's face. Isobel screams, and we all stretch across the table with icing on our fingers, spreading it everywhere, until Violet, the cleanest of the group, declares a truce.

"Game over," she shouts, pulling her chair away from the table and grabbing a damp cloth.

"Let's play another game," Isobel says when the icing is cleaned off.

They all nod in agreement, and Isobel and Violet settle onto the couch while Tilly slides into the armchair.

"There was this game show on the radio in Capedown called *Dreamhome* that Mother and I used to listen to," I say. "It was Mother's favorite show. People had to guess the price of things and if they guessed the right price, they got the prize, and if they guessed enough things right, they got a whole house."

"They got a house, just for doing that?" Violet says.

I nod, grabbing a knife and holding it to my mouth like a mic, as Isobel tosses me a pillow. "Ladies and gentlemen, what we have here is a King's Court Pillow. Made of the finest upholstery on the Mainland. Violet, what would you say this fine-looking pillow is worth?"

Violet smiles, straightening up and pretending to be nervous. "Well, I don't know. I mean, a pillow like that . . . I'd . . . I'd . . . have to say . . . two dollars."

When I tell her she's correct, she cheers and the girls beg for more. They bid on spoons and cushions and Miss Charlotte's tea-cups, and when they guess a number, I either tell them they're correct or ask them to try again later. We keep an imaginary score, and at the end of the game, Violet's declared the winner. I give her a fork as the key to her new home, and when I ask her what she's looking forward to most, she leans in to the microphone-knife and says, "I'm just looking forward to getting the hell out of Riverside."

We all laugh, and when they beg for more games, I invite the girls to show off their talents, like they do on the Mainland pageant shows.

"Abracadabra," I say, tossing a blanket out of sight and smiling as though it has disappeared into thin air by magic.

"Good magic," Isobel says, holding on to her belly and laugh-ing hysterically, while Tilly and Violet boo with their hands cupped around their mouths.

I ask one of them to come up and present her talent next, but all three of them shake their heads.

"It's my birthday," Violet says.

"And I don't have any talents," Tilly says.

"You must have some talents," I say, smiling and gesturing toward the dining area, which has become our stage.

"Tilly tells good stories," Isobel says, and we all clap and shout because it's true.

"Tell a story, Tilly!" Violet yells, and when the three of us continue to beg, Tilly raises her hands in surrender.

"Okay, okay, okay," she says, rising slowly and taking a deep breath with her hands on the sides of her belly.

When she starts to tell the story of Jimmy Bean, a boy she knew back at the academy, Isobel claps and cheers, like she's heard this one before and wants to hear it again.

"Now, Jimmy Bean was sweet like chocolate," Tilly says, licking her fingers and using fancy adult words and funny hand gestures to describe every part of his body.

"He was fine as wine, and every girl wanted him. But he wanted me," she says, smacking her hand against her hip, so we all know he liked her curves.

"We had this shed on campus, a little wood room full of tools and broken machinery, and when Jimmy Bean took me out to that shed, the night was as pretty as a painting."

She describes the moon and the stars and every sound that made her sweat while the three of us hold on to our bellies, begging her to keep going.

"He made a woman out of me, let me tell you," she says, swiveling her hips as far as they'll go and puckering her mouth.

"Tell them about his name," Isobel shouts at Tilly, who smiles with her eyes and her ears, like she knows this is the best part.

"They called him Jimmy Bean, cuz he was five foot nothing and barely one hundred pounds."

Isobel claps, giggling into a pillow, while Violet and I look at each other, our eyes big and round.

"He was the size of a bean, but he told me he liked his girls big and round," Tilly says, with her hands raised out to the sides. "And, what can I say, I like to give my man what he wants."

We cheer and we shout, and Tilly tilts her head forward in a bow before sitting back down.

"Will you go back to Jimmy Bean?" Isobel says softly, and Tilly shrugs, the curves of her mouth sinking low.

"I don't know. Who knows if I'll ever see him again? Maybe he'll be gone by the time I get back. Maybe this is the only thing I've got left of him, you know?" She pats her belly and shrugs. "I know I shouldn't get too attached, but I've been calling this child Baby Bean from the start. Seems as good a name as any, don't you think?"

We nod and smile, quiet for a moment, and for the first time, I wonder what I would name my own baby, assuming Lulabelle's right and it's a boy.

"The babies will be okay, right?" Isobel says with a soft, small voice, but no one responds, and when the music on the radio turns into a happy tune, Violet stands.

"Let's dance," she says with a big smile.

We move our bellies and our bodies to the beat, waving our hands in the air. I show them how Duncan taught me to dance, and when the song is done, Isobel shows us the way Ruwai people move, her hips swinging side to side, her hands gliding beside her.

"Sing, Isobel," Tilly says when she's seated back down on the chair.

"Tilly," she whispers, her face turning red, like she's too embarrassed or nervous.

"It's my birthday," Violet says, and when we all beg again, Isobel reluctantly moves to the stage.

I sit down on the couch next to Violet as Isobel drapes her

long hair over her shoulder, her body still thin despite the round-
ness of her belly. When she opens her mouth, Isobel sings words
in a language we don't understand, but it's almost like we can feel
it, like whatever she's saying is magic.

When she's done, Tilly and I clap and holler, as Violet holds
her hands to her chest. "Oh, Isobel," she says. "That was really
beautiful."

Isobel smiles, lowering her chin, her face bright red. "I'm
sorry, I don't know Mainland songs. Only Ruwai songs, Violet."

"What does the song mean?" Violet says.

"It is about a girl who can move through darkness with her
light," Isobel says, and Violet stands and squeezes Isobel tightly.

WHEN WE GET into bed, Violet lies on her back, staring up at the
ceiling. "Elimina, I think that's the very best time I've ever had."

She reaches out and when I put my hand in hers, I feel tiny
flutters move across my belly. I close my eyes and think about the
baby moving and growing inside me. I make a point of memoriz-
ing everything about tonight—how it sounds, how it smells, how
it feels to really be happy.

24

TILLY IS SITTING AT THE TABLE WITH A LOAF OF BREAD and a slab of butter when I step into the kitchen one afternoon. Her legs are sprawled wide under the table, so I can see her feet and ankles, which are thick and swollen in ways that look terribly uncomfortable.

She's been ordered to rest for the last month of her pregnancy out of concern for the health of the baby, so she takes short walks around the yard twice a day and focuses on chores where she can remain seated. Isobel says that Tilly hardly sleeps, which is evident in the puffy pockets under her eyes and the way the stairs creak when she makes her way down to the kitchen in the middle of the night.

"No bread. No sweets. No sugar whatsoever," Miss Charlotte told Tilly before leaving to take Violet for a checkup.

"Tilly," I say, pulling the plate toward me. "Miss Charlotte said no."

"I don't need a babysitter, Elimina," she says as she pulls the food back.

I sit down across the table, watching her butter the bread and chew each bite slowly, pausing each time like she's not even hungry.

"Tilly, Doc Luca says you're going to hurt yourself . . . and the baby if you don't slow down."

"I'm fine."

"But the baby . . ."

"It's the baby that I'm thinking about, Elimina."

I shake my head as she takes another buttered slice in her hand and opens her mouth. "I don't understand."

"I don't want them to take the baby," she says.

I sit up tall, massaging my belly gently as Tilly sighs and leans closer to the table.

"I thought I could just have the baby, give it up and get back on Redemption track like they want. Keep moving forward, you know, for my family and everything. But every day, I feel a shaking from this baby that says, *Don't leave me here. Get out.* I hear this baby begging. *Please, please. Don't leave me with them.* It keeps me up at night."

I nod, unsure whether to admit out loud what I've known since my first appointment when I heard the baby's heartbeat: I don't want to give this baby up either. Something in me feels the way Rosalind must have felt that night when she went into labor, when Duncan and Lulabelle came to deliver the last baby in the project. *This baby belongs with me.*

"Have you said anything to Doc Luca and Miss Charlotte?"

"They're the last people I would tell," Tilly says. "Sarah, the girl who was here just before you, she wanted to keep her baby. She wanted to go back to the Gutter, and she told Doc Luca and Miss Charlotte what she was thinking a few weeks before she was due, how much she wanted to go home."

"What did they say?"

"They told her how great it was to see girls who love their babies, who want to be mothers. They told her they'd look into some options. But the next day when I woke up, she was gone. I went to look for her in town, and I saw her sitting in front of the clinic all dazed, waiting for a driver, surrounded by two Mainland Guards. She was a mess, and the baby was gone. I asked her what happened. I asked her where the baby went, whether it was a girl or a boy, and she just turned to me with glazed eyes and said, 'Don't tell them anything, Tilly.' I didn't really know what she meant when she said it. But I do now."

I lean back and think about how we're expected to give our babies up as soon as they arrive, how nothing we have is ours except our debt.

"Miss Charlotte tells us it's for the best," Tilly says. "She says the babies are in good hands. And I believed that at the start. I really did. I was ready to go back and work off my debt. But, Elimina, something inside is telling me otherwise. Like giving this baby up isn't right."

I gesture toward the plate, where only a few crumbs remain. "But how is this supposed to help, Tilly? You're making yourself sick."

She looks up at me, her eyes sad and determined. "They won't take a sick baby. Or a sick mother. They only want us if we're healthy. They'll add a fine to my debt if I don't deliver a baby for them, but we'll be able to go home together. I don't care about Redemption Freedom anymore, Elimina. I just want my own life with my baby."

"And you think this can work?" I say.

"I come from a big family," she says, closing her eyes as she massages her leg to keep it from cramping. "My momma was big when she had me and I've been big from the start. But I turned out healthy enough to get approved for academy track. I turned out alright. I'm just working with what I got."

Tilly raises her empty glass, and I take it to the fridge, where I fill the glass with milk and rest it on the table.

"You heading back after this, Elimina?" she says, before taking a sip.

"There's a couple up on the Hill who've offered to hire me. I've got a friend who's already there. I'm thinking of seeing if they'll allow me to bring the baby too. Kind of like Isobel."

Tilly shakes her head, wiping milk off her lip with a napkin. "Isobel's not going back to those Healers," she says.

"What do you mean?"

"You think they're going to want her around, having everybody see that the baby looks a little too brown in the sun, a little too like that girl who cleans up the Healers' house? That woman is not going to want Isobel around after she's been with her husband and is the real mother of that baby. They're probably on some trip right now, hiding the fact that Lady Ann isn't pregnant. They're going to pass that baby off as theirs, as a Mainlander. I'll bet you anything, Elimina. I'll bet you that's why they hired her from the very beginning."

I stare at Tilly, shaking my head because I don't want to believe her. "They wouldn't do that. Isobel's just a kid. She was twelve when they took her in. She's got no one."

"Which is exactly why they did it and why it's so damn cruel," Tilly says. "They raised her to trust and believe them. Then they used her, and they're going to toss her out like she's trash."

I place my hands on my belly, where the baby is flipping around like a bird in a cage.

"And if your baby is healthy, Elimina, your headmaster will send that baby wherever he wants, hiring you out to whoever will pay the most. Maybe that's the Hill and maybe it's not. But you and Isobel, you have no idea what's ahead. And no control over it either. I'm not going to let them do that to me."

Tilly reaches out and takes my hand, squeezing it tightly.

"What you got to think about now—what I started to think about after I saw Sarah—is whether Redemption Freedom is going to feel good if you lose everything to get it, whether you'll want to be at the Hill knowing your baby is lost somewhere, being raised at some academy or working for some Mainlander."

I swallow hard, staring down at the table, thinking about Rosalind in that alley, about growing up alone, having no one who looked like me, no one who could tell me who I was or where I was from.

"I'm tired of being without my family," Tilly says. "I'm tired of doing everything they tell me."

I think of all the women who gave their babies up for the project—babies who died when they were apart from them—and I wonder what they would tell me to do if they were here, what Rosalind would say to me. I lower my head, and I hear a sound that's so clear it's hard to believe it's not Tilly, a voice that's so loud and distinct, it frightens me. *Run.*

I stare up at Tilly, who's watching me strangely, like she can tell that I'm stirred. "I . . . I gotta go, Tilly," I say, pushing my body up from the table and heading for the stairs.

When I step out of the kitchen, I see Isobel in the shadows, her eyes brimming with tears.

"Isobel, did you . . . how long have you been there?" I say.

"Do you think it is true, what Tilly said?" she whispers.

I bite my lip, unable to give her an answer, and she runs down the hall that leads to the backyard, letting the door slam behind her.

25

SOBEL OPENS THE DOOR TO OUR ROOM ON A NIGHT WHEN the house is hot and stiff from a heat wave that makes sleeping more uncomfortable than usual.

"Tilly's water broke," she whispers, her face red and puffy. "I don't know what to do. She's in so much pain."

Violet and I move quickly, following Isobel quietly across the hall and crowding around Tilly's bed. She's lying on her side, her skin shiny with sweat, her chest rising and falling so quickly it's clear why Isobel's scared.

"Help me," Tilly whispers, clutching a pillow tightly.

I get down on my knees and hold one of her hands. "I'm here, Tilly. It's okay."

"Do you think they'll shoot me if I'm running the other way, if I'm heading for the Gutter?" she says.

"Tilly," I say, and she closes her eyes and nods, like she already knows she's in no shape to go anywhere.

For the last week, Tilly has been in pain and constantly uncomfortable. Her knees and her back have been so sore that she hardly leaves her bed, begging us to bring her extra food, which she hides all over the room and eats without Miss Charlotte knowing, apologizing to Isobel whenever she can.

"I didn't mean it, Isobel. I'm sure the Allisters are nice people. I'm sure they'll take you back," she told her.

But what made Isobel so sad, and what had aged the young girl somehow, was the fact that what Tilly said is probably true. And there is nothing Isobel can do about it.

"I gotta go," Tilly says, suddenly trying to sit up, but when a rush of pain hits, Tilly stiffens and squints, biting down hard on the pillow.

She squeezes my hand and when the pain finally fades, she relaxes a little. Isobel places her hand on Tilly's leg and starts weeping, and Tilly cries too.

"It's okay. It's going to be okay," I say.

But when the door to the bedroom opens, and Miss Charlotte is standing there, Tilly drops her head back in frustration. Her only hope now is that the baby is too sick to go to an academy, but healthy enough to make it to the Gutter.

DOC LUCA ARRIVES with his medical kit, checking on Tilly while I cool her face with a cloth. I see the concern on his face, how he frowns with his lips pressed tightly together, and I can tell by the way Tilly holds my hand a little bit tighter that she sees it too.

"It's going to be fine, Tilly. Everything will be fine," I whisper, hoping it's true.

"Is . . . everything set, Charlotte?" Doc Luca says as Miss Charlotte enters the room, squeezing past Violet and Isobel and waving a paper fan.

"Everything's set," she says. "They'll be here soon."

"Good. We need to move now," he says, taking one of the towels from the pile we stacked on Isobel's bed and wiping the sweat from his head.

"Miss Charlotte, can you clear the room, please," he says as Tilly twists and moans.

"But I want them here," Tilly says.

"Doc Luca needs room to work, Matilda," Miss Charlotte says. "The three of you can go wait outside."

"But, Miss Charlotte, it's not even light out," I say.

"It will be light in due time, Elimina," she says, standing in the hall with her hands on her waist. "Just stay on the porch. The Mainland Guards will be watching you."

A PAIR OF Mainland Guard vans are parked in front of the house as a thin strip of orange light cracks along the horizon. Four guards are standing on the edge of the driveway watching us closely, just like Miss Charlotte promised. Violet leans against a post while Isobel and I sit on one of the benches. From the open windows, we can hear Tilly moan and sob, like she's in agony.

"That's it, Matilda. That's it. I know it hurts, but you're doing great," Doc Luca says.

When Tilly shrieks louder, like the pain is getting worse, Isobel looks over at me and grabs my hand.

"I'm nervous," she says.

I can't tell if she's worried about Tilly or if she's worried about suffering through all of this herself in a few weeks when her baby is expected to arrive. I squeeze her hand to encourage her as a sleek gray car pulls into the driveway, driven by a Mainland woman with black hair that's white at the temples.

One of the guards moves toward the car, and she rolls down the window and smiles.

"You delivering?" he says, and the woman nods.

"How soon until the baby comes?" she says.

"If her shouting is any indication, it shouldn't be too much longer," the guard says with a nod toward the window where Tilly lets out a sharp scream. "But who knows. Sounds like it's a tricky one."

"Well, I'm used to waiting," the woman says, adjusting the bassinet that's resting on the front seat and pulling out a book as the guard steps away from the car.

Tilly's contractions grow longer and closer together, and I can tell from the screams and the shrieks and the coaching of Doc Luca that she's exhausted.

"Come on, Tilly. Come on. That's it. That's a girl," Doc Luca says. "Just a little bit more."

"I can't. I can't," Tilly says.

"Push, Matilda. Push!" Miss Charlotte shouts, and Tilly groans loud and hard until we hear a baby crying.

"Good job, good job," Miss Charlotte says. "It's a beautiful, healthy little girl."

"She's healthy?" Tilly says, her voice full of disappointment as Doc Luca and Miss Charlotte move about and make plans. "Can I hold her?"

Two of the guards head toward the house, talking casually as Miss Charlotte mumbles a response that's too quiet to be heard.

"No. You're not leaving," Tilly shouts. "I want to hold my baby."

"Tilly, you need to calm down," Doc Luca says. "You just had a baby."

Something crashes to the floor, and when we hear a scream, this time from Miss Charlotte, the two guards run quickly, push through the front door and stomp up the stairs.

"Tilly," Doc Luca says, his voice filled with warning.

"Give me my baby. Right now," she says as the third guard stands in front of us with a gun.

"You three, on the grass," he yells, nodding in the direction he wants us to go while the fourth guard stands near the gray car.

"Put it down, Tilly," Doc Luca shouts.

"Put it down!" yells one of the upstairs guards.

"Tilly, you're bleeding. Please, put the knife down," Miss Charlotte says.

"Oh, Tilly," Isobel whispers, pressing her hand against her mouth.

"Give her back!" Tilly yells, and the baby cries louder.

"You're scaring the baby," Miss Charlotte says.

"You're scaring her!"

"Tilly, we just need to clean her up," Doc Luca says, calm and slow. "Just let Miss Charlotte through, and we'll clean the baby off for you. Go ahead, Char. Go on."

"Miss Charlotte!" Tilly begs. "Please. Please bring her back."

"She'll be back, Tilly. She'll be back," Doc Luca says. "Let me have a look at that hand."

We listen to Miss Charlotte move down the stairs, followed by one of the guards. Miss Charlotte sings gently with a voice that ripples in the air, and for a while, that's the only thing we hear. But when the baby cries again, piercing and loud, Tilly's panic returns.

"What's wrong with her? Where is she? What's taking so long? I want to see her now," she shouts.

A few moments later, Miss Charlotte rushes out of the house, carrying the baby. She moves quickly across the porch with one of the Mainland Guards, heading directly for the gray car.

"Wait. Where are you taking her, Miss Charlotte?" I say, stepping toward her.

"Get back," the guard yells.

"She just wants to hold the baby," I say, stopping in my tracks as the woman steps out to greet her like they're old friends.

The two women exchange a few words as Miss Charlotte leans forward and hands her the baby, which she places in the bassinet in the car.

"Thomas will send along the paperwork as soon as he's back in the office," Miss Charlotte says with a low voice, and the woman nods, waving to her and the guards before climbing back into her car and driving down the road.

WHEN TILLY APPEARS at the front door, led by one of the guards, her eyes are veiny and red. There're bandages on one hand, and she pauses in the doorway, gripping the frame.

"You said I could see my baby. You said I could hold her," she shouts as another guard leans in from behind, pushing her out.

Isobel gasps when she sees her and she drops down on her knees like she can't stand up any longer.

"Tilly!" I shout, and she looks over at me, then at Isobel and Violet, her face hollow and tired.

"Where's my baby? I want my baby," she shouts as the guards force her toward the driveway, pushing from behind and pulling from the front as she leans back to slow them down.

A few neighbors in thin cotton robes stand on the sidewalk, watching everything and shaking their heads as Miss Charlotte and Doc Luca stand on the front porch.

"Where is she? Where did you take my Baby Bean?" Tilly shouts, but they don't say anything.

Two guards push her up the ramp that leads into the van, while the others stand by for support. When she's inside, they slam the door shut as Tilly sobs and bangs on the walls.

"Please, please," she begs as the van pulls away and heads down the road.

When the van is gone, I kneel down in the grass with Violet and Isobel. We huddle close, weeping for Tilly and her baby, weeping for each other.

26

STAND IN THE DOORWAY OF DUNCAN'S TAILOR SHOP WITH a letter for the Hill tucked deep in my pocket. Duncan is hunched over a pair of pants with a needle and thread, tapping his foot to the music, which is playing so loudly, he doesn't hear me enter the store.

"Duncan?" I say.

He looks up and moves toward me. "Elimina. You alright?" he says.

I can't tell if he's frightened by my arrival or by the way I appear, but I can tell by the way he's looking at me, the way he moves in slow and careful, that he knows I'm not okay at all.

"Is this about Tilly?" he says, and when I nod, he leads me to a chair. "She okay? I saw some vans at the house. Figured she was next."

"They took the baby, and then the guards took her away . . . She pulled a knife on Doc Luca. Miss Charlotte says she's in real trouble."

Duncan turns down the radio, and I tell him about the way they loaded Tilly into the van and the woman in the gray car who took the baby.

"It was awful. What do you think is going to happen to her?"

"I don't know," Duncan says, shaking his head. "Hard to say. There's a jail in the Gutter, but not too many women there. It'd be rough. But Tilly's a tough girl. I'm sure she'll come out alright."

I think about how badly Tilly wanted her baby and how much she wanted to go home, and I shake my head because I don't know if I agree with Duncan. I don't know if she'll be okay at all.

I pull a letter out of my pocket, addressed to David Hamble, and hand it to Duncan. "The headmaster at the academy told me not to tell anyone I'm here. But the driver who brought me here said to come to you if I need to send a Network letter. I need to see if the Freemans can help."

"Help you how?" Duncan says.

"I want to keep my baby." Just saying these words feels like a breath of fresh air.

"And how is this letter going to help you do that, Elimina?"

"Maybe they'll take both of us," I say, but when I think about what Tilly said about the Allisters and what I know about Mr. Gregors, I feel the same doubt I see on Duncan's face.

"The Hill's a long ways away. It's going to take time to get this to them."

"I don't want to give up my baby, Duncan. I want family. Like you and Lulabelle have."

Duncan sits down and places his head in his hands, like he knows this is partly his fault, that what I want and what I need is tied to the day he and Lulabelle brought me into the world and took me away.

"If the Freemans don't come, Miss Charlotte and Doc Luca will deliver the baby and just give him away. Like they just did with Tilly. Like they did with Sarah. I can't do that, Duncan."

"I know you're scared, Elimina, and I wish I could help . . . I mean, I hope this letter helps, but—"

"Wait. Wait," I say, pausing in the middle of the shop and looking at Duncan as an idea begins to grow. "What if you and Lulabelle deliver the baby? Instead of Doc Luca? In secret, you know?"

He shakes his head back and forth, like he doesn't like this plan at all.

"If you deliver the baby, maybe I can get to the Hill myself."

"Elimina, it's not that simple," he says. "Delivering a baby here so no one knows, then making it all the way to the Hill? It's impossible."

"Duncan, please. Help me."

"Okay, let's say we do this, Elimina. Let's say me and Momma and you, we all do our part. How are you going to get to the Hill?"

"Couldn't the Network help? They get letters there. Couldn't they get people there too?"

"A baby and a woman who just gave birth are a little harder to hide than a letter. Trust me, there's no way you're going anywhere north of this town, especially the Hill, without getting shot or found some way. And there's no way I'm helping you die, Elimina. I can't do that. Not after what Momma and I already did."

I place my hands on my knees, breathing deep and slow, while Duncan watches me.

"If you want to keep the baby, and that's your concern . . ." he says, sighing and shaking his head like he's not sure if he should go on.

"What? What should I do, Duncan?"

"Your best bet is heading the other way, to the Gutter."

"The Gutter?" I say.

"We'd have to find a way to make it seem like you're not much worth to Mainlanders. We'd have to find you the right paperwork.

But that's the best way I can think of. Assuming Momma and I help with the delivery."

I place my hand on my belly as the baby flutters and kicks. "I'd have to go to the Gutter?"

"You don't *have* to go to the Gutter, Elimina. There are other ways to pay down that debt. Momma and I, we have some money. It won't pay everything. But it's a start. You don't have to give up. You could get Redemption eventually."

"But what about the baby, Duncan? I don't want to end up like Rosalind or Tilly. I want to keep my child with me."

"What about the Hill, Elimina? You got a life to live too."

"I want to go to the Hill, and I hope this letter gets there and that the Freemans can come for us both. But I can't rely on hope, Duncan. I don't want to go to the Hill if it means I go alone."

Duncan wanders the room, pacing and rubbing his head while I sit there thinking about life in the Gutter.

"Maybe the Hill was never meant to be," I say, clearing the thickness in my throat. "I was born in the Gutter. Maybe Lulabelle was right. Maybe you never should have taken me from there. Now I'm just going back. Starting over. Making things right. Maybe that's where I belong."

Duncan shakes his head, squatting down in front of me and holding my hands. "Where we are is where we belong. What you got to think hard about right now, Elimina, is what kind of life you want to live—where you want to be and who you want to be with. You got to be sure on that. Because debt, it can hurt just like a wound."

"I want this baby. I want a life with my son. Like you and Lulabelle have. I'm willing to go anywhere to get that."

He rubs his hand over his mouth like it's not the response he wants. "And you're *sure* it's not better for your boy if you go to the

Hill alone? I know how one choice can eat away at everything that comes after. It can swallow you whole, Elimina. Trust me."

"Duncan, how can this baby survive if he's alone, if he thinks the person who brought him into this world gave him up? I know what that's like. He'll wonder about me forever. He'll think about me every day and feel a hole, even if he pretends he doesn't. Tilly, Isobel, Violet, the project cases, every person I ever met at Livingstone Academy—they all lost their families this way. It's not good. We're not good, Duncan. And the girls who come here, to Riverside, to Miss Charlotte's—we're doing it all over again. Giving our babies away. Growing up apart. This is my only family. And what if he's all the family I'll ever have?"

Duncan looks out on Main Street and watches the marked vans come and go.

"You're healthy and good and loving, Duncan, and your mother is right here. Like she's always been. What if that's what I need to do? What if that's what *we* need to do, stick together? No matter what," I say, holding my hand on my belly and thinking of Josephine and David and our nights in the Fieldhouse, of Saturday nights with Violet, Tilly and Isobel. "What if greatness only happens when we're together, when we don't let them pull us apart?"

Duncan turns to me, head tilted to one side, chewing his lip and rubbing his beard.

"Duncan, if I don't do anything, they'll take him, and I won't ever see him again. And I don't think I can live with that. I need your help. Please."

Duncan reaches out and pulls me close, and I cry into his chest like he's the father I'll never know.

27

A MONTH AFTER TILLY'S ARREST, I WAKE UP ONE MORN-
ing to find the door to Isobel's room wide open and the
sheets stripped from her bed. Her mattress is bare and
sunken in the middle, like an invisible body is there. I
wake up Violet and we hurry downstairs as quickly as we can. Miss
Charlotte is standing in the kitchen making breakfast, yolk dripping from a broken shell.

"Where's Isobel?"

"Well, good morning to you too, Elimina," Miss Charlotte
says, eyebrows raised like she's expecting an apology that I refuse
to give. "I was waiting to tell the two of you the good news over
breakfast."

"What good news?" Violet says, her voice sharp and angry,
like she already knows anything but good news is coming next.

"Isobel had her baby last night."

"She's gone?" I say, and Miss Charlotte nods, humming a
happy yes.

"When? How? Where did she go?" Violet says.

Miss Charlotte cracks another egg, letting the yolk ooze into
the bowl. "She's fine. She asked me to say goodbye to both of you."

"I didn't hear any noise last night," I say.

"When I checked on her, she said she was feeling a little pain, so I took her down to Doc Luca's. Her water broke, and by morning the baby was out. Things go rather smoothly when you stay healthy and do as you're told," Miss Charlotte says, grabbing a fork and whipping it through the eggs.

"Did she go back to the Allisters?" Violet says.

"That's not something I can discuss."

"Why?"

"That's between Isobel and her employer, Elimina," Miss Charlotte says. "It has nothing to do with the two of you. What *you* need to know is that Isobel has been suitably compensated, and that she's at a good place of employment. That's all I want for you ladies. That is why you're here."

But I can tell by the way she turns away from us that what happened to Isobel is exactly what we all feared: the Allisters took the baby and sent her somewhere else. And all I can think about is how lonely and scared she must have felt delivering the baby alone, how horrible it would have been to see her baby go and to know the Allisters didn't want her.

When Miss Charlotte asks us to set the table, Violet and I slowly gather dishes and cutlery, carefully arranging three place settings at a table that suddenly feels empty.

"Are the new girls coming soon?" Violet says, as Miss Charlotte leans the frying pan forward and distributes scrambled eggs on each plate.

"There are no new girls just yet," she says, dropping the empty pan in the sink.

"Why?"

"I think it will be good for the two of you to have your own rooms. It will make things a little more comfortable," she says, sitting down at the table and spreading a napkin over her lap. "I know how much you like the river, Violet, so I figured you might like to take the room across the hall."

"I'm not changing rooms," Violet says, her jaw rigid and tight as I scoop eggs into my mouth. "And neither is Elimina."

Miss Charlotte finds me on a stool in the front yard assembling flower baskets, while Violet plants near the bench in the back. She sits down on the front porch and watches me from the same place I sat on the morning of Tilly's delivery, and I try to hide my anger and frustration. I don't want to get taken away in the middle of the night like Sarah. I don't want her to know I resent her.

"Elimina, why don't you come and take a break?" she says.

I sigh with my back to Miss Charlotte, pushing up from the stool and leaving the small gardening tools on the ground, while Miss Charlotte pours a glass of cold tea.

"I know the last few weeks have been difficult," she says, handing me the glass. "I just want to make sure you're ready to go back to Livingstone. I know you have big plans for the Hill."

"I'm ready," I say, slow and careful, so my words sound calm and certain.

"I know you were close to Tilly," she says. "And Isobel."

"We're all close," I say, as though they're not significant attachments, even though they are. "Gutter folks are always saying goodbye, Miss Charlotte. You just get used to it eventually."

But this is a lie. Every goodbye hurts, sharp and deep, and suddenly I understand why Ida stays in the basement of the academy and prefers to live alone.

"I know it's hard to see them go," Miss Charlotte says.

I nod, sipping tea that's cold and bitter on my tongue. "Is that why you aren't bringing in any new girls?"

She stares down into her cup. "It's been a hard month. I could use the rest. Maybe a little vacation," she says. "Trust me, Elimina, I only want you and Violet to be comfortable. I thought Violet might like her own room. The water seems to calm her."

I nod because it's true. Violet sits on the bench every day and watches the river, collecting her rocks.

"What happened to Tilly was not what I wanted," Miss Charlotte says. "But she's a stubborn girl, and that stubbornness was bound to get the best of her eventually."

"She just wanted to be a mother," I say.

"Is that what you want, Elimina? To be a mother?"

"No, Miss Charlotte. I don't want a baby at all. I want to go to the Hill and pay off my debt. That's all."

She smiles and nods, and I can tell this makes her happy and that she believes what I've said.

"You've got an excellent opportunity there," she says. "You'll be out in no time."

"Duncan and Lulabelle are the only people I've ever met who've actually done it. Do you think I really have a chance?"

"I'll be honest. It's hard, Elimina. But not in the way you might think. It's not any more difficult than working here or being a tailor like Duncan or even a doctor like Thomas. But there are just so many temptations for you. Distractions that can get in your way. Which is why I think you will do it. I think you, more than anyone, know how to avoid those temptations."

"Temptations?" I say.

"Relationships and bad influences that can lead you astray. You have to know what's really important, so those kinds of distractions don't add to your debt. I think you're the kind of girl who's learned an important lesson by being at a place like this."

A Gutter man with a foot that curves inward makes his way

down Main Street, and we sit there for a moment, sipping tea, as I watch him limp down the road, toward the bridge.

"Do you like it here, Miss Charlotte?"

"I think it's no better or worse than anywhere else. But yes, I like it. I like it a lot."

I think about the gentle weather in Capedown and the paved roads, the fancy buildings and the boardwalk. I think of all the people in town who hated that Mother picked Capedown as the place she wanted to live and raise me, how she had to fight so hard and give up so much. And even though I wish I'd known more, and that things had been different, I wonder if I have what it takes to be that kind of mother.

"Do you think Tilly could have been a good mother, Miss Charlotte? If things were different?"

"A baby requires structure and safety and discipline, Elimina. Tilly couldn't provide any of those things. She didn't even demonstrate them herself. It would have been very difficult to go back to work after what she did to herself, don't you think?"

"She loved that baby," I say, trying hard not to show how much I despise everything Miss Charlotte says and does. "I should get back to work. Thank you for the drink, Miss Charlotte."

She smiles at me, but when I step down to the yard, Miss Charlotte stands too, like there's something else she wants to tell me.

"What Tilly did was not love, Elimina. It was selfishness. She could have really hurt the baby. And she certainly hurt herself. That's not what good mothers do."

I nod like I agree with her, like I don't see what Miss Charlotte can't accept—that Gutter life requires us to make impossible decisions, ones she'll never understand.

28

A GROUP OF GUARDS GATHER ON MAIN STREET ON SATurday night, yelling and laughing so their voices rise and spread. I read a few poems to Violet while she sits on her bed, watching the guards move about. When I'm done, she sits quietly for a moment, like there's something she wants to say but doesn't know how.

"You remember those guys who hired me?" she says.

"Yeah."

"Well, they didn't hire us to help with travel."

I tell her that Rowan had a bad feeling about them, and she smiles as though this is funny.

"Rowan's a genius," she says, and we both laugh.

"How bad was it?" I say, because I can tell by the way she's sitting up in her bed, twisting her bedsheets, that she finally wants to talk about it.

"We lived in this crummy place that felt cold and wet—like the basement at the academy, only worse. My bones always hurt," she says.

The men outside start shouting someone's name—Marianne or Mary Ellen. They're laughing and screaming as though they're calling out for her, and I wonder if she was one of the girls before Sarah or if they're lost at the wrong end of town.

"Mainland men would stop by and we would dance with them or talk . . . More if they wanted. Whatever they were willing to pay for," she says. "That's why I hate this place. These men. They remind me of them. They smell like them. I can't stand it."

There are two places in Riverside where men go to meet with women, places where the windows are always covered and the front entrance is never used, only the one in the side alley. And my heart breaks at the thought of Violet paying her debts that way, with her body.

"Some of the guys who came to see me were just lonely, you know. And it was weird. Because they were married. They had kids. And they were still so lonely. But some of them were awful. Ugly. Like them," she says, nodding toward the street, where the men are still shouting. "I could tell when they looked at me that they hated me, and I hated everything about them—the way their hands felt like straw. I hated the way they rushed and pressed with their sweaty, red faces all twisted up. But I tried my best to make them feel good, like they were wanted. Like they were special. Because isn't that what everyone wants, to feel wanted? All I wanted was their money."

I climb onto Violet's bed, and she leans her head against me. We sit there for a while without saying anything, but when I ask her if her debt manager knew what was going on, she huffs and shakes her head, like the very thought of him makes her angry.

"Jameson Wells," she says, pursing her mouth, so her face looks pointy and sharp. "I told him I couldn't do it, that I wanted to find somewhere else to work where I could make more money, where I didn't have to be doing . . . what I was doing. He told me that if I left, I would get a fine. That it would ruin my chance at Redemption Freedom. He said it was best to stay with the Jungs and find *creative ways of making money.*" She turns to me, her eyes sad, like she's apologizing. "I didn't want to give up on Redemption Freedom, Elimina. I couldn't. I don't have what Josephine and David have. A real family. I don't have anything or anyone back there. And you saw how it went at the fair. I didn't think I had any other options . . . So I did it."

"Did what?"

"I was making decent money with the Jungs. But it was going to take a long time. And how long could I do that kind of work? The other girls were saying that when you couldn't do the work anymore or when the men didn't want you, they would just send you back to the Gutter. They can do that, you know. Jameson told me that if I was willing, I could cut my debt in half, maybe more. He couldn't pay me in cash. But he could . . . he could fix the books, he said."

I squint one side of my face so she knows I don't understand.

"Adjust my debt so it looked like I was making more. He said he could get me debt-free in just a few years if I just did a few things for him." She shakes her head back and forth, like she doesn't believe her own words. "So I went to him whenever I could. In his car when we were supposed to be meeting. In the rooms meant for clients. 'Yes. Oh yes, debt-free. Debt-free, baby,' he would say before and after and during. It was awful. I kept asking him how much, how much more, and he would just say, 'Trust me, you're going to be free before you know it, Vi.' That's what he called me. Vi. And I hated it. The name. The feel of him. The look on his face when he grinned. I hated all of it."

Outside the window, the streets are quieter now, except for one man with yellowish hair and a messy, undone uniform, who wanders down the road singing as loud as he can: "*Baby, you got me for life. Baaaybeee, you got me for liiiiife.*"

"I'm so ashamed," Violet whispers, shaking her head.

"Violet, it's not your fault. None of this is your fault. You have nothing to be ashamed of."

"But I believed him. I did all of that because . . . because I wanted a way out so badly, and I thought he could give it to me faster. But I wasn't smart. I wasn't careful."

She looks down at her belly, like she wishes the baby wasn't there.

"Is the baby his?"

She nods. "The Jungs were very strict about . . . protection. For good reason, it seems. But Jameson didn't want to. That was part of the deal. Do you think he knew this would happen? Do you think he's done this before?"

I squeeze her tight as she covers her face with her hands.

"Did he give you those bruises?" I say, and she looks up and shakes her head.

"No. *That* was the Jungs. They wanted the other girls to know what happens when you don't follow the rules. 'There are no shortcuts for Gutter girls. Only *dead* ends,' they said. So maybe I'm lucky. At least I'm not dead."

"I'm glad you're here, Violet. I'm glad you're okay."

"I'm not okay, Elimina," she says.

"You know what I mean."

In the street, the man's voice wails even louder.

"I'm going to try and get the best hiring package I can. A new one. The Jungs won't take me back, so it's up to Mr. Gregors. He has to decide if he'll take me back and find a new contract or if he'd rather just keep the money from the original deal."

"*Baaaybeee, you got me for liiiiife,*" the man sings.

"When will you know?"

"Should hear back any day now."

"MPS?"

"Of course," she says, rubbing the side of her stomach and squinting like it hurts. "I could walk back to Mainland City before one of those Network letters gets here."

I nod, thinking about my letter, wondering if Mr. Gregors chose Miss Charlotte's for that very reason—to make it harder to reach out to the Freemans.

"I don't know what I'll do if I don't get another job on the Mainland," she says.

"*Baaaybeee, you got me for liiiiife.*"

"I'm sure everything will be okay, Violet," I say.

She nods, closing her eyes and rubbing her belly, listening to the man on the road.

A LETTER ARRIVES for Violet a few days later, and she spends most of the afternoon gathering rocks and adding them to her collection. I don't ask about the contents, but when we lie down in our beds later that evening, I start talking about how nervous I am about having the baby, hoping she'll stay awake and share something.

"I know you have plans," Violet says.

"What do you mean?" I say, taken aback.

"I see you rush off to the Manor. I see the way you smile and rub your belly when Miss Charlotte isn't looking. I know you, Elimina. I know you want that baby."

I've been visiting Lulabelle and Duncan every day after chores, making plans with hushed voices at Cranberry Manor and inside Duncan's shop. We talk about the baby's arrival, and whenever we have time, Duncan tells stories about the Upper End neighborhoods or the Corridor and the blocks in the Lower End.

"The Network will look out for you. You're not in this alone," Duncan said.

I don't write our plans down out of fear that Miss Charlotte might see it or find it in my drawer. But when I go to bed each night, I repeat the things I've learned over and over so I won't forget, just like the story Ida shared at the academy.

"You don't have to tell me your plan, Elimina . . . but if you wind up in the Gutter . . . you could look me up," she says, her voice soft and cracking.

"Why? What did Mr. Gregors say in the letter?"

Violet sits up carefully, rotating her belly as she retrieves a few sheets of paper from under her bed. "'Upon careful review of the case, it has been determined that due to medical reasons, Violet Masters, Case Number 73956, has been determined to be unemployable.'"

"*Unemployable?* What does that mean?"

"It's from Jameson's agency. Mr. Gregors sent it back with his response. He said that because of this letter, I'll never find work anywhere on the Mainland. Ever."

"Ever?"

She nods and her lips begin to quiver. "After the baby is born, I'll be going back to the Gutter for good."

"They can't do that, Violet. They can't just declare you unemployable when you're willing and able to do the work."

But I know, even as I say this, that they can do whatever they want.

"Why is it so hard for them to care about us, Elimina? Don't they know how hard it is already? Why do they make things harder? Why do they enjoy being cruel?"

I climb onto Violet's bed and let her cry into me. "I don't know, Violet. I don't know," I say, shaking my head.

"It's all over for me, Elimina. Miss Charlotte will take the baby and then I'm done. Back to the Gutter," she says.

"It's not over, Violet. It's not over at all. We can do this together now. We're going to find a way to be okay together over there. It's not over," I say, and she looks at me with wide teary eyes as I rub her back in slow circles.

29

ON MY LAST SCHEDULED VISIT WITH DOC LUCA, HE shakes my hand and pats me on the shoulder as if he's proud. He tells me that the baby is healthy and strong and should arrive in the next week—that before I know it, I'll be on my way back to Mainland City and on to the Hill.

"Thank you," I say with a big smile, trying hard not to look nervous and afraid, hoping I don't give anything away.

"If the baby doesn't want to come on its own, there are ways to help things along. Sometimes, these little ones need a nudge," he says. "But I have a good feeling about you, Elimina."

LULABELLE PLACES HER hands around my stomach later that morning in her yellow room at Cranberry Manor. She squeezes my belly like it's fruit and listens with her ear pressed against it, as though the baby is talking to her at a frequency only she can hear.

"Baby's right about ready," she says. "This fella's an early riser, Little Lima."

She smiles the way she does every time I visit, as though just seeing me brings her joy, and I tell her what I didn't tell Doc Luca, about the strange pains and the squeezing that happens throughout the day.

"Those are the beginnings," she says, when I describe the tightness and the slow letting go that I feel in my belly. "Next, we wait for the pain."

"The pain? Lulabelle, it hurts already."

"That's just tickles, Little Lima. Just you wait."

THE REAL PAIN comes two days later, during Saturday night dinner. I try not to jolt or choke as I swallow down mashed potatoes, but I feel a sharp fire that starts in my back and pulls tight around my waist like a rope.

"Don't leave the house for any reason. Keep an eye on each other," Miss Charlotte says before leaving for poker.

When she's gone, I hunch over and bang on the table, startling Violet. "The baby's coming," I say.

Violet pushes her chair back and waddles upstairs. She returns with my bag, the carving and the blue book of poems, which she holds out to me.

"That's your book, Violet. That's yours from home."

"Home means nothing to me, Elimina. You know that."

"But it's yours."

"When I come, we'll read them," she says. "But you'll need this till I get there. It will help. Plus, I practically have them all memorized."

"Then you keep the statue. We'll put it in our new place when you get there."

"Our place," she says, and we both smile.

A burst of pain comes, and I hunch over while Violet stays

close, rubbing my back and reciting a poem about a baby that lives across a wide river to help me stay calm. I breathe in and out in short little huffs, and when the poem is done and the pain is gone, I stand up with Violet's help.

"Don't forget to fill the bed with sheets in case she checks on us tonight," I say. "But not too much. Not too obvious. Because—"

"I know, Elimina."

"In the morning, you tell her that I went into labor, that the phone was broken, and that—"

"That you insisted on going to Doc Luca's alone," she says, grinning widely.

"Why are you smiling?"

"Because you've turned into a mother already, Elimina. I'll be fine. I'll remember everything you told me. I promise."

I smile, and I try to think of something meaningful to say, something more, but all I can think of is thank you. "Thank you for everything, Violet."

"Yeah, yeah, yeah. You gotta go, Elimina," she says, ushering me out the door and handing me a bag she grabs from the yard with one of my dresses soaked in blood.

"Where did you get this?"

"You're not the only clever one, Elimina," she says. "Put this in an alley on the way, past Duncan's. We want them to think you had the baby, right? That something happened to you after the baby was born?"

I look at the dress, remembering the rat she placed in my bed at the academy and the blood she smeared on the wall.

"Violet, what if something goes wrong?" I say, taking the bag and standing there, like I'm not ready to go after all.

"You'll be fine," she says, holding me tight as I nod into her shoulder.

"I'll see you at the bridge?" I say, stepping away.

"At the bridge," she says with a small smile.

IT TAKES ME twice as long to get to Duncan's shop with all the pain and contractions. I pass by guards who hoot and holler, and I make sure to be seen by a few who are sober. I place the dress in the alley next to the Country Store, and I double back to Duncan's, hiding in the shadows along the way.

Duncan is waiting in the shop in a fancy suit, his hair and beard neatly trimmed, and when I'm safely inside, certain that no one has noticed me, I lean up against the wall to catch my breath. "I think you're overdressed," I say, grunting at the pain and holding my waist.

"Told the nurses I was taking Momma on a date," he says, as he guides me to the back of the shop. "You ready?"

I nod, and he opens the door to a room full of fabrics and baskets that have been pushed to the side to make room to deliver the baby. The counters are clear, except for an iron, and there's a small table against the wall covered in clean blankets and fresh towels.

"I'll be right back, Elimina," he says, before stepping out of the room and locking the door behind him.

When a contraction comes, I lean against the table with my hands clasped around the edge, grunting with my face pressed into the blankets. I count to ten, then down again. When the contractions start to come quicker and the squeezing pain gets worse, I feel certain that I'm going to die, just like Rosalind, but with my baby trapped inside me.

"Hurry up. Hurry up, please," I say, hovering over the table with my belly hanging down, my hips swaying in the air.

"This place is a mess. But I've seen worse. I have definitely seen worse," Lulabelle says when the door to the storeroom finally opens.

"Momma, I did what I could," Duncan says.

She places her hands on my belly and clicks her tongue at her son. "Well, looks like we're going to have a baby today. Let's get you up on this table so we can see how soon."

Her voice is calm and clear, and Duncan smiles proudly. "We're almost there," he says.

Lulabelle coaches me through the contractions, paying careful attention to the changes in my body and adjusting my position so that I'm as comfortable as possible when she finally instructs me to push.

"Gotta use all that energy to press out, right here," she says, with her hand inside my body. "No screaming. Just push."

I close my eyes and press as hard as I can, grunting and groaning, over and over, until it feels like I've come unplugged, like a piece of me that was stuck inside has slipped out. When Lulabelle places something small and slimy on my chest, I open my eyes to see a tiny brown face.

His eyes open and then they close, and I stare at his tiny fingers and the wiggle of his mouth.

"He's so quiet," I whisper as Lulabelle and Duncan watch.

"Babies only cry when they need something. It seems this one's got everything he wants," Duncan says, and when I look at my son, satisfied in my arms, I cry messy and hard.

As soon as Lulabelle takes the baby, I know we have to move quickly, that I can't rest or wait until I feel strong. I've got to get through those gates before morning, just like Duncan said, before Miss Charlotte knows I'm gone.

"Get through those gates as quickly as possible and you're fine. No matter what your headmaster wants, or what happens with

Miss Charlotte and Doc Luca, it's near impossible to get folks out once they've gone back inside. Debt is all Mainland governments care about. Giving it to you and holding you to it," Duncan said. "So just get in there quick as you can."

But when I look over, he and Lulabelle are whispering over the baby, not rushing at all.

"We've got to go," I say, trying to sit up.

"Whoa, whoa," Duncan says, turning to me, while Lulabelle gently washes the baby with a sponge. "The boy doesn't even have a name yet."

"You've got to name him, child," Lulabelle says.

"Duncan Jackson Dubois," I say. "Little Duncan."

Duncan pauses, scratching at his beard and his head like he's not sure what to do with his hands. "I'm grateful. I certainly don't deserve it after what I've done."

"Well, Lulabelle didn't seem like quite the right fit," I say, and we all laugh as Duncan fiddles with the iron.

"Duncan, is everything okay?" I say, but he doesn't respond, and when I hear a sound like meat frying in a pan followed by a loud, sharp cry from the baby, I try to sit up again, groaning at the pain in my belly and between my legs.

"Duncan, Lulabelle, what's wrong with him?"

Lulabelle scoops the baby up, bouncing him up and down until he calms, and when I reach my arms out to hold him, Duncan moves toward me with something in his hand.

"Just be still, Elimina," he says, and before I can say anything, he grabs my wrist and I feel it—a searing pain as a hot piece of metal burns an X onto my left hand.

THE GUTTER

30

O N THE ROAD INTO CAPEDOWN, THE SIGN THAT stretched over the highway read, "The Most Beautiful Town on the Coast." But from the peak of Dead Man's Bridge, all I can see is "GUTTER" painted in white across a gate that's red like blood. I feel the weight of my child, and the pain of his birth, and the feeling of every one of my possessions piled on the bend of my back as I cross over the river in darkness.

I stop on the bridge, facing the wall that runs around the Gutter, filled with overwhelming doubt. *Maybe Miss Charlotte was right. Maybe I don't know how to be a good mother. Maybe I shouldn't go any farther. Maybe I should go back.* But when I place my hand on DJ's body, hidden under a long black cloak, and when I feel his tiny bones and the slow rise and fall of his chest, I know that I have to keep going.

"Move fast. And when you get to the top of the bridge, move slow," Duncan said. "Pretend like your body is broken, like no employer on the Mainland would want you."

But I don't have to pretend. My body is split open, bleeding and burning from the fresh push of a child who was marked and scarred the moment he came into the world.

A sharp pain rushes through, and I place both hands on the

railing of the bridge, listening to the rush of Freedom River, the sound of the cool water below. I hold my breath and wait for the pain to leave just as a Mainland Guard van heads toward me, covering me in white light.

Are they coming for us?

The van passes, and I let out a deep, shaky breath.

Move.

I watch the red taillights as the van stops in front of the gate. The driver climbs down and opens the back doors, letting four Gutter men and one Gutter woman pour out, rubbing their backs and their necks.

A tall guard with a sharp nose moves toward them, counting the passengers and waving up at the wall. "Five coming through," he yells.

"Five coming through," someone shouts back as the red gates swing open like a hungry mouth.

"Let's go. Keep it moving, Gutters. Straight through," he says, and when he sees me hobbling toward them, he groans and shakes his head. "*Six* coming through. I repeat, *six* coming through."

WE WATCH THE gate close from the other side of the wall while I look around for signs of someone from the Network and the building that could be the Reporting Office. But all I see are Mainland Guards walking around a large area enclosed by a tall metal fence with barbed wire curling across the top.

"Alright, we're going to head to that brick building up ahead. Slow, so we don't lose anyone," the guard says, and I know that he's talking about me. "Stay on the main path and under the lights. If you move to the left or the right, I'll be right here to make you sorry for it."

We pass armored tanks and emergency vehicles parked along the wide oval road that loops around a large grassy field with a brightly lit General Covey statue in the middle.

Before I left Riverside, I asked Duncan every question I could imagine about the Reporting Office and what might happen when I get there. "What if they don't believe me? What if they just want DJ? What if they want to send us both back to Miss Charlotte's?"

"Just give them the letter," Duncan said, handing me two envelopes, which I slid into each of my pockets.

The first letter looks just like the one that came from Violet's debt manager. Only this one says that Lima Jenkins Sinclair is medically unfit for the Mainland, with the forged signature of Dr. Thomas D. Luca. There's a second letter for DJ, but the goal is to get into the Gutter without anyone knowing he's here.

I walk gingerly as the burn between my legs grows stronger, and when we reach the brick building, the guard stands in the doorway, holding it open. He instructs the rest of the group to sit while I climb the stairs slowly, sweaty and drained from all of the walking, my bandaged hand sore and pulsing.

"Don't touch anything. Just sit and don't move until I tell you," he says when I'm finally inside.

"Is this the Reporting Office?" I whisper.

But the guard doesn't answer. He just points at the chairs.

I use the long counter at the front of the room for support, hobbling to the end of the waiting area so I'm as far away from the guard as possible, standing next to the woman from the van.

"Sit," the guard says.

"I . . . I can't," I say, because even though I want to sit and rest my legs, I worry that too much moving and bending will wake DJ.

"What do you mean you can't sit?" the guard says while the five passengers from the van watch me.

"I just can't," I say, closing my eyes and leaning against the wall, shifting side to side to manage the discomfort and to keep DJ quiet.

"You want to stand, then stand. Just stand," the guard says, raising his hands in the air before stepping outside for a smoke.

I take two long, deep breaths, and when the door shuts completely with the six of us inside, the four men from the van lean their heads back and close their eyes as the guard watches us from outside.

"Name's Molly," the woman whispers, standing up and stretching her arms, twisting side to side.

"Lima," I say, remembering to use the same name that's on the letter, the one Rosalind wanted me to have. "Do you know what we're doing here? Or how long this will take? Do you know if this is the Reporting Office?"

Now that we've stopped moving and we're in a quiet room, I can hear DJ's every grimace and see every movement, and I wonder how long it will be before someone else notices.

"I'm not too sure," Molly says. "Shouldn't be long."

"What are we waiting for?"

"Processing. Get our docs all up-to-date for return. That's my guess."

"Docs?"

"Documents, honey," she says, waving her letter, and I nod, reaching down in my right pocket.

But what if this doesn't work? What if the Network doesn't come?

"How old?" Molly whispers.

"Me?" I say, and she shakes her head, pointing at my cloak and leaning close.

"I'm gonna guess by the way you're walking and the way you're holding your chest that there's a baby in there that's fresh."

I look at her wide-eyed, my eyes spinning around the room until I'm certain no one else has heard or noticed. "He's very new. Very fresh."

"They're precious then," Molly whispers, letting a little smile come to her mouth, as the guard comes back in.

"Don't you worry," she whispers. "If that baby stays good and quiet like it's doing right now, these men won't notice. And if the baby grunts, I'll just blame it on gas."

I laugh into my hand as a tall guard with a thin mustache and a crooked mouth enters. He steps behind the counter and pulls out some paper, a pen and a pad of ink from a drawer.

"How many we got?" he says to the guard at the door.

"Six. But only five listed. The one at the end's a medical," he says, handing him a clipboard and nodding in my direction.

The new guard looks over the list, studying each name. "Alright, who's first? Which one of you is Gerard Smith?"

A man in grease-stained overalls looks up, peering down the row of chairs at the rest of the passengers from the van.

"Come on, Gutter. Let's go. I got other things I'd rather be doing this early in the morning. Don't slow me down."

The man moves toward the counter and slides the guard his letter. "Um, sir. It's Gerald, not Gerard. Sir."

"Gerald Carter Smith? Is that right, then?" the guard says, and when the man nods, he continues. "Fine. Great. Sign right here."

When the rest of his information is confirmed—his school, his employer and the reason for his release—the guard presses Gerald's fingers into the ink, then onto a paper, before calling the next person on the list. "Martin Lewis."

A young man in a crumpled brown suit moves to the counter, and when I pull out the collar of my cloak and peek down, I find DJ smacking his mouth.

"Where you headed, Lima? Where you from?" Molly whispers.

"I . . . um . . . I don't really know," I say.

"What do you mean you don't know? You don't remember where your family is at? I mean, shoot, it can't be that long since you been here. You got to remember who your people are."

But when I look at her with teary eyes, she looks almost as worried as I am, and I wonder if I've made a horrible mistake coming here like this, alone.

"You live in one of the blocks, honey? Or in the Upper End?" she says, looking back at the guards with concern that only adds to my nerves.

I shut my eyes, breathing in and out like I might faint if I don't get fresh air.

"Breathe, honey. Breathe," Molly says, rubbing my back, while I lean into the wall.

"Alright, ladies," the guard says when all of the men have been processed. "Which one of you is Molly Highwater?"

Molly raises her hand and moves toward the guard slowly, looking back at me, like she wants to make sure I'm okay.

"Academy?" the guard says.

"Kingston House."

"Job?"

"Well, I been working as a maid since graduation."

"And what brings you back?"

She tells the guard that her boss gambled away his money and had to cut some expenses, and I wonder if she's making the story longer to give me more time to get ready.

"Couldn't afford me. But if you're looking for someone to take care of your bunk or clean up around here, I'm very afford-able," she says, but he just points down at the ink, waiting as she rolls and presses each finger on the paper.

When Molly is done, the guard looks at his list, carefully counting each name before motioning for me to come.

"Alright, your turn," the guard says, tapping the counter with his pen. "Name?"

I move slowly toward the counter. "Lima," I say, as the door to the Reporting Office swings open.

Everyone turns and looks at an older Gutter woman standing in the doorway wearing a white apron with a red X on the chest. She has a badge around her neck, a mask over her face and rubber gloves that reach to her elbows.

"I'm looking for Lima Jenkins Sinclair," she says, studying Molly before moving toward me, like she knows I'm the person she's looking for. "Are you Lima?"

"Yes," I say softly, because something about the way she looks at me makes me afraid.

DJ shifts and grunts, and when I rest my hand against him, I see how the sternness in her eyes softens, how she notices what none of the men seem to see.

"Come with me," she says.

"Now, wait just a minute," the guard at the counter shouts out. "She needs to be processed."

"What she needs is to go straight to Medical," the woman says.

"You got docs to say so?" the guard says, and I nod as he holds his hand out toward me.

"We were told to expect a Medical Alert Case this morning, but I didn't receive a call. Did any of you call?" the woman says as I place the letter in his outstreached hand.

The guard at the door shrugs and the guard at the counter lowers his head to read the letter while the woman urges me to move toward her with a quick wave.

"I'll process her at the Medical Center, and I'll bring her docs back as soon as they're ready," she says when I get to the door. "You're supposed to call Medical from the gate so we can test them at the Center, so they don't go contaminating everyone if they've got something serious. This is exactly how that virus spread the last time when half of your guards went down. You-all brought folks in here instead of sending them to us because you didn't want to wait, and look what happened. A good handful are in that graveyard on the other side of the Base."

The men from the van wiggle in their seats, and both of the guards stand taller. But Molly pounds her chest and coughs like whatever I might have has gone inside her. I bite my lip to hold back a smile as I follow the woman in the white apron out of the Reporting Office.

THE GUTTER MEDICAL CENTER is a pale-green building just beyond the Base. When we pass through the front doors and into the lobby, I shake my bag off and unbutton the cloak, letting the cool air touch my skin as DJ's eyes flutter at the light.

The woman in the white apron removes her mask and her gloves, tossing them in a bin, and when I ask her if she's with the Network or if she knows where I'm supposed to go next, she just looks at DJ and shakes her head.

"My name is Geneva Jackson. I'm not with the Network, Lima. I'm Rowan's mother," she says. "And you're coming with me."

I can tell by the cold tone in her voice and her stony expression that even though she came to get us, she's not happy we're here, and when I look down at DJ, I don't know whether to feel relieved or worried.

31

THE STREETS BACK IN CAPEDOWN CURVED IN NEAT PAT-
terns and rows with names like Mary and George. But in
the Upper End, the houses are different sizes and colors,
twisted along straight roads with signs that only use numbers. Everywhere we turn, people with faces just like mine smile
and say hello, and I realize that even though I may not be welcome
at Geneva's, I finally look like I belong.

Geneva doesn't say a word during the walk from the Medical
Center, and despite the food and supplies that boosted my strength
there, all I can think about is lying down in an actual bed for the
first time since yesterday.

When Geneva turns up the front steps of a small yellow house,
two girls in pink pajamas come out to greet us, their hair braided
in neat sections with pink plastic bows on the ends.

"Nana G!" the girls shout, wrapping their arms around Geneva.

"Good morning, girls," she says as she kisses the tops of their
heads.

"Daddy's here and so's Mommy," the smaller girl says, and I
close my eyes, tired at the thought of meeting more strangers today.

"Of course Mommy's here," the older girl says. "How would
we get here if she wasn't, dummy?"

"Beula, don't call your sister names," Geneva says, and the older girl scowls at her sister.

"Is that a real baby?" the smaller girl says, and when I nod, her eyes grow wide as she looks at her sister.

"How old?" Beula says.

"About half a day," I say.

The two girls look at each other with big toothy grins, and I think about how lovely it must be to have a sister, how nice it would be to grow up with someone just like you.

"Can I hold it?" the smaller girl says.

"It's not an it, Reina. It's a . . . Is it a boy or a girl?" Beula says.

"His name is DJ."

"It's a boy," Beula says to Reina, and when I remove him from the wrap, the two girls move even closer.

Geneva shoos the girls away and scoops DJ up out of my arms. "Everyone . . . this is DJ," she says as she carries him into the house, cradled against her chest.

"I want to see the baby! I want to see him, Nana G!" Reina shouts, and I stand on the porch with sweat leaking through my clothes, unsure whether I should follow them inside.

"Well, come on now, Lima. Don't just stand there. Everyone's waiting," Geneva says.

I turn to enter the house, pulling gently at my shirt and flapping it in the air in the hopes that it'll dry.

Geneva's front door opens into a small living room with a green couch and a large window that faces the backyard. The house smells of bacon and fresh bread, and when I step into the room, the soft carpet squishes under my tired feet.

A young woman with copper hair is sitting on the couch next to a man with a little girl snuggling on his lap.

"I can't believe Ma is doing this, Roger," the woman says, shaking her head.

But Roger doesn't respond. He just leans in and speaks softly to the child. "Haddy, say hello to Auntie."

The little girl pulls her thumb out of her mouth with a small *pop*. "Hi, Auntie," she says, and I smile at this small bit of kindness.

"Shirley, take Lima down to Rowan's room, please," Geneva says. "See that she gets some fresh clothes."

"Ma," she says, trying to protest, but when Geneva raises a finger and points down the hall, Shirley reluctantly obeys.

"Should I . . . take DJ with me?" I say, stepping toward Geneva, who immediately waves me away.

"You just fed him at the Medical Center. He should be fine for a little while. Get yourself tidied up," Geneva says, like I'm being dismissed from a job.

I follow Shirley down a narrow hallway, and I study the pictures on the wall. I lean toward a picture of young Rowan wearing a pair of oversized boxing gloves and a tall girl squeezing his shoulders while Shirley waits, tapping her foot and crossing her arms. "So, you're Rowan's sister?"

"I am," she says, like all she wants is for me to hurry up so she can get back to doing something else.

"And those girls, the ones in pink . . . those are all Rowan's nieces?"

She nods, showing me the shower and the bedroom and handing me a pile of her old clothes.

"Shirley, did I do something? Should I . . . ?"

"Don't play that game with me. You've got some nerve coming here," she says.

I want to tell her that I didn't ask to come here, that I was supposed to connect with the Network, but I don't know where to begin.

"Don't stand there and try to act innocent. You know what you did. You and that kid have just ruined everything," she says, and when she closes the door, I climb onto a bed that's meant for a young boy and cry into the pillows.

I WAKE UP from a nap thick with sweat in a blue room with a shelf of tarnished trophies and a pair of old boxing gloves that hangs from the wall. I pull on a fresh T-shirt and step out of the room, worried about where DJ has been while I was fast asleep and how much time has passed since I last fed him.

When I reach the kitchen, Shirley is holding DJ and Geneva is washing dishes. I can hear the girls outside, but there's no sign of Roger, and the dishes from breakfast are all cleared.

"I forgot how small they are when they just come out," Shirley says. "Look at all those wrinkles. It's like he's an old man. Maybe Roger and I should have another one, Ma. Try for a boy."

"Absolutely not," Geneva says, and Shirley laughs.

"Where did everyone go?" I say.

They both turn to look at me but no one says anything as DJ wiggles and stirs, like he's the only one who really cares that I'm here.

"You could have woken me up. He must be ready to eat," I say, moving toward Shirley, who hands him to me without a word.

After my shower, I shoveled down a small plate of eggs and a slice of bread before taking him to the bedroom to be fed. But after he ate, I felt more tired than before, and Geneva insisted I rest, carrying him out of the room before I had a chance to protest.

"Use the chair in the corner to feed him. It's much better for you than the bed," Geneva says.

I sit down in the chair, pulling my shirt up and holding DJ to my chest while Geneva slides pillows underneath him. He clamps down tight, and I try not to show how much it hurts.

"You'll get used to it," she says, returning to her sink full of dishes.

Shirley stands a few feet away, staring out the window at the girls, who are playing with a few boys in the backyard.

"I get to be the boss next," Reina shouts.

"You're too little to be the boss," says one of the boys.

"You can be the boss with me, Ray," Beula says, and when the two girls start to count, Haddy stays and tries to count too while everyone else runs away.

"Roger coming back before he heads out?" Geneva says as DJ guzzles loudly.

"I don't know, Ma," Shirley says, like the question itself makes her tired.

"Oh, don't get all emotional, Shirley. He's fine."

"He's not fine, Ma. Roger is . . . Roger's going to be done at the factory next month," she says, and I can tell by the way Geneva's shoulders sink low that she doesn't approve.

"He's quitting?" Geneva says, dropping a bowl in the sink with a loud thud, so water spills on the counter and over the edge. "We've had this conversation before, Shirley."

"Yes, and it's always the same argument. 'Think of the girls. Think of the girls.' But we are thinking about them, Ma!"

"I think Roger is only thinking about himself."

"Three of his friends died last year from that sickness. Three. In one year. And they all started at the same time. It's a miracle he's still alive."

"You can't beat the pay at the factory," Geneva says. "Or the benefits."

"I know, Ma. But he's gone all the time. He only sees us on weekends. I don't know why they built the factory down in the Lower End and then set us up way up here. It's like they don't want us to even be together."

I watch DJ guzzle, thinking about Rowan, wondering if he knows about the baby, curious if he would ever have a problem being apart from us like Roger.

"The factory is down there because that's where the resources are, Shirley. And you're up here because nobody wants to live in the Lower End."

"Lots of people like living there, Ma."

"No. Lots of people live there because they have no other choice. Mainlanders couldn't care less about how much time a Gutter man gets to spend with his children. But you get a nice house and good money. You can manage."

"I don't want to *manage*, Ma. I don't want Roger working down there."

Geneva looks at her daughter, shaking her head.

"What's wrong with the factory?" I say, swapping DJ from one side to the other as Geneva comes to readjust the pillows.

"There's *nothing* wrong with the factory," she says.

"Ma, you can't be serious. Have you seen the yellow smoke coming out of those pipes? That's what Roger breathes in every time he goes to work. Five days a week, that's what's going into his lungs," she says. "The air is so bad you can taste it in the back of your throat."

"That's a little dramatic," Geneva says.

"When was the last time you were down there, Ma?"

"I've been there plenty of times, Shirley."

"Since Pop left," she says, and Geneva doesn't say anything. "How many times you been to the Lower End since Pop left, Ma?"

"What Shirley isn't telling you, Elimina, is that that factory offers the best-paid work anywhere in the Gutter. The men get Redemption Freedom for their entire family if they put twenty-five years in—and that's on top of their pay. If it wasn't men only, I'd be there myself," Geneva says.

"Ma, do you know how many people have even gotten that Redemption Freedom bonus?" Shirley says, watching her mother. "Do you want to guess how many, Lima?"

I stare up at her, startled by the use of my new name, unsure if she really wants me to answer.

"Since this whole Gutter System nonsense began, there have been nine factory workers to get Redemption Freedom. Nine. It's like they just pick one every so often so folks still believe it's possible."

"Oh, Shirley, that's nonsense and you know it," Geneva mutters.

But all I can think about is the Hall of Heroes at Livingstone Academy—how difficult it must be to get Redemption Freedom if only eight men ever did it, and how impossible it seems for a woman to get it at all.

"Hundreds of men die in that job every year," Shirley says. "And Ma knows better than anyone. She sees them at the Medical Center. She treats them. She's there when the black in their lungs makes it impossible for them to breathe anymore, like they're drowning in their own bodies. And that's what she wants for Roger. That's how much she cares about the father of my children."

"You're talking like the Network, Shirley. Like you have truly lost your mind. What you're doing is shortsighted and it's wrong," Geneva says.

"If they don't finish their twenty-five years to the day, we get nothing, Lima. Not even if it's twenty-four years and 364 days," Shirley says. "One guy finished his twenty-five years sick as a dog. He did everything he was supposed to, but he couldn't pass Mainland medical tests. So they didn't even give it to him then. Didn't want whatever he had spreading on the Mainland. They refused him Redemption Freedom based on a sickness they gave him. Imagine doing all that, and working right to the end, and still not getting out?" Shirley says.

Geneva shakes her head like this is a rumor that's not worth believing—a story that doesn't change anything.

"That's why Roger's leaving, Ma. Because it's a horrible place. Because it will kill him before it ever lets him out."

Geneva spreads a towel out on the counter and places wet dishes on top.

"Do you know what they make down there?" Shirley says.

I shake my head, pulling my shirt down as DJ lies across the pillows, arms limp and dangling, mouth open.

"Shirley, stop with this," Geneva says. "The last thing Lima needs is to get caught up in your conspiracies."

"Guns," Shirley says, raising her eyebrows and nodding her head when I look at her surprised and confused. "That's what they make at the factory. Guns for guards and whoever on the Mainland wants to have them."

I think of the headhunters around Miss Charlotte's and the sound of their guns shooting into the dark.

"They'll sell guns to people across the ocean. But no one in the Gutter is allowed to have a weapon. Nothing sharper than a butter knife. Right, Ma? We make the very bullets they use to shoot us and the guns that do the shooting, but we can't be trusted to have our own. And you know why? Because they're worried about another rebellion. And maybe they should be. I mean, what do we have to lose?"

"So what are you going to do, Shirley? You going to move down to the Lower End and join the Network? Or live on Subsidy?" Geneva says. "For heaven's sake! He's just got ten more years."

"That's ten more years, Ma!" Shirley says, the skin on her forehead stretching as though each crease is filled with a new worry.

"Fine. Be Subs. Ruin your life, Shirley. I don't know why I even bother," Geneva says, and Shirley growls in frustration.

"Subs?" I say.

"Subsidy Cases," Geneva says. "They'd live on government support, collecting checks that are barely enough to survive on. And every check, Shirley, will add to your debt. Remember that."

"I know how it works, Ma."

"But do you get what that means?"

"Of course I do, but—"

"If you become Subs, your debt will be so impossible so fast that your girls will never have a chance at Redemption Freedom. Never. And any children *they* have would have to go to an academy to even have a chance."

"Ma, we can find work. Roger can work. I can work. The girls will work. People do that, you know. We don't have to go on Subsidy," Shirley says.

Geneva places her hand on her chest like her daughter is breaking her heart. "You know what it's like down there, Shirley."

"Ma, this is hard enough."

"Oh, you don't know what hard is, Shirley-girl. You don't think I've had it hard?" she says, nodding in my direction, and I feel my face get warm. "You don't think I want to give up?"

"Ma—"

"You really want to become Subs like Elsa May and those friends of hers? Is that what you want? Fine. Except remember, you won't have a nice house in the Upper End, Shirley. You'll have a crummy apartment down there. Because let me be clear: if Roger quits that job, you-all are not living up here with me. Not so long as I'm alive. You won't bring that life in this house. I won't tolerate it."

"I would never move in here," Shirley says, and the two women stop talking as Geneva unplugs the sink, letting the water drain out.

"My daughter. A Sub," Geneva says eventually, spitting the words out of her mouth.

"Ma, we don't want to become Subs!"

"Then have Roger put in more hours. They say that if you get out at a certain age, there's a lower risk of sickness. Make him work."

"He doesn't want to work there, Ma!"

"Who cares what he wants, Shirley! You know as well as I do that finding another job like that is near impossible. Please. Think this through."

"Am I just supposed to let Roger die? Force him to live down there all week and see his girls only on weekends, and then tell him, 'Oh yeah, by the way, any day now you could start coughing up blood!'?"

Geneva steps closer to Shirley, her voice so low I can hardly make out the words. "Let me tell you something: I couldn't care less what happens to Roger. Do not make his weakness their curse. Let him work, like he should. Keep him healthy as long as you can, as best you can. But don't let him quit."

"It's that simple, is it, Ma? Did you tell Pop to keep working? Did you keep him healthy? Did that work? Cuz I don't see him around here!"

"He didn't have a factory job. But if he did, yes, I would have told him to do that instead. Because all those boxing wins got us nothing but a bunch of worthless trophies. What the hell am I supposed to do with those?"

I sit quietly in the corner as the two of them yell, and I wonder if this is what Shirley meant about ruining everything, if my being here reminds them why Rowan is gone, and why he might never come back.

"I don't work at the Medical Center because I like it," Geneva says. "I don't go out and do twelve-hour shifts six times a week because I *want* to. I do it because I *have* to. Because it gave you and me and your brother the best chance at getting out. That's what my parents wanted for me, and I promised your brother when he left that I would work hard and save too, that it wouldn't all rest on him."

"And how's that working out for you, Ma?" Shirley says. "What are you going to do now that she's here?"

Geneva presses her lips tightly together, pausing for a moment to gather her words. "I have no tolerance for weak men," she says sharply, pointing at her daughter. "And neither should you."

"I'm not like you, Ma. I'm not going to push my family away," Shirley says, stepping outside and calling for the girls without saying goodbye to her mother.

Shirley tells them it's time to go home, and when Beula and Reina complain that it's too early, that they've almost won the war and killed the monsters, Shirley tells them it doesn't matter, that they're leaving anyway, and Haddy throws herself on the ground.

"This is so unfair," Beula says.

"This is so unfair, Mommy!" Reina echoes, while Haddy cries louder and louder.

"Well, sometimes life is just incredibly unfair," Shirley says as she nudges the two girls down the road with a screaming Haddy tucked under her arm, legs kicking in the air.

32

ETWORK LETTERS APPEAR IN THE GUTTER BY WAY OF
Runners, who hide notes from the Mainland inside grocery containers or special deliveries. My first letter arrives
in Geneva's vegetable box—a note from Duncan informing
me of the arrival of Violet's baby three weeks ahead of schedule.

"It was a close call, but the baby is holding on so far," he
writes. "Unfortunately, due to the smallness of the child and some
other complications, little Jewel was declared medically unfit and
will not be going to an academy. As soon as Violet and Jewel are
safe to travel, they'll both be heading your way."

I pause when I read this, staring at each word. Violet didn't
want to come to the Gutter and she didn't want to keep the baby.
Now she has to do both.

"Violet is adjusting to the news," Duncan writes. "But I wanted
to let you know she'll be there a week from today. She'll be fine in
time, Little Lima. Don't worry."

But all I feel is worry. For Violet and for Jewel.

"I hope all is going well and that you've found a place where
you're getting all the rest and Sossi love you deserve. You did
good. Best, Duncan."

I cry over these closing lines because even though we're safe with Geneva, I worry that someone from the Mainland could show up any day and take DJ away.

THE STREETS IN the Upper End run in parallel lines, forming a neighborhood grid. The lower-numbered streets lead to the bridge, while the higher-numbered ones lead toward the main road that curves down to the Lower End. Odd numbers run east to west, and even numbers run north to south, so that by the time I take my second walk with DJ, searching for a place to live with Violet, I feel a confidence and comfort I've never known in any of the other places I've lived. As though no matter where I go, I'll never be lost again.

Geneva's house sits on Fifth, near Eighth—around the center of the Upper End—near a convenience store and a tiny park where hundreds of birds perch in tall trees.

On a hot, blue-sky day, when Geneva is at work, I take DJ to the park to study the birds. I hold him tightly to my chest, watching their wings, imagining what it might feel like to be light enough to soar all the way to the Hill.

"Lima!" a woman says.

I stop at the end of Geneva's walkway, looking in every direction for the person who called my name.

"Lima!"

A woman is standing on the front steps of a lavender house, waving her arms and trying to get my attention.

I cross the street and climb up the steps to a porch where four ladies in floral dresses are seated on white chairs, sharing a pitcher of lemonade.

"I'm so glad to finally meet you," the woman says, adding

74

another chair around the table while the others adjust to make room. "I'm Elsa May. Please, please, have a seat."

Elsa May introduces me to her longtime friends Cecily Smith and the Harper twins, Marley and Marnie. The twins wave hello, almost in unison, while I stare at their hair and their matching green dresses, trying to figure out a way to tell them apart.

"You all know Lima—Rowan's lady," Elsa May says, and the three women nod.

I consider telling Elsa May that I'm not Rowan's "lady," but the women have already moved on.

"May we see the baby?" one of the twins says, smiling and leaning toward DJ, who's tightly wrapped in a thin blanket. When I tilt his face toward them, they all sigh.

"What's the little man's name again?" Elsa May whispers.

"Duncan Jackson," I say. "DJ."

"I tell you, isn't he just the spitting image of Rowan when he was that age," Elsa May says.

"You know, we practically raised Rowan," Cecily says as she takes a sip of lemonade.

"Really?"

"Every time Geneva had to work and Shirley was off doing something, I looked after him," Elsa May says. "Rowan spent just as much time here as he did at his home, if you ask me."

"Mm-hmm. He was something, that Rowan," Cecily says, and the twins nod.

"Kid had muscles on his arms and legs coming out of the womb, just like this one," Elsa May says, squishing DJ's tiny arms between her fingers. "His father had him dancing around that yard from the start. Kid could practically do push-ups and punch before he could walk. Everyone knew he'd be just like his father."

"Do you know about his father?" Cecily says, and I shake my head.

"Champion boxer down in the Lower End. Part of the Gutter Boxing League," Elsa May says. "Everyone knew him here. I mean, he was something. There used to be a ring in every block of the Lower End. Not all of them are still standing, but back in the day, that was where we would go to see all the matches. People thought Rowan Senior might go to the Mainland, that folks out there might hear about him and give him a shot. But he had troubles of his own, demons he couldn't quite punch out, if you know what I mean. Geneva and I were quite close back then."

"How's Rowan? He must be quite handsome," Cecily says, handing me a glass of lemonade.

I smile politely, unsure whether to tell them that it's been almost a year since I last saw him or heard from him, that I have no idea whether he even knows he has a son.

"Guess Miss Geneva ain't getting out like she thought. Least not anytime soon," Cecily says, pursing her lips while Elsa May raises her eyebrows, like she knew this day would come.

"What do you mean?"

"It's not important," Elsa May says.

"But it is important. What did you mean by that? Why isn't Geneva getting out like she thought?"

"She doesn't know," Elsa May says to the other ladies as she watches me closely. "She's a project case. Probably has no idea what she's done."

There's a collective hum of agreement as I wait for them to explain.

"Don't worry," Elsa May says. "It's nothing to be ashamed of. Most folks around here don't want to think about the project. Some have forgotten all about it. Back in the day, there were some up here who hoped to get selected. Filled out the forms and waited, thinking that we legacy families had an advantage, that they'd want to take our babies first. Well, as you know, it was quite the opposite."

The three other women shake their heads with their lemonade glasses resting in their hands.

"My kids are off doing lord knows what. But at least they're alive," Cecily says.

The Harper sisters nod, chattering about how their adult children might have fared on the Mainland.

"My George would have been fine, I think," one of them says. "But your Ebony wouldn't have lasted a year. She would have cried her way back home."

"That may be, Marley. But you're wrong about George. He wouldn't have lasted a week. Look at the way that child eats," Marnie says, and all four women laugh.

"I don't think any of that would have mattered," I say, scowling down at the lemonade. "The project kids didn't die because they were homesick or hungry."

Elsa May and the twins shift in their seats while Cecily sucks in her cheeks.

"You're right, Lima. It turned out to be a terrible tragedy. We should never forget that. May those souls rest in peace," Elsa May says, raising her glass in the air.

"Elsa May, why is Geneva not getting out like she thought? Can you please tell me?"

Elsa May pauses for a moment, sitting up in her chair. "There are two types of folks in the Gutter, Lima," she says. "There are folks who are happy here, who see this place as home, and there are folks who believe home is somewhere beyond those walls."

I nod so she knows I understand.

"Geneva is part of that second group. She believed she could get out of here if she worked hard enough. She's worked at the Medical Center all her life, covering all her bills on her own, paying down what she can and avoiding new debt. I've known all along that her plan was doomed to fail. And if we were still friends, I would have told her as much already, just like I did when we were young. You see, this house is mine, and when I'm gone, one of my kids will live here, and so on and so on. Our family debt is so big they probably don't calculate it anymore, but that doesn't matter much at all. Because this is home. This house and this little bit of land belongs to me and my family. Truth be told, sometimes I think my eldest boy, Frankie, is just waiting for my heart to stop," she says. "When he and his wife come to visit, I swear I've seen that girl measuring for curtains and swapping my medications."

The four women laugh even harder, and when Cecily comments on the sweetness of the lemonade, they start talking about gardens and fruits and vegetables.

"The tomatoes are just not growing as large this year," Marnie says.

Her sister nods. "It's the rain. There's been almost no rain."

"And the heat," Cecily says, dabbing her face with a napkin, as though the very mention of heat makes her warm.

"By the way—"

"What does Geneva's plan have to do with me and DJ?" I say, interrupting Elsa May.

All four women turn to me, mouths slightly open.

"I'm sorry. I didn't mean to interrupt . . . I should go," I say, holding on to DJ with one hand and using the other to help myself stand up.

"Geneva sent Rowan away when he was seven years old

because he had a gift," Elsa May says, placing one hand on my leg so I don't go. "She thought boxing could solve everything. Thought if she could limit her debt and he did well at fighting, they could get out once and for all. And now you're here and that's not going to happen."

I sit back down as I think about my conversations with Rowan back at Livingstone Academy—about his plans to get Redemption Freedom for himself and for his mother.

"Now that Rowan's got himself a son, he's got to work to get DJ's debt and your debts paid off before he can help Geneva," Elsa May says.

I place my fingers to my forehead, trying to understand. It's as though each word is coming in one by one—too slow to assemble and process all at once. "He's got to help us before Geneva? Why?"

"Because they say so," Elsa May says.

"There was a man from the Gutter some time ago—I was just a child when it happened. You remember that, Elsa May?" Cecily says, and Elsa May nods. "I remember Mommy talking and laughing about it with her friends, full of all kinds of hoots and hallelujahs."

"Mm-hmm," the twins say.

"The man had fifteen children with eight different women," Cecily explains. "Took nearly twenty years, but he paid off his debt, and brought along a friend too, by forcing those kids into all kinds of work that was rather . . . unsavory, according to what folks say. And he left all of those kids and all eight mothers behind when he got his Redemption Freedom—each child more messed up than the next."

"No one could stop him from getting out," Elsa May says. "But Mainlanders passed a law after that saying that a man had to bring along his biological children, and their mamas, before he could redeem anyone else."

"Men started making babies far more carefully after that," Cecily says. "No man looking to get out and help their family wants to be tied to a Gutter woman they don't care about. There's enough obstacles without adding all that."

I look down at DJ, who's sleeping quietly in my arms. "Do you think Rowan knows . . . about us, that I'm here?" I say, so quiet it's almost a whisper.

"Oh, yes," Cecily says. "There's a whole department of the Mainland government that handles that. Finds them and lets their debt manager know as soon as a woman is pregnant with their child."

"Too bad they can't seem to find my Oscar," Elsa May mutters.

"Or Rowan Senior," Cecily adds.

"Is that why you and Geneva don't talk?" I say, wondering if Geneva will be angrier than usual if she comes home and finds me with Elsa May.

"That no-good Rowan Senior disappeared at the same time as my Oscar," Elsa May says. "Geneva blames me, thinks I know where they went, but I've told her time and time again I had nothing to do with it. Oscar worshipped Rowan Senior, thought he was the man's personal manager—always by his side, always trying to book the next gig. I didn't care much for Oscar, so maybe I wouldn't have done much even if I knew something. But the fact is, I didn't. I had no idea. That's the truth. I was as surprised as she was when they were gone."

"We were all surprised," Cecily says, patting Elsa May on the leg.

"Truth is, I'm not even sorry about it. Oscar was not a nice man. And Rowan Senior was no prize either. He was supposed to be the one that boxed the family out of here. Not Junior. There was a lot of fighting about that before he left. She blames Rowan Senior for everything."

"Well, now I guess she has me to blame," I say, and the women all pucker their lips tight and look away.

"I will die here, Lima, and that's just what it is," Elsa May says. "Truth is, I'm fine with that. I mean, I'd like the Mainland government to fix the streets and get us better stores and train up some actual doctors so I don't die before I have to. But Geneva was not prepared to die here at all. She thought she was going to get out of here someday. And now she knows that everyone was right and she was wrong. She's got no one to blame but herself."

I look down at DJ, thinking about what this means for the two of us, and for Violet, who arrives tomorrow. I wonder if Rowan will resent me for coming here, and if Violet will resent me if I go.

"Way Geneva figured it, Rowan would be getting her out in a few years, once he got fighting," Elsa May says. "I suspect that if the money for fighting is what they say it is, it probably wouldn't be more than a few years before he'd have what he needs for you two, depending on your debt. So long as he does it before DJ turns five, DJ would be able to come out too. So that's some good news for you."

"One big happy family," Cecily says, and I try to smile at the thought.

I WRITE A letter to Rowan later that night when DJ is sleeping in the bed. I try not to sound desperate for his approval or his forgiveness, even though I'm in need of both.

"I'm so sorry I spoiled your plans. I'll do whatever I can to help. Can you tell me how you are? Please let me know you're okay."

I tell him about his sister and his nieces, and about Cecily and Elsa May, and when I seal the letter, I take a long, deep breath to calm my hopes and fears.

In addition to Rowan's letter, I prepare a letter for the Hill. I include a note for David and one for Josephine. "Please tell me how you are and what you're doing."

The last thing I think about before I go to sleep is what to do about Violet and Jewel.

33

I T RAINS THIN, SHARP DAGGERS ON THE DAY VIOLET IS released to the Gutter. The morning is hot and the sky is so gray that even though it's nearly noon when I set out, it almost feels like it's nighttime.

When I get close to the Base, I see Geneva standing in front of the Medical Center under an umbrella, tapping her feet. "What took you so long?" she says.

"I came as quick as I could. I'm sorry," I say as she hands me a white apron with a red X.

"Put this on," she says, taking DJ from his wrap and carrying him into the Medical Center while I tie the apron over my clothes.

"What's going on? Why did you take DJ in there?" I say when she comes back empty-handed. "Geneva, you know I don't like to leave him with strangers."

"The nurses will watch him, and I don't have time to explain," she says, starting toward the Base.

"Geneva, what's going on?" I say, running to keep up with her pace.

But Geneva doesn't respond. She just turns into the Base as a guard steps out, raising his hand so we stop at the fence.

"Where the hell do you think you're going?" he says, adjusting his hat so it shields his face from the rain.

"To the gate," she says.

She shows him her badge, and when he nods for her to go ahead, she tries to pull me along.

"Badge," he says.

"She forgot hers at the clinic," Geneva says.

"That's not my problem."

"No, but what is your problem is that you've got an emergency over there. You really want us running back to get a badge? You want to be the one who holds things up?"

She looks over at me, and I know right away from that rare look of concern that this has something to do with Violet.

I told Geneva about Violet early this morning—how her baby is sick, how she had been declared unfit to work by a debt manager who wasn't kind. "She has no family. She needs help."

I explained how I had promised to look out for her and find us a place, and how I would do that as soon as I could. Geneva just listened, straight-faced and serious, while I rambled about all of my problems, trying to forget about hers. "I was going to ask Elsa May, but—"

"Elsa May?" she said, like the very mention of her former friend offended her.

"She said she has a room but—"

"When did you talk to Elsa May?"

"Yesterday. She invited me—"

"Look, Lima, if the baby is sick and your friend is too, they're both going to need proper help," Geneva said as she stood up and prepared to leave for work.

"What should I do?"

"We'll make room until you can find something proper," she

said, and if she had been open to a hug, I would have thrown my arms around her.

We move quickly toward the red gate where guards are moving about in formation, facing the bridge and standing on the wall, guns pointed at a figure in white standing on the railing with a baby strapped to her chest.

"Is that your friend?" Geneva says.

I cover my mouth and nod, but Geneva grabs my hand and pulls it back down.

"Hold yourself together," she says as a wiry guard approaches us.

"Guards are in position, ready to move on her. But we called you, you know, protocol and all," he says. "She's been standing there for a while now. And it's slippery out. I'm not sure what else we can do."

"I assume we can retrieve her, that we have your permission to do that, officer?" Geneva says. "I think it's best if one of us goes out there without a guard, given her state."

"You expect me to let you go all the way out there alone? You people are cleared to help Gutter folks inside the Gutter. But that right there," he says, pointing at the bridge, "is not inside the Gutter. It's *outside* the Gutter. You do understand how inside and outside work, right?"

"Officer, we're cleared to help any Gutter folks who require medical attention," Geneva says, forcing a tight smile. "I would argue that that woman very much needs medical attention, and since she's living here, or will be soon, she's our responsibility. She's certainly not one of you. And you know as well as I do that most times, when someone's ready to do what she seems prepared to do, you-all are the last people they want to see."

"Well—"

"Look, officer, our job is to make sure she gets to this side of the gate safe and healthy. I've got clearance, so if you need to get yours, hurry up, because we're wasting time."

The guard shakes his head, squeezing his holster before heading into the booth to make a call. While he talks, Geneva takes my umbrella and gives me a shove. "Move fast, hands up. You'll be fine," she says.

Before I have a chance to think or protest, I move quickly past the guards toward Violet, hands up, just like Geneva said.

"Stop. Wait. Shit. Son of a bitch. Hold your fire, hold your fire!" the guard from the gate shouts over the rain.

VIOLET IS STANDING on the rail with her blue bag on her shoulders and her toes curved over the ledge.

"Violet," I say, looking up and shielding my face from the rain with both hands.

She turns and looks down at me, like she's sad and relieved at the same time, and I try to hide my surprise. She looks worse than she did when she arrived at Miss Charlotte's. Even though there are no bruises or cuts, her skin is pale and her bones are sticking out through her skin, like she hasn't eaten or slept since I left.

"Violet, please. Let's just talk about it. Just come talk to me."

"I can't go back," she says.

She looks past me, toward the red gate, her hair pressed flat against her face as the rain picks up even harder. When I take a few steps closer, she yells for me to stop.

"Violet, please," I say.

She leans down and places the statue from David on the ledge. "I wanted to make sure you got this," she says.

"Violet—"

"Don't come any closer," she says.

"Okay," I say, lifting my hands and stepping backwards, trying to figure out what Geneva would do to make this go better. "Violet, listen to me. Just come down. Please. Come down and talk to me."

But Violet just stares at the water as Jewel starts crying, shrill and loud.

"Is that Jewel? That's her name, right?"

"She's so sick. No one wants her," she says as she looks over at me again.

I can see in the tilt of her head and the frown in her eyes that she's exhausted, and I wish Jewel would stop crying, because I can tell that the noise is too much for Violet.

"I've got this place, Violet—it's a really nice spot in the Upper End. A nurse who's really good with babies, she's going to help us. I promise, Violet. Just come down. Please. Let me see the baby."

"She just cries and cries like this. All the time. Because she knows what's coming. She doesn't want to go in there either," she says, looking toward the gate and the guards.

I follow her gaze, watching the wiry guard inch closer with Geneva, and I feel nervous for Violet but grateful that Geneva will be able to help.

"You're both going to have to come with me," the guard says.

"Please. Please, just give us a minute," I say. "Geneva, please help me."

But when I turn back, Violet's gone.

I rush to the ledge and when I look down, I see Violet tumbling toward the water as tiny stones and large rocks slip out of her bag like rain.

34

FOR WEEKS, I SLEEP POORLY. EVERY NIGHT, MY EYES STAY
wide open as I think about the rocks falling around Violet,
about the way her white dress floated up as she went down.
When exhaustion hits and my eyes close for a moment, I
dream that I'm falling from the bridge, never hitting the ground.

I barely leave my room, taking short rests throughout the day
while DJ naps. I watch him learn to smile, roll over and grow his
first teeth in a blue room that swallows me whole.

When a long letter arrives from David, tucked in the milk
delivery, I hold it against my chest, grateful and ashamed, worried
about what he might say now that he knows where I am.

In the letter, David thanks me for writing and apologizes for
not writing sooner. "The first letter you wrote seemed meant for
Josephine. I didn't know if it was my place to read it or respond
and by the time it came, it was too late. I'm glad to know that you
and DJ are okay. I always knew you were brave, L." I smile at this
nickname, the way he bridges my two names in this way.

David tells me about the Freemans and the Hill and about
the work he's doing as a carpenter. I read this good news over
and over, feeling both proud and envious. But other than his ref-
erence to the letter, there's no mention of Josephine. I find it so

strange that David would share so fully about everything else and say so little about his sister. Was Mr. Gregors still looking for her? Would he be looking for me too?

"I think of you often," David says in closing, and I wonder if he thinks of me the way I remember him that night we sat together behind the Fieldhouse and on the way to the employer fair.

When DJ falls asleep, I write back to David, adding details about DJ and life in the Gutter, and asking more questions about life on the Hill. "Is it warm there? Are there others like the Freemans? What does everyone do all day?"

I ask about Josephine, and I tell him about Violet and Jewel, about the funeral and the women in white who danced and sang them to their final resting place.

"I find myself sleeping a lot these days, and I've been thinking about this word, *rest*. Because I don't feel rested here. Maybe I never have. Is it different at the Hill? Do you feel rested there? Much love, L."

I WAKE UP from my nap, and I can't find DJ. I pat the mattress frantically, turning things over and checking to see if he rolled onto the floor. I pat the bed again and again, lifting and turning everything, calling his name. When I open the door, I head to the end of the hallway, where I find him sleeping on Geneva's lap, holding a large wooden spoon.

"Geneva, what are you doing here?"

"I beg your pardon? This is my house."

I shake my head because that's not what I meant. I grab DJ quickly, holding his sleeping body close. "Why aren't you at work? You're usually at work right now. Didn't you hear me calling for him?"

"I thought you could use the sleep," Geneva says. "I opened the door to check on you, and DJ was just lying there, wide awake while you were asleep. So I played with him. And now he's worn out."

I straighten my shoulders and take a deep breath. "You shouldn't come and take him from me like that. I appreciate the help . . . but I don't need it anymore."

After Violet's death, Geneva changed her shifts at the Medical Center to start at noon and finish by dinner. She prepares breakfast for us in the morning and helps bathe DJ at night, but I don't want her to help me anymore. I need to prove that I can be a good mother, that Miss Charlotte wasn't right.

"Come with me," Geneva says, grabbing a cushion from the couch and moving it onto the kitchen floor.

When I sit down at the table, she takes DJ and lays him down on the cushion. She puts a tray of vegetables in front of me and hands me a sharp knife.

"You need to get yourself together," she says. "I'm starting you off simple. Cut."

I pick up the knife, grab a carrot and begin peeling back the skin while she tends to the stove.

"Elsa May and the ladies have a job for you, and you're going to do it," Geneva says, and I wonder how she knows this when she hasn't spoken to Elsa May in years.

"Did you hear me? You're going to be a Runner in the Lower End. Starting tomorrow."

I want to tell Geneva that I'm too sick or that I'm too tired, because both of these things feel true. But instead, I just nod and grab another carrot to peel.

35

I REST MY FOREHEAD AGAINST THE WINDOW AS THE BUS DIPS and curls toward the crowded streets and tall buildings of the Gutter's Lower End. The journey takes an hour, and when we pull into the Lower End bus terminal, people pour into the Corridor like a fast-moving current that's forceful and strong. I place my hands around DJ, who's strapped against my chest, as tightly packed bodies bump us in the rush.

"Keep him in there," Geneva said, showing me how to wrap DJ in a way that would allow me to carry him safely and feed him whenever I want. "Don't take him out unless you absolutely have to."

Her voice was firm when she said this, not annoyed or irritated, and it was this statement and this tone that terrified me the most about taking the job as a Runner in the Lower End for Elsa May, Cecily and the twins.

The young man who used to be their Runner got a job at the factory, and while they were hesitant to send a woman to do the work, and while Geneva wasn't thrilled with the idea of DJ going along with me, all five women agreed that I was capable, and that doing the work would provide a helpful solution to their problem—Geneva was looking to get me out of a rut, and the Subsidy women were desperate.

Without a Runner, they would have to wait until later in the month to get their Subsidy—when all the checks that aren't picked up in person are put in the mail. And it was well-known throughout the Gutter that Subsidy checks marked for Upper End legacy homes had a strange way of disappearing or getting delayed along the way.

In the Corridor, guards are stationed on every corner of the narrow lanes that break out from the main row. As I make my way through the marketplace, toward the cone-shaped building at the far end, I spot a Gutter man in all black sitting on a low wall, chatting to a small group outside the Subsidy Office. A woman in black encourages others to join as two Mainland Guards watch them both closely.

THE LINE TO get into the Subsidy Office curves down a narrow side street, even though it's the third day of the month, and when I join the end of the line, I see the words "SOSSI" and "RESIST" spray-painted above me in black on the cracked brick wall.

According to the ladies, it's best to come on the second or third day of the month, when those who need the checks most are already enjoying their monthly allowance.

"Every Sub is told not to leave a penny in their pocket at the end of the month. Did you know that?" Geneva said on the day Shirley and Roger packed up a truck with their belongings, bound for the Lower End. "Gutter folks think the government tracks everything. And they panic about it all the time. Especially Subs. 'Spend every last bit,' they say. People who are sick and dying in the Medical Center worry about how much money they have on them. And not because they want to save it or because they need it. It's because they want to find a way to spend it before the month ends. They think that if they have anything extra, the government will start giving everyone less."

I think about Geneva's words as the Subsidy Office line shuffles forward into a large room with grimy floors. When I reach the front of the line, a teller calls me over just as DJ starts to wake, stirring and twisting like he's tired of being confined. I pull out the documents for Elsa May and the ladies, plus six additional Upper End legacy families who hired me when Elsa May took me around the neighborhood. With every new name, the teller sighs, her long nails gripping each sheet like claws.

"These folks can't come down themselves?" she says.

"They're quite old."

"They're not that old," she says, looking at all of the paperwork. "They're just legacy. Legacy families don't like to come down to the Lower End. It's like we got something they're worried they might catch."

DJ wiggles and squirms, and I try to feed him, thinking he might be hungry, but he tightens his lips and turns his head.

"You know, my momma got sick and had to travel an hour both ways just to get help," the teller says. "Took twice as long when the checkpoints were slow or when the road just up and disappeared during rainy season. Shouldn't be too worried about catching anything if you can just walk up to the Center whenever you feel like it."

DJ squeals, his face reddening, as the teller examines each document. Occasionally, she looks up at the long line and sighs so it's clear that I'm a bother to everyone.

"Ain't nobody running for folks around here, but you Upper End Runners just think we got all the time in the world. You don't see how long this line is?" she says as I stand and rock DJ.

"Betty Sayer comes down in her wheelchair. She gets herself

into the line and all the way up here. On her own. Doesn't ask for any help or complain about anything. And plenty more like her. But these legacy folks, they gotta send someone else to do it for them cuz they got all that extra money."

When the teller slides the checks and the paperwork toward me, I prop DJ on my hip and place the papers inside the bag while she watches.

"You know, we really don't recommend bringing children here," she says.

I open my mouth to apologize, but the teller is already looking past me, waving for the next person in line.

ELSA MAY AND the other ladies pay me in cash, and when I sit down to write a letter to David, I spread all of the bills out on the bed like a fan. Fifty dollars, after bus fare and a small snack.

"I know it's not a lot, but I understand why Geneva works and why you must love what you do at the Hill. I get it now," I write as I look at the bills. "It's not much, but it's mine. And I don't have to give it to anyone, David. I can't even describe how this feels."

I think about what Ida said back at Livingstone about the way Sossi people were meant to live, how the Gutter System changed us. And when I look down at the money, curved across the mattress, I vow to work hard, so that one day I can pass some of this on to DJ.

36

ON THE DAYS BETWEEN LOWER END RUNS, I VISIT UPPER End customers and offer discounts and meat rolls from a popular bakery in return for referrals. In addition to Subsidy runs, I take on special deliveries throughout the month, bringing groceries door to door with DJ strapped to my back or against my hip as he grows thick and stocky like his father. And I keep all of the money I make in a box.

During my second trip to the Lower End, I stop in for a short visit with Shirley after finishing at the Subsidy Office. When I return home, I sit down to write another letter to Rowan.

"Shirley tells me that you're doing well on the circuit, and there's a woman named Harriet, who sells lemonade, who says that for a while, no one could beat you. Does it feel good to know that people here are cheering for you, that they love you and wish you well? Does it help to know that you have fans back home, or does it add pressure?"

I tell him about my job and all the money I'm saving, and about the people in the Lower End who look at DJ and see Rowan Senior.

"Can you please just write something . . . anything . . . so that I know that you're okay? Yours, Lima."

x

FOR MY THIRD run to the Lower End, I take an earlier bus to avoid the crowds. Even though the marketplace is less busy, the Subsidy line is still slow, and as I lean over the stroller Geneva gave me to use on my runs, I check on DJ, who's stuffing a toy car in his mouth.

"Watch it," a woman says when we collide.

I start to apologize, but when I see the short woman with thick black hair, I stop with my mouth wide open, unable to hide my surprise. "Josephine?"

"Elimina? What are you doing here?"

She looks down at DJ, who wiggles his legs and flaps his arms at both of us. "Is he . . . yours?" she says, looking back up at me. "Is this why . . . ?"

"This is DJ," I say, nodding. "Duncan Jackson."

Josephine leans down closer to DJ and shakes her head. "Well, he certainly looks like his father."

I place a hand on DJ's head, trying not to show the hurt that comes whenever someone says this. It's hard to see his father present in our child's face when he's absent in every other sense.

"I suppose I shouldn't be surprised," Josephine says. "I knew you didn't stand a chance the first day you met him. I tried to warn you."

"And then you left. And we were alone," I say, shrugging my shoulders like this is a story with only one possible ending, one she should have known. "What are you doing here? Why aren't you at the Hill with David?"

She looks down, and I can't tell if she doesn't want to talk about it or if she just doesn't know what to say.

"I missed you," I say.

Josephine reaches out her hands, her eyes brimming wet, and when I lean my face into her shoulder, we cry so hard that DJ cries too, and we force ourselves to stop.

JOSEPHINE AND I head to Johnny's Restaurant, a small place across from the Subsidy Office, where they sell three meat rolls for a dollar. When our order is ready, Johnny brings the food to our booth while Josephine holds DJ on her lap.

"How long have you been here?" I say, eating a roll and breaking off small bits for DJ.

"Longer than you," Josephine says.

"Did you know I was here?"

She shakes her head, and I think about the day she left Livingstone, how she made me believe that she was sick and that she was sad to see David go, how I could never tell what was true with her.

"I wasn't faking, Elly," she says, and I turn away frustrated because she always seems to know everything that's on my mind just by watching me. "That last day. At Livingstone. I didn't lie to you. Not exactly."

"What does that mean?"

"I meant every word I said. It's just that . . . I wasn't sad about David. I was sad to be leaving *you* . . . I was sick to death about it. That part was real." She leans over and places one hand over mine. "And it wasn't because I couldn't trust you. It wasn't even because I thought you'd tell, even though that's what I told the boys. I knew you wouldn't do that. I just couldn't tell you I was leaving. I couldn't say the words."

I look up at her, and when she bites down on her lip, I do the same, my throat sharp and stuck with all of the things I want to say but can't.

"I'm sorry. I'm really sorry, Elimina."

"It's . . . it's Lima now," I say softly, and she nods.

I swallow hard, focusing all my efforts on feeding the meat roll to DJ, who smiles and licks his lips with every bite.

"I hope Mr. Gregors didn't give you a hard time," Josephine says.

"He took the coat back."

Josephine covers her mouth. "You loved that coat," she says.

"I did," I say, and when we both laugh, DJ laughs too, which makes us laugh even harder.

When Josephine asks how I got here, I tell her about Riverside and Violet and the day on the bridge, hoping she'll do me the same and tell me why she's not at the Hill. But when I finish talking, Josephine just nods, like she has nothing to add.

"What happened, Jose?"

She leans back against the booth, holding DJ close while he tugs at her hair. "David's fine, if that's what you're asking. He's always fine," she says, and for the first time I hear hurt and bitterness at the mention of her brother instead of need and adoration.

"That's not what I meant," I say.

I want to know why they're not together and what happened at the Hill. But just as I'm about to ask, a young boy enters the restaurant and heads our way.

"Auntie," he says, "I was worried. I was asking everywhere for you."

"I'm fine. I just ran into an old friend," she says.

The boy has tight curly hair and skinny legs, and when he climbs into the booth, Josephine pulls him close while DJ stares.

"William, this is El—this is *Lima* and her son, DJ," Josephine says.

William says hello, but he keeps his eyes on DJ, holding his small hands and squeezing the folds of his legs like they're dough. "Hi, baby DJ," he says in a small voice, and DJ smiles and flaps his napkin like a flag.

"Would you like something to eat, William? My treat," I say.

He looks over at Josephine, and when she nods, I give him one dollar and he runs to the counter to place his order.

"William is a family friend," she whispers. "Found him living in an abandoned apartment all by himself after his parents died. I've been looking out for him since I got back."

"So, you're here for good?"

She nods. "Have you heard from Rowan? Is he coming for you? They've got rules about that, you know. He can't just abandon you and go off to the Hill by himself."

"I haven't heard from him since Livingstone. But he's still boxing," I say, as I look out the window at the busy streets and crowded marketplace.

"So it's still possible? Your plan to go to the Hill?" she says, but I don't say anything.

I was supposed to go to the Hill to be with her and David, and I'm not sure what to think now that she's here.

When William returns with three rolls, Josephine takes one and breaks it up for DJ, while William scarfs down the other two.

"If he's doing what he's supposed to, I imagine it shouldn't be too long," Josephine says. "I mean, how hard can it be to punch Mainlanders for money, you know? If they gave me that job, I'd be rich."

JOSEPHINE TAKES US to a park in Block 1 with a playground built out of slabs of concrete and metal pipes. On the way, DJ falls asleep in the stroller, and when we arrive, William makes friends with a long-haired young boy while Josephine and I sit on an old bench.

"It wasn't what I thought it would be," Josephine says, like she was only waiting until we were alone. "At the Hill. It just wasn't what I imagined. They made us work hard all the time, and I know how that sounds. But somehow working at the Hill felt . . . different. I couldn't get over all the stuff they had and how they wanted us to work for them, like they were Mainlanders. Do you know that Mabel Freeman has never had a job? Never. Not like a real job where she goes and does something hard and sweaty. She just . . . supervises things, like she's a Deco or something. But not like Ida. She's nothing like Ida. That woman just sits around reading books all day, talking like she's a star in a movie: 'Helloooo, David,'" Josephine says in a voice that's meant to sound high and sultry like Mabel Freeman's.

"She lives this whole other way, Elimina. They have so much money. They have this big house. And then they have other houses that are just for people to come and stay in when they're traveling on their fancy boats. And these Mainlanders who visit and the regulars who live on the Hill, they expect us to do everything for them. We tie up their boats and we clean them. We say hello, but only when they want us to. Some of them like to act like we're not even there. We had to call them sir or madam, and we had to wear gloves all the time. Like folks don't know who and what we are and where we come from. Like they don't know what's underneath."

I look down at my hands, the old scar that's messy and worn, and the new one that never feels like it belongs.

"They had us doing every kind of job you can imagine," Josephine says. "Did you know that there are things Mainlanders buy that you can only get on the Hill—that they do business with them?"

I nod.

"Well, the Freemans are involved with almost all of it. Coffee and this chocolate bean that Mainlanders use for their skin. They've got their hands in everything. They have so much money, Elimina!"

Josephine looks out on Block 1, squinting into the sun. I move DJ into the shade and fan him with my hand so he doesn't get too warm.

"You know they could have hired you right there at the employer fair? Violet too. They could have afforded both of you. And whenever David talked about that day, how lucky we both were that it was them, I asked him why they didn't save you right then. If they're so great, why didn't they save us all? Imagine how different things would be. You'd probably have your debt mostly paid off, and Violet would still be alive."

I think about this imaginary life and what it would be like, but when I look down at DJ, I wonder if I could ever enjoy a life that doesn't include him now.

"What did David say when you asked him that?"

Josephine growls and stands, waving her arms as though the very mention of David infuriates her. "I didn't share half of what I'm saying with him because I couldn't. He adores the Freemans. He thinks they hung the moon in the sky with their bare hands! Whenever I criticized them, he would ask me why I hated them so much. He would beg me to keep my voice down because he was afraid they would hear. But I couldn't care less if they could hear. Maybe if they heard, they would do something about it."

"Josephine—"

She holds her hand out, like she doesn't want me to say anything, like she knows what I'm going to say next.

"I love David, Elimina. But when we got there, he changed. Or maybe I did. I don't know. All I know is that I couldn't get past who they were. Those people on the Hill surrendered to the Mainland and then left our families here with nothing. They just paid for themselves and left. Now there's this whole Gutter System that we're stuck in, while they're making all the money they can. Sure, they've got their David cases and their Hill Coalition, where they do some good here and there. And sure, they took me in. But what about this? What about what they did to all of us?" she says, gesturing toward the whole Gutter. "I don't know how to explain it, but working for them made me feel far more like a fool than I ever did working for Mainlanders."

When William comes over and asks if he can go down the block with the other boy, Josephine tells him not to be gone too long and not to go too far.

"Stay away from the guards," she says, and William nods and runs away quickly. "Did I ever tell you how David and I got to Livingstone?"

I shake my head, and she takes a long, deep breath, looking out on the park.

"My parents tried to pay their way out for years. They worked and their parents worked and their parents' parents worked. They all took the best-paying jobs they could to stay out of debt. They saved and they saved, passing money down like a torch they said would light our way out someday. Every generation added and saved, placing money all over the house in special hiding places, in case of money raids, so that one family could get out together. But when I was ten, there was a fire, and suddenly everything was gone. Our house. Our money. All that we saved. Gone. Just like that," she says, snapping her fingers in the air.

I think about the money tucked under my bed, the payments I've earned over the last few months, how hard it would be if all of that saving was suddenly gone, let alone generations of it.

"The fire destroyed the home my parents' great-great-great-great-grandparents built, and my parents were devastated. They came down to the Lower End on a bus with nothing but their children in their arms, a legacy family who had lost everything their family had ever owned and earned. They couldn't bear to look at us. That's why they sent us to the academy. They were too ashamed to live with us as Subs and give us debt."

I look down at DJ sleeping in his stroller, unable to imagine the pain I would feel sending him away, not knowing if I would ever see him again.

"A month or so after I sent you the letter at Livingstone, I got word that Mom and Pop weren't well, and I knew I had to come back. I needed to see them again. I kept thinking about what my family had always wanted—for us to always stay together—and I had to be here with them. But the Freemans didn't understand."

"They wouldn't let you go?" I say, and she shakes her head.

David had mentioned the passing of his parents, how hard it was, how he often thought about me losing Mother at fourteen, but he never mentioned knowing they weren't well.

"They said it was too dangerous, and David agreed with them. Can you believe it? He said Mom and Pop knew this could happen, that what they wanted more than being together was for us to find success," she says. "I was so angry at him. And the Freemans too. But I had nothing. No money in my hand, just some imaginary debt I was paying down . . . So, I took some things, to help me get home . . . and to help Mom and Pop once I got here."

"You stole from the Freemans?"

"I figured Mom and Pop might need medicine. And all that money I earned was just sitting with some debt manager. But it was mine. I earned it. They owed me."

"So you just took things?"

"Just a few gold items and some dishes. They have so many dishes. Some they don't even use. Some just sit in bookcases, like trophies or something."

I place one hand on my chest, like I'm not sure what to say next. "Did you get caught? Did they find out? Josephine, why would you do that?"

"David was just as mortified as you. He begged them to be lenient, and the Freemans arranged for my punishment to be coming here with a large fine instead of going to jail."

I sit back and rub my hand across DJ's hair.

"It's fine. Really. Life's a lot simpler," Josephine says. "I have William, and we play music in the Corridor and do deliveries for the pharmacy. We're Subs, but we try to make a little extra so that it's not so tight. And I like it. It feels good, you know. To be here at home."

I close my eyes and listen to the wind moving between the buildings, rustling the leaves of two nearby trees with roots that burst through the concrete.

"Don't stop going to the Hill on account of me, El . . . Ell," she says, stopping at a shorter version of my name. "It just wasn't for me. David would love the company. Especially if it's you."

I hear the choke in her voice, the way she clears her throat, like she misses David more than she wants me to know.

"Did you get here in time? To see your parents?"

She smiles a little with her lips tucked tightly together. "I said goodbye just in time."

We sit quietly and watch the sun slide down, and when Josephine leans over and rests her head on my shoulder, I wrap my arm around her, grateful to have my friend back, grateful not to feel so alone.

37

THE FIELDS ON THE WAY TO THE LOWER END ARE USUALLY empty, but on my fifth run to the Subsidy Office, they're packed with green tents and people moving about like busy ants. The ride takes twice as long as usual on account of the steady stream of buses and backed-up checkpoints, and when we finally arrive at the terminal, Mainland Healers are pouring out of buses wearing red shirts with "We Come to Heal" written across the chest in bold white letters. I stare into the chaos and my heart races quickly as I remember the fear that comes with being outnumbered by Mainlanders.

In the Corridor, Mainlanders are hanging lights from tall poles and setting up barriers and tents along the lanes. Tight groups of Mainland Healers stare up at buildings and point, while guards lead them through the marketplace. When I reach the lemon stand where Harriet usually works with her daughter, Sondra is working alone, smothered by a crowd of young Mainlanders.

"Seems like a bad day for your mother to be away," I say, and she smiles and shrugs like she doesn't mind.

"Healing Days. Biggest three days of the year in the Gutter," Sondra says. "They'll have real doctors and dentists packing the lanes and doing free appointments by tomorrow. Momma's resting so she can line up real early for the dentist."

In the Gutter, there are a few small clinics set up in the Lower End to treat minor injuries like broken bones or small wounds, but the Medical Center, where Geneva works as head nurse, provides the most significant medical care. According to Josephine and Duncan, the long bus ride combined with the cost of treatment prevented most people in the Lower End from ever going there. Most people preferred to trust local home brews and remedies they got from neighbors and whatever they could find in the Corridor—most of it focused on reducing pain, not treating it.

"Momma wants to line up at four in the morning to be sure she gets in on the first day," Sondra says, serving two more lemonades to a pair of Mainland girls who giggle and point at my hair.

"In the morning?" I say, and Sondra nods.

"Wish us luck," she says, handing DJ a small glass of lemonade, which he lifts slowly to his mouth and laps like a dog.

WHEN WE ARRIVE at Johnny's, Josephine and William are waiting in the same booth where we always meet after I visit the Subsidy Office. I apologize for being late, telling them about the traffic and all of the Healers in red shirts who got in the way, and Josephine begs me to stay late for celebration night in order to make it up to her.

"You should see it. I mean, it's something. I can't believe they don't have this on the Mainland," she says.

"So long as you have a birth card saying that you were born on the Mainland, there are doctors and hospitals open whenever you want," I say.

"What about you?"

I shrug. "Most of them refused to see me or insisted that Mother pay double."

"Well, maybe this is one thing that Mainlanders are missing out on," she says as we watch a group of Healers on the other side of the street set up a ladder and organize cans of paint.

"Have you ever had red pickles, Auntie?" William says, and I crinkle my nose at the thought.

"Pickles soaked in red sugar," Josephine explains, shaking her head and squinting her face like they taste as gross as they sound.

"They're the best," William says, rubbing one hand across his belly and squeezing DJ's chubby hand. "You want a pickle, DJ?"

DJ smiles as he watches William and tries to move his mouth the same way.

"Pic-kles," William says slowly, and DJ pauses for a moment, then laughs as though the very sound of the word is funny.

"When I was little, our family would always go to Healing Days," Josephine says, in a way that sounds both sad and happy. "Our parents would pack us up and we'd spend a few days down here, staying with family friends. We'd get our teeth checked and we'd go to the celebration shows each night. It was the only time of year when we got to stay up really late. The shows didn't mean much, but it was fun to watch."

I place my hand over hers and when she squeezes back, I feel how much this memory hurts now that David and her parents are gone.

"We can't stay the night, but I'll stay as late as the bus will allow," I say. "Hopefully, Geneva doesn't send the Mainland Guard or switch the locks."

Josephine smiles and William cheers, picking up DJ and squeezing him tight as the Healers across the street cover the words "SOSSI" and "RESIST" with seven purple letters outlined in white: "BELIEVE."

x

BY THE TIME it's dark, the Corridor is crowded from the bus terminal to the Subsidy Office, with guards perched on all the rooftops. People flood to the Corridor, including families with small children, factory workers in uniform and a group of Gutter folks wearing black.

"No, no, Healers go!" the group in black shouts until dozens of Mainland Guards wearing masks and holding shields push them back.

DJ sits in the stroller next to William while Josephine and I sit on a low wall, and when the lights onstage turn up, Healers in red shirts take the stage, welcomed by loud applause. They sing songs, and they clap and dance, and when the music gets slower, the crowd sways, stretching out their hands as though the music is a cure they can touch.

I close my eyes and try to feel what they feel, but nothing happens.

When the singers are done, a thick man with a bushy gray mustache takes the stage. He talks into the mic about the Mainland doctors who've come to the Gutter and about the people they're going to save, shouting so loud that the crowd claps whenever he stops, begging him to go on. "Do you believe?" he shouts, and everyone cheers. His eyes seem to find me in the crowd, so it feels like he's staring right at me. "Do you believe?"

The Healers back in Capedown visited the hospitals regularly, and when Mother got sick and the doctors told me she would die, I sat by her bed and prayed for her to come back. But nothing happened. When I saw an old woman in a red shirt making rounds, offering prayers, I asked her if she could help me.

"Can you heal my mother?" I said to the red-shirted Healer with white hair and bony shoulders.

"I suppose anyone can be healed," she said, standing a few feet away and smiling with a strange curve of her mouth.

She spoke differently with me than she did with the nurses and the Mainlanders who were ill. I saw how she held them close and wept over them, and I saw how she took a step back when I approached. She didn't come in Mother's room and she didn't pray for her, and when Mother died the next day, I wondered if prayer only worked for Mainlanders, or if that Healer let her die so I would leave Capedown.

The Healer with the mic and the mustache invites a young man in a factory uniform to join him onstage as the other members of his crew stand nearby, shouting and hollering in matching coveralls.

"Way to go, Tommy," they shout.

"Atta boy, T," they say as the man moves across the stage, waving at the crowd, his hair neatly braided in rows.

The Healer with the mustache places his arm around Tommy and shares how Tommy got an appointment with the dentists last year during Healing Days. "Is it true you had a mouth full of problems?" the Healer says.

Tommy smiles with his lips pressed tightly together, his brown skin glistening under the lights. "I did, sir. I had a mouth full of problems," he mumbles into the mic.

"He needed new teeth and that's what we gave him," the Healer says, and he points at Tommy and shouts, "Show them, Tommy!"

The young man smiles, and when he stretches his mouth out wide, everyone applauds because his teeth are impressively straight and white.

"Are you a believer, Tommy?"

"I'm a believer," Tommy says, still smiling and shaking his fist in the air.

Tommy steps down as his coworkers pat him on the back and give him high fives, passing a Gutter woman who heads onto the stage with her young son.

"This is my friend Dellianah," the Healer with the mustache says to the crowd, inviting the woman forward with a wave of his hand. "Am I saying that right, Dellianah?"

The woman smiles. "Oh, yes, sir," she says.

"Dellianah and her son were here last year, and you know what? I'm going to let her tell you the story. Because she tells it so well."

He places his arm around the woman and points the mic toward her mouth. She shares how sick her son was, how she was certain she would lose him, and how the medication the doctors brought during Healing Days saved his life.

"I believe, and you should too," she says, and everyone claps and shouts.

"Who else is a believer?" the man with the mustache says.

People wave their hands, jumping up and down, as the singers return and the music starts up again. Only this time, the Healer stays too, talking and walking while the singers shift and move to the music. "*We come to heal*," they sing when the music pauses, their voices softer and quieter than before. The man talks about believing and purpose, about why they're *really* here, and when DJ fusses a little, I pick him up and hold him on my hip so I can still hear and see the show.

"We didn't just come here to *heal*, to bring doctors and dentists," the man says. "We came here to *help*. We came here to help *you*."

I feel a tingle down my spine, like somehow this message is for me.

"*We came to help*," they sing softly, changing the words, and I close my eyes and listen as the man lowers his voice.

"Who needs help? Raise your hand if you want help," the man says, and I feel my arm float up in the air.

"Can I help you?" a young woman in a red shirt says, and when I open my eyes, I see Healers everywhere, whispering in people's ears and touching their foreheads as the music floats around us. "*We came to help.*"

"Can you take away my debt? Can you take it away if I believe?" I say, and when she shakes her head, sad and perplexed, I just cry into her shoulder, because I realize that more than anything, that's what I want—this debt off my chest, these scars off my hand, a freedom I've always wanted but never had.

"Ma'am," she says, when I've been crying a long time. "Is there anything else I can do to help?"

I look around at the people raising their hands and singing along. "*We came to help.*"

"My son would like a pickle," I say, clearing my throat.

The woman smiles and reaches into a pouch, handing me a large pickle soaking in red sugar and wrapped in clear plastic.

She tickles DJ's knee, and when she leaves, I lean my forehead into him, tired and overwhelmed as he sucks on the red pickle. I tell myself that everything will be fine and I repeat this over and over. "Everything will be fine."

When a bright light flashes, I turn to see a camera pointed at the two of us. But when I move closer, the man disappears into the crowd, clutching his camera.

Everything will be fine.

38

I WAKE TO THE SOUND OF GLASS BREAKING AND FIND GENEVA standing in the kitchen, surrounded by broken dishes. She's staring at the mess, panting and out of breath, her robe dangling off one shoulder.

"Geneva?" I say.

She looks up at me, her face and her eyes red like she's been crying. "Stay out," she says as DJ crawls out of our room and into the hallway.

He smiles when he sees his grandmother and moves toward us with a grin.

"I'll grab the broom," I say.

"No," she shouts, so loud and so harsh that I have to pick DJ up quickly to keep him from crying.

"No," she says again, this time quieter. "Go down to the Base. Take DJ. I don't want him crawling around in this mess."

"The Base?" I say.

She presses her fists into her hips. "Rowan is here."

"He's here? Right now?" I say, but what I really want to ask is if he's here to take us away.

When I don't move, when I just stand there trying to figure out what this means, waiting for her to explain, she waves her

312

hand toward the door and shouts, "Go to the Base, Lima! It's best not to keep a man waiting."

ROWAN IS LEANING up against the fence with one small bag at his ankles when I arrive. He's wearing brown dress pants with a fitted beige shirt and dark sunglasses. When he sees us, he removes his glasses and smiles. His steps are long and slow as he moves toward us while mine feel short and rushed, like I have somewhere important to go and he's taking his time.

"Took you long enough to get here," he says.

"I could say the same thing," I say with a smile that fades when I see how this comment seems to hurt him.

Rowan pauses in front of me, staring and smiling before pulling me in for a hug. He's more handsome than I remember, and the smell of him and the feel of his arms around me remind me of the first day we met.

"You look good," he says, and I feel a shiver down my spine as he places one hand on the curve of my neck.

"It's really good to see you too," I say, blushing and grateful no one's around.

"Up," DJ says as he wiggles in the stroller, hands outstretched, like he's tired of going unnoticed.

"Well, look at you," Rowan says.

I lift DJ out of the stroller and when I lean him toward Rowan, he reaches out for his father, who holds him out in front of him so his legs dangle in the air.

"Wow. Couldn't claim he wasn't mine if I wanted to," he says.

"Is that what you thought—that he wasn't yours? Is that why you didn't write back?" I say with a scowl, but Rowan doesn't respond.

We start toward the house, and it's not until Rowan slows

down at the first turn that I realize he doesn't remember the way. I point down Eighth Street. I think about the day I arrived, how everything was new, and I wonder if it's harder for Rowan to return to a place where the only thing that's changed is him.

"Did you get my letters?" I say.

"I did."

"Why didn't you write back?"

He shrugs. "How's my mom? How was she when you left?" he says as we make the final turn down Fifth Street.

"Strange. But I think—"

"Strange how?"

I think about the sound of glass breaking, her hair out of place, her robe and her red eyes. "She seemed upset," I say, turning to study his expression as he kicks a stone down the road.

"Rowan?" I say.

"Not now, Elimina."

"It's . . . it's Lima," I mutter.

"Oh . . . yeah, right," he says as DJ chats and points at everything that flies.

"Bird," DJ says.

"No, baby, that's not a bird. That's a butterfly," I say with a long sigh.

GENEVA IS WEARING a long purple dress by the time we arrive, and when she sees Rowan, she opens her arms and he buries his face in her shoulder. When Shirley and Roger show up with all of the girls, Shirley cries tears of joy as she holds her brother for the first time in twelve years.

I try to feel happy. I try to be glad for Rowan. But all I can think about is DJ and my debt and when we're all going to the Hill.

The house fills up with neighbors and boxing fans as news of Rowan's arrival spreads, and he soaks in all the attention and adoration in the tightly packed living room, drinking whatever people put in his hands.

He pulls me into his arms and squeezes me in a way that reminds me of our nights in the Fieldhouse, and I feel the same heaviness and need I always feel when we're together.

"You remember how you used to wear Pop's boxing gloves everywhere?" Shirley says.

Rowan raises his glass and nods.

"He wore those things everywhere. Drove Ma crazy. He wouldn't even take them off to go to the bathroom," Shirley says, laughing and squeezing her brother. "He would call for Ma to go in and help him so he wouldn't pee all over the floor."

"Whoa, whoa, get the story right. Ma had to help me because I didn't want to pee on Pop's gloves. I couldn't care less about Ma's floors," he says, and everyone laughs.

Rowan smiles at me, but I don't smile back, and neither does Geneva, who stays in the kitchen most of the night like she's not in a celebrating mood either.

When the last guest is gone, I place DJ on a flat cushion on the floor, listening through the walls as Geneva and Rowan begin arguing.

"What was it, Rowan? What the hell did you do?" Geneva yells. "Was it women? Booze? You know what this means, don't you? You know what this means?" she screams, whacking him at the end of each question, like punctuation. "How could you?" *Thump*. "How could you?" *Thump*. Her voice goes shrill and she repeats things over and over. "How could you do this to us?"

When I step out into the hall and peek around the corner, Geneva is hovering over Rowan, slapping and punching him as he covers his face with his hands. I watch her hit him, her face clenched with rage, and I know that Rowan is back for good—that there will be no Redemption Freedom for any of us.

"You're your father's son. A no-good failure at everything," she says, her veins pulsing at the temples like she might explode.

When the shouting stops, Rowan opens the door to his old room and climbs into bed with me. He whispers in my ear and wraps one arm around me, saying my name and kissing every part of me, pulling me in tight. "I'm sorry," he says. "I missed you."

I don't say a word or make any noise. I just hold my breath and close my eyes, remembering the way it feels to be wanted and touched, longing for David and the Hill.

39

THE CROWDS IN THE CORRIDOR MOVE SLOWER THAN usual, or maybe it's just Rowan who's slowing us down. His shirt is off and tucked into his belt so the "SOSSI" tattoo he got on the circuit glistens across his back. We haven't talked about the fight with Geneva or what happened between the two of us last night, but I keep thinking about what it means now that Rowan is here for good, how my life feels more uncertain and impossible than ever before.

The guards watch us closely as we make our way through the marketplace, while Gutter folks whisper and point. I realize that while I've spent all my time in the Gutter avoiding attention, especially from guards, Rowan welcomes the feeling of being noticed.

A bald man with a long gold beard guides Rowan to a table covered in thick chains and brassy rings. "I've been following your career. You're the spitting image of your father, and he was a good one. It's good to have you home," the man says.

"It's good to be back," Rowan says.

The man takes a gold chain and lifts it over Rowan's head, letting it fall so the X-shaped pendant hangs between the curve of his chest.

"That's it. That's the look. You want to look sharp, I'm your man. Tell everybody about me, okay?" he says, patting Rowan on the back.

"You do the same," Rowan says, fingering the chain.

A young man selling brightly colored T-shirts hollers for us to come. "Big Man," he shouts, and when Rowan heads his way, they hug and slap each other's shoulders like they're old friends while I wait.

"You back here for good?" the young man says.

"Yeah. Yeah, I'm back," Rowan says.

I bite down hard on my lip because hearing him say this out loud makes my heart feel tight and sharp.

"Good, good, Big Man. Good to have you. Welcome back to Sossi Land," the man says, shaking hands with Rowan before we move on.

At the lemonade stand, Harriet cries over Rowan like he's her long-lost son. "I knew when I saw your boy's face that he was yours," she says. "I used to know your father. He was a good man. You look like him when he was your age. Little one looks just the same. This young lady's been taking good care of him. She's quite the Runner."

"Harriet, you don't have to say that," I say, and when she smiles and nudges me with her elbow, I notice how the spaces between her teeth are all fixed.

Rowan orders two lemonades, and while Sondra prepares the drinks, Harriet tells us about a fight where Rowan Senior took another boxer out with the toughest left hook she ever saw. Rowan smiles, and when the drinks are ready, he pulls out a large wad of money. He hands a few bills to Sondra and quickly raises his hand as she begins to dig for change.

"No, no, no, you keep it. That's yours for being so pretty," he says, and I watch her cheeks turn red.

"Just like your father," Harriet says, smiling with her arm linked through Sondra's as the three of us walk away.

"Where did you get all that money?" I whisper.

Rowan shrugs, puffing his chest out and strolling through the Corridor as two guards with thick necks follow us all the way to the Subsidy Office. On the wall, "SOSSI FOREVER" has already been spray-painted over the Healers' purple "BELIEVE."

"Shirt on, Gutter," one of the guards says as a crowd begins to gather.

"Come on, officer. It's a hot one out. No big deal if I just try and stay cool, right?" Rowan says, turning toward them with DJ perched on his arm.

"Rules are rules, Jackson."

"Oh, you know who I am? Are you fans? Do you want me to sign autographs?" Rowan says, pretending to search his pockets for a paper and pen.

"Why would we want your autograph? When was the last time you won a match?" the taller guard says, stepping so close to Rowan that Rowan has to lift his chin to stare at his face.

"The rules are still the same, Jackson. No Sossi signs or symbols of any kind," the other guard says as the tall one pokes Rowan in the chest with his finger.

"Not on shirts, not on necklaces, not on walls and not on bodies. You can put your shirt on or you can come with us. It's that simple."

Rowan steps back and slides his shirt on slowly, but when the guards move away, he laughs loudly, like his fear and obedience was all pretend. "I was making them look bad," he says, flexing his muscles.

Everyone in the crowd applauds, including DJ, who claps and smiles like he's proud.

Josephine and William are waiting in the restaurant when the three of us arrive, and when Josephine sees Rowan, she looks at me sadly, like she knows exactly what it means to see him here in the Lower End.

"Rowan! I didn't expect to see you," she says in a tone that makes it clear she's not impressed.

"I could say the same," he says, leaning in for a hug. "It's our own little Livingstone Academy reunion. Too bad David couldn't be here."

"To be honest, I half expected to come here one of these times and find that Ell and DJ had gone to meet you, you know, debt-free," Josephine says. "At the very least, I thought we'd get news that you'd gone on to the Hill. Isn't that what you always said, what you always bragged about, Rowan? Didn't you say you'd be the first one to get it?"

Rowan runs his tongue across his teeth, like he's holding back the words he really wants to say.

"Yes, well, you know how it is, don't you? Things never seem to happen quite like we plan. How is David, by the way?" he says.

"Good," she says, nodding her head. "David's good."

"He still at the Hill working hard?"

"Always," she says.

"Good for him."

In his last letter, David thanked me for all the news about Josephine. He told me about his work and his increased responsibilities, which increased his pay. He also mentioned a few places I might like to live—neighborhoods well-suited for DJ—and I don't know how I'll find the courage to tell him that it will be a long time before I get there. If I get there at all.

Josephine and I climb into the booth with the boys, while Rowan grabs a chair, swinging his leg over the back and tilting it toward the table so he's balancing on two of the legs.

"Are you famous?" William says. "I think you must be famous, because your muscles are the biggest I've ever seen."

"Bigger than the Mainland Guards'?" Rowan says.

William waves for him to come closer, and Rowan leans in. "Auntie says they're not *really* that big," the young boy whispers. "The uniforms just make them look that way. But I can tell yours are real."

Rowan laughs, rubbing his hand on William's curly head. "For that, you can order anything you want," he says, dropping a few bills on the table. "It's on me. And that goes for everyone. Including you, Jose."

Josephine looks at the bills and then at me, raising her eyebrows. I try to seem like everything is okay, but my face feels too heavy to smile.

"Can I get a milkshake?" William says. "I've always wanted a milkshake."

"Have these ladies been depriving you of milkshakes?" Rowan says, and when William nods, Rowan hands him another bill.

"Get one for DJ too," Rowan says.

"Seriously, Rowan, how the hell did you end up here?" Josephine says when William is gone. "What happened?"

"Missed my mom and my boy, I suppose," he says, kissing DJ on the forehead.

"Not *Lima*?"

"I knew she was okay," he says. "She's tough. Plus, she was sending me letters, felt like every day."

"And did you write back?" Josephine says.

Rowan scowls and shrugs, and Josephine shakes her head.

"I'm shocked. You're usually so thoughtful, Rowan," she says.
"Screw you, Jose."

"So are you going to tell us why you're really here, Rowan?
How are you going to take care of your little family now that your
boxing plan didn't work out?"

"Look, I didn't tell her to keep the kid and come here," he says.

I press my hand into my forehead, rubbing it gently, while DJ
bangs on the table, reaching for all of the cutlery.

"Well, maybe you should have been a little more careful with
your you-know-what then," Josephine says as William returns.

"What do you want from me, Jose?"

"I want to know what the plan is now," she says, as I hand DJ
a spoon for him to suck on. "I mean, are you going to get a job at
the factory or something?"

"I'm not getting a job at the factory," he says, shaking his head
like he's both annoyed and offended. "And I don't need a plan. I
just got here."

"So you're just going to hang around doing nothing, wishing
you were back on the circuit?"

"You know what, I'm actually glad to be home. You have no
idea what it was like for me out there. It feels really good to be
here, where people get me," he says, reaching out and taking my
hand.

When Johnny brings a large plate of meat rolls to the table,
along with two giant milkshakes, Rowan grabs one of the rolls
and takes a huge bite, closing his eyes and savoring each bite.
"Man, I missed these. They don't make meat rolls like this on the
Mainland," he says.

Josephine looks out the window, while I help DJ with his
milkshake, lowering the glass off the table so he can drink from
the straw.

"You know what, ladies? I'm just going to take another one of these and go," Rowan says, standing suddenly.

"Go where?" I say.

"Maybe Josephine's right. Maybe I should go find some work."

I hand DJ's milkshake to Josephine and follow Rowan as he heads out of Johnny's.

"Where are you going?"

He stops and turns toward me, raising his hands and his voice. "I'm going to find some work. Isn't that what you want? That's why you have Josephine grilling me, right?"

"I didn't tell her to do anything," I say quietly, hoping he'll lower his voice.

"I just got here, Elimi—Ell—Lima, whatever. It hasn't even been a day. Give me some room to goddamn breathe."

I reach out and grab his arm. "But where are you going to look for work? Aren't you coming back with us?"

He pulls his arm back. "The Mainland isn't the only place that pays boxers. Half the boxers here are better than those Mainland guys and the pay is good. It's good enough. I just gotta find my way in," he says. "I'll just have to show them I can hang with these guys."

When I return to the table, DJ is sucking on the straw of his milkshake so hard and so fast, I have to pull the whole cup away to get him to slow down. He licks the shake off his face, smacking his tongue against his mouth and smiling like he's tasting bits of heaven.

I can feel Josephine watching me, and I don't look up because I don't know what to say in return. *I'm sorry. You were right. I don't know what I'm going to do. I don't know what to do with my life.*

40

CRAWL OUT OF BED AND TURN ON THE LIGHTS IN THE kitchen to find Rowan sitting on the tiled floor, leaning against the cupboards in the middle of the night. His clothes are torn and bloody, and when he turns to look at me, I notice a gash across his forehead and a fat lip caked in dried blood. It's the first time I've seen him since he left us in the restaurant two days ago.

"Rowan, what happened?" I say, wetting a cloth before bending down to clean him up and check his wounds.

"Sorry, sorry, sorry. I'm sorry, Elimina," he whispers with sour breath. "I didn't mean to wake you. I'm sorry."

"Where have you been?"

But he doesn't answer. He just keeps on shaking his head.

I grab ice from the freezer, place it in a cloth and dab at the wound before holding it to his mouth. I think of that day in the barn when I first saw him cry, and when he pulls me close, wincing at each painful touch, I know he's thinking of that night as well.

"Sing," he says.

"Rowan, please. Tell me what's going on."

He places his elbows on his knees and drops his head low between his legs.

"Rowan?" I say, sitting next to him on the floor.

"I don't know how," he says, looking down and choking on his words.

"You don't know how to what?"

"I don't know how to fight anymore."

I wait for more, and he lets out a long, deep breath.

"I fought hard out there, Elimina. I swear. I know Momma doesn't think that. I know you probably don't think that either. You probably don't think much of me. And you'd be right. But I fought hard."

"I know you fought hard," I say, ignoring the way he always refuses to use my new name.

"I did what you said and I used what I felt, and I got them. They thought they could bring this Gutter kid up and that I would just fight bad and mean, that I would lose and everyone would be happy. That's what the MBC thought. They think we can't be good at anything. But I proved them wrong. I beat all of them Mainland boys—even the big ones. I was good. Just like folks say."

"That's why people love you. That's why they're so proud. You did good."

"Yeah. Too good," he says. "Turns out . . . they didn't want me to win. They wanted me to fight, but they didn't want me to win."

I lift his face and clean the blood from the fleshy cut on his forehead, handing him the ice. "Hold it on your eye," I say, and he nods, leaning his head back and holding it gently against his skin.

"They said people would pay a lot to see a Gutter kid get beat up in the ring. So they offered me a deal."

"What kind of deal?"

"They paid me to lose, and they said they would send me back if I didn't do it. I had to let all of their boxers beat me. But only barely. I had to make it believable. My trainer, my debt manager—they were all in on it. They all made money by telling me which round to lose in and how to do it so people would believe."

I reach out and touch his hand gently where the bruises are purple, the knuckles split and raw.

"I'm a loser, Elimina. And you should know this."

"Is that why you're back?"

He shakes his head. "They would have paid me to lose forever. Sent me around as the Great One from the Gutter, only to watch me get beat up. It never got old for them. I mean, I almost had Redemption Freedom. I was close."

We sit there for a moment as the ice drips in his hand, melting into a puddle on the floor.

"I was in a fight that I was supposed to lose with this Mainland kid," he says. "Cory Flake. He was a terrible boxer, and I was supposed to let him win. I mean, it wasn't hard to fake losing. But this guy was bad. For the whole fight, he kept whispering, 'Gutter, Gutter, Gutter.' He kept whispering it under his breath like he knew he was going to win. Even though he was terrible. He really believed he was better than me. And I let him win. Just like they wanted. He grinned when it was over, like he earned it. And I was so mad. I've never felt angry like that before, Elimina."

I take the cloth and soak up the small puddle. I wring out the cold water in the sink while Rowan remains seated on the floor.

"After the match, I went to the bar. I'm walking down the street, and this guy calls me Gutter under his breath. He was skinny, really cocky, like Cory Flake. Only he was just a regular guy. And I snapped. That's what it felt like in my head, Elimina. Like one of those branches that breaks apart in your hands." He snaps his fingers, letting the *click* sit in the air for a moment.

"I turned and punched him hard, and I kept punching and punching. I just remember thinking, *I don't have to lose now. I can win this fight.*"

I lean back against the counter, while Rowan stares down at the floor. "Is he okay?" I say, but Rowan shakes his head.

"He survived. But only barely, which some say is worse. His head and his mind aren't the same, you know. He was a good-looking guy, well known. Some important government kid."

"So that's why they sent you back."

He bobs his head up and down, like he doesn't quite believe it yet. "The MBC told me I couldn't fight anymore. I've been banned. That's why Momma's so mad. I've got nothing. Less than nothing. They took all the money I made. Everything but the cash I had tucked away."

Rowan puts his hands on the floor and rolls to his side, and I move to help him stand up. "You have nothing?"

"All the money I earned since I started boxing is going to that guy and his family," he says.

I place my hands over my mouth. If Rowan has all of his debt, it means that unless we send DJ to an academy, he'll inherit all of our debt.

"And now. Now I'm just a fucking loser. I got in the ring with a guy in the Lower End last night or tonight. I can't remember. He was untrained. Bad feet, weak block. But I couldn't beat him. I couldn't beat this kid. It's like I didn't know how to win anymore." He pulls me close, gripping my arms. "I get why Violet did what she did, Elimina. I get it."

"Rowan, stop it. Don't say that," I say, pulling away.

He leans into me and grips me tightly, burying his face in my chest and weeping the way DJ does when he's tired himself out.

When I lift my head, I see Geneva standing in the shadows, watching us from beyond the light as Rowan sobs. I think about what Ida said back at the academy—how the hardest battles to fight are the ones that come for our minds. And I close my eyes and hold him tighter.

41

ROWAN SPENDS MOST OF HIS TIME BOXING IN THE LOWER End. There are rumors about his gambling that I try to ignore because money is hard to come by and he rarely offers anything to help with the costs of raising our child.

Elsa May tells me that Rowan is visiting other women in the Upper End, taking clothing, jewelry and the leftover subsidy their dead husbands left behind in exchange for favors she can't bear to mention. Lola Ferguson, who lives five doors down, sees him more often than I do—a woman who's the same age as Elsa May and Cecily but who, according to the ladies, "likes them young."

Rowan's behavior makes everything worse with Geneva, who feels the shame of seeing what happened with Rowan Senior happen all over again with her son. For all of his boxing accomplishments, Rowan Senior was known for being familiar with women who didn't mind knowing they weren't the only one.

But if Geneva was to blame for Rowan Senior, then I am to blame for her son, and she takes every chance she can get to remind me of my failures as a wife and a mother.

"You better keep an eye on that man of yours," she says, shaking her head as she sits on the couch on the sixth night of his absence—his longest so far.

When DJ is asleep, I sit down to write a letter to David, only I don't know what to say or how to start. I want to tell him about Rowan, about what he's like and how it feels to live with Geneva, but I just send a poem from the blue book about a weary, troubled woman instead.

I feel the difference it makes to share someone else's words, how it makes me feel less alone, and I sign the bottom, "Missing you terribly, Love L."

WHEN I FIND out that I'm pregnant again, I feel so ashamed. I stop writing to David, and I skip my visits with Josephine, rushing back to the Upper End to lie down in a blue room that seems to get smaller and tighter every day.

When I tell Rowan that we're having another baby, he smiles— as though a baby offers proof that he's still a man and that we are a family, when neither of these things feel true. He is broken, and I am breaking too.

I don't tell Geneva about the baby, but when she finds me throwing up in the bathroom, she lays into Rowan about how he ought to find himself work and how we better be out by the time the baby arrives. "I'm not raising two more babies when the two I have are such disappointments," she says.

There's so much hate and anger in her voice, like she's yelling at Rowan and the husband who left her at the same time.

"You are a no-good mess of a father," she says.

"Don't worry, Elimina. I'll find us a good place," Rowan says when he crawls into bed and finds me crying.

But this doesn't help at all. If we move, we won't survive long on the money I make. If Rowan can't find a real job, Subsidy life will be the only life DJ and the baby ever know. And the heaviness of passing down all of our mistakes presses hard against my bones.

"I want to give them something better, something more," I say to Rowan, choking back tears.

"We will, we will. We'll give them everything," he says, holding on to my belly and kissing my shoulder, like everything is going to be okay.

WHEN I RECEIVE another letter from David, I open it alone, treasuring each line as though it might hold some cure for my unhappiness. He writes about the progress he's making on a house he's building for himself on the Hill, and I read each word slowly, trying to imagine his life in this whole different world.

"It's a small place. But it will be mine," he says.

The letter is full of happy thoughts and good news about the generosity of the Freemans, who have promised that if he works for them until he's thirty, they will give him Redemption Freedom.

"So soon, L. I can almost touch it," he says. "Please write back. I've been so worried about you since you sent that poem."

I cry so hard when I read these words because I have nothing good to send back to him. But when I think about all of the letters I wrote to Rowan, waiting for a response, I force myself to write something.

I tell David about the gambling rumors and the stories surrounding Lola Ferguson. I tell him about the baby, and all of the pain and fear that I've been feeling, and I beg him not to be angry.

"Please, don't worry, David. I'll be okay. I miss you terribly. Love, L."

x

I WAKE IN the middle of the night to the sound of cardboard scratching across the carpet as DJ sleeps next to me. I blink my eyes, thinking it's Rowan, but when I see Geneva dragging a box from the closet, then returning for the trophies on the shelf, I sit up. "What are you doing, Geneva? What time is it?"

She hesitates for a moment, but she doesn't answer. She just pulls the boxes down the hall, closing the door behind her. I climb out of bed and follow her outside, where she's dumped all of the trophies and the boxing gloves into a metal garbage bin that she's pulled onto the front lawn.

"One day, when we have our own place, we'll put them up on display," Rowan had said to DJ soon after he arrived, handing him a medal he won on the Mainland, which DJ rammed into his mouth.

Geneva pours gasoline over everything. She lights a match and tosses it into the bin, and the flames rise so high she laughs while I shield my face from the warmth.

When Rowan comes running down the street in an oversized pair of sweatpants a few minutes later, I can tell by the smirk on Geneva's face that she knew he was with Lola Ferguson, whose bedroom window looks out on her front lawn.

"Ma, what the hell are you doing?" he yells, breathing heavy, sweat dripping off his chin.

"I should never have let you box," she says as she watches the flames chew up everything.

I stare at the fire too, pushing my hair back over my shoulder as everything crackles and burns.

"Are you crazy, Ma? Do you want the whole house to burn down? Elimina, get some water."

But I don't move. I just watch the trophies bend and curl as Rowan runs into the house. He returns with a pot of water, which he pours frantically over the flames. Everything sizzles, and when the smoke settles, Rowan curses and kicks the bin because it's too late. Everything is destroyed.

"This is why Pops left and why we're leaving too," Rowan yells, slamming the pot on the ground. "You're crazy. Totally nuts. And you're going to make her crazy too."

I look at Geneva and then at him, wondering if this is true. *Is this how crazy feels?*

"Let's go, Elimina!"

"Where are you going?" Geneva says, stepping toward him, and I wonder how she does it—how she stands up to him without any fear, just like she does when she talks to the guards. "Who the hell is going to take you in? How are you going to pay for food or rent? You going to be Subs like your sister?"

"I have money," he says, and she laughs.

"Today you do. Today you have Lola Ferguson's money, but what about tomorrow, Rowan? What about tomorrow?" she yells.

Across the street, Elsa May peeks her head through the curtains, while other neighbors step out of their houses to examine the source of the noise. But Lola Ferguson's porch remains empty, her bedroom dark, like she wants us to believe she's not there.

"Where are you going to go, Rowan?" Geneva shouts, and he turns around and points at his mother, taking a few steps closer to her.

"Pops was right when he walked out on you," he says, and when Geneva takes a swing, Rowan grabs her arm and pushes her away with a small shove.

"That's it, Ma. I'm done," he says, storming back into the house.

Geneva stands on the lawn, and for a moment I stand with her, staring at the mess of burnt trophies and what's left of an old pair of boxing gloves before joining Rowan in the house.

42

OUR FIRST APARTMENT IS LOCATED IN THE SOUTHWEST building of Block 15—the block farthest from the Corridor and closest to the factory. It's filled with painters, musicians and artists who sleep in and stay up late, and factory workers who put in long shifts and return to the Upper End on Friday nights.

We arrive with a few bags piled on Rowan's shoulders and DJ slumped in the stroller when the sun is barely lifted in the sky. When I see the mural on the side of the building, I cry because I know right away that this is the block where I was born and Rosalind died.

During the day, the painting looks like moving bodies, black and yellow, graceful and strong. But at night, neighbors say the dancing wall bends and curls in eerie ways, like terrible monsters reaching out in the dark.

Rowan leaves DJ and me alone in the empty apartment to search for furniture. When he returns, he brings a stained couch he found in a drop-bin and a mattress from an abandoned apartment down the hall.

I don't tell Rowan about Rosalind or about what happened in

the alley. But I can't help but feel that I am reliving my past. Like my entire life is moving backwards.

When I ask him why he picked this building and this block, Rowan tells me that he almost picked a different place because the mural makes the building look poor.

"It's why it's got the cheapest apartments," he says with a disapproving shake of his head. "Like everyone who lives here is too poor to get anything more."

"Well, we are poor," I say, looking down at the clothes I pulled from Rowan's drawers, everything baggy and long. "And we can't afford anything more."

I reach for a cup from a bin of dishes that a neighbor brought over while Rowan was out and he grabs me by the arm, pulling me hard, so the cup crashes to the floor.

"Don't you ever say we're poor," he shouts. "I got this place for you, didn't I? Can't you just be grateful for once?"

When Rowan leaves, I look out the window and watch as he disappears into the shadows. I think about his words and his expression, about the feel of his hand pulling me hard, and I wonder if Rowan is just like those murals, someone who is two things at once, depending on the light.

JOSEPHINE LIVES ONE block away from our apartment, and when I knock on the door, she answers wearing a black dress with her hair braided in skinny rows. It's been three months since I've seen her, and I bring a small bag of meat rolls and hold them out in front of her as my first attempt at apologizing.

"Well, look who it is," she says, snatching the bag and leaning against the door frame.

My heart breaks because I recognize the expression on her face right away. It's the same way I felt when I came home from the employer fair—like she misses me and hates me for how I disappeared without any warning.

"I'm sorry," I say, and she nods and moves to the side to let me into her apartment.

"You okay?" she says, like she knows from the expression on my face that something is wrong. Only I'm not sure where to start.

"Auntie," DJ says, leaning out of my arms, and Josephine reaches for him and squeezes him tight, holding his cheek against hers.

When William hears DJ's voice, he comes to the door, and when I tell him that we've moved to the Lower End, he cheers and pats DJ on the back. He takes DJ to his bedroom to show off his train set and his stuffed bear, and when the two of them are settled, Josephine and I sit down on the yellow couch in her living area.

Her apartment is just like ours. It has the same gray walls and the same brown carpet, but her place has plants in the window and pictures on the wall, like a home.

"Is this why you've stayed away?" she says, pointing at my belly, which is noticeably round even under my oversized T-shirt.

I nod, and when she shakes her head I can't tell if she's mad at Rowan or mad at me, or if there's enough anger to share between the two of us.

"Does David know?" she says.

"Why would you say that?"

"I know you two have been writing, Ell."

"How?"

"He wrote to me trying to figure out if you're okay," she says. "I have to say, it helped to know you weren't talking to him either."

I look down at my hands, where the two scars are starting to look similar.

"Does he know about the baby?" she says again, and this time I nod.

"But you couldn't tell me?"

"Telling David is easy, Josephine. I don't have to look at him and see his disappointment."

"I'm not disappointed," she says with a long sigh. "I'm surprised. And worried. I'm hurt that you didn't come sooner. That's all."

I nod and we listen for a moment as William explains what the conductor of a train does from the other room: "Can you say *conductor*, DJ?"

"So what are you going to do, Ell?"

"I don't know. I never imagined being here forever. It was always going to be the Hill. I just thought somehow I'd get there. But now we're here. Now there's just no way."

I bury my face in my hands, and Josephine reaches over, resting her hand on my back. "You can always make a home here. Be happy or a version of happy with me," she says.

"I know. It's just . . . I just don't feel like I belong," I say, shaking my head. "This isn't home for me like it is for you. And I think I'll always feel that way."

"You think you don't belong because you were raised that way," she says. "It's what the project did when they gave you to that Mainland woman. It's what Mr. Gregors did with that coat. They made you believe that you were one of them. They tell us all the time that the way the Mainland does things is somehow best. That the Gutter System is how we become great. But you know better, especially now. You don't see this as home because it was taken from you. This *is* home, and they took that from you from the start."

I think about her words, wondering if it's true—if the Gutter can ever really feel like home for me the way it does for Rowan and Josephine.

"But what do I do, Jose? I don't know what to do," I say, and I hear in my words the same helplessness I've seen in Rowan since he returned from the circuit, like I was raised to lose too.

"Is it wrong for me to want Redemption Freedom, to have what Mainlanders have? I don't want this debt. I don't want it, Josephine."

"No one *wants* debt, and you can want that, Ell. But just know that you're not really free if the Gutter System still exists. That debt they gave you when you got to Livingstone, it isn't yours to pay. You don't owe them anything. They owe you. They owe all of us."

Her face is strong and intense, and I can tell that she's waiting to see if I get it, if I understand.

"Where is all this coming from, Josephine?"

She stands and turns, stuffing her hands in the pockets of her dress. "I've joined the Network, Ell. I'm not going to Healing Days and begging for money anymore. I'm going off Subsidy. This is my home," she says, pressing her hand to her chest. "This is Sossi territory, and we want it back."

"When did this happen?"

She shrugs and looks away. "I guess it started when I was waiting for you one day at Johnny's. This lady came in, and she was with this man, and they were dressed in black. I knew they were both part of the Network. They sat in the booth next to us. And the woman spoke in a way that sounded just like those poems we read. There was this fire in her voice, and I listened to everything she said. Her name is Cat Cole, and I've been going to meetings and doing work with them since that day. It's what I was meant to do, Ell. I just know it."

I take a deep breath, unsure what I should say next. I worry about Josephine's safety, but I also envy her purpose, the way she is fighting for what she wants.

"Look, Ell, I'm not asking you to join or anything. But you should know that this is a war. And we all have a part."

"What does that mean, Josephine?"

She sighs and moves to the kitchen, where she opens one of the drawers. She pulls out a small black box and hands it to me. There's an *E* engraved on the top, and the box is filled with clippings from Mainland newspapers. At the top of the pile, there's an article with a picture of me holding DJ—the one the photographer took during Healing Days. The title reads, "Heartbreak at Healing Day—Who Is the Woman Who Wept?"

The story is about the "destitution and despair" of the Gutter. It addresses the Gutter System and the Subsidy Cycle and a few medical success stories from Healing Days. I turn to the other articles—"Woman Who Wept Pregnant by Failed Boxer Rowan Jackson," "Woman Who Wept Sends Poems to Secret Lover," "Woman Who Wept Fears for Her Future," "Woman Who Wept Facing Subsidy Crisis."

When I read the articles, I realize the stories all come from the letters I wrote to David, the stories I shared with him privately. I feel my stomach bend and tighten at the thought of my letters being shared in newspapers all over the Mainland.

"Who . . . How did they get these? How did you . . . ?"

"The one with the picture came out in a Healer magazine. Apparently, there were tea-drinking Mainland ladies who saw it and cried with guilt just at the sight of your face and the story that went along with it. They wanted to know more. So the Network found a way to give it to them. They've been using your letters to raise sympathy. They're trying to get rid of the Gutter System and make this place ours. No more Subsidy. No more Mainland Guards."

"Josephine, these are my words. These are my private letters. I sent these to David."

"I know, Elimina," she says quietly.

"And if they're everywhere, if this picture went everywhere, then people know where I am. If Mr. Gregors or Doc Luca or Miss Charlotte recognize me, they could come for DJ," I say frantically, terrified at the thought.

"I know," she says, lowering her head.

"Are you a part of this, Josephine? Is this the kind of work you do? Stealing people's words? Why are you showing this to me?"

"Because you're my best friend. And because David is my brother, and when I heard the Network talking about you, when I saw this, I thought you should both know—"

"David knows?"

She nods.

"Is he angry?"

"All David cares about is whether you're okay. He would do anything for you, Ell."

I shake my head, remembering the night Josephine went missing and I learned about their plan. It felt like nothing was real, like everything was a lie. And I sit there quietly for a moment, trying to figure out why this feels different and the same.

"I'm risking a lot by telling you," Josephine says.

"What do you want me to do, Josephine? Am I supposed to stop writing to David?"

Even as I say this out loud, I know that I can't, that writing to David gives me joy and hope in a life that often robs me of both.

"David loves you, Ell. From the time he met you at Livingstone and even more so now. I know it. He'd be heartbroken to lose both of us."

I nod, tears burning my eyes, because I can't imagine life without him either.

"Besides, if you stop writing, they'll know that I told you. They'll figure it out."

Josephine watches as I look through all of the articles, reading each word carefully.

"What are you going to do, Ell?"

I think about all the letters, about all the things I confessed and all the stories that are spread out across the Mainland, being read by people I don't know who are interested in my life.

"Do you have a piece of paper and a pen?" I say.

Josephine nods, pulling a few pieces of paper and a thin black pen out of one of the drawers.

She sits the boys down, and they all eat meat rolls while I start to write a letter to David, where I talk about being a mother again.

"David, I'm worried I'll do it all wrong."

I share the stories of Tilly and Isobel and the things Miss Charlotte said at her Home for Troubled Girls, and when I'm done, I tell David how much he means to me, and how grateful I feel to be heard.

43

I LIE DOWN ON THE COUCH IN THE MIDDLE OF THE DAY, wearing one of Rowan's old boxing shirts and a pair of ratty underwear, while DJ naps in the bedroom. The changes in my body are happening faster than they did the first time I was pregnant. After yesterday's run to the Upper End, which felt twice as long as usual, my back and knees are still sore.

I sat with Elsa May and the ladies for some time, listening to them argue about plants, and before I left, I could tell that they knew as well as I did that I'll need to stop running sooner than we thought. But if I stop running, I won't have enough for rent.

I receive a letter from David, and I smile at the sight of his words, grateful that his letters always seem to arrive when I need them the most.

"I'm so sorry about Tilly and Isobel. But I know you are a wonderful mother," he writes. "I know DJ and the new baby are lucky to have you. Because I feel that way as well."

I read about his new projects and the things the Freemans are up to, and I fall asleep with his letter held close to my chest.

x

I WAKE TO a loud knocking, and I sit up quickly, wondering if someone is really at the door or if I woke up in the middle of one of my nightmares where someone comes to take DJ away.

"Elimina Dubois?" a man says, knocking louder.

"Who's there?" I say, my voice quivering at the sound of my old name.

"We'd like to speak with Elimina Dubois," the man says with his mouth pressed close to the door.

"Just a minute."

I pull on a pair of shorts and slide into a robe, tightening it with one of Rowan's belts, my heart pulsing loud and hard. When I open the door just a little, the chain pulled taut, I see two well-dressed Mainlanders—a man with a briefcase and a red-haired woman with her back to me who's speaking to a pair of tall guards.

"Can I help you?" I say, trying to sound as normal as I can.

"I'm looking for Elimina Madeleine Dubois," the man says.

". . . Well, my name is Lima," I say, stumbling over my own name, hoping they don't know who I am.

"We just want to talk, Elimina," the woman says, and when she moves toward the small slit in the door, I recognize the woman who left me at Livingstone Academy and never returned.

"Just give me a minute."

I close the door and lean against it, staring at my apartment, which is scattered with toys and clothes. I pick up the laundry and pile it in the corner, placing everything from DJ at the bottom. I hide all of his toys and place a cover over the box of diapers, then close the door to the room where DJ is napping.

When I open the door to the apartment, the man with the briefcase enters ahead of Miss Femia, leaving the two Mainland Guards outside.

"It's so good to see you," Miss Femia says, walking into the middle of the apartment and looking around. I nod, even though I don't feel the same way.

Miss Femia places her hand on the back of a wooden chair from a kitchen set donated by a factory worker who got sick and took a turn for the worse and is expected to go any day. "Take good care of it. It's been in my family for years," he said with a sad look in his eyes, and I promised to try my best.

"Elimina, I'd like to introduce you to Mr. Richard Rhodes," Miss Femia says, gesturing toward the man in the black suit and tie who's staring at the cupboards and the ceiling as though he's making notes on all the things that need fixing.

Miss Femia sits down on the edge of the couch, while Richard Rhodes grabs a chair from the kitchen.

"Why don't you sit next to me?" Miss Femia says, patting the cushion.

"What's this about?"

"It shouldn't take too long," Rhodes says, grabbing a file from his briefcase.

"Richard just has a few questions. Have a seat. Please, Elimina."

I sit down slowly, leaning on the arm so there's plenty of room between me and Miss Femia.

"Elimina, I work for the Mainland government. So does Miss Femia, which you already know. Miss Femia works in Family Services, but my role centers around Policy and Implementation, particularly as it relates to Special Projects."

I adjust the cushion, moving the pillow so my lower back feels more comfortable.

"The Gutter Enhancement Project has been part of my portfolio from the start," he says. "And we're here to finalize a report on the project."

"You're here to write a report?"

"Yes, we're speaking with all those who were involved," he says.

"That's going to be a pretty short report, don't you think?"

The two of them pause for a moment, unsure how to respond.

"I know what happened. To all of them," I say.

Miss Femia lowers her eyes while Richard Rhodes coughs into his fist.

"Yes, well, we had planned to do a report when you were twenty-one. That was the original scope of the project—to see how everything unfolded. But there is some new urgency in speaking with you now—"

"What new urgency?" I say before he's finished his thought.

Richard Rhodes opens the folder on his lap and pulls out a black-and-white photograph, placing it on the coffee table. I stare at it for a moment before picking it up, even though I recognize it immediately.

The picture that appeared in the paper had been grainy and brown. But this copy is sharp and shiny—DJ biting into the pickle, juice dripping down his chin, our foreheads tilted together in black and white as the crowd lift their hands.

When I look at it, I remember all of the feelings I had in that moment—the fear, the unbearable worry—how all that only got worse when Rowan arrived.

"This photo appeared in a Healer magazine a few months ago," Rhodes says. "And then in Mainland newspapers and a paper on the Hill. It's been getting a lot of attention. You're quite famous, in fact."

I tilt my head, pretending to be surprised.

"It's a very powerful photograph," Miss Femia says. "I knew it was you as soon as I saw it. I thought, *Oh my god, look how strong she's become. Look how grown-up.*"

"So, you came because of this picture?"

345

"We're here to find out how you're doing, Elimina," Miss Femia says.

"How I'm doing?" I say, reaching my hands out to show my scars, waving them around. "I'm in the Gutter. I live in the Lower End, next to a factory that's killing people. How do you think I'm doing?"

Miss Femia sucks her cheeks in like she's swallowed something bitter.

"Elimina, why don't we start with how you got here? What happened in Riverside?" Rhodes says, holding his pen up like he's ready to write. "You were sent there straight from the academy, is that correct?"

"Yes."

"And you were set to deliver your baby with a . . . Dr. Thomas D. Luca."

"Yes," I say, swallowing hard.

"According to our records, that never happened. The delivery with Dr. Luca, that is."

"That's correct."

"Can you tell us more about what happened? We have a notice of a pregnancy, we have the father's name, but no name for the child. No record of birth," he says.

I look at Miss Femia, then back at Richard Rhodes. "Am I in trouble?"

"I'm just here to collect information," Rhodes says. "What happened at Miss Charlotte's Home for Troubled Girls, Elimina?"

The door to the bedroom creaks open, and the two of them look in that direction while I close my eyes, wishing he would have just kept sleeping a little longer. When I turn, DJ is standing in the doorway to our bedroom, wearing only his diaper, his face scrunched and confused.

"I wet, Mama," he says, closing his eyes and shielding his face, like the room is too bright.

I place him down gently on his back to change him as he continues to watch the two strangers with a mixture of fear and curiosity. It's the first time he's ever seen Mainlanders who weren't Healers or guards, and it's the first time a Mainlander has ever been inside the apartment, sitting on the couch like they belong.

"It's okay, sweetheart. These are Mama's guests," I say, leaning over and kissing his head. "Can you say hi?"

"Hi," he says, covering his face with both hands.

"Is this your famous son? The boy with the pickle?" Miss Femia says, smiling with a gooey kind of grin.

"Yes," I say, but I don't smile back.

I remove the cover from the diaper box and change him on the floor while Richard Rhodes adjusts his papers and continues with his questions.

"His father, Rowan Jackson, do you know where he is?" Rhodes says.

"He's out."

"But he lives here with you?" he says, and I hear the surprise in his voice.

"Yes."

I don't tell him that Rowan hasn't been home in two weeks and that I have no idea where he is, because it's none of their business.

"Are you aware of the circumstances that brought Mr. Jackson back to the Gutter?"

"Yes, I'm aware," I say.

"You're aware that he has violent tendencies, that he's considered armed and dangerous on the Mainland?"

"He's not violent or dangerous or armed," I say. "He's a boxer.

347

He's been boxing his whole life because you-all asked him to. He doesn't hurt people for fun. He's just—"

"But you're aware of what he's capable of?" Rhodes says, and when I think about the twist of my arm and the time Rowan punched a hole in the Fieldhouse wall, I nod. I know more than anyone what Rowan Jackson Junior is capable of.

"I'm curious, Mr. Rhodes. If you thought he was so dangerous, why did you let him come back here?" I say. "Why would you send him back and then blame me for taking him in? Where is he supposed to go?"

"No one is blaming you for anything, Miss Dubois. I simply want to understand your decisions."

"For a report on the project?" I say.

I use the table to stand up, holding DJ and placing him on my lap as I sit back down on the couch.

"My bibby. My bibby. My bibby," DJ says to Miss Femia as he rubs my belly gently, and I move his hand away, adjusting the robe.

"You're pregnant?" Richard Rhodes says.

"Yes. I'm pregnant," I say with a sigh, and Miss Femia smiles.

"You look wonderful," she says.

"And this baby is with Mr. Jackson as well?" Rhodes asks without looking up, ready to record my response.

"That's not really your business. Although for the record, yes. This baby is also Rowan's."

"Miss Dubois, I'm only trying to help you," Rhodes says. "There's no need to be hostile. And there's certainly no reason to lie."

"Well, perhaps that should go both ways."

"I'm not sure I understand," he says.

"Why would you come all the way down here to do a report? Why would you come to my home in the Lower End? Have you come here to take my son?" I say, looking at Miss Femia so she knows this last question is for her.

There's quiet in the room while Rhodes scratches his pen across the paper.

"Elimina, I haven't come to take your son away," she says. "But why don't I take DJ while Mr. Rhodes finishes with you. I can walk around with him outside. It might make things easier."

She reaches out like she wants DJ to come to her, wiggling her fingers and leaning in close as I hold DJ tighter. "You're not going anywhere with my son, Miss Femia."

Miss Femia sits up taller, her lips pursed tight like she's hurt, and DJ squirms in my grip, fighting for more room.

"I need to understand a little bit more about your life, Miss Dubois . . . for the report," Rhodes says. "That's why we're here— to understand your circumstances and your living arrangement and how you came to be here. So can we get back to that? Can we work our way through some of these questions, please, ladies?"

I nod because all I want is for them to leave us alone.

"Are you on Subsidy?"

"No. We're not Subs, Mr. Rhodes."

"Have you ever been to a meeting or gotten involved with the Network?"

I pause and think about Josephine, about the letters I've written knowing that the Network would use them. "No, I've never been to a meeting," I say.

"And do you know anyone who's involved with the Network?"

"What does the Network have to do with a report about the project, Mr. Rhodes?"

"I simply ask the questions and write the report. It's not up to me to determine the questions or the significance of your response."

"But if a person was involved with the Network, what would

that say about them? How does that relate to my circumstances or my living arrangement or how I came to be here—the very things that you say you want to know?"

Rhodes looks over at Miss Femia, who's trying to get DJ to laugh by tickling the top of his hands with her long, painted fingernails.

"It might say that, in terms of their circumstances, they've become a danger or a threat to the community here or the Mainland at large."

"The Network is not a danger to this community, Mr. Rhodes. Quite the opposite."

"So you've joined them?"

"No, I haven't joined," I say again. "I told you, I've never even been to a meeting."

"What happened at Miss Charlotte's, Miss Dubois?" Rhodes says, and this time I hear a tone that's full of accusation, like he's growing tired with being patient and polite.

"Elimina," Miss Femia says, her voice sweet and high like a song. "Just tell us what happened."

"They were going to take my son. I didn't want to be separated from him," I say. "I didn't want to give him up. I wanted to be the one to raise him."

"Did you ever mention this to . . . Dr. Luca or Miss Charlotte?" Richard Rhodes says.

"No," I say, shaking my head.

"Why not?"

"Sarah. Tilly. Isobel," I say, raising three fingers, one at a time.

"I beg your pardon?"

"Because they would have taken him away and I wouldn't have been able to stop them. Just like they did with Sarah, Tilly and Isobel. Am I in trouble, Mr. Rhodes?"

Richard Rhodes opens the file and pulls out a letter, placing it on the table in front of me.

"Do you recognize this letter, Miss Dubois?"

It's the letter I brought on my first day, the one Duncan forged, the one I handed to the guard with the crooked mouth the day Geneva came to get me at the Base.

"Do you know that it's a crime to produce false documents?"

I shrug.

"Do you know who produced this?"

I shake my head, my heart pounding so loud I can hardly hear anything.

"Elimina, this is quite serious," Rhodes says. "We're here to do a report, like I said at the start. But you should know that there's also a claim that you breached your contract, and we're being asked by a judge to use this report in that case as well."

"A claim?" I say, trying to remain calm. "Who's making a claim?"

"It's led by Mr. Gregors, Dr. Thomas Luca and Miss Charlotte Harris," Richard Rhodes says, reading from the file. "They've charged you with forgery, kidnapping and endangering the life of a child."

"Endangering the life of a child?" I say. "I mean, if taking my own child is endangerment, then what is it called when you take one hundred and ninety-nine die? Are you facing any charges, Mr. Rhodes? What about you, Miss Femia?"

"Miss Dubois, I'm not here to have a debate."

"What do they want from me? Why don't they just leave me alone?" I say, shaking my head and holding DJ close.

"You should know that their claims have merit, and that they've demanded the return of their property in keeping with your contractual obligation," Rhodes says.

"The return of what property?"

Miss Femia and Mr. Rhodes exchange a glance before he responds. "Your son, Miss Dubois."

I look at DJ, my stomach twisting and turning so tight, I feel like I might faint.

"The report will be used to determine whether their claim has any merit."

"Well, what are you going to say, Mr. Rhodes?"

"We're trying to figure that out," he says, sliding the letter closer. "Do you remember this letter?"

"Just tell the truth, Elimina," Miss Femia says. "It's okay."

"It's not okay! If I tell you the truth, then I'm a criminal. And if I lie, then I'm a liar, and then I'm a criminal too. Either way, you're going to make me guilty, and then you're going to take my son. Your project took me from this place when I had no say, even though my birth mother wanted to keep me. You gave me to a woman who loved me as best she could, who raised me in a place where no one wanted me around, and when she died, you—you, Miss Femia—drove me to Livingstone Academy and you left me there. You just left me with Mr. Gregors, and now you're here telling me that he wants to take my child and charge *me* with kidnapping. Isobel was right. You're all thieves. Not just now but from the start. You built this whole system to ruin us, and I'm done. I'm so tired of it all."

The two of them sit there, and I see fear mixed with pity in their eyes as DJ stuffs three fingers in his mouth and sucks on them, his eyes wide at the sound of my raised voice.

"I can't address the past here, Elimina. So let's just focus on the situation we're looking at right now. I don't know if you realize it, but this report is very important."

"If I'm just supposed to forget about the past, then why am I still paying debts? If I have to pay for what Gutter folks did way back then, why can't you be held accountable for what you took from us? I mean, you're still taking right now," I shout, holding DJ tight against my chest. "You're still trying to take everything from me."

"Mama, don't cry," DJ says. He wipes the tears off my cheeks, kissing my lips with both of his hands pressed against the side of my face.

"Elimina, I know this is hard," Miss Femia says.

"You have no idea what hard is, Miss Femia!"

"I understand you're upset. But we want to help," she says, and I bite down on my jaw to keep myself from letting everything I've ever felt toward Mainlanders come out.

"If you want to help, then either leave us alone or fix what you've done. But don't come here judging my life and the way it's turned out."

"Miss Dubois, it would help if you could let us know if you're involved with the Network. The people who are pressing charges are using that against you."

"How?"

"They're saying you're an agitator," Rhodes says. "They're saying that you're a disruption. You're facing criminal charges."

"They want to take my son and send me to prison?"

"I'm not saying it will come to that. But I need to know, are you with the Network?"

"I'm writing to my friend. I don't control what they take and what they do with what I say. I didn't even know they were doing it."

"Perhaps if you can provide some information about the Network, I can put in a good word in your case."

"I don't know anything."

"How do you get the letters out, Elimina?" Richard Rhodes says. "Who shares them? Just give me a name."

I sit back, because something about where he's going doesn't feel right. "What department do you work in again?" I say.

"Miss Dubois, your answers could really help your case. If you could share a name or anything you know about the Network, we could make a recommendation to the judge."

I look at Miss Femia and she looks down at the floor.

"I need you to leave," I say. "I'm not helping you take down the Network. Even if it hurts my case. Because there's nothing that I can say that's going to change what you think about me, and I won't hurt other people to make it possible."

The two of them look at each other, and when they stand and prepare to leave, I rise from the couch.

"Let me ask you a question, Mr. Rhodes."

"Of course, Miss Dubois," he says, closing his case and letting it drop by his side.

"What was the plan when we turned eighteen—the project cases?"

"I don't see why that's important."

"I just turned eighteen. I think it's very important."

"But you went to the academy. You have debt now," he says.

"But if I hadn't."

"It's a moot point," he says as the two of them approach the door.

I stick my hand out to keep it closed, leaning against it with my back. "It's a simple question, Mr. Rhodes."

He lets out a deep, loud exhale, like he's tired and wants to go. "If they met the criteria—if they stayed out of trouble and did well in school—the plan was, theoretically, to let project cases live and work like Mainlanders."

"Debt-free?"

He nods, and I look at Miss Femia. I think about how Mother kept me in all the time after I turned ten, after the night we lit all those candles, how I spent so much time with her alone. I thought she was ashamed of me, but maybe she believed that whoever hurt the others would try to hurt me as well.

"Do you think that's why people killed them? Because they didn't want that to happen?"

"I don't know, Elimina," Miss Femia says softly, her face red and swollen like she's about to cry.

I move away from the door, and Richard Rhodes turns the handle to open it.

"Mr. Rhodes, what are you going to tell the judge? What are you going to say about me?"

"I'm going to tell the judge the truth about everything I heard and saw here, Miss Dubois. And I'm going to tell them about the things you didn't say and that I didn't hear also. I will tell them whatever they ask me and whatever they need to know. It's not my job to be emotional or take sides," he says with a glance at Miss Femia. "But I will share the facts, Miss Dubois."

THAT NIGHT, DJ plays with his toys while I write another letter to David. I tell him the story of the project and the one hundred babies, and the twenty who died in the fire. I tell him the plan for what would have happened when I turned eighteen if Mother hadn't died.

"Do you think they will ever honor *their* promise, David? It's so frustrating to follow the rules that they make when they never follow through with theirs."

When I finish, I sign the letter the same way I have since I arrived in the Gutter, even though Doc Luca, Miss Charlotte and Mr. Gregors know where I am.

"Love, L."

44

ROWAN HAS BEEN GONE FOR NEARLY THREE WEEKS, AND I try not to worry about rent even though the box under my bed is empty and I can no longer do my runs. I spend the afternoon asking about him in the marketplace, talking with Harriet and Sondra, the man with the gold beard and the kid who sells the X T-shirts. They all tell me the same thing with the same pity on their faces: they rarely see Rowan anymore and they only ever see him at night.

"Be careful, Elimina. He's not himself," Shirley says when Josephine and I leave William and DJ with her and the girls on our way to a Network event.

Shirley's face is pale and there are dark pockets under her eyes. I can see how registering for Subsidy and taking on all the burden and guilt that it carries is weighing on her body and her mind. I see in her what Geneva always said and what I've known since I arrived: the Gutter System is killing us.

JOSEPHINE AND I pass Gutter folks in bright clothes and colorful wigs that seem to glow in the dark, the night loud and electric around us, full of music and noise. In the Corridor, people lie on mats made out of boxes, with old sheets and garbage bags stretched out for blankets. Some laugh and eat, while others sing under a sky that looks dark and wet, like the ink from the blue book of poetry.

At the south side, near the Subsidy Office, people sit on crates and along a low wall. Some are members of the Network, others are casual observers, wearing black for support.

"That's Cat Cole," Josephine says as a woman with black hair and dark, painted lips stands to speak to the group.

She talks about the people on the Mainland who are invested in our lives and our stories, and the work being done to increase support in the Gutter, as Mainland Guards look on.

"The Mainlanders who support us are few, but they are passionate," Cat says. "And they will be critical to whatever happens next. But the hardest work, the most important work, starts here. Living every day and fighting for what is ours. We need to get our land back and govern better with our own set of rules."

People nod and clap.

"Independence!" she shouts.

Josephine joins in as the crowd shouts back, "Independence!"

After the speech, members of the Network serve soup in small bowls. They hand out packets of washcloths, toothpaste and toothbrushes while others play music on plastic drums. Josephine dances, moving around and laughing, and I try to keep up, holding on to the sides of my belly and moving side to side like I did with Duncan and at Violet's surprise party.

When my back and my belly get sore, I watch Josephine sit with people in the Corridor. She asks questions about the kind of work they do, whether they've been to an academy or whether they've always lived here, and I see how she listens, how this is what she was missing on the Hill—the opportunity to help people who need her.

"Martin, good to see you again. You been home? You seen Leeza?" she says.

"That girl kicked me out," Martin says, frowning and rubbing his hands against a shirt that was once white but is now gray with dirt and sweat. "Won't even let me get my clothes."

"We've got some nice stuff down at the Swap Shop," she says. "I want you to come by tomorrow. If you don't, I'll have to bring something here, and I can't promise you're going to like what I pick, Martin."

He promises to come tomorrow, holding out his hands and squeezing hers tightly.

"The Network, they do this *every* weekend?" I say.

"Different people speak. Sometimes they organize marches. There's a whole other set of people who come every morning to help with breakfast. Same with the soup."

She turns and helps a thin woman who's leaning against the wall as a man in a blue shirt argues with someone from the Network about a second serving or a bigger bowl. The man starts yelling and the guards come rushing through, ordering everyone to move on.

I feel a hand on my shoulder and I turn to see Rowan. Only it doesn't look like him at all. His beard and his hair are long and messy, and he smells as though he hasn't bathed in days.

"Rowan," I say.

His eyes are glassy and his shirt is off and tucked into his belt, so that the soft muscles of his body and his Sossi tattoo are visible. I know right away that it was pointless to come looking to him for money.

"What are you doing here?" he says, his words watery and blended together, slippery in his mouth.

"I came with Josephine."

"You shouldn't be out here," he says.

"Do you know how long you've been gone? Do you know how worried we've been?"

He flips his hand at me like it's not a big deal, turning and walking through the crowd. "Don't waste your time worrying about me," he says over his shoulder, and I follow him quickly, not wanting to let him out of my sight.

He turns down a quiet alley, where the noise of the Corridor only hums, where people are huddled in groups, smoking pipes.

"Go home, Elimina," he says, closing his eyes.

"Is this where you go? Is this where you hang out, Rowan?" I say, looking around as he shrugs. "What are you doing for money?"

He shrugs again, running both hands across the top of his head like he wants to get away and doesn't know how, growling without saying any words.

"What the hell, Rowan?"

"I saw the picture, Elimina," he says, pacing across the alley. "Of you, crying. The Woman Who Wept. That's what they call you. The Woman Who Wept. Did you know that you're all over the Mainland? Articles everywhere. The Woman Who Wept knocked up by failed boxer."

"I know, Rowan," I say, but I don't lower my head or turn away. I just stand there with my chin up like Geneva.

"You knew?"

"I've known for a while."

"You've been writing to David all this time? Sending him letters and poetry? How do you think that makes me feel?"

"I don't know, Rowan," I say. "How do you feel?"

"I'm here trying to put food on the table and keep a roof over your head, and you're writing to him? Trying to go to the Hill with our kids?"

"Our kids? You hardly even see DJ. You missed the first months of his life and now you're here, but you're still never here, Rowan. And when was the last time you gave me any money?"

"I can never do enough for you," he says, shaking his head.

We stand there, leaning against the wall for a moment, feeling so much but saying nothing, like we both know it's all falling apart.

"Rowan, Mr. Gregors and the doctor at Riverside, they want me arrested. They found me. Miss Femia and the Mainlanders involved with the project, they came to the apartment."

"Well, you're not doing a very good job of hiding, Elimina."

I smile for a moment. "They want to take DJ and put him into an academy. They want to send me to jail."

Rowan shakes his head, like it's not true, like it just won't happen.

"I don't know what I'm going to do, but I thought you should know that."

"Is that why you're out here with Josephine? To join the Network and protest? You think that's how you're going to get your independence?"

"I told you. I came out here because I wanted to make sure you were okay."

"I'm great. I'm fine," he says, but when he looks down the alley and wipes his fingers along the side of his mouth, I start to walk away because I know that he can't help me at all.

"Elimina!" he shouts as I head back toward the Corridor.

"Forget it, Rowan. Just be careful, okay?"

"Elimina," he says again, chasing after me as a crack and a loud popping sound come from somewhere near the Corridor.

Pop, pop, and *pop, pop, pop, pop,* and *pop, pop, pop.*

When the popping sounds stop, the screams rise and grow louder as a crowd heads down the alley, wild and frantic, some covered in blood. They bang into one another, trampling over the ones who fall, and as they get closer, Rowan uses his body as a shield, pushing me against a wall. I close my eyes and tuck my head into his shoulder, crying loud and hard because all I can think about is Josephine, Cat Cole and the Network, and everyone still left in the Corridor.

IN THE MARKETPLACE, pieces of broken wood and trampled cardboard are scattered everywhere as Mainland Guard vehicles with red flashing lights and alarms squeal down from somewhere beyond the bus terminal. In the middle of the mess, four bodies lie in spreading pools of red—two young boys, an elderly man and a young girl wearing only one shoe, her white sock soaking up blood.

"Elimina!"

Josephine runs toward me, and I feel so much relief at seeing her alive that we both cry and hold each other tightly.

"Josephine, what the hell happened?" Rowan says.

We pull apart, and Josephine looks out on the bodies and the mess with her hand resting on her chest.

"This boy, Jamal, was shouting about how Malachi owed him ten dollars, and they started pushing each other," she says, standing in the center of the Corridor and looking around, still in shock. "They're friends. They were just shoving, like they do, like they always do . . . But then the guards started shooting . . . into the crowd."

When the Mainland Guard medic team roll in, they order us to get out of the way. They run tape around the whole area, and

361

they push us down the lane, along with members of the Network who are already treating the injured on the tables that used to be filled with bowls of soup.

"Back up, Gutters," the guards yell, trampling through the blood, and everyone moves away from the bodies, toward the low wall.

But I can't.

I feel a pain under my belly like an anchor pulling me down, and I close my eyes and try to breathe, long and slow.

"Elimina, are you okay?" Josephine says.

I look at her and open my mouth to say something, but nothing comes out. I look down at my legs, and I see blood everywhere. All over my feet. Red. Blood. I try to move toward Josephine. I try to hold on to Rowan. But the blood keeps following me until I can't stand up anymore.

45

W

E CALL THEM THE CORRIDOR KILLINGS — THE DAY four people were shot and killed by guards because a boy named Malachi owed his friend Jamal ten dollars. The event is added to the Network calendar as an official day of mourning, so I can always remember the day I lost a child I never wanted.

I'm not sure if I'm sad or relieved about losing the baby, and this thought brings on dark clouds I can't seem to break through, like a storm with no clear ending. Because maybe I did this. Maybe I didn't want her enough. Or maybe I knew this life would kill her and I wanted to spare her from the start.

I call her Rosalind, after the mother who never knew me, and I bury her outside the Lower End with Violet and Jewel under a tree that's filled with red gavanje birds who will always be there to look out for her.

THE MAINLAND GUARD call it a riot, and that's the story that's told in the papers that the Network smuggles into the Lower End the following day: "A riot broke out in the Gutter, after gangs and looters tore through the dangerous night Corridor. Guards stopped the violence from spreading, but four were wounded in the process and later succumbed to their injuries."

But that's not what happened at all. Friends were arguing over ten dollars and guards began shooting, wounding eight and killing four: Jamal Smith, Malachi Foster, Betty Vaughn and Jeffrey Cooper.

When I see the articles from the Mainland paper, knowing what I heard and what Josephine saw with her own eyes, I wonder about all the papers Mother and I read when I was younger, about all the lies I believed about who I am, where I'm from and where I belong.

THE REAL RIOTS come after the Corridor Killings, when the Network marches through the streets, setting fire to the Subsidy Office and to the marked vehicles of the Mainland Guards. They spray-paint "SOSSI" on buildings and signs.

"This is Sossi Land," we shout as we march. "Redemption Freedom for all!"

The Network sets up blockades on the road to the Lower End, shutting down all work at the factory and preventing the Mainland Guard from entering the Corridor. They demand the elimination of the Gutter System and the return of Sossi territory—starting with the area known as the Gutter—under a document entitled the Sossi Independence Act, which Cat Cole and the other leaders have been drafting for months.

When no one from the Mainland responds, the protests continue to escalate. The Network pushes the Mainland Guard back toward the Base, occupying the Upper End as well. Marches take place in the streets and speeches are held every night in the park near Geneva's house, where the Network presents their hope for independence to crowds of legacy families.

While the Network's breakfast program continues in the Corridor, and the midnight soup service does as well, all the Mainland papers focus on are the riots, the roadblocks, the graffiti and the fires.

"Mainland Guard Kept Out: Gutter Descends into Chaos," the papers read, as though no one cares about how the chaos really began or the prospect of stopping it by giving Gutter folks what we want and deserve: freedom instead of scars at birth.

WHEN FOOD BECOMES scarce and the first day of the month passes with no Subsidy checks, Gutter folks in the Upper and Lower End get restless and beg the Network to negotiate with government officials who arrive three weeks into the riots, concerned about the prospect of a lengthy closure of the gun factory and the displacement of the Mainland Guard.

In the negotiations, officials agree to improve medical support by training and hiring more nurses. They agree to increase Subsidies by a dollar per day, and they promise to improve conditions for factory workers by providing masks and conducting air quality tests regularly.

When the Network reads the Mainland's offer to a crowd of people in the Corridor, folks applaud, smiling and holding on to one another, relieved that this might finally end. But I stand there with Josephine wondering how this will change anything, wishing for an entirely different ending.

"What about the Sossi Independence Act?" I say to Josephine, who frowns as the crowd around cheers.

Cat Cole suggests making a counteroffer and asking for more—

for the removal of the Mainland Guard and for a clear progression plan toward independence. "Our focus is on the elimination of the Gutter System," she says.

But people in the crowd shake their heads, worried about further delays and thinking about their hunger instead.

"We need food," they say, and when the crowd's demands grow louder and more insistent, the Network agrees to accept the offer based on the wants of the overwhelming majority.

"A system can't be broken in a moment," Josephine says somberly as we hold each other close.

WHEN ALL THE roads reopen, and deliveries to and from the Mainland resume, I send a letter to David telling him the true story behind the Corridor Killings, knowing it will be read by people across the Mainland and the Hill. I tell him about the ten dollars and about those who died in the crossfire, and I tell him what really happened during the protests that followed—how we marched in the streets and cried out for justice and independence on behalf of Jamal Smith, Malachi Foster, Betty Vaughn and Jeffrey Cooper.

"But everything feels the same now. Just like it was before. I'm trying not to lose heart, but I feel like we're trapped, as Cat often says, 'in a cage of injustice.'"

I tell David about the loss of Baby Rosalind, and the terrible guilt I feel, about the worry that swallows me up at night when I lie down with DJ.

"I worry that I'm going to jail and that DJ is going to an academy, and I don't know which is worse, the thought of being separated or the thought of him facing this terrible world alone and in debt always. I don't want to lose DJ too, David. I don't want to lose everything. But I don't know how to hope anymore. I don't know how to believe in anything."

I move in with Josephine one month after the Corridor Killings, as the truth about that night in the Corridor draws attention across the Mainland.

"Mainland Guard Massacre Kills Four."

"Woman Who Wept Continues to Mourn the Loss of Her Unborn Child."

I store the articles in the box from Josephine, along with all the others, and when David responds with accounts of the protests he attends on my behalf, I read each word carefully, overwhelmed by what he shares about the response to the Woman Who Wept.

"There are people who care about you and DJ. We are fighting hard," he writes, and this gives me a small bit of hope, a spark I can believe in, without knowing how it will end.

Josephine and I find work wherever we can as Runners, refusing to take Subsidy checks when the Subsidy Office reopens, based on the encouragement of those who have been working with the Network for a long time.

"We do not need them to survive. We need each other," Cat says.

I do runs and I serve meals whenever I can, recording stories while I await news of my fate, and while Rowan becomes unrecognizable, lost every night in the Corridor.

At first, I feel overwhelmed by this loss, filled with a longing to fix whatever seems to haunt and torment him, whatever pulls him away from us. I am learning to let go of the things I can't control so I can hold fast to the people I need most.

"Never lose sight of the promises we deserve and the things that are rightfully ours," Cat says.

This is what I begin to include in the letters I write to David—stories of people working hard in a system that was meant to punish and destroy us, stories of people who fought, and are fighting, for their dreams.

Because we are still here.

I CLIMB INTO bed every night surrounded by a handful of my most prized possessions: a black box full of articles, a blue book of poems, a wood carving of a mother and child, and the boy who changed everything about me—one item from every one of the Gutter children who became my family when I found myself alone in the world, lost and without a home.

Each night, DJ begs for a story, and when he does, I clasp his fingers down so they all link together, telling him the most important one while we await news of our future. "A long time ago, the world was good and happy—land, ocean and sky, all together," I say.

We nuzzle closer as the night grows dark and smooth, and I tell him the story of his people—our people—the people of the Land, and how we were meant to live.

Acknowledgments

I CONSIDER WRITING TO BE A LONELY, SOLITARY ACT. WHEN I finish a book, I always feel deeply indebted to those who were affected by the way I tucked myself in a corner to read the manuscript "just one more time" and to the people I stepped away from to fix "just one more little thing."

To Mark, who treasures me in a way that makes me grateful to be exactly who I am; to Edan, who regularly reminds me with so much pride that writing is what I was meant to do; to Josh and Maddy, who were there for part of the journey and remain with me always, who came to me when I longed for more children and changed me forever by becoming a part of our family.

To Mom, Dad, Skye, Damon and Derryl, who have known me from the start and who have made me who I am, who root me on with so much love, support and applause.

To Kafi, Bo, Vernley, Beris, Karen, Jed, Ahmeda and Kylan, who came into my life along the way and who have taught me so much about the abundant blessing of family.

To Amanda, who carried me through the final stages of this project with such grace and generosity—professionally and personally.

To AJ, Dante, Justice, Asher, Marcus, Zuriel, Jibril, Jobim, Yohannes, Reina, Jotham and Judah: may you grow up knowing the incredible power of your story and your voice.

To Christina, Lamoi and the members of the Ontario Arts Council jury who read this book in its very early stages and whose encouraging words helped me press through at times when I thought I wouldn't finish this at all.

To Helen Humphreys and those at the Sage Hill Writing retreat I attended so many years ago, who contributed thoughts and ideas that impacted the shape of this story.

To Canisia, Léonicka, Bianca and Jay, who fill me with strength and courage by being phenomenal Black women I treasure and admire, whom I regularly turn to for strength.

To Jennifer and Carly, who believed in this work from the start and who helped this story become what it is now.

To my Creator, who fills me and equips me and guides me through every minute and with every word.

x

Poems mentioned in this novel are drawn from the work of Langston Hughes.